About the Author

South Africa provided an idyllic childhood of wild exploration, fostering a great love for the outdoors, where shoes were reserved for church. The travel bug bit at eighteen, where following a year in the USA as an au pair for four beautiful children, I moved to the UK. The nature of my degree allowed for eighteen glorious months in New Zealand. I found forgotten summits, wild beaches and dense woodlands, the ideal locations for disappearing into the colourful worlds conjured up by my imagination. Putting pen to paper, and bringing these worlds to life, would only come later, after graduation.

River of Ice

Ankia Scott

River of Ice

Olympia Publishers
London

www.olympiapublishers.com
OLYMPIA PAPERBACK EDITION

A CIP catalogue record for this title is
available from the British Library.

ISBN: 978-1-78830-970-7

First Published in 2021

Olympia Publishers
Tallis House
2 Tallis Street
London
EC4Y 0AB
Printed in Great Britain

Dedication

This one is for you Mum.
Love you always.
"tu se manques.'"

Chapter One

She felt at odds with herself; like a piece of meat being dragged in opposite directions by two equally hungry and deserving wolves. The white creature with its blue eyes was calling her home, to her sanctuary in the woods, to the place where she felt safe, and protected, from the harshness of the world.

Stilling herself, she lifted her eyes to the peaks on the horizon, willingly offering their extraordinary colour as a sacrifice to the mountain gods. Kira allowed her eyes to slip closed for just a moment and opening them again focussed inward, allowing the stillness to wash over her and settle her doubts. The two blue pools carried within them the picture of steep mountainsides, ice-capped peaks and blue-grey sky, reflected in its glacial, ice-coloured surface.

The air was cold, stinging her skin and making her lungs burn with each inhalation as protective moisture leaked from the corners of her eyes, spilling over her lids and rolling down her face. Her cheeks once more carried a blush from the cold, bringing healthy colour back to her skin that had been so pale only days ago. Refusing to take her eyes off the bright summits, Kira blinked away the moisture, aware of the cloud of breath hanging in the air in front of her. Her feet were back where they belonged, in the cold snow, the movement of ice crystals comforting beneath her leather moccasins. She closed her eyes, losing herself in the familiar.

The pull of home was strong.

She could smell the smoke from her fire, feel the heat seeping into her bones. The arms of her wooden home were stretching open in a warm welcome, trying to hide the darker shade of a shadow, lurking in the corner of her mind.

Kira opened her eyes against the brightness of the sun, her body turning back towards town. The other creature was pulling her in that direction. The green of its eyes shone like emeralds against the brown patches of fur as it pulled, vehemently, fighting against its blue-eyed nemesis. They were friends, these beasts, and yet they had different needs which were pulling them in different directions.

Her heart yearned for the comfort and norm of her own home. She needed to return to it, the way she had left. The circle had to be completed. This journey would not be complete, until she returned to the home she had left behind over two weeks ago. The home her parents had created for them. They were of course no longer there, she knew that. The memory of their profound presence on the Glacier, a week ago, was fresh in her mind.

Was that it? A week ago?

Kira turned her body back towards the mountains and allowed her feet to carry her up the valley, towards her home. The blue-eyed wolf running ten steps ahead, leading her.

The journey had taken its toll on both her and Adam; they had both paid a heavy price for the privilege of burrowing deeper into the heart of the mountain.

They had stood on the ice; the frozen blood of her veins. They had plummeted into her depths only to crawl back out; colder, weaker, damaged, but somehow stronger and enriched. She had touched their lives in a way that she had touched no other.

She was not the same person as the one who had left her home before the journey, and she would not be returning as such.

She had been tested.

She had dug to the very bottom of her reserves to punch through this boundary, unbreached by man. She had grown in experience, offering her body as sacrifice in payment for this opportunity. She returned to her home, smaller in stature but so much bigger in knowledge and experience. Her life had been enriched by this journey and she knew that nothing would ever be the same again.

The dominant emotions of comfort and relief she always felt, drawing closer to home, were underlined by a narrow thread of longing and sadness. Her isolation and solitude had allowed her to focus on nothing other than herself, for years. She had been able to utilise every hour of every day in bettering herself, in training, in sharpening and honing her skills into a perfect razor-sharp blade. Her reactions far outshone any other, her physical speed, thought processing and problem solving an asset in this environment. Adam had been right in recognising these skills as a massive asset on the expedition he had planned and had taken the time to teach her the technicalities of winter expeditioning which were not already within her skillset.

This had saved his life.

She had grown, as an individual, in solitude, into

something almost supernatural in her abilities, but she had blossomed in the presence of like-minded company.

Today, she missed the crunch of snow beneath her feet. She was light, with no bag on her back, and no heavy boots to weigh her down. Harvey had repaired her damaged cloak whilst she was in hospital and she was making her way home as herself. Her white hair hung loose against her back, a contrast against the dark leather of her cloak. Light strands of the distinctive colour dancing to the music of the breeze as she floated over the layers of ice on the ground. Her nostrils filled with the scent of pine, her vision filled with the colours of the forest. Shades of red, green, yellow and even black lichen sheltered beneath the canopy of brown and green needles under the covering of snow.

She stilled for a moment.

She was alone.

The air was quiet, allowing the forest to sing its song. It reached her ears on a wonderful medley that filled her up from the inside, causing her eyes to close and her lips to curl into a smile. She had missed the sounds of the forest, the movement of snow on the branches, the needles brushing up against one another, wings flapping, snow sifting, floating, dripping. The sun played a musical tone on her skin as the rays danced across her closed lids, ducking between the heavily laden branches of the trees. The variety of texture filled her senses as she allowed her fingers to drift over the bark of several trees, smooth, rough, dimpled, crevassed, flaky, papery. The snow was cold and hard, then warm and smooth as it melted in her hands, the liquid glistening in the rays of the sun. Snow crystals sparkled around her as the music filled her senses.

'I'm home,' she whispered into the thick of trees, before changing her course in the direction of her sanctuary.

The door still moved the same way, she noted, scuffing against the floor before squeaking to a halt. She stood in the doorway of her home, much as she had done before they left.

The fireplace had been cleaned and reset, matches lay at the ready on the hearth. The electric kettle was waiting patiently beside the solid fuel stove.

The silhouetted figure in cloak and moccasined feet, long white hair and startling blue eyes, stepped over the threshold allowing the home to envelop her in a hug. Memories ran through the house, footsteps, laughter, and the smiling faces of her parents. The smell of iron-rich blood filled her senses, the warmth of extensively worked leather enveloped her. She could hear the sound of knives being sharpened and wood being chopped. The colour of herbs, and smell of potions, drifting up from the kitchen.

She had come home.

She had brought a small part of them home with her.

Kira stepped inside and closed the door behind her, drawing comfort from the familiar scuff of the door and the loud click as the latch slipped into place.

She had returned the way she had intended, as someone the house would recognise.

Deep down inside she knew she had changed, and stood for a moment waiting, listening for sounds of rejection or acceptance from the house. Individual moments of silence, strung together like beads on a chord, formed a pleasant bracelet of acceptance. Breathing a quiet sigh of relief she strode over to the fireplace, removing her boots before stepping up onto the hearth. The cold of the stone seeped through her socks, grounding her as she sank down onto her haunches. The scratch of the match-head on the hearth reverberated through her bones. She smelled the puff of ignition as an orange flame overwhelmed the match, and after a moment lowered it to the tinder. The flame tentatively took hold of the fine pieces of wood, and highly flammable material, before suddenly bursting into life, igniting the kindling in a whoosh of heat and colour. Kira smiled, allowing the sound, colour and heat to enfold her in its comforting embrace. The flames danced in front of her eyes, bringing memories of the journey, pieces of information that had been lost in the cold corners of her exhausted mind. Moving to retrieve some logs from the neat pile against the wall, Kira carefully placed them on the growing blaze before stepping away and removing her cloak. The house was cold, having been devoid of life and heat for weeks. She shivered against the chill of stone beneath her feet but, feeling the need to be one with this familiar place, she removed her socks. Her toes curled away from the ice of the floor, making her smile before she pressed the bareness of her feet against the cold surface and, closing her eyes, took a deep breath allowing the connection to be re-established.

Her eyes fluttered open after a few moments, roaming unbidden over the house before coming to a rest on the stove in the kitchen. Her feet moved without being instructed, her body taking up the familiar pose in front of the stove as she knelt to light the fire, also laid ready to be restarted. She enjoyed the scratch and whoosh of the match just as much as she had the first time. Placing it inside the stove, she watched the kindling take fire and waited to feed it some more fuel.

The house would take a while to rewarm, but with both the stove and the fire going it should be warm by tonight. The day was still awakening around her, slowly drawing itself out of a lazy slumber and nosing its way into mid-morning.

Straightening her legs and stretching herself to her full length, Kira allowed her eyes to drift over the space again. It was as she had left it, nothing added, nothing taken away, and yet it felt empty. The quiet rose up out of the floorboards and drifted down from the rafters.

She had not been alone in weeks. In reality she had not been alone all year, and she was no longer accustomed to the sound of this silence.

The green-eyed wolf pulled her flesh in the direction of town.

His face appeared in her mind, the smell of him filled her nostrils, the ache in her heart, the fear and the concern she had felt on the journey returned.

He was her friend.

She was no longer alone.

Perhaps she never had been.

Shaking her head to clear the vision of him she stepped back over to the fire. It was going well, devouring the fuel like a hungry bear. Banking it up with coal and wood she did the same to the fire in the stove before stepping back into her moccasin boots and cloak. Her arms slipped through her outer layer, the leather settled comfortably around her body. Drawing the cord tighter around her waist, she slipped her sheathed knife into its place, braided her hair and tucked it beneath the outer layer, before moving to the door.

She glanced back once to the warm glow of the fire, a smile tugging at her lips, before turning away and moving through the door.

Some ptarmigan would be lovely for dinner tonight.

She was flying, wings spread like an eagle, soaring. A creature of the forest, home at last.

White hair in flight, blue eyes piercing, focussed. Muscle memory had taken over, allowing her to flow freely through the trees and around obstacles. The forest welcomed her home with open arms, and she was pleased to find that her agility had not taken a beating like her body. She wasn't moving as fast as she had before the journey. She knew it would take time for her strength to build back up, but she was pleased to find her movement still smooth and accurate through the trees. Slowing to a stop, she smiled to herself, joy and appreciation filling her mind and body. She was so fortunate to live up here, to have these skills, to have been brought up with appreciation and knowledge of the environment around her.

'Thank you,' she whispered, lifting her head to the sky and the mountains in the distance.

'Thank you.' She wanted to shout it, hear it echo off the walls of the hills. She wanted the sound to reach her parents all the way on the river of ice, but she respected her environment and the need for quiet reflection. Dropping her head, she changed direction and like a coiled spring was released back into the woods. She headed towards the clearing, higher up, where she might be lucky enough to find some meat for tonight. Ptarmigan liked open plains in winter, where its white winter feathers can disappear against the backdrop of snow. It would need some cover though, from bigger birds of prey, and Kira knew exactly where they liked to frequent.

She would have liked the cathartic practice of a big kill. Something to reassure her of her skill, a celebration for her homecoming, but the realist inside of her won out. She would struggle with dragging home a big deer, she would have to preserve or dry the meat and work the hide to prevent it from going to waste. It would be lovely, encouraging and exhilarating, but it was not sensible. She didn't have the time, energy or inclination to focus her attention on these tasks at the moment. She just wanted to be home, eat her own food, sit in front of her own fire, and tonight, sleep in her own bed.

Her heart was pulling her back towards town. Adam could not make it up the valley, as much as he wanted to, he would not be coming up to visit her anytime soon. The responsibility lay with her. She was going to have to make the trip to town and back if she wanted to see him, and she did.

Her eyes focussed on some movement in the snow, her body stilled as all thoughts evaporated from her mind. Everything else was going to have to wait. The bird was scratching in the snow, unaware of the threatening presence downwind of it. Kira's fingers found her knife, slowly removing it from its sheath. Her fingers found its familiar position on the weapon, slipping into its old hold as her hand lifted, and dinner looked up, a moment too late.

Kira was sitting cross legged in front of the fire, finding the plucking of the bird therapeutic. It wouldn't take her long to prepare it and she usually did it in the kitchen, but today she sought the warmth and comfort of the fire. She felt grounded, sitting here, on the floor. She placed the feathers straight in the fire before placing the bird on a large chopping board on the ground. Standing up she placed her feet on the wings, right next to the breastbone, her big toes tickling the breasts at the joint. Folding her fingers around the legs she slowly pulled up and out until it slipped away from the body, leaving only the breast with the wings still attached. Crouching back down she twisted and broke the wings free, leaving only the breast before carefully removing the organs. Her hair slid over her back and, spilling over her shoulders, tried to soak up the blood of the bird. She pushed it away with the back of her hand, the ends coloured red with the warm life of the bird. She'd run home, swiftly after killing it, and the body was still warm in her hands. Cutting the breast away she got up to move the operation to the kitchen, where she folded half of the meat into some hide, tying it together with string before hunching down to drop it into the hatch in the floor. It was still early afternoon, there was no gnawing hunger inside of her and the meat would benefit from a marinade. A simple saltwater solution would enhance the flavour of the meat and allow it to retain more moisture during cooking. She enjoyed this pure raw taste of the meat and felt like that is exactly what she needed tonight. She would not be making it into a stew or a roast like she sometimes liked to do, tonight she wanted a strong flavour to bring her home. She did away with the intestines and extra bits of the bird, saving it for when she went high up in the mountains where she could leave it as an offering to the animals, appeasing the mountain gods. Her parents had taught her to put something back into nature when she had taken from it, and this was a practice she obeyed with gratitude and appreciation.

The kettle signalled its readiness with a cloud of steam

exploding from its spout and a loud bubbling. Lifting the heavy container, she poured hot water over the prepared herbs in her cup before replacing it to the cooler part of the stove and making her way back to the fire.

She sank away in her favourite chair, drawing her knees up and leaning back in a manner that allowed her to see both the window and the fire. She sighed, closing her eyes and putting her lips to the mug; the scent filled her nostrils, wafting up into her brain and stoking the memories back into life. The sound of the fire crackling, the flames licking hungrily at the dry wood, gave way to the howling of the wind and the loud slap of the tent bending and buckling to its will. She opened her eyes to stop herself from drifting off as she sipped leisurely at the warm drink, allowing it to heal her with its comfort and warmth.

She wanted to go back to the glacier; her heart was aching to find what was buried in its dark icy depths. She would go back tomorrow if she was less sensible. The journey had weakened her, and she knew her mind was not in the right place. She would like to think that she would be able to go back up tomorrow and still think clearly, still hold herself back and behave appropriately. Years of training and conditioning had her believing that she would be able to slow herself down, move at a steady pace and do everything right, but deep down inside she knew that without Adam's steady presence she would rush ahead, unable to control herself. She needed him to be there to drag her out of pools or crevasses, without him she would have nobody to press her back up against in the cold of the dark night. She needed him, as much as she hated to admit that she needed anyone, she needed him to go with her, and he was certainly in no state to be climbing mountains.

The feeling of her parents' presence swirled around in her mind. She had felt them so intensely up there, so near.

Adam had seen ice screws in the wall of the glacier, hints that they might have been there.

Did they get out of the crevasse? Did they even fall in? Was it them?

It had to be, didn't it?

Who else could have been up there so recently for the screws to still be untarnished with rust, and visible against the frozen walls?

Were there karabiners clipped in? Quickdraws?

Why didn't she think to ask Adam these questions? They could have got out, they could have made it further.

Kira closed her eyes against the thoughts as they burned like tears behind her lids.

She needed to find them.

There had been an aerial search for days after their failed re-appearance, but by that time, Kira thought, it would have been too late. Had they fallen into the crevasse, it would have happened roughly four days into their journey. Nobody had started looking until two weeks after that. That was a long time to spend in the jaws of an ice monster with nothing to do but wait, wait for rescue from an icy hell, one way or another. If they had both fallen, as evidence might suggest, what with the ice screws, the likelihood of injury was high. They would have had great difficulty climbing out and surviving with injury. There were no signs of any shelter they might have constructed, which only led her to believe that they were still down there, trapped in the jaws of the beast, this river of ice. Their souls were restless, still on this earth, she could feel them all around her.

She needed to find them.

She needed to lay them to rest.

***

Home, for Adam, was smothering.

The clutter of his Uncle George's house was closing in on him after the minimalism of Kira's, and the basic pureness of the tent.

He was frustrated, unable to do anything for himself. He could walk with crutches but could not carry a cup of tea at the same time. He could make himself a sandwich and transport it on his lap whilst in the wheelchair, but again he could not carry a cup of tea. This small detail was what was getting to him, tugging at the edges of his frayed nerves. He got impatient with George hovering over him, checking on him, constantly making sure that he was okay. He wasn't allowed out. George was scared he would slip on the ice and hurt himself more, so he snuck out beneath the cover of night.

Slowly, carefully placing the feet of his crutches in the snow he hopped out, over the threshold of the door. He felt confined in this space, like a criminal more than just an injured mountaineer. He closed his eyes and breathed in the cold night air, feeling it crystallise in his lungs. The feeling reminding him of the sharp stabbing pains Kira must have felt in her lungs as she gasped for air, coming out of the freezing water. His heart jumped at the memory, the vision of her, drenched and frozen. Her lips blue, in a race to match the colour of her eyes, her body ice cold against the warmth of his skin. He sighed as his eyes opened and his head dropped. He hadn't seen her in days, not since they returned from the hospital.

He missed her strength and companionship. He missed her grounded ways, and suddenly felt guilty about his frustrations and tantrums at the inability to do anything for himself. Adam sighed; if she was here, he doubted that he would be so irritated, she had a way of calming him, soothing his frayed nerves. He was sure that part of his growing irritation was because he had not seen her. They had spent so much time together, in such close companionship that it felt wrong to be without her. He didn't even know how she was doing, he felt... empty.

He thought about her constantly.

He dreamed about her.

They were connected in a pure and profound way, and the distance between them was working on both their minds.

His eyes dropped to his leg, as thoughts of her filled his mind, again.

The injury had confused and astounded the doctors, he smiled as he remembered their inability to grasp what he was trying to tell them.

They were unable to believe that Kira had set the bone in his leg, asking him time and again where the wound had come from.

'It is from the broken bone,' he had said, his voice growing in annoyance as he found himself having to repeat his answer for the third time.

'We know your leg is broken Adam.' The doctor was looking down at him, talking to him as if he was a small child, drunk on pain. 'What we are trying to figure out is

22

where the wound had come from. Can you remember? Did something fall on your leg? Did you fall on something?'

'Yes! I fell down a bloody crevasse!' he said angrily. 'My crampon caught against the wall of the crevasse and got stuck whilst my body continued past. My leg snapped and the bone came through the skin.' He was trying to control his breathing, speaking through gritted teeth as the doctor looked at him disbelievingly.

'That is not possible Adam.'

'Well, that is what bloody happened!' he had roared. 'I told you! Kira set the bone and dressed the wound.'

He was angry, agitated, he hadn't been allowed to see Kira, he didn't even know how she was doing. The last time he saw her was in the helicopter being flown out. She was asleep, her face sunken and ashen with only the fever to colour her cheeks.

'Adam, it is not possible for one person to set a bone if it has penetrated the skin. It requires specialist surgery, it cannot simply be manipulated back into place.'

'So how did they do it in the Stone Age or the Iron Age?' he asked, glowering at the doctor through narrowed eyes. 'Or did they simply not have open fractures back then?'

The doctor had looked at him with confusion, staring down at his leg once more before sitting down next to his bed.

'Okay, tell me again exactly what you think she did.'

He had to take a deep breath in order to stop the frustration from bursting out of him in a scream and reverberating through the hospital corridors.

He told him what he remembered. How he had felt the protrusion of the bone, the pain, Kira's words and the calming effect of the drink.

'What was in this drink?'

Adam wasn't sure, the only ingredient he remembered being the hemp. 'It must have had some kind of sedative effect because I don't remember her setting the bone, but I woke up with it back in place, bandaged and splinted.'

'Hemp is historically known to be used as a sedative, even a kind of anaesthetic.' The doctor marvelled quietly before tilting his head to the side and fixing his eyes on Adam again.

'Setting a bone which had been broken this badly would take incredible strength and technique,' he pondered out loud. 'I've not known it to be done without surgery, and certainly not by one person alone. It would be a superhuman effort.'

'She dragged me for five days over those mountains,' Adam said, throwing daggers at the doctor with his eyes. 'Over glaciers, through blizzards and down near sheer drops. That is a superhuman effort. Kira is no ordinary person Doctor; I'm telling you she did this.'

The doctor had looked into his eyes for a long time, reading the truth and sincerity in them. The doctor knew that had this young woman set his broken bone from an open fracture, it would have taken hours of extremely hard work. He had read about this being done in prehistoric times, but he hadn't for one second thought that any person today would be able to do something like this. She had probably saved his leg, if not his life, in setting it so well. The doctor had no concerns about Adam's leg. They had cleared the infection and set it in a cast with a window to allow for redressing of his wound. He was confident that it would be healing well, with no long-term damage. He should regain the full use of it

24

in time and would be back to his normal self by next winter, if not before.

The cold finally broke through his reverie, making him shiver against its embrace. He allowed himself one last look at the mountains before carefully turning around and making his way back inside.

Any sleep he got these days, was with compliments from the painkillers. He didn't like taking them, they rendered him pretty much unconscious, and so he didn't sleep very well. The aching in his leg was growing less with every passing day, but the aching in his mind and heart grew stronger. He didn't know how he was ever going to be able to thank Kira for everything she had done for him. She had given up so much, her own strength and body, for his safety. He hopped over to a seat in front of the fire, carefully lowering himself down into it and closing his eyes against the burning. It was late, he felt sick form the pain radiating out of his leg, but he did not want to take the pills. His head was so full of thought, full of her, that it felt like a lead weight on his neck. The sound of the crackling wood being licked by flames reminded him so much of her. The smell of the coal filled his nostrils with the smell of her.

Blue, sky, navy, indigo, cobalt, azure, cerulean, lapis, denim, admiral, arctic, white, scarlet, earth, the colours flashed through his mind.

Her colours.

Green, teal.

An undefeatable spirit.

Resilience, beyond comparison.

Strength, beauty, compassion.

He drifted away on the waves of her attributes, his admiration for her. The smell of herbs filled his senses, the touch of her cold fingers against his warm wound. Her gentle touch against knots of muscles, her pain, her cold, her suffering.

His eyes shot open on a gasp as the vision of her, falling to her knees in the snow in front of him, jumped into his mind. The sudden movement send stabbing pains down his leg, making him grit his teeth against the cry of pain.

He dreamed of her. Every time he closed his eyes, he dreamed of her, it always started out with her strength and ended the same way; her body beaten but her spirit undefeated.

He hated this dream. He hated waking up with this vision of her; broken. It tore at his heart, send his head in a spin until he could not make out the top from the bottom.

He didn't sleep well, because of the pain, yes, but also because of this dream.

He ran a hand through his hair and pushed himself up, he was going to have to take pills tonight; he needed sleep. He was becoming increasingly agitated with his uncle, and tomorrow he was going to have to go out; being stuck inside all the time, not sleeping and having his mind filled with Kira, and visions of the expedition, did him no good.

Swallowing two of the strong painkillers he returned to the fire and put more fuel on it. Lying down on the sofa, he could let his mind drift back to her and not be afraid of the dreams. These pills pounded him into another world of pure, quiet darkness. A place where he could hide.

***

The quiet darkness outside was in stark contrast to the screaming of her dreams. Kira's eyes opened to a deep darkness, chased from the blue and white of her dreams, the cries still echoing in her head, spilling over into the room around her. Her heart was beating fast, a film of perspiration covered her brow but she did not move. She knew it was just a dream, she was used to these dreams. Waves of snow had been haunting her since her first attempt into the mountain six years ago. She lay very still, allowing the emotion of her dream to spill over her lids and roll down the side of her face as she focussed on the cold darkness beyond the glass of her window. The snow was still there, but it was the blue of the ice that had been haunting her subconscious since they returned. Two faces that sometimes appeared in her dreams have turned into three, and it was this third one, with its echoing cries of tortured pain that woke her. Kira lay quietly in bed, unmoving. The depth of darkness outside confirming her suspicions that the sun was still warming the other side of the world. Sitting up, she pushed the covers away and quietly padded through the house and into the cold night air. The stark difference in temperature had her folding her arms around her against the cold, as she lifted her eyes to the sky. The moon was still high in the sky, illuminating the snow-capped mountains in the distance and casting her slight form in an eerie light. She looked almost ethereal in the light of the moon. A creature of the night, with her impossibly blue eyes and snow-white hair, her bare feet clinging to the raw wood of the porch. The moon cast its gentle glow over her, allowing the stars to look down and smile upon this creature of their own. She belonged in these woods, her form was as familiar to them as the shape of the trees and the sharp angle of the mountains. They had called her out tonight, wanting to smile upon her form, fill her with the heat of their fires and remind her of her home. The howl of a wolf in the distance tilted her head, as another answered. Kira stood quietly listening to the conversation. She didn't know the call of wolves as well as her dad had. He had tried to teach her, but she was always more interested in the medicinal values of the herbs in her mother's box.

They're mourning, her father's voice carried through the still air.

'What are they mourning?'

She was suddenly seven years old again, standing beside her father on the porch, listening to the wolf song.

The loss of one of their own.

Kira watched her younger self slip her small hand into her father's as the mournful tone of the wolf choir echoed through the valley, bouncing off the hillsides and reaching up to the sky; sending the spirit of their friend into the afterlife, amongst the stars.

'They will be looking for a new member, to fill the place of the lost one in the pack,' she whispered, that much she remembered. The tone of the howling will change in the next few days. A shiver ran down her spine, shaking her body with the cold and breaking the spell. A moment later she turned away, moving back inside and closing the door behind her. That lingering feeling of emptiness washed over her, again, as she stood looking at the fire. She missed the laughter that had filled her home over the summer months. She missed the quiet companionship of him beside the fire as they read or stared at maps. She missed the aggravation he ignited in her, the obstinacy, the fire he lit in her soul and the warmth of his eyes on her. She didn't know what to do with these emotions. She had never felt like this, and didn't know what to make of it. They were friends, undoubtedly, but the experience of this expedition had brought them so much closer. They were so much more than just friends. There was a bond between them, complete trust, unlike she had ever felt with anyone besides her parents. Her home felt empty because he had been a part of her life, her home, a constant presence within these wooden walls for a year and now, suddenly, he was gone.

Only, he wasn't.

He was just an hour's walk down the valley, and all she had to do was get dressed and make the trip.

Wrapped in a blanket, in front of the stoked fire, Kira drifted off again. The dreams kept themselves at a distance, allowing her these precious few hours of peaceful slumber before the orange light, streaming in from the eastern windows fell across her face and gently pulled her lids apart.

Her eyes fell on the coals glowing in the fireplace, the heat rolling over her in gentle waves. The house was quiet. So quiet.

Outside the birds were offering a half-hearted morning song. Snow was falling again, gently, dancing in the music of the breeze. She pushed herself up, hunching in front of the fire to stoke it back into flames. The bottom of her hair was still stained with the blood of the ptarmigan she had hunted a few days ago. Her eyes fell on the dark colour, having turned a rich brown against the white, as it tickled the hearth she crouched on. She liked it, this connection with the land. She carried its lifeblood in her hair, as an offering. It was part of her. The heat of the flames pushed her back, making her rise to her feet and find her way to the kitchen where she moved the kettle onto the hot part of the stove. She hadn't made much dinner last night, and yet she could not even finish that. She struggled with the food, her stomach rebelling violently, contracting into vicious cramps that reminded her of the icy pool beyond the second ridge. The rich meat of her normal diet disagreed with her digestive system after all the scientifically prepared expedition meals. Kira was acutely aware of the protrusion of bones on her body. She didn't like it. She felt unhealthy, weak. She was doing her best to build herself back up to her former self, but found herself struggling. She had tossed the packages of supplementary nutritional shakes that the hospital had given her aside. She did not think that she would need it. She has never needed them before, she had spent her whole life fuelling her body with wholesome home-grown food, and meat from the land. Why should that change? What reason could there be that, that would not be enough? She had never thought for a moment, that the food her body knew so well could cause her so much pain and discomfort. Her expedition rucksack was still in town, at Harvey's. She had not wanted to carry it back up the mountain. There was nothing in it she needed, but now as she thought of what to wear into town, she regretted leaving it behind. She could have worn the comfortable technical clothing, with the thick insulated jacket into town instead of her normal, dated attire. Suddenly, just for a minute she missed the brightly coloured jacket she had thought so garish at first. Its warmth and colour had grown on her, filled her with happiness. How could you not smile, wearing a bright purple jacket? Adam must have been having a laugh to himself when he picked it she thought, making a broth for breakfast. Her life was dominated by the colours of nature, and he had brought the splash of colour into her life, a colour which had stood out like a smile in the dull brown room. The only other colour being in the blanket her mother had made, dulled by time and use. The sea of white that had dominated their lives for eleven days had brought a yearning for colour into her life. She had always been content with the colours of nature, the colour of summer flowers bringing brightness into the house over the warmer months. Winter was cold; white and brown with hues of green. She used to love everything about winter, until this expedition. The dominance of white had filled every nook and cranny in her mind and body, and she was struggling to get rid of the monotone colour of her emotions. Even the broth in her cup, which she loved so much, was brown and she was tempted to add fresh sprigs of indoor herbs, just for a splash of colour.

She sat in front of the fire, still in her night clothes sipping at the broth and wondering what to wear into town. She did not have much choice of attire and had never before felt this concern about what to wear. The more nondescript she could be when going into town the better. She had wanted to stay below the radar, remain unnoticed by society, and simply live the life she wanted to live in peace, alone. She drained the cup looking into the fire, but now things have changed. She had a reason to go into town, she had dreams, ambitions and she could not accomplish them on her own. She was smart and realistic enough to realise that there were some things she simply could not do by herself, no matter how much she wanted to. The sun had risen above the horizon when she tilted her head to look out of the window.

Soft snow was still coming down in a gentle veil, unhampered by wind or warmth. She had known, last night when she was standing on the porch, drowning in the sad choir song of the wolves, that she could not spend another day alone. She needed to talk to someone. This feeling was a foreign one in her mind, struggling to find a place to settle. She had never felt the need for human company before, but now it struck her suddenly, without warning, knocking her off her feet. This desperate need to see another human being, to make her voice heard and to hear the laughter and chatter of something other than the trees and the animals, overwhelmed and confused her. She needed to feel the presence of another body and bathe in the warmth of his voice. Pushing herself up she moved quickly, purposely through the house; rinsing her dishes, banking the fires and getting dressed. She had on her feet her own moccasin boots, tied around the bottom of the worn jeans which now hung loosely on her hips, even with the woollen leggings underneath. She braided her hair down her back, having found over the years that the tidy look detracted from the strange colour that had people staring. She always pulled her hood over her hair when she went into town, but today she wasn't going to do that. Her and Adam's dramatic return into town had focussed everybody's attention on them. The townsfolk who had not known about her or who could only ever speculate about her existence now had a firm picture of her in their minds. She was the strange child of those mountaineers that went missing years ago. Rumours were rife through town, speculations of how she lived and survived. Precious few knew the truth and she wanted to keep it that way. Leave the townsfolk to their speculation, it had nothing to do with her. The air was very cold and she found her feet moving faster and faster over the snow, willing the exercise to create heat within her muscles. She hated how much she struggled with the cold now that she was so worn out, her reserves depleted and her body reduced in size. She was determined to gain her weight and strength back, no matter what it took. She had been going for runs to aid in the rebuilding of her fitness. She was pleased to find that through sheer determination she could still go as far as she had before the expedition, even if she was more tired by the end of it. She fell asleep in the early darkness of the evening only to be woken by the white and blue of her dreams, hours later. The lack of peaceful sleep and excessive exercise did nothing to help her put the weight back on. She didn't want to resort to the nutritional supplements provided by the hospital, but she might need to.

Her feet stilled on the bridge as her mind came into focus and her eyes fell on the town; the road that she had dragged the sled onto. The last time she had come this way, facing this direction she was at the very edge of survival. The sled had been heavy behind her, pulling at the already raw flesh that had been torn off by the hard work. The lights of town had swum in front of her eyes as she struggled over the bridge and came to a stop in the middle of the road. Kira was pulled along with the memory, drowning in the pain and emotion seeping out of the cracked edges of the visions. She could feel the exhaustion tug at her limbs as she stumbled into the centre of the main road. She stopped and lifted her head before looking down at the snow-covered road that today was bathed in sunlight, rather than the painted black of the memory. The snow was still the same and the smell from the bakery enticing, as it had been on that night.

Kira started as somebody pushed past her, sending her stumbling forward out of the memory. She had to shake her head and focus her eyes on the sign above the bakery before her feet would start moving again.

The whispers and stares went over her head as she focused her attention on her destination. Her white hair exposed her for who she was, and by the time she pushed through the back door of Harvey's a crowd had stopped to watch her, pointing and whispering in admiration.

'Kira!' Harvey looked up at the cold wash of air blowing into the bakery. She had been on his mind constantly since she had returned to her home. He had held himself back from calling her, not wanting to break the promise of their agreement. He understood her need for life to return to normal, and if he suddenly started calling her at home things would change. She stood in front of him, blue eyes overwhelming her tired face as the emotion tried to spill over the edge. He could not stop himself from stepping forward, out from behind his baking table and wrapping his arms around her. She felt warm and slight in his arms, her hair cold where she laid it against his chest and closed her eyes.

'How are you kid?' He didn't let go as she mumbled her response into the folds of his apron. She felt so safe, here. Warm and protected.

Adam's green eyes flashed through her mind as she remembered his fingers lacing through hers, the gentle touch sending electric currents up her arm, jolting her heart and making her stomach do a backflip. She pulled away and shook the vision of him from her memory.

Harvey held her at arm's length, looking her up and

down. 'Have you been eating properly?' The concern in his voice mirrored the look in his eyes. She still looked very small and although he knew it would take more than three or four days for her to build herself back up, he didn't like her looking like this. Her nod turned into a shrug as she lowered herself into a seat. 'I've tried, but it's hard.' She had been trying so hard not to allow the sadness to overcome her, fighting to keep it at bay. She tried to keep active, to blow away the darkness with runs in the cold air or to keep the endorphins flowing by chopping wood, clearing the snow from her porch, walking through the woods, anything. She was keeping busy by making ointments and salves, reading books in an effort to increase her medicinal knowledge, and yet she was losing the fight. She had been out hunting, but it wasn't the same as before; she felt tired and sad, unable to keep her parents out of her thoughts.

'I think you should use those things the doctor gave you,' he said, moving to the kettle to make her a hot chocolate. 'Your bag is at my house. You can come and have dinner with me tonight.'

'No, it's all right.' Her voice was low, heavy with melancholy as he turned to look at her,

'Thanks Harvey,' she finished, looking at the melee of people just beyond the window. The bakery was suddenly very busy, and they could hear the sound of growing voices beyond the door of the back room.

'I'm going to go see Adam,' she said pulling her eyes away from the snow, trying to ignore the voices. 'Have you seen him?'

Harvey added cream and marshmallows to the mug, making Kira smile. 'I've been round yesterday,' he turned his attention back to her, passing the mug over. 'I think he feels a bit like you,' he said watching her thoughtfully. 'Trapped inside, at a loss of what to do with himself.'

Kira nodded along with the words, she knew exactly what he meant.

'He looked tired,' Harvey continued. 'I don't think he's getting much sleep.'

'Harvey!' The bakery assistant tumbled in through the door looking stressed and harassed. 'I need your help. There is so many of them and nobody seems to know what they want.'

Kira looked up and then at Harvey. 'It's my fault,' she said. 'They saw me come in.'

'No worries kid.' He smiled and ruffled her hair. 'Any publicity is good publicity. Now that they are in here, they will be buying something.'

She smiled a wry smile pulling an apologetic face as he walked away, cajoling the assistant with him. She glanced back curiously, familiar with the presence of the white-haired girl but suddenly interested in the stories that had been told about her.

Kira sighed, putting her lips to the hot chocolate as she hid from the enquiring stares and excited whispers of the townsfolk. Harvey's booming voice filtered through the closed door, as he joked with the customers, convincing them to buy some treats, as he took their minds off the reason they had come into the bakery in the first place. She was only halfway through her hot chocolate when it occurred to her that whilst they were all in here, being nosy, she could escape unseen. Regretfully she placed the half-drunk drink on the counter, scribbling a *Thank you* in the flour on the table.

Hitching the deep leather satchel she had brought down the valley with her, over her shoulder, she slipped out through the back door. Her feet leading her around the perimeter of town, the same way that Adam had first shown her to his uncle's house.

Her eyes were trained to notice everything around her and even as she travelled past, her mind focussed only on reaching the house, her conscious picked up on the lone figure just inside the line of trees. Perceiving no danger, she continued past and found herself around the back of the house which contained her friend. She was standing just inside the treeline looking out towards the back garden, frozen in time and space. The memory of her first day out there flashed through her mind. She had questioned the wisdom of setting out on this expedition, even back then. Looking up at the majestic peaks she currently had her back to, she had seen danger in this trip. She had felt it in her bones and she had been right.

A cry of frustration roared out of the house before the back door swung open, bouncing on the hinges as it slammed against the wall of the house.

Adam looked tired, harassed, angry even as he stumbled out of the door on his crutches. He tried to slam the door behind him, his injury preventing him from having full control over all his limbs. Denied even this small satisfaction he groaned again and hopped over to the garden chairs where he had to lower himself into one, instead of just collapsing like he would have done three weeks ago. He looked defeated as he stared at his lap before slowly, on a sigh, lifting his head.

His heart stopped and skipped a beat, allowing his

stomach to do several somersaults before falling back into rhythm.

His eyes fixed on the impossible blue of hers, her calm presence washing over him like a cool cloth over a fevered brow. She was watching him like she had that first time he had come to her house, and knocked on her door with purpose.

'Ki.' Her name was a whisper over his lips. He didn't think that she would come to see him and he loathed the time he would have to wait before being able to get up the valley to her home.

She stepped forward out of the trees, like a child out of a hiding place, moving towards him. He watched her move, finding comfort in the silent progress of her moccasined feet. She was herself again, floating over the snow; smaller, more tired, but herself.

'Hi.' He wanted to stand up, fold his arms around her, kiss her lips, or at least her cheek, but he couldn't find the control over his limbs.

'Hi.' She half smiled against the flutter in her stomach, feeling slightly uncomfortable as her eyes darted to movement beyond the window. Adam wondered if she could feel the intensity of his feelings for her radiating out from his pores.

'How's your leg?' She half perched in the corner of the porch were the railing met the house, not wanting to be seen through the window.

Adam noted the leather bag she had removed from her shoulders and placed on the deck, wondering about its contents as he lifted his eyes back to hers.

'It's all right.' Kira could see the lie in his eyes and

narrowed her own, wondering why he would feel the need to lie to her. He couldn't move away from her piercing stare, she knew he was lying and he looked away, running a hand through his hair as he sighed. 'It's frustrating,' he admitted. 'The pain stops me from doing anything but when I take painkillers that work, it knocks me out.'

He had dark circles beneath his lids that made her believe he had not been taken the pills very regularly at all.

'Is it really bad now?' The softening of her tone alerted him to the guilt she was feeling.

'No, it's all right.' He wanted to take her hand. She was so close, he could feel the heat of the blood pumping through her veins, his heart rate increased as his eyes dropped to her lap, where her hands were resting. The skin looked smooth as it curled around her narrow wrist and covered her hand in a silky embrace. Her nails were clean and clipped short, her fingers looked strong as he knew them to be.

'Can you walk?'

His eyes lifted back to hers. He had always found her attractive, he had always wanted to touch her, be with her, but he had never felt it more acutely than now. He struggled to concentrate on her words as his eyes focused on the movement of her lips, deeply coloured by the wind and cold.

'A bit.' His voice had dropped in volume when he finally found the words as Kira fought his intense stare, swallowing past the lump formed in her throat by her own beating heart. 'The crutches struggle on the snow, I can only go very slowly.'

Kira nodded. 'Slow is better than nothing. Let's go for a walk.' She pushed herself away from the house, desperate for the anonymity of the woods as Adam looked at her with trepidation. 'I don't know if I can.'

'Don't be stupid.' She brushed past him. 'Of course you can. Where are your boots?'

The words 'I can't' were not part of her vocabulary. He looked at her, wondering what it was that made her believe that anything was possible whilst others struggled with even the smallest tasks.

'Inside, by the front door.'

Kira took an internal breath and opening the door kept her eyes focussed on her goal. The rooms around her were warm and cluttered as she moved through them, aware of the other presence in the house, the eyes and the drop of his jaw. Spotting his boots, she reached down for them before unhooking the coat from behind the door.

'Here.' She tossed the coat on his lap, quickly followed by the hat that she had found beneath it.

'We should put something around your foot.' She stood looking at the cast. 'To keep it dry.'

'Bin liner?' His eyebrow lifted as she smiled down at him, a thought occurring to her.

'I've got a better idea. Get those socks on,' she said turning away to her bag in the corner of the porch. Adam watched as she pulled out a package wrapped in animal skin and releasing the first large layer, returned the bundle to her bag.

'What's that?'

'What does it look like?'

His eyes dropped to her feet and suddenly he knew what she was doing; she was wrapping the leather around his foot in a makeshift moccasin. It would be warm, dry and waterproof. She used the piece of twine which had held the package together, to tie the material around the cast.

'There we go.'

Adam shook his head, once again surprised by her ingenuity, as a smile spread across his lips. He struggled with his other boot until she bent down and tied the laces for him.

'Thanks.'

'Come on.'

She wanted to get out of here. George was peering curiously out of the window, now that he knew she was there. Adam hadn't told him much about the expedition and he had tried to respect his privacy, but he was astounded at the appearance of this child; John and Ava's daughter.

He knew that she had gone through a great deal to get them back, he knew that she was to thank for the survival of his nephew, but he did not know how to thank her.

Kira was standing beside Adam, her arm around his back as she tried to help him up. She was strong, he realised. As slight as she was, she was strong.

He watched as she carefully helped his nephew down the couple of steps, taking care to make sure his crutches were stable. A roar of laughter suddenly erupted from the young man and George saw the smile on Kira's face as she looked back at him. She must have said something funny, her lips were still moving, making Adam laugh again. George moved away from the window as they disappeared behind the trees, relieved for the laughter that she had coaxed out of his nephew. He had never known Adam to be so impatient and angry, the frustration of his condition wreaking havoc on his emotions. He hadn't realised that there was more to it. He didn't know how much Adam had missed Kira, how concerned he was about her and how desperate he had been to see her.

Chapter Two

The moving air felt good on his skin. The feeling of his muscles working together, consuming oxygen provided by the rich blood in his veins was encouraging, filling him with hope. He knew that eventually the break would heal, the cast would come off and after a while he would be able to move as he used to, what he didn't know is when that would happen. Six weeks at a minimum; that was what the doctors had said, and then rehabilitation which could take a lot longer. The lack of movement was frustrating him and being stuck inside was beyond what he could handle. He needed to be outside, he needed to feel the wind on his skin and the cold between his fingers. Kira understood, Uncle George didn't.

Kira had never let injury stop her from doing what she wanted. Even at the age of four with a bandaged hand after nearly slicing a big chunk of it off, she was still making kindling. Her mother was not amused, but her father had encouraged her to keep doing what she wanted to do. Nature was a great healer; she was a firm believer in that. Sitting inside, drugged up to the eyeballs took away the ability to appreciate nature and all it had to offer. Pain was part of life and although she did not advocate battling through severe pain for the sake of proving something, she did not think that there was anything wrong with accepting it and learning from it. She had often practised new medicinal remedies on herself, experimenting with which herbs offered the most pain relief in which manner and for which ailments. One herb could be used in several different ways for different ailments. She had experimented with everything from grazes, cuts, colds, headaches, muscular pain and even menstrual ailments. One consistency that she had found was that no matter what, it was always better to spend some time outside, to lift your mood and allow for the release of endorphins, rather than to stay locked up inside.

The gentle fall of snowflakes as it drifted through the air and settled soundlessly on the objects around them, emphasised the quiet of the woods. There was no sound other than the crunch of their movement through the snow.

Kira was patient as she walked beside him, feeling content at just being outside, and not being alone. Their solitary walk in the woods created the illusion that they were far away, lost in a world where no others dwelled. Kira drew comfort from this illusion along with the fact that they were indeed not alone, or lost. She had enjoyed the adventure of being at high altitude, isolated from the world where they had only themselves and each other to rely on. The risk had excited her. She had been confident in her belief that they could deal with anything that was to be thrown their way and they did, but she would not like to repeat it, ever, never mind right now. So, she looked back to the edge of the trees, thankful that they were indeed not alone or at risk.

'Are you okay?' Adam lifted his head from where he had

been concentrating on the placement of the crutches, fixing his eyes on her profile. She took a couple of small steps past him before drawing to a halt. She was staring into the distance, thinking deeply about her answer. She did not just rasp out a common response, like others did. She put thought to the questions he asked her as if they carried a deeper meaning.

'I feel different,' she whispered, her voice settling quietly, like the snow around them. 'Changed.' She turned to face him and found the comfort and support of a tree behind her. Adam's head dropped slightly, tilting as his eyes drifted over her, unable to settle on any one place.

'I feel... weaker and somehow stronger, enriched but altered.' She half smiled at the garbled explanation.

'Altered in what way?' His eyes bore into hers, filling her body with liquid warmth.

'Like, I'm not the same person as the one who had walked out of my home on the first day of the journey.'

'You're not,' he said, he could see it in her eyes, in the way she held her body. She was proud and confident yet hesitant and unsure. She had discovered something about herself that she did not know how to deal with.

'Should I be?' There was genuine concern in her voice, confusion in her eyes. 'I feel like I'm somehow dismissing my teachings, going against everything my parents strove for, in answering this need for...' She stopped and shook her head.

'Need for what?' His heart was hammering in his chest. He wanted her to express the same emotions he was feeling, but he had no way of knowing if she would. He couldn't tell if she felt the same or if she just saw him as a friend. Her only friend, other than Harvey.

'I don't know.' She shook her head, she just didn't want to be alone anymore. She loved her life and her home, but she felt lonely. Now that she had a friend, a partner, a companion who understood her, she felt the need for conversation. She felt a need to share her thoughts in a way she had never done before. She had always been content with being alone. She could entertain herself, she had no problem with dealing with her own thoughts. So why has all of that now changed?

'I guess I'm just used to company now.'

She started walking again and Adam was forced to move his crutches forward and swing himself into motion.

'How's your wounds?' he asked after a while, feeling a need to break the silence. He was not prepared for her to come to a stop and peel the layers of clothing away from her skin as her head tilted down to look at it, as if she hasn't seen it in days.

His heart quickened at the exposure of her flesh, but his heart ached at the sorry state her beautiful body was in.

'Better, I think.'

His eyes rested on the scabbing, hugging her body above protruding hipbones. Dull yellow bruising surrounded the wounds, showing evidence of healing. She dropped her top, making him tear his eyes away.

'Have you been drinking that stuff the doctors gave you?'

Kira sighed and shook her head. 'I left it at Harvey's, I didn't want to but...'

'Ki, I think you need to.'

She looked up at the concern in his voice, seeing it

45

mirrored in his eyes. She was painfully thin and it worried him.

'I'll pick it up on my way back.' She closed her eyes against the pull of his. She had been coming to the same conclusion over the last twenty-four hours.

'How about you? Are you having any trouble eating?'

He couldn't lie to her. He couldn't preach to her, be so concerned about her health and then lie to her, so he nodded his head in truth.

'I don't seem to have an appetite. I try but it's a struggle. I think it's because I've been feeling so trapped as well.'

Kira nodded. 'I've been hunting, less than normal, but I can't seem to finish anything. I seem to be living on broth at the moment.'

They looked at each other with worried expressions, until a giggle started to tickle in her stomach. A smile spread across her face moments before she let out a laugh. It was comical really. The two of them staring at each other, worried about the other when they were in exactly the same position. Adam found his stomach swirling at the sound of her laughter, a smile breaking through his own defences before quickly giving way to laughter. She would have given him a friendly push if he weren't on crutches.

'Come on,' she said. 'I've brought some ptarmigan and vegetables. I'll cook you a stew.'

Adam turned, slower and more laboriously but with a smile on his face.

'Well, I can't say no to that.' He was suddenly hungry, his mouth already watering just from the thought of it.

His heart felt lighter, his mood lifted from this short walk in the woods but more so because of her presence. He glanced in her direction as she walked close to his side, the heat of her body mingling with his. Her arms brushed against his every so often as she walked with a content smile on her face. She hadn't realised how close they had grown, how much the existence of his presence meant to her, how much she needed it. She hadn't thought about how much time they had spent together over the past year. The number of days they spend apart up until the expedition could be counted on two hands. He had become such a close friend, somebody she felt comfortable with to be herself.

They reached the back garden, too soon for his liking but probably just in time for the ache in his leg. He sat down on the chair with a grimace, the slight change in muscle tension lifting Kira's eyes to his face as he bit back against the pain, allowing her to unlace his boot and remove the cover from his cast.

'Come on.' She reached down, winding her arms beneath his shoulders and around his body, helping him up. There was no thought in the process as his arms lifted, folding around her small body. His face was buried in her hair by the time he became aware of the intense hammering against his chest; unsure whether it was his heart or hers that was threatening to pound a bruise into his skin. She smelt pure and clean, like the trees of the forest and the air of the mountains. Her hair was like malleable ice, bending and flowing over the lines of his face in a cold wave. He was losing himself in the warmth when her arms suddenly disappeared, her heat ripped away as if doused by the coldness of her hair. She handed him his crutches as she moved away, her eyes darting aimlessly in the space around him, unwilling to come to rest. His heart was still hammering in his chest as he watched her move away, her own chest visibly moving up and down. Kira pulled the door open, trying to calm the beating of her heart, dancing to the drumming rhythm of his heat.

'Thank you,' he placed the feet of his crutches inside the house before hopping over the threshold. Kira had to turn to the mountains, ask them to provide her with strength and calm presence of mind, before she stepped through the door and froze; George was there, in the kitchen, staring at them.

Adam became aware of the tension in her muscles before he noticed the presence of his uncle, and tearing himself out of the well of his increasingly uncontrollable feelings, he found his voice. The door was still open behind them and Kira was on tenterhooks, ready to dash at any second.

'Kira, you remember my Uncle George?' He fixed his eyes on her, daring her to make a run for it. He waited until she had stepped inside, closing the door behind her before looking away. 'Uncle George, I'm sure you remember Kira?'

'Of course.' He stepped forward, freezing when he saw her body move back. George looked at her with warmth in his green eyes. 'Thank you,' he said softly, the intensity of his gratitude dripping from the clear edges of the words. 'It seems we both now have you to thank for our lives.'

Her eyes lifted to his, reading the emotion on his face before giving a small nod of acceptance. Adam frowned at the growing silence and tension in the room, acutely aware of Kira's discomfort next to him, scared that she was going to turn around any second and disappear back up the mountain. He fixed his eyes on his uncle, lifting an eyebrow in quiet question. George took a moment to pull himself out of the intense gaze of those icy blue eyes before clearing his throat.

'I was just on my way to tell you that I'm going out,' he said finding Adam's eyes again. 'I have a dinner date with a friend, will you be all right with finding yourself something to eat?'

'We'll be fine, thank you.' Adam willed his uncle out of the room if not the house, intensely aware of the sensitivity of Kira's discomfort.

'All right then,' he turned, reluctant to remove his eyes from this extraordinary creature in his kitchen. 'I'll see you later.'

Adam managed to voice a farewell to his uncle, the majority of his attention on Kira still measuring the level of her discomfort, and wondering how likely it was for her to want to bolt.

'Would you like a drink?' He moved behind the counter, still aware of the tension in her body.

'Please,' she whispered, as the tension slowly started to ease from her muscles. She dragged her eyes away from the door through which George had disappeared and moved to a seat, wearily sitting down. Leaning forwards onto her arms she dropped her head, her hair spilling forwards over her shoulders and onto the counter. She felt tired, drained and annoyed with herself. She didn't understand why she had to get so tense around people. Taking a deep breath, she lifted her head to find Adam staring at her hair.

'What's this?' He reached for the lick of iron colouring the ends of her hair, and running it through his fingers enjoyed the way it moved on his skin. He lost himself for a moment wondering what it would be like to run his fingers through the length of her hair.

Her breath had caught in her throat as his fingers

touched her hair, he was so close, leaning forward to scrutinise the unexpected colour. She could smell the familiar scent of him, the smell she had fallen asleep to in the confines of the tent. Her heart skipped a beat as her pupils dilated and she struggled to find the words in the sudden emptiness of her mind.

'Blood,' she whispered, starting at the violent acrobatics of her stomach as his eyes lifted to hers. She could feel his breath on her cheek. His eyes drifted down to the bright colour of her parted lips. Their hearts were beating to the same rhythm, desperation, before she blinked and pulled herself away. 'Ptarmigan blood,' she said clearing her mind with a deep breath, banishing the visions to a dark corner and locking the door.

He didn't ask how it got there as he pulled himself away and stood up, righting himself on the crutches. He liked it, it suited her; this connection to the land.

'I like it,' he said when he finally found his voice and smiled. It seemed very much a part of her.

She was quiet for a long time, her eyes eventually leaving the movement of his body around the kitchen and settling on the view beyond the window. Adam liked the fact that she didn't rush to help him and wasn't concerned by the time it took him to do small, simple tasks.

'Did your uncle know my parents?' The words were difficult to move over her lips, heavy with emotion as she forced them out. Her eyes were still on the mountains beyond the window, but he could see the fight in her eyes as she tried to keep the emotion at bay.

He wasn't really sure how well George had known John and Ava Roche. He'd only ever heard him speak of them once, that night when they took shelter in Kira's home. George had said nothing of them, or of Kira, since that night and Adam had thought nothing of it, until now.

'I'm not sure.'

Kira's eyes found his as he placed a mug in front of her before drawing up a seat, folding his hands around his own warm mug. 'He's not said anything to me.'

The colour of her eyes changed as she thought back to that faithful night last winter when George had spoken of them with comfort and confidence in using their Christian names.

'He mentioned them by name.' Her voice was low and quiet. 'He said that he'd been up there before, didn't he?'

Adam nodded at the confusion on her brow. 'He did.'

'So he must have known them. I don't remember ever seeing him up there. I don't remember anybody ever being up there.'

'It might have been before you were born,' he offered, 'or when you were very young?'

'Maybe.' Her voice had changed, her eyes darted to the table top as she lost herself in thought, just for a moment. Kira remembered playing barefoot in the woods and splashing in the creek at the age of two, when words were precious few from her lips and body contact was the overwhelming method of conveying her love and emotions. She would have remembered George if she had met him.

He saw the moment she pulled herself away from the world behind her eyes and took a cleansing breath before facing the world again.

'I'll get this meat on now,' she said suddenly, ducking down to the bag on the floor. 'It will need some time to soften.'

Pushing away from her seat she moved around to his side of the counter, her arm brushing against his body as she passed and ducked down to where he was pointing out the pots.

He loved watching her work, finding comfort once again at the confidence and grace of her sure hands, losing himself in the memory of the touch of her fingers against his skin. She had healed him more than once, she had touched the aching, damaged parts of his body with her healing hands and brought them back to life. She pulled several bags from the leather satchel, amusing him each time her hand reached in to pull something different out. She had brought everything she needed with her.

'What?' She glanced across, aware of his eyes on her and frowned at the smile on his face.

'Is that a Mary Poppins bag?' his eyes were twinkling as she looked at him with confusion, making him laugh.

'Do you not know Mary Poppins?'

'No,' she stated, turning her eyes back on the preparation of vegetables. 'Who is she?'

Adam smiled, loving how removed she was from this world of his. She had grown up with tales of Stone Age healers and Iron Age warriors, the music of the wind and water, a constant backdrop to her life. She did not know of these fictional characters that had filled the background of his early years.

'She is a magical nanny,' he smiled when she looked up at him with a quizzical brow. 'She owns a bag from which she can pull almost anything to make the children's wishes come true.'

Kira's hands stilled as she looked at him. 'It's a musical fantasy film created in the 60s in America.' He smiled the answer to the unasked questions in her eyes, realising that while he was watching children's films she was running through the woods, climbing up the steep sides of mountains and killing deer. Whilst he was being read fictional stories, losing himself in the fantastical characters of children's books, she was learning about ancient medicines and healing methods. There was a hint of understanding below the colour of confusion as she lowered her eyes back to the food she was preparing. She'd never watched films; they had never owned a television. Her entertainment was climbing trees and watching young animals play in the sunshine. She swam naked in the spring, unperturbed by the movement of fish against her skin. She missed being a child, being carefree and cared for. She missed being enfolded in the strong arms of her father and the gentle trace of her mother's fingers against her skin. She missed being part of a family, she missed being loved.

'Is there anything I can do?'

Her stomach lurched at the timeliness of his words, throwing her off kilter and colouring her cheeks at the thought that jumped into her mind. Looking into the pot she shook her head, keeping her eyes averted and her face away from his enquiring eyes.

'No thank you, this is as much as we can do at the moment.' She lifted her head when she was sure the colour had left her cheeks and covered the pot. 'We'll just leave it for a few hours.'

The room was thick with the need radiating from both of them. Kira stepped away, the void she left immediately filling with the confusion of emotion that poured out of her like a open tap. She shivered at the intensity of Adam's eyes on her and moved away. 'I'll go check the fire.'

Adam watched as her long lithe limbs carried her away at the speed with which he was accustomed. He was pleased to see her strength having returned to at least this part of her, which he knew so well, but sighed at the haste with which she had pulled herself away from him. He had felt the tension in her limbs earlier as well, the hesitation with which she had helped him to his feet.

Confused and slightly demoralised he pulled himself to his feet and laboriously made his way over to the front room where she was hunched in front of the fire, coaxing it back to life with small pieces of wood.

The familiarity of this pose drew him back to her home and the time they had spent their, together. His eyes glanced across the room, littered with the evidence of a lifetime's activity, and longed for the calm order of Kira's home in the woods.

He understood the need she had shown for her home and wished that he too could return there. Those wooden walls were more his home than this one of his childhood. He had spent more time up there with her than he had in town with his uncle, and he felt the ache of longing as she had in the hospital.

'I miss your home.' The words made her turn, her eyes recognising the sudden embarrassment in his as he realised, he had spoken the words out loud. Her eyes were darker in here, shining by the light of the fire as they drifted down to his leg. Her mind pondering the possibility of him making it to the house. She missed his presence up there. The house was mourning his absence by casting deep empty shadows in the corners he frequented. She didn't need to say anything, he read her thoughts on the lines of her face and by the flash in her eyes. She turned away, placing a log onto the fire before moving back into a seat. There was so much going on inside of her that she found it hard to distinguish between her emotions. Thoughts of the expedition, memories really, was so fresh in her mind they plagued her day and night. They took over her life, invading her quiet time and infiltrating her dreams. Kira lost herself in the sea of white, as she stared into the dancing flames. Letting go of the present she allowed it to take her back to the cold, hard surface beneath her feet and the moving air on her chilled skin. The sky was blue when they had set out, only the unease in the pit of her stomach tinting it with red and black in her mind. She had been driven by a desperate need to reach the heart of the mountain. She had carried within her an understanding and appreciation for the world they were entering, but on the fringes, there was something else, an obstinacy, almost an anger as she ploughed on, ignoring all the signs, all the warnings. She knew something wasn't right and she still chose to continue, even after falling through the ice she pushed on. Forcing the growing fear to the back of her mind and thinking that they could beat the mountain. She closed her eyes, aware of the warmer air around her and the presence of a strong body beside hers. Adam had sat down next to her, respecting her time of thought and need for this quiet. He had often seen her do this, disappear into herself with the help of the dancing flames and knew that she was struggling with something inside of her. She didn't tense when his arm came around her shoulders and he breathed a sigh of relief as she leaned into him, accepting his offer of support. Kira was reminded of the way his body had felt against her back, supporting her, warming her after she fell through the ice. She trusted him, but she didn't understand her own emotions. She didn't know if it was guilt, or trust, or friendship that made her heart ache for his acceptance and presence. She didn't know if the offer of his support was out of duty, friendship or something more. She wished for someone to guide her through this confusing time, to explain the turmoil inside of her.

There was an immense sense of relief that escaped from their bodies and enfolded them as they sat together on the sofa. They had come full circle. They had made it back and they were safe. This relief she felt was different from the weight that had been lifted off her shoulders on the evening of their return. There was a comfort in being wrapped in his arms, pressed against the warmth of his strong chest as his heart hammered against his sternum and his lungs filled with air. They were alive. She derived great comfort from the life within his body. Her mind stilled as her breathing matched his, his heart slowed to a calm rhythm in her ears as his head came down on hers, warming it with its gentle weight.

It was Kira's dream that startled them out of their slumber as she flew out of his arms with a loud gasp. Her breath coming in ragged gasps as the jolt of surprise send a pain shooting down Adam's leg. He clenched his teeth against the pain, aware of the sudden loss of her heat and a sense of great fear. The fear dissipated as his eyes focussed on her heaving form. She wanted to shout in anger at the dark dominance of the dream, its blunt unforgiving challenge on her senses. She had not been able to save him, as she had not been able to save her parents.

'Ki?' She jumped at the touch of his hand on her shoulder making him quickly retract it. 'Are you okay?'

'Yes, sorry.' She wiped the palms of her hands on her jeans, aware of his movement behind her as she moved her gaze to the window. The light was failing, the fire was low in the hearth and she realised that they must have been asleep for at least a couple of hours. 'I'll go and check the stew.' She pushed herself up, ignoring his questioning gaze as she left the room, battling through the remnants of the dream, dark edges lingering as she turned the heat off beneath the pot of stew. The food was of a pleasantly thick, rich consistency, the meat falling apart as she ran a spoon through it. Why was she dreaming about Adam, about not being able to save him? There was no rhyme or reason to this dream, she had not dreamed it before. There was no snow and ice, no cold crevasse, just torrents of water. They were swimming in a river when suddenly it turned into a raging torrent pulling him away in a rush of water. She couldn't get to him, no matter how hard she tried, she didn't seem to be getting anywhere. Her arms were slicing through the water, she was a strong swimmer and yet she didn't seem to be able to move. He was shouting her name, crying out for help and all she could do was watch in horror as he disappeared over the edge of a waterfall.

'Is it okay?'

'I'm fine.' She started, the words spilling over her lips, her eyes flashing to his and then back to the food. Adam frowned at her reaction. 'Are you all right Ki?'

'I'm fine.' She turned away, pulling open cupboards in

search of some bowls, relieved when his next words were to direct her to the bowls and not pry any further into her startled state. She went through the process of dishing up, drawing comfort from the familiar pattern of movement and taking the time to bring her emotions under control. She did not look up to him until she was sure that she could do so without the fear and guilt showing.

'This is great.' Adam spooned another heap into his mouth and savoured the familiar taste. 'Thank you.'

She nodded her acceptance before returning her eyes to her bowl, the feeling of the dream lingering. Her eyes moved to the window. In another hour it would be dark.

Adam watched as she sat with the spoon halfway to her mouth, staring at the bowl with vacant eyes.

'Tired?' He put the spoon to his mouth trying not to look at her.

'I guess,' she answered after a moment, bringing the spoon to her mouth. Adam watched thoughtfully as she slowly chewed and swallowed the mouthful of food before staring at the spoon in the bowl, unmoving. No wonder she wasn't gaining any weight, she probably wasn't eating.

'Do you dream about the expedition?'

His words pulled her out of the thoughts she was drowning in, refocussing her attention on the movement of his spoon between his bowl and mouth. He seemed to be enjoying it, at least one of them was eating. 'Sometimes,' she admitted forcing another spoonful into her mouth. 'It's hard not to, I suppose.' She returned the spoon to the bowl and faced the window again. 'It's such a big event in our lives, it would be more surprising if I didn't dream about it.'

'What do you dream?' His voice was gentle, enquiring,

his eyes warm and brimming with emotion. Kira's eye darted to his, for just a moment. 'Bits and pieces, nothing really identifiable.' She paused for a moment thinking about this. 'It's more like the emotions are given physical bodies to roam through the landscape we had covered.' She frowned slightly then shook her head. 'I don't know. It will go away, I'm sure.'

Adam nodded, wondering if he should be admitting to his own dreams, or nightmares rather, which woke him with terror filling his heart. She looked small and lost, hunched over her bowl of barely touched stew.

'I know what you mean,' he said finally, his words carried on a sigh pulling her gaze in his direction. 'I dream about it nearly every time I close my eyes.'

He held her steady gaze as understanding drifted between them. 'It's nearly always the same for me though,' he admitted. 'Like a memory, haunting me with the emotion intensified and almost tangible.'

She dropped her head, guilt forcing her eyes to the counter as his emotions washed over her, 'I'm sorry,' she whispered making him do a double take.

'What for?' He tried to catch her eye, feeling the pain behind her words, almost seeing the guilt in the visible corner of her eye as she turned away from him.

'It's my fault,' she said. 'I should have listened to you, we should have turned back when you said, then you would not have got hurt.'

His spoon dropped into his bowl as he reached over to take her hand, forcing her eyes onto his. 'Kira this is not your fault.' His words were strong, loud in the quiet room, as his face tried to convey the earnestness of his emotion. 'I wanted to keep going just as much as you did, I wouldn't have kept going if I didn't want to.'

He saw the flash in her eye, the hesitation to believe him, the guilt still burning behind the glimmer of emotion. 'Ki, I turned around a hundred metres from the summit of Everest because I knew it was the right decision. It saved my life and those that chose to turn around with me. I will not continue on any route if I perceive it to be too dangerous. If I wanted to turn around, I would have.' He was gripping her wrists trying to force the words into her, trying to force her to understand and accept that this was not her fault.

'Would you have left me then?' Her words were steady as she looked into his eyes. 'Because I would not have turned around. Would you have left me and gone back alone?'

Her words were swimming in his mind, he knew he wouldn't have left her. He dropped his head in the realisation that she knew this as well. Her eyes were still on his when he looked back up.

'No,' he admitted. 'I wouldn't have left you, but that doesn't mean that it was your fault.'

Pushing her chair away she stood up looking for her bag.

'Kira, it could just as easily have been my fault, for not being vigilant enough, for being complacent and falling through, down that crevasse. If you want to blame yourself you need to blame me as well.'

She wasn't listening to him. She was hooking the satchel over her head and looking for her shoes by the back door.

'Kira!'

She lifted her eyes to his once she had her boots on. 'If it wasn't for me, we wouldn't have gotten as far as the glacier, and you wouldn't have fallen through.'

'Ki, it's not your fault!' He wished that he could jump to his feet and chase after her as she opened the back door, disappearing through it into the dark night.

'Kira!'

His voice carried into the night, racing through the trees and reaching her ears on an aching note of despair. The moon was full, lighting her way as she headed home through the familiar surroundings. She would have to come back for her rucksack, she wasn't stopping at Harvey's now.

'Dammit!' Adam slammed his fists on the counter, making the bowls jump in response. She could be so bloody pig-headed.

***

Harvey was only partially surprised as a flash of white, quickly followed by startling blue eyes fell into the bakery on a strong gust of cold air. Outside it was obvious that the sun was still bidding a fond and laborious farewell to the other side of the world. The light was creeping into the early morning like a small child reluctant to get out of bed.

'Good morning.' He smiled, enjoying her presence for a second day in a row. Last night as he watched her cross the bridge with her determined gait, eyes focused on the horizon, a part of him had thought that she might be back today. He'd come back to an empty baking room, her half-drunk cup of hot chocolate and some hastily scribbled words in the flour the only evidence that she had ever been. He could only assume that she had been at Adam's for the rest of the day.

'The wind is picking up,' she said by way of greeting, the snow on her clothes melting in the heat of the bakery ovens. 'The clouds have been building all night.' Removing her cloak, she hung it on a peg next to his own before turning her clear blue eyes on his. 'This snow is set to last.'

A small sigh escaped his body as his eyes moved to the window, aware of the thick layer of white already covering the town in a blanket of purity. 'How long for?'

'The wind is coming from the north.' There was a slight pause as she thought about it. 'Seven days, maybe more.'

Harvey let out a long low whistle at her prediction. 'This heavy?'

'Probably not.' She shook her head, pulling up a seat. 'This will last for a couple of days at most with this wind. Longer if the wind drops and the clouds stay, but the snow will be around for a while.' Her eyes followed the movement of the dough as he slapped, pounded and stretched the mixture, filling the room with animated sounds and actions.

'I brought your bag.' His eyes indicated the red bag in the corner of the room. She had left without collecting it the day before and he wanted her to start drinking those meal supplements. He would put his foot down if he needed to, in the vain hope that she would listen. He had a few cards up his sleeve to convince her of taking them, should she resist, but she was a sensible girl. He could see it in her eyes, now, as she looked at the bag. The carrier bag, containing a large supply of these supplements, were sitting next to it, and Harvey watched as she wearily got up and moved towards it. He could see it in the hunch of her shoulders and the manner of her step that she did not want to take them. She perceived it to be a failure, having to resort to these modern medicines. He could sympathise with how she must feel. She prided herself on her strength and independence. She had never to her knowledge had to rely on modern medicine. She had spent her entire life on the other end of this spectrum, living only off what the land provided and she felt a sense of guilt for having to resort to this. She felt like she was failing her parents and her teachings as she stood with a packet in her hands, reading the instructions.

Harvey watched as she went through this at length, quietly turning the packet over in her hand several times as she stared at it. She seemed so small with her hunched frame and he realised once more the huge toll the expedition had taken on her body. He was so proud of her for the strength and resilience she had shown in getting them both off the mountain. He gathered, from the bits of information that made it to his ears, that they were five days into the journey when the accident happened. She must have pushed herself beyond the boundaries of endurance in order to get them back in roughly the same amount of time, and this despite the feverish illness that had pushed her over the limit and rendered her unconscious. Kira had not told him about the event of her falling through the ice, it was Adam who had informed him of this. Harvey's heart had dropped into his stomach as a great sense of guilt and utter uselessness had overcome him. He had to send an apology into the realms of the night, hoping it would reach John and Ava and return to him with forgiveness on its wings. He knew that he had no power or authority in the world that Kira lived in, he never had. He had admired his friends' bravery and tenacity but had never really understood it. Kira was a child of the earth as her parents had been, if not more so, and it would have been wrong of him to remove her from it when her parents had passed on. He had known it even then, all those years ago, and today these thoughts were once again tangible in his mind. He worried about her, like he had never done before the expedition, because for the first time it seemed that her world was not providing her with what she needed, neither physically nor mentally. She seemed not only smaller in stature but lesser in personality. Her words were edged with weariness, trimmed with loneliness and confusion. He wondered if she felt about Adam the way he felt about her, maybe she was just struggling to come to terms with these new emotions in her life.

'Have you got a blender?'

His eyes snapped back into focus as the determined, yet resigned, tone of her voice reached his ears, moments before the words registered.

'Of course.' He pointed to a long bench on which, amongst other sizable pieces of equipment, sat a large blender. 'What else do you need?'

Kira shrugged. 'Just milk I think.' She was pulling a face. 'It says you can put other things in, but I guess milk is fine.'

'What other things?'

She handed him the packet before moving to the fridge in order to retrieve some milk.

'I haven't really got any of this.' He looked up apologetically. 'I do at home.'

'It's all right, I'm sure it will be fine.'

'Hmmm.' His eyes moved over the package. 'You can make this into a milkshake,' he said thoughtfully. 'That would probably taste better than just the powder and milk.' He looked up for a moment, thinking. 'What else have you got in there? Is this all they gave you?'

'No.' She moved back over to the bag and emptied it onto the table.

Harvey's eyebrows reached for his hairline as a whole myriad of packages in different shapes, sizes and colours assaulted their senses. He moved to catch a brightly coloured bottle, which he could only assume was a ready-made supplement, before it rolled off the table.

'Yikes.' He pulled a face. 'I see why you went for this one.'

There was a wry smile on her face; she had picked the simplest packet which did not have a mass of instructions or confusion of colours surrounding it.

'It is probably worth going through all of these though.' Harvey looked up into her furrowed brow. 'They are probably for different times of the day and have different ways of working.'

'I know,' she sighed. 'I just thought I should get something down myself, I haven't been able to eat very much.'

Harvey took a deep breath scanning the packets. 'Right, okay.' His hands were rifling through the mess, sorting them into piles of corresponding size and colour. 'I think this one is for when you are out or maybe between meals or something.' He pulled a face as he read the back of a bottle. 'Why don't you try one of these?' he said handing her the bottle before returning his attention to the other packages.

'I think the rest of these will be better if you can add some ingredients to it, make it taste a bit nicer.' He thought for a moment. 'You could add some of the things you like.'

He looked up to see her pulling a face at the taste in her mouth. A spark ignited in his eyes moments before a laugh roared out of his belly, making his whole generous frame shake in jubilation; she looked like a child having been given a sour sweet.

'No good?' he chortled as the intense blue of her eyes met his in defiance. She took another sip trying not to pull a face. 'It's all right, I suppose.' She pulled the bottle away from her lips, handing it to him.

Harvey allowed a small amount of the liquid to roll over his tongue and coat the lining of his throat. It tasted of tropical fruit, a flavour Kira might not be familiar with.

'It's nice,' he smiled. 'I'm sure it will just take a bit of getting used to.'

She accepted the bottle back from him and brought it back to her lips. It was all right, actually. She allowed the taste to linger on her tongue, closing her eyes as she tried to decide if she liked it. A moment later her eyes popped open. 'It's all right.' She glanced up at him. 'I can make myself drink it.'

'Good.'

Harvey finally returned to his baking, pummelling the dough into submission as Kira sat quietly, intrigued by the drink in her hand. She wondered how many of them she would need to take in a day, and how long it would take for her to build herself back up to full strength. She wanted to go back to the glacier as soon as possible; she knew enough to know that the ice was constantly moving. They were lucky, or unlucky, to have found that particular crevasse still there. She was sure that her parents were down there, her resolve to this fact grew with every hour of the day. They had to be. She knew that they had gone that way. Adam had found evidence of climbers having been there. She had felt them. They had to be down there, she was sure of it.

She knew that this winter was out of the question, neither she nor Adam would be strong enough to go up again before the end of the season. She was hoping that she would not have to wait much longer than next winter, and she could only hope that Adam would be strong enough to go with her.

A gust of cold air brought them both out of thought as the bakery assistant stumbled in, in a whirl of snow. She was ferociously shaking the snow off her body, stamping it off her feet as she animatedly expressed her feelings about the weather, oblivious to Kira's presence. Her eyes were drawn to a flash of blue making her freeze, her arms suspended in mid-air as she shook the snow from her hair. Her eyes were locked on the deep clear blue of Kira's, as she felt herself trapped, unable to withdraw from the well of emotion she was being dragged into.

Kira had caught a glimpse of the sun on the horizon; morning had dragged itself across the lives of the townspeople who were moving about, bravely facing the weather with determined walks and layers of warm clothing. She suddenly longed for the comfort of a warm fire, her own at least an hour away. She had not come down the valley only to see Harvey or to collect her bag, she had also come to see her friend. She hid behind the sense of responsibility she felt towards Adam, unable to deal with this unidentifiable pull to see him. She looked away, allowing the assistant's eyes to stumble bewildered and unsupported around the room.

'I should go.' Kira rose to her feet, unaware of the effect her presence was having on the woman, who was stunned by the unrivalled beauty of the girl, enhanced only by the stories of her strength and valour. She had known about Kira, but had only ever known her as the girl who stopped in once a week, her black hood pulled over her head, her eyes always lowered to the ground. Her visits had been brief, and she had been so quiet in those days.

Everything had changed now, after the expedition, after she had stumbled into town with the sled attached to her back. Rumours and tales of happenings both historical and present had blown through the town like a wild fire, painting Kira as both a heroine and mysterious creature of the woods. Few people had known about the house in the woods, even fewer of the girl who had remained there after her parents' disappearance.

'Take those things with you kid.' Harvey stopped her before she could leave, indicating her rucksack and the supplements. 'I don't want you leaving them behind again tonight. I'm sure there are stuff in there you would find useful.'

Kira nodded and moved to the bag, making the bakery assistant scramble in the other directions, much to Harvey's amusement. Her hands were sure and fast as she packed the supplements into her bag and shouldered it, the familiar weight on her shoulders taking her back, for just a moment.

Harvey saw it.

He saw the sudden intake of breath, the flash through her eyes, before they closed, and the rapid beating of her heart against her chest.

Shaking her head, she cleared the visions, her eyes filling with the haunting they left behind as she said her goodbye and disappeared into the whirl of snow.

Kira was glad for the cover of snow. The townsfolk had their heads down, hiding behind the protective covers of their hoods, eyes fixed firmly on the ground. Kira walked, for once, without the fear of being seen and with her white hair loose around her brown cloak, she melted into the surroundings of wooden buildings blanketed in snow. Her blue eyes were the only thing that gave away her presence as she moved around the perimeter of town, unseen. Only one pair of eyes met hers with a deep need accompanying the curiosity she was used to. The pull in them stopping Kira in her tracks. She could feel the plea wash over her skin, as they turned away and continued on their course to the local school. Kira found herself staring after the girl long after she had disappeared, her tracks no longer even visible in the snow. There was something in her eyes, in the size of her small frame, a hunger, a longing in her eyes that she could not quite identify. She had sought out Kira's eyes; her eyes had already been fixed on Kira when she looked up. A small shiver shook her body, alerting her of her surroundings. Kicking her feet into motion she focused on reaching her destination. Yesterday she had rushed off in the heat of emotion, Adam's shouts smacking her square between the shoulder blades. She had not known what an effect the emotion in his voice could have on her.

Today, she found him where she had the day before; on the porch, his eyes fixed on the woods as if he was waiting for her to appear. She saw the flash through his eyes as she came into view, the muscles in his face relaxing, the darkness of his eyes turning to a lighter green as he relaxed onto his crutches, watching her approach.

'Morning.' She said it first, catching him off guard. 'I brought you some of the dried meat you like.'

She did not stop to meet his eye; she did not want him to

see the emotion in hers. 'I can do you a broth if you like.' She stomped the snow off her moccasins before looking into the woods, '… or we could go for a walk first, if you like.'

Adam sighed, realising that the rush of words was meant to be a barrier between today and yesterday, she was not going to talk about it. She wasn't ready to admit to her guilt any more than he was, and he wasn't going to do anything that might drive her away.

'A broth would be really nice, thank you.'

She met his eye, silently thanking him for this concession before smiling awkwardly as she pulled the back door open. Adam noted the rucksack pulling on her shoulders, following its progress as she allowed it to slip off the narrow breadth and fall to the floor with a loud thud. His heart dropped with the sound, taking him back to the time she had been wearing it, exhausted and beaten by his incompetence. He felt an aching pain in his gut, a tight ball formed in his throat, preventing him from swallowing properly. He had to turn away, closing the door behind him to hide the pain in his eyes. He loathed himself for the direct result of his injury on her. He owed her so much. How was he ever going to repay her?

He had dreamed of her again last night; events of the expedition having been rearranged and altered. In his dream she had been dragging him on the sled, for days, her body wasting away to a dull shadow in front of his very eyes. He had been trapped on the sled, unable to help her when she stumbled onto the ice and fell through. She had shouted his name, begged him to help, as he was overcome by a heavy burden of complete uselessness, feeling utterly helpless, trapped on the sled, unable to move. A heavy weight pinned him to the sled, his body frozen, forced to watch as her limbs slowly stiffened with the cold until her voice disappeared and her eyes froze into immobility. He had woken with a start, shouting her name as anger and guilt overwhelmed him.

He was going to have to talk to her about this. He knew, deep down inside, somewhere within the rational part of his brain that he was not to blame. He knew that it was circumstances beyond their control that had forced them into the position they had found themselves, but if they didn't talk about it, it would consume them. It could take over their lives and eat them up from the inside. He had to make her see that she was not to blame, and he had to accept the same.

They had to come to the realisation that these events had been written in the stars long before they even set off. Kira had known that something was not right, and it was their combined decision to ignore this instinct, that had allowed them to fulfil this destiny. They were never going to complete their journey on this occasion and neither of them was to blame for that.

The familiar smell of the broth filled his senses, washing over him like a warm comforting shower.

'Is the fire going?' The euphonious tone of her voice pulled him back, allowing his head to nod in affirmation. 'I'll go check on it.'

'I'll bring these through in a minute.' She was adding the last herbs to the broth, allowing it to gently infuse as she found two bowls and spoons. She was comfortable enough in this house, but there were too many things cluttering the rooms, threatening to take over her mind as the street noises infiltrated her senses, making her long for the quiet of her own home.

The fire was warm and inviting as she entered the room, its orange tongues licking hungrily at the wood, grounding her, making her feel at home.

'Thank you.'

Adam revelled in the close heat of her body, more than the aromatic scents of the bowl in his hands. He felt comfortable, at ease in this setting, with her body pressed up against his on the small sofa and the atmosphere of the fire reminding him of her home. Her presence was like a staple to his diet, he struggled to function without it, without her. The closeness of their friendship allowed them to feel at ease with each other, to not shrink away at the accidental contact of their legs or the bumping of their arms as they ate. The silence was in no way uncomfortable and he realised that they quite often spend large stretches of time in silence, simply being together, doing different things. He liked that, he liked that they could be together without discomfort or awkward silences. They felt no need to fill the quiet with strained words, or uncomfortable glances.

'Did you sleep any better last night?'

It was Adam's voice that carried the words, but the thought was in both their minds as they stared into the fire. She had noticed the dark smudges beneath his eyes and knew that he had had as bad a night as her. She had hardly slept, every time she closed her eyes he was there, telling her that they should turn around.

Slowly, she shook her head, allowing it to move from side to side as her eyes remained on the fire. He wondered what she read in the flames, if they were revealing the past or the future to her. She hadn't even made it to her bed, she had remained in front of her fire, wrapped up in the worn blanket made by her mother's own hands, all night.

'Ki, it's not your fault, you do know that, right?' His words were like a cooling balm on a burn, and a nettle sting at the same time. He didn't blame her, but she blamed herself.

'Kira?'

The only indication of his words having reached her mind was the closing of her lids as a small breath escaped her, a moment later she opened them again returning her gaze to the fire. 'It's not my fault that you fell down a crevasse, but it is my fault that we were on the glacier.' Her voice was even with acceptance as she finished her broth and sat with the empty bowl on her lap, mesmerised by the dancing of the flames.

'Kira.' He put his hand on her arm willing her to listen, to accept his words. 'It is not your fault that we were on that glacier, it is not your fault that we kept going. In fact,' he pulled his hand away drawing her attention with the sudden movement '… it wasn't a fault to keep going, I wanted to do it as much as you did.'

'You wanted to turn back.' There was pain and guilt in her voice. 'You were ready to, it's only because I said I wouldn't that you kept going. You know it's true.'

'No, it's not.' His voice was growing in determination. 'I kept going because I wanted to.'

'Adam, you said it yourself; you would not have left me.' Her words lost their power towards the end of the sentence as it knocked on something deep inside of her.

'That's right,' he admitted forcing her to look at him. 'and I still mean it, I still feel exactly the same as I did in that tent. I would not have left you to continue on your own, I would have dragged you out by your hair if I had to.'

The image sparked a smile into her eyes as his own lit up with humour. 'I wanted to continue on as well Ki.'

Her eyes dropped to her hands, which were tightly woven together, as she fought the anxious beating of her heart against a torrent of emotion. His hand, big, heavy and warm folded over both of hers as she sat staring at them. 'It wasn't your fault. It is only because of you that I am here today, that we are both here. I would never have made it out on my own.'

'You would have.' She whispered unable to tear her eyes away from the fingers, now gently caressing hers.

'No Ki, I don't have your grit and determination. I would have stopped long before you did.'

'You'd have done the same if it was me.' She lifted her eyes to his, her voice stronger now. 'You would have done everything you could to get us back, would you not?' The emotion was swimming on the surface of her deep blue eyes. The power of it taking his breath away as all he could do was nod. His hand was still on hers, their eyes locked as the beating of their hearts filled, first their own ears before spilling over into the room around them. Everything else disappeared, they were alone, as they had been on the mountain. Kira's lips parted as her body demanded more oxygen in its frantic state, every inch of her skin was tingling with the closeness of his heat. Their thighs were still pressed together, upper bodies tilted towards each other. Adam felt himself move forward to the beating rhythm in his chest, adrenaline pumping, he didn't know how long he could stand this. His body was screaming out for hers, his hunger growing by the beauty of her eyes, her lips, and now beneath his fingers the smooth skin of her cheek. The air was thick with tension, their bodies coiled like springs ready to explode at the slightest touch.

'Adam!' The sound of the door banging against the wall preceded the call making them jump apart. Kira quickly jumped up and started gathering the dirty dishes, escaping through the door just as George stepped across the threshold. He started but before he could even utter an exclamation she was gone, disappeared into another room.

'Adam? Are you all right?' George stepped into the room, the tension still palpable in the space surrounding him. The fire was low, begging for more fuel and George stepped up to feed it as Adam sighed running a hand through his hair.

'I'm fine.'

George watched him carefully, '… and the girl?'

'Kira,' Adam corrected him, waiting for the brief nod of the older man's head before he continued. 'She's fine, I think.'

He pushed himself up, hoping that she had not run off as George rushed to help him.

'I'm fine,' Adam ground out from between clenched teeth, resenting having to rely on others for help. George stepped back, the hurt evident on his face.

'Sorry,' Adam whispered, pleading forgiveness with his eyes. He wanted to offer an explanation but there simply wasn't one so instead offered another meaningless word of apology before hopping through the door in search of Kira.

She was gone, but her bag was still in the kitchen. A wealth of mixed emotions swam through him. The only way to show her that he didn't blame her was to start planning their next journey. Resolute and with his face set, he turned around and returned to the living room where he picked up the phone without thinking.

He knew a few people who would be interested in this trip, people that could help them.

Chapter Three

Kira's head was spinning. Driven by the rapid beating of her heart she stumbled into the woods, fighting against the power of adrenaline. She had never felt anything like it, this powerful need to be with someone, this overwhelming need to press her lips against his. She had wanted to kiss him so badly, everything inside of her was screaming at him to do so and then, suddenly, the gods spoke. They were ripped apart by the same noise as a clap of thunder, her heart jumping into her throat. Was she not supposed to be doing this?

She didn't want to go home, she couldn't, she had fled the house with nothing more than her boots, pulled on hastily as she crossed the porch and slid down the steps. She didn't even have her cloak. Her mind whirling like the steady fall of snow from the sky, she cursed herself for being so stupid. It was not like her to act so hastily, without thought, to be so unprepared and unobservant. The only thought in her mind, as she ploughed through the snow towards the trees had been escape. She did not even see the girl until she was on top of her, literally.

Kira was pulled out of her race of emotions with a sudden jolt and thud as she stumbled to the ground. She was back on her feet in seconds, staring down at the small frame compressed in the snow. Fear and surprise registered in her mind before she stepped forward and with one swift pull yanked the girl back to her feet.

'Are you okay?'

The girl, her hair as black as Kira's was white, stumbled back a few steps, finding strength from a tree against which she pressed her back. She had no time for this. Kira was about to turn away when something stopped her, those eyes. A different blue to Kira's but powerful in the emotion behind them.

'Are you following me?' There was amusement in her voice, reaching the heart of the young girl, allowing her muscles to relax. She wanted to be like this woman in front of her. She wanted to be strong and beautiful, but she was weak. Her head dropped slightly in guilt, her hair tumbling forward, covering her face. A moment later she lifted her eyes back to Kira's, unable to look away. There were rumours in town. Rumours, about her strength and beauty.

'They say you were kissed by the mountain gods.' Her voice was barely a whisper over her pale lips. 'That's why your hair is as white as the snow.'

Kira's eyes narrowed, as the girl's words continued. 'They say the gods favour you, that's why you are so strong.' There were questions in her eyes, as she looked up at Kira. 'Is it true?'

'I am strong because I train.' Kira eventually found her voice. 'As for my hair, my mother's was the same.'

There was a sudden light in the girl's eyes. 'Is it true that the gods took them, your parents, so they could have you all to themselves?'

A thud of her heart so violent it could be seen in her eyes threw Kira forward towards the girl. 'Who says all of this?' She was trying hard not to scare her, but the anger was evident in every tense muscle of her body. The girl did not move, she hardly breathed as Kira's dominant presence hung over her. She did not know what to think of this woman, she knew only that she wanted her strength. She was even more beautiful than the people said, her skin was smooth and even, coloured only by emotion and the cold air, blemished by no impurity. Her cheekbones where high and strong, framing the stunning blue eyes that nobody seemed to be able to come to grips with. Small wisps of white hair were blowing in front of her face, forming a bridge across her straight nose, below which was full red lips.

The colour of her eyes changed as she stepped away, her muscles relaxing. 'What do you know of the gods?' she whispered dismissively. 'Townspeople no longer believe in these and you are still young, a child.'

'I know more than you think.' The sudden strength in her voice, the confident means with which she stepped forward surprising Kira. She allowed her eyes to settle on the girl again.

'Perhaps,' she whispered, sensing a strength inside of her that she had sensed in few others. 'Shouldn't you be in school?'

'Perhaps.' The cocky reply raised a bubble of laughter in Kira's throat which spilled over into the cold air. The girl's eyes widened, as if she could not quite believe what she had just done, before she spun around and without a second glance disappeared into the veil of snow.

Kira was still smiling to herself when she returned to

Adam's. He was not on the porch and she was forced to make her way inside, by herself, despite her reservations.

'I'm sorry,' she said, her voice drawing his eyes to where she stood in the doorway. Lowering the phone, he looked into her eyes, doing his best to conceal the concern within them. 'I don't know what you are sorry for,' he smiled, cutting through the tension, 'but I have something to show you.'

A breath of relief escaped her body as she felt her muscles relax. 'What is it?' She was already making her way across the room to where he sat at the table. The same table that months ago, had been covered in maps as they planned their journey.

'You want to go back to the glacier, right?'

Her heart skipped a beat, but he wasn't looking to see the flash through her eyes. 'I think there is an easy way to do it.'

'An easy way?' She pulled up a seat, turning her eyes to the computer screen, his words sitting uneasy with her. There was no easy way to do this. Nothing worth doing was easy.

'Yeah.' The excitement in his voice made her eyes drift up to his face. 'I know a few people,' he said pointing at the screen. 'These guys can probably fly us up there and work with us.'

'Fly us up there?' She reeled back, his words were like a physical punch to the stomach. 'What are you talking about?'

Surprised, Adam looked up to the utter horror on her face. He was so sure about this. It was an easy way back up, she could do what she needed to do and they would be safe. They would have a whole team around them.

'I just thought…'

'Adam, don't you get it?' A frown was covering her brow, pain in her eyes. How could he not understand this, did he not know her at all? 'This isn't something that should be easy. We shouldn't be going up there with a 'team', demanding from the mountain what we want!' She was incredulous. 'We have to ask for permission.' She paused looking into his eyes, trying to establish if any of this was sinking in. 'We have to work for it. It will not just be given to us, that is not the way it works.'

He shook his head, confused. 'It can be though Ki, that's what I'm saying. Don't you want to feel safer? Get up there with less effort?'

'No!' she shouted. 'No, I don't, and I certainly don't want anybody else up there.'

'These guys are scientists,' he offered. 'Mountaineers. They will respect it in the same way that you and I do.'

'How do you know that?'

'I know because I've worked with them. Sally is a gifted glaciologist, she's worked several seasons in Antarctica.'

He didn't see the second punch land, taking her breath away. She was staring at him, wondering where she had gone wrong, how she could have been so badly mistaken. Where had her judgement failed her?

She was shaking her head in disbelief. He would actually take somebody else up there? Had he not felt the power of those mountains, had he not felt the connection in the same way that she had?

'I've known her for years…'

The rest of his words eluded her as a sickness overcame her. How could she have been so wrong? She was no longer angry, but the pain inside of her was threatening to spill over the edges and she could not let him see that. Turning away, her back to him, his continuing words washed over her like a subliminal stream. She did not even notice them, or him, as she focused her mind on what was needed.

Shoes. Cloak. Bag. Breathe. Door. Breathe. Cold. Snow. Breathe. Trees.

She was gone.

Adam was staring after the shadow that had disappeared into the woods, at a complete loss. Where had he gone wrong? He thought she would have appreciated the effort he was going through to plan this. It would mean that they could go sooner. They wouldn't have to wait until they were at full strength and fitness. Going up in a helicopter and getting the job done would take no more than two days. It would require no more than one night on the ice. He thought she hated the ice. He thought that she would appreciate not having to spend so much time on it.

Kira was shocked, hurt and confused as she stumbled into her home. She did not have to think, her limbs went on autopilot as she removed her outer clothing and stoked the fire before stumbling through to the shower. Her limbs were cold and stiff from the time spend outside. The muddled state of her mind had made her journey home both longer and shorter. She had stumbled through the woods behind his house for ages before focussing her mind and changing her course for home. Now, with the hot water flowing over her, pounding away the knots in her muscles, soothing the aches, she wished it could soothe the ache in her heart, or scratch the itch in her mind.

What was he thinking? Fly up there? A team of people? Did he not realise that she wanted to do this alone? She wanted to go to find her parents' bodies, and he thought it a good idea to bring a team of strangers!? What the hell was wrong with him? Her arms slammed against the wall, a sharp pain suddenly shooting up her limbs as her eyes opened wide, a gasp of pain escaping her.

'Dammit.' She felt like crying as she brought her arms away, wanting to cradle them against her breast.

'No.' The word was a quiet decree of resilience. 'I will not allow others up there before I have found them.' She felt the iron will straighten her spine as she dropped her arms, still throbbing with pain, and thrust her face into the hot water. She would train, she would eat, and when she was strong enough, she would go back up, alone, and lay them to rest. She was not going to let him ruin this. The mountain gods would not allow them up there, that much she knew.

**

A week had passed before Adam finally admitted to himself that Kira was not returning. He had offended her in some incomprehensible manner and now, once again, they were apart. He hadn't so much as replied to an e-mail from any of the people he had contacted regarding this next adventure he had wanted to plan. He didn't fully understand why Kira was so riled up about this and he wouldn't unless he could talk to her. He had to make peace with the fact that she was not going to be coming back down the valley, so he was going to have to find a way to get to her.

Another dawn broke after a sleepless night and despite the issues of guilt having been resolved between the two of them, Adam's mind still plagued him, preventing him from sleep.

He had been through it a hundred times, and he could not understand where he had gone wrong. He could not identify what it was that had offended her so much. Pushing the blanket off his body, he carefully manoeuvred the stiff, casted leg over the threshold of the sofa. There was only one person he could think of, other than Kira, that might be able to answer his questions.

It was not the heavy awkward bulk of the young man that Harvey expected to be coming through the back door of the bakery. The cold air forced its way in, snow whirling in the warm environment as Adam struggled with the crutches. Harvey quickly stepped out from behind the counter, making his way over to help the young man, closing the door behind him.

'Thank you,' Adam heaved, falling into a seat. 'Sorry.'

Harvey brushed his apology away. 'No problem son, it was a bit too hot in here anyway.'

Adam smiled a wry smile as Harvey patted his back before turning to put the kettle on. 'What brings you here at this ungodly hour?' Harvey lifted an eyebrow at the man. 'I thought it was only Kira that braved the pre-light hours of winter.'

There was a flash of pain through the young man's eyes that made Harvey stop and count his words.

'I guess she must have rubbed off on me.' Adam's voice was weak and low, filled with confused emotion.

'There are worse things, I gather.' Harvey smiled, trying to lift his spirits. 'I wouldn't mind a bit of her drive to rub off on me.'

'No, indeed,' Adam returned the laugh. 'Sometimes I

think she has a bit too much of it.'

Harvey nodded sagely, filling the mugs with boiling water and stirring the teabags inside.

'So, what brings you here?' he asked handing Adam a mug of tea before pulling up a seat of his own. The weary sigh emanating from the man had Harvey's eyebrows raised.

'A girl, aye?' Harvey winked. 'I suppose, being that you came to me, it's the one we both know all too well?'

Adam nodded. 'I think I've offended her, badly.' He grimaced. 'She ran out last week and I've not seen her since.'

Moving in his chair Harvey tilted his head, trying to think of the last time he had seen her. 'She's not been by, if that is what you were going to ask.'

'It's not.' Adam shook his head. 'I just need some help.'

'Help?' Harvey chuckled. 'With Kira? She is a law unto herself that one.'

Adam couldn't help but smile. She certainly was strong willed, but there was also a vulnerability within her that few had seen.

'I thought you might be able to help me understand where I went wrong.' Adam ventured. 'You know her better than anybody and short of actually going up there myself, you are the only chance I have of understanding her reaction.'

'Hmmm.' Harvey breathed in deeply. He wasn't sure that he necessarily knew Kira any better than Adam did, the boy should give himself some credit. 'All right, I'll give it my best. Tell me what happened.'

Adam retold the story, feeling the rush of confused emotions wash over him all over again. When he finished, the agonising emptiness he had felt after her disappearance was filled with anxiety and nerves. Harvey's eyes bore deeply into Adam's, trying to see beyond them, into his soul. Adam had to know why Kira was so hurt by his suggestion, if he didn't, then maybe he was wrong about their connection. He had seen love and longing in their glances. Friendship and trust, but if he didn't even understand this basic need of hers, then maybe he was wrong.

'Adam,' Harvey said sitting back, his body leaning slightly to one side. 'I want you to think very carefully about everything you have just told me.'

'I have!' Adam exploded. 'I've gone over and over it in my head and I just don't get it!'

Harvey held his hand up, taking the mug out of Adam's hands. 'I'm going to make you another drink, then I would like you to just sit and think about the words you have used, and her response. I want you to think about it without the cloud of emotions; just the words.' He refilled the mugs. 'Think about the words. Then, think about Kira, who she is, what she is, why she is. Think about why she went up there to begin with.'

Adam was looking at him with apprehension. 'I think you know the answer to this, and if you don't...' He shrugged, almost sadly. '... then perhaps you should just let it go, let her go.'

The thought shocked him, hurt him. Slapped him across the face and kicked his mind into gear. Harvey was right, if he didn't understand her thought process, her feelings then he didn't understand her, and he thought that he did. The mug in his hands did not hold tea, it was filled to the brim with hot chocolate, whipped cream towered far above the edges of the mug and small marshmallows forced brown liquid over the rim with displacement. He smiled. He could practically see her drinking it, he wondered what she was like as a little girl. The drink was probably bigger than her head. The thought amused him and saddened him as he thought of this young girl, losing her parents. Suddenly it hit him, like a rock between the eyes.

'Fuck.'

Harvey saw the light come on in his eyes and silently let out a breath of relief. 'How could I have been so stupid?'

He hadn't thought about it from her point of view, only from his. The mountain was sacred, pure. The only people who had ever set foot on that glacier, as far as they know, were the two of them and her parents. Of course she didn't want anybody else up there, of course she didn't want to do it the 'easy' way. It was not their way. A blanket of despair descended upon him. What must she be thinking of him? It was callous of him to make such assumptions on her behalf. He had seen the emotion play across her face but he had not understood it until now.

'Ah shit.' He ran a hand through his hair. 'I have to see her.' He said lifting his head and finding Harvey's eyes. 'I'm going to have to go up there.'

'How?' Harvey looked at his broken leg and Adam followed his gaze. 'I don't know. I'll have to find a way. I don't think she's going to be coming back down for a while.'

'I think you're right,' Harvey admitted. 'I'd offer to help you, but I don't think I can make it myself, in this weather.'

Adam shook his head, pulling himself to his feet. 'It's all right, I'll figure it out.' He pulled the door open allowing the snow to be blown in on a gust of wind. 'I won't be going until this has passed anyway,' he grumbled, reluctant to sit on his own words for too long.

His mind was much further up the valley, with her, as he slowly made his way through town. Maybe somebody would take him up on a snowmobile, if he paid them. No, Kira wouldn't want anybody else to know where she lived. They could drop him on the path, and he could make the last few hundred metres on foot. He grimaced, or hands and knees maybe.

'Shit, sorry.' He nearly ploughed straight into the girl.

'You're her friend, aren't you?' She hadn't seen Kira in town for a long while.

'Pardon?' Adam looked confused. The snow was coming down heavily around them as this small girl stood in front of him, preventing him from moving.

'The mountain woman. You're her friend,' she stated. 'She dragged you off the mountain.'

He tilted his head at this curious creature, he knew that much. 'Where is she?'

Adam shook his head, wondering if he was dreaming. 'I'm sorry, who are you?'

'My name is Raven.' His eyes went to the jet black of her hair. Apt.

That still didn't answer his question and he was getting cold, his leg was aching and his arms were sore from the crutches.

'Well, it's nice to meet you R...'

'Where is she?' The words were harsh, almost harsh enough to disguise the frantic need in her voice.

'I don't know,' Adam said cautiously, shaking his head. 'At home, I suppose.'

There was something in her eyes he couldn't quiet

decipher, the snowflakes blocking his view of her face. Raven only knew she lived in the woods, high up in the valley. She had never been up there herself. She wasn't allowed to; her heart was too weak. Adam watched as without another word the girl disappeared, very quietly, into the snow. Her stealth like movement reminded him of Kira and for a moment, he wondered if the girl had actually been there. Shaking his head, he leaned forward on the crutches starting his slow progress home.

***

The wolves were howling into the night, their song had changed just as she knew it would, and they were closer. Shivering, Kira pulled the blanket closer around her shoulders. She had never known them to come this low down in the valley, aside from once. She remembered the first lonely weeks after finding out that her parents were gone, the wolf song had vibrated against the walls and doors of the house. They had come right up to the house, howling. She had been terrified at the time, but now she realised that they were mourning, mourning the loss of one of their own. No, two. Her parents were part of the mountains as the wolves are, as she is, and their loss had hurt more than just one child.

Kira felt better, stronger. She had been consuming the supplements along with her own food; forcing herself to eat despite the pain. She was determined to win her strength back and go up the mountain. She had been training every hour of the day, practising everything from endurance and knife skills to medicine. Next time, she would be prepared.

A loud howl made her jump as moments later the glow

of eyes could be seen a few yards away. A second pair of eyes joined the first, and then another, until the land in front of her was awash with them. She sat quietly, her heart beating loudly in her chest as she watched their every move. Her knife was inside. She stood no chance, should they attack. Their howling echoed around her, completely enfolding her in their song, as she slowly felt her heart return to normal. They did not look aggressive and their howling was of a pleasant, almost mournful tone. What were they mourning? One wolf, with bright blue eyes moved forward from the line, just enough to distinguish himself. He made sure her eyes were locked on his before he let out a howl quickly followed by a short yip. She started at the change of tone. She couldn't look anywhere else now. The rest of the wolves could be closing in on her, but she was transfixed by this one. His head moved, his eyes disappeared as he looked back into the trees. A second later his eyes were on hers again, giving a short yip.

'I don't understand,' she whispered, intrigued, willing the wolf to understand her. He turned away as if giving up on her and trotted away. The rest followed shortly after and Kira let out a breath of relief. Standing up, she moved forwards, pressing her hips against the railing as she leaned forward on the support. The night had gone eerily quiet, something was not right. Lifting her eyes to the sky, she tried to read the stars, willed them to share their knowledge with her, show her what they could see. When she looked back, he was there, right in front of her. She jumped back with a short scream of surprise. The intense blue eyes did not waver as she found her courage and moved back to the railing. He was sitting down looking at her.

'What is it?' she whispered. 'What are you trying to tell

me?'

He yelped and standing up started to trot away, only to stop a few metres away from her looking back. He yelped again, making her frown. 'Do you want me to follow you?'

There was of course no reply as he sat back down, looking at her.

'Okay,' she breathed out oddly, unsure of herself. 'Let me get my cloak.'

Slowly, backing into the house she withdrew her cloak, throwing it around her before sheaving her knife and pulling on her boots. Her progress over the porch was slow as the wolf stood up and trotted closer towards her, making her freeze. Could he smell her fear?

Impatient now with the ignorance of this woman, the wolf yelped once more and turned away, trotting off. He looked back once to make sure that she was following.

Kira had no idea what she was doing, why she was running after this wolf in the middle of the night. If Adam was here, he would probably have tied her up to stop her from doing it. Her eyes closed involuntarily, but Adam didn't understand, she thought sadly. Not like she thought he did. The night was cold and still, the snow having stopped for a temporary reprieve as the clouds still lingered. There were no stars or moon in sight; she could only grab brief glimpses of far-away fires as the clouds separated. Her mind automatically kept track of where she was going, it was strange that the wolf was taking her on the path. Suddenly, skidding to a halt her heart jumped into her throat. The rest of the pack was there, a great mass of furry bodies on the ground. They lay still, watching her as her eyes settled on a streak of black, so dark it did not fit with any of the wolves.

The wolf by her side yapped out a command and slowly the pack began peeling themselves away from the body on the track.

'Oh my God.' Kira rushed forward, any fear forgotten as she pushed her arms beneath the small familiar frame lifting her off the ground.

'Thank you,' she whispered to the wolves, then lifted her head to the sky. 'Thank you.' There was no hesitation, as without a second thought she set off, running up the hill and back into her home.

Her heart was beating fast in her chest, adrenaline coursing through her veins. She was barely aware of the weight in her arms as she ran up the hill. There was nothing she could do out in the snow, she had to get her inside, by the fire. The wolves were at her heels, following them home. She didn't have time to wonder about who they were protecting; her or the girl, or both? Bursting through the door she kicked it shut behind her, striding over to the fire and laying the girl down on the ground in front of it.

'Okay,' she breathed, she was focused. Her eyes scanned the body in front of her. Small, young and frail. Her skin was a sickly ashen colour with perspiration covering her brow, despite the cold outside. Kira put her hand to the girl's brow and frowned. No fever. The skin on her hands was cold, but not freezing. The wolves had kept her warm.

'Thank you,' she breathed again, almost unaware of her own words. She had no idea how long she had been lying outside, or why she had collapsed, anything could be wrong with her. She could see no obvious signs of injury, and turned her attention to the finer details. Tilting the girl's head back she put her ear to pale lips, trying to establish the state of her breathing. Looking carefully, she could see her chest rise and fall with slow equal breaths. Putting her fingers to the small wrist Kira allowed her eyes to scan the body again for any obvious signs of injury, coming up empty. She could barely feel a pulse. She wasn't even sure if what she was feeling was real, or just her desperate need for the girl's heart to be beating. Moving her hand to the throat she gently pressed her fingers against the cold skin, relieved at the stronger pulsing against her fingers. Okay, she thought, she was breathing and her heart was beating, now she just had to figure out what was wrong with her.

'Help me,' Kira implored. 'Please.'

Check for bleeding.

There was no blood on the snow and nothing on her clothes, but she could be bleeding internally. Unzipping her clothing Kira lifted her shirt to check for injury to her chest and abdomen. None. She rolled her over doing the same to her back and coming to the same conclusion.

'Good.'

The sense of urgency had left her as she did a careful examination of the girl, periodically checking her pulse and breathing, both of which remained stable.

Her hand touched something cold and metal as she checked the opposite wrist and arm for signs of injury. Frowning Kira pulled the clothing away to reveal a medical bracelet on the girl's wrist. Turning it the right way around she tilted her head to read the words in the firelight. Her eyes closing as the words sunk in.

It was her heart.

Opening her eyes Kira looked down at the girl once more. That is why the wolves had found her, they can sense weakness or injury in people and, more often than not, are drawn to it. Kira knew only one natural product that could help with heart problems and she was in no hurry to use it.

Digitalus purpurea better known as Foxglove was a very effective heart medicine in the right dose, but it was also poisonous and not recommended for human consumption. She has never had to use it and had hoped that she never would. Checking the girl's pulse again she found it weaker. She had two choices; she could call for help now, her eyes darted to the window, with the snow which was once more falling, it would take somebody at least two hours to get up to them and more to get back down. She didn't think the girl would make it. Her only other options is to try the *Digitalis*. Knowing what was wrong with the girl, she moved her to the sofa covering the small body with her mother's blanket, hoping that it would provide some kind of healing power. She would call for help, somebody would be looking for the girl, and then she was going to have to administer the drug. Her father had installed a phone when they built the house, believing it would come in useful one day. The phone was hidden in a cupboard and after pulling several things out of the way she pulled it from its hiding place. She knew only one number, Harvey's.

Lifting the receiver to her ear she felt her heart drop, there was no dial tone.

'Shit.' Fumbling around she tried to figure out what was wrong with the phone; she had no idea how long it has been broken for. She pushed and pulled at cables to no avail, finally deciding that she needed to check the line outside. She checked on the girl before pulling her cloak around her shoulders and pushing her feet into her boots. Confronted with a sea of eyes patiently watching the house Kira stopped, her heart hammering in her chest. The wolves had settled themselves in front of the house, their bodies resting close to one another as their eyes followed her progress. 'She'll be okay,' Kira whispered as she carefully skirted around them. 'She'll be okay.' There was no time for fear, besides these wolves had helped them; they had come to get her, knowing that she could help the young girl. Finding the phone line proved impossible in the snow and a while later, with her hands frozen from digging in the snow, her clothes soaked and her mind on the sick girl, she resolved to fix this problem in the spring. Right now, the girl was her priority. She briefly wished she knew her name. She should have asked for it when she had run into her in the woods. She had seemed so alive, so fiery and cheeky. Sighing, Kira opened the medicine cabinet, the same one her mother had always used and looked in the back. The *Digitalis* was still there in the corner, where it had always been. She had replaced it year on year, like her mother had taught her, to make sure that it was fresh and strong. Placing the medicine on the kitchen counter she turned back to retrieve an ancient-looking book. She could not do this by herself, she needed her mother's help and advice, and this was where she was going to get it.

Taking her time to carefully read all the information on this dangerous medicine Kira made sure that she understood everything, and knew what she was doing, before she worked out the dose she was to give the child. This was by no means a miracle cure, she knew that, but it would last until she could get the girl back into town. She needed to be stronger for the trip into town, and so did Kira.

Her heart was hammering against her chest as she picked

up the measured dose, moving across the room without thought. She was sure it was right, it had to be. Her feet redirected her to the door. She wasn't thinking when she pushed the door open and stepped outside. She had to know that this was right, there was so much at stake. Lifting her eyes to the sky she willed it to clear, for the stars to give her a sign, any sign that what she was doing was the right thing. She didn't want to kill the girl, but if she did nothing she would die anyway.

'Tell me if this is right,' she whispered into the night, praying for anything, to anyone and everything to give her an answer. 'Give me a sign.'

She wanted to hear her mother's voice, she wanted the clouds to clear and the stars to shine down on her, telling her that she was making the right decision, but after a prolonged period of no change, no sign, she dropped her head. Her eyes met those of the wolf, his blue eyes almost the same colour as hers at this point.

'I don't know,' she whispered to the wolf. 'I just don't know if this is right.'

Rising to his feet the wolf moved forward, his eyes remaining on hers before coming to a stop a few metres away. Raising his face to the skies he let out the most gut-wrenching howl, sending shivers down her spine. Moments later the rest of the pack joined in, filling the valley with their howls until the skies cleared, for just a moment. Her heart lifted as relieve flooded her.

'That's good enough for me boys.' Turning her back on their howling she re-entered her home to the soft moaning of the girl.

Kira rushed to her side and kneeling down tried to rouse

her, thinking it would be easier to administer the drug with the child awake. She stirred and moaned, the sweat beading on her brow, but she did not wake.

'Okay.' Kira closed her eyes offering a prayer before taking a deep breath and administering the drug to the child. She kneeled beside the girl for a long time, checking for any signs of change either good or bad, anything that might give her an inclination of the dose she chose to use. Hours later with the child's pulse stronger, barely, but definitively, Kira fell asleep in her chair, wrapped in the comforter she had pulled off her bed.

Raven woke to the orange glow of gently smouldering coals, the warmth of it holding her gaze for a long moment. Blinking, she pulled her eyes away from the fireplace, allowing them to drift around the unfamiliar room. She was not exactly accustomed, but definitely not unfamiliar, with the sensation of waking up in strange places, usually hospital rooms. She preferred this room to a hospital room she decided, the calming earthy smell of herbs on the fire soothing her, rather than frightening her. She tried to remember what she was doing before she collapsed. It was dark outside, and she must have missed her evening dose of medicine, that would be why she collapsed. Weakly pushing herself onto an elbow her eyes fell on her opposite and yet her equal. Kira stirred as Raven suddenly remembered exactly what she was doing when she collapsed. She was walking up the valley, searching for *her* house. The wolves had come down from the mountains and trotted alongside her until the combination of fear and exhaustion had become too much for her weak heart. She thought for sure that she would be dead. The wolves would probably eat her before anybody could find her. Raven didn't really know why she was so desperate to find Kira, or even what she would do when she did, but everything inside of her shouted out for the woman. Just being in her presence made her feel stronger, like she could do anything. The smooth flesh of her lids moved, slowly peeling away from the intense blue eyes that fell on her own. The sense of movement or maybe the intensity of her gaze is what had pulled Kira out of her light sleep. Judging by the glow of coals in the corner of her eye, she must have had at least two, or three, hours of sleep. She breathed an almost visible sigh of relief. That was three hours without any dreams or nightmares.

'So,' Kira felt her lips tug into a smile as she looked at the young girl. 'Are you following me?'

A blush rushed across the otherwise pale face as the girl's lips tucked into a rueful smile before she gave a small nod.

'Why?' Kira did not think the child needed reprimanding, she has probably never been allowed to come up this high, and embarking on such a journey would have been incredibly brave, or foolish.

Raven shrugged. 'I'm like you,' she whispered, her voice weak. 'I don't belong down there. I thought, maybe if I came up here, I could...' Her voice trailed off as she shrugged.

'I guess I was wrong. I don't belong up here either.'

'Why do you say that?'

'I didn't make it, did I?'

Kira's head tilted to the side as she observed the strong set of her shoulders. 'I'd say you did.'

'Not by myself. How did you find me anyway?' She was

sitting up now, drawing the blanket close around her shoulders, giving a small involuntary shiver.

Kira pushed herself out of the warm cocoon of her chair and moving to the fire started to stoke it back to life. 'Do you have to do everything by yourself?' There was only a hint of amusement beneath the query, she saw a familiar fire in the girl's eyes.

'I can't do anything by myself,' she said bitterly. 'That is the problem.'

'Why?'

'Because of my heart.'

Kira turned to face the girl, reading the resentment in her eyes.

'What is your name?'

'Raven.'

Kira's eyes moved to her black hair as a small smile tugged at her lips. 'How very apt, I like it.'

Raven shrugged. 'I guess it's because of my hair, it's the only strong thing about me.'

Kira's eyes narrowed slightly. 'I don't know.' There was an inner strength that the girl did not realise she had. 'There might be more to it than you think.'

'Huh?' The girl pulled a face as Kira smiled.

'Are you hungry?' Her mind was already mulling over the child's name as she watched her shake her head. 'No, neither am I,' she smiled. 'I think I'll make us something anyway.' She strode away to the kitchen her mind already filled with the memory.

As a young girl Kira had wondered about her name and one night as she was being tucked into bed, she looked up at her mother and asked the question. 'What does my name mean?'

Ava had smiled down at her daughter, this special child whom she knew to be blessed, and stroked the hair away from her face. 'It means, "beam of light",' She had whispered and kissed her forehead. 'You are a child of light.'

Kira's eyes had widened, the blue of her mother's eyes no longer reflecting in her own. She was taking charge of her own personality and the change of colour in her eyes resembled her mood and independence.

'Why did you choose it?' she had whispered as her mother stood up from the bed, moving to the window.

'We didn't.' Her eyes were fixed on the heavens, the stars clearly visible on the clear night. 'You see sweetheart,' she addressed her daughter, 'people think they choose the names of their children, but it is the gods that decide. They look into the future of the child, and into its past, before whispering its name into the hearts of parents. Your name is a symbol of who you are, a prophesy or a history.'

Kira's eyes had drooped at the gentle whisper of her mother's voice. She had thought no more about this until now. The Raven was closely associated with the Norse god Odin, who was believed to have been the wise king of the gods and bringer of victory. He was mainly seen as a shamanic god, a guider of souls, a healer and was closely associated with magic. The gods would not have chosen this name for this girl if she did not have strength within her. Perhaps her illness enhanced other parts of her mind, body or both.

Raven had gently dropped back off to sleep, her half empty bowl of broth still in her hands as she stared at the fire, mesmerised by the flames. She was sure she could see figures or faces in the flames, it soothed her and frightened her at the same time. Kira did not necessarily believe that the hypnotic dancing of flames could provide you with information of the past or the future. Her mother had hinted as much to her and although she saw things more clearly and understood them better after allowing her mind to wander, being pulled away by the steady flicker of the orange tongues, she wasn't convinced that the fire itself had revealed something to her. Perhaps she was wrong. There is evidence that suggest fires when fed with certain herbs allowed druids and seers to see into both the past and the future but for Kira it was more therapeutic. She did not dismiss it, neither did she sit in front of it day after day trying to see the future.

Raven had not woken by the time Kira was ready to move, her pulse had weakened again and Kira was reluctant to give her any more *Digitalis*. The best thing was to get her back down to town and give her some of her own medicine. Wrapping the girl in her warmest cloak she lifted her from the sofa, holding her close to her heart. She could feel the reassuring drum of the weak heart against her own. It wouldn't take her long to get down into town, she thought as she descended the steps of her porch. One lone wolf rose to its feet as she approached, making her scan the surrounding area for the others. The emptiness of the small clearing brought her eyes back to the lone animal, the colour of its eyes stunned her and she could not help but believe that all three of them were somehow connected. Shaking her head, she kicked her feet back into motion, she had to get Raven home. The wolf fell into step behind them, occasionally disappearing into the denser woodland only to re-appear a short while later. She no longer carried any fear for this animal, nor its pack. They had protected Raven until they could find her and lead her to the child. The wolf stayed at their heels until they reached the lower limit of the treeline, where it stopped so abruptly it caught Kira's attention. Turning to face the animal she took a moment to thank it before looking up to the mountains and doing the same. When she looked back, the animal was gone.

Kira was right, she could see the bright bulk of a helicopter already parked in town. An army of people wrapped in warm clothing stood around, stamping their feet against the cold whilst blowing heat into their cupped hands. It was not until she was on the bridge that somebody noticed her. Moments later it became clear that she was carrying the child and with a cry of surprised relief she heard somebody shout.

'There she is!'

The entire mass of people turned in awe as Kira approached with the child in her arms. The hood had blown off her head and with her arms full, she could not replace it. The white of her hair was a stark contrast against the black of the child's, her blue eyes proved impossible to look away from as the paramedics rushed to her side.

The loss of heat, as the child was taken from her, made her wrap her arms around herself against a sudden emptiness as she herself stood rooted to the spot, feeling lost.

People were surrounding her, shouting questions at her as she felt her world spinning, her eyes locking onto the black of Raven's hair. She was unaware of the figure pushing through the crowd until he was standing in front of her.

'Come with me.' A strong hand gripped her arm and led her through the crowd, pushing her through the nearest doorway. The paramedic had heard Adam's shouts, and nodding he had moved to pull the young woman from the crowd. He was stunned by her beauty, the white of her hair and the intense blue of her eyes.

'Are you all right?' Kira's eyes were focused outside, on the girl being prepared for flight.

'What happened?' Pulling her eyes away she fixed them on the paramedic. 'Can you tell me anything about what happened to her?' There was another slight pause as he watched the colour of her eyes change right in front of his very own, before she nodded. Her lips parted and the euphonious tone of her voice washed over him like a warm embrace. Nodding along with her words he noted down the times, pulse rates and dose of medicine that Kira had given the child.

'Are you a doctor?' He looked up when she had finished speaking, the quiet leaving him feeling bereft of the sound of her voice. Kira shook her head. 'No, my mother taught me.'

'You probably saved her life,' the medic said reassuringly. 'Thank you.'

His eyes darted outside to where his colleagues were given him the thumbs up, they were ready for departure.

'Thank you,' he said pushing himself up and away from her.

Kira felt a great sense of loss as she watched the door being closed, the crowds pushed aside and the helicopter lift off. She wanted to go with her.

'Ki, thank God.'

Her attention was drawn from the window to the door, where Adam's form filled the entire frame. 'Are you okay? What happened?'

She hadn't seen him in over a week and she almost despised the way her heart jolted, and her body jumped to attention at the sound of his voice. She didn't move from her seat as he approached, her lips remaining shut, the words trapped in her mind. She wasn't purposely shutting him out, but the confusion inside of her did not allow any words to travel over her lips. She was still confused about his complete disregard for her feelings in relation to the glacier, but she had channelled these emotions into training, into forcing herself to get better, stronger.

'Kira?' His hand was on her shoulder, burning a hole through her clothing and, blinking, she forced herself to move away from the heat.

'I'm fine,' she sighed, pushing herself up, unwilling to meet his eyes as she carefully moved around him.

'Wait.' His voice was strong, stopping her as her stomach did a somersault. 'I need to talk to you.' He hopped forward as she turned to look at him. 'I'm sorry,' he said hastily, forcing his words into the empty space between them. 'I wasn't thinking about what I was doing, how it might seem, and how it might affect you.' He saw the narrowing of her eyes as the colour changed. Kira didn't want to talk about this now. She wanted to go home, she wanted to run into the woods and clear her mind, allow the dancing of the flames to bring things into perspective.

'I can't do this right now,' she whispered, turning away again.

'Kira, wait, please,' he pleaded. 'I just want to talk to you. I want to understand.'

'Not now,' she whispered, lifting her feet off the ground. There were too many prying eyes, too many whispered words and questions, she needed to get out of town.

Frustrated, Adam wished he could stamp his feet or slam the counter with his arms, but his injured state prevented him from this. All he could do was watch her leave as the anger and frustration built up inside of him. He felt like an angry bear, wanting to roar in fury and exhume this frustration from his body. It was crawling around inside of him, making him wiggle with discomfort and growing irritation. He hated the fact that he had no control over the situation. His face was set in angry lines as he hopped out of the store and into the cold air. She was already gone, having disappeared beyond the trees, and he didn't know what to do. His mind was on a journey of its own as his body took him to the only place that made sense at that moment.

Harvey's was still closed; the townsfolk had appeared en masse to look for the missing girl and as a result all businesses were still closed. Adam found himself standing outside of the bakery, his body cold but his mind burning by the time Harvey approached.

Shaking his head Harvey unlocked the door with a sigh. 'Come on then.' He indicated for the young man to follow.

'If you have come for advice, I think you will find yourself disappointed.' Harvey shrugged out of his coat before turning to the kettle.

'I don't know why I came, to be honest.' Struggling to a seat Adam wrestled with his coat for several minutes before giving up and, with the coat at his feet, he hung his head, disheartened for a minute. 'I don't know what to do, she won't listen to me and as long as I am in this state, I can't make her.'

'I don't think you could make her listen if you threatened

to throw yourself into another crevasse.' Harvey half smiled. 'She has got a mind of her own and she won't listen unless she wants to.'

'… and she obviously doesn't want to,' Adam finished, running a hand through his growing hair. 'If I could only make her stay for long enough to hear me out…' frustration was evident in his voice. '… but she keeps running off and I can't chase after her.'

Kira's gut reaction was always to turn and walk away from something she didn't like, from things that went against her will and beliefs. She didn't waste her time with things she didn't believe in. The only way he had been able to make her listen in the past was by physically stopping her from running away, not something he was currently capable of, or facing her on her own territory. She felt safer, stronger when in the woods or in the mountains, it was what she knew, and she drew her strength from them. He had a minimum of another four weeks before they would even do another X-ray on his leg. There was no guarantee that the cast would come off and he didn't want to go four weeks without seeing her. He didn't want to allow her the time to build a wall between them. He needed to speak to her, make her listen, make her understand and if she wasn't going to come down to him then he was going to have to go up to her.

'Have you got a snowmobile?'

Harvey's eyes lifted at the question. Most everyone had a snowmobile in these parts, everyone apart from Adam it seemed.

'How exactly are you planning on getting on one of them, with one of those?' Harvey's eyebrow disappeared below the fringe of hair as he pointed at the cast on Adam's leg, reaching well beyond the knee.

Adam's eyes dropped to the cast. 'I don't know yet,' he admitted before lifting a determined gaze to meet Harvey's. 'Rest assured though that I sure as hell am going to find a way.'

Harvey was shaking his head. 'The two of you deserve each other,' he mumbled. 'You're both as crazy as bats.'

Adam couldn't help but smile. 'So you'll help me?'

Harvey frowned and shook his head. 'I won't be able to take you further than the path.' He looked at the young man, the guardian in him pleased with the effort he was willing to go through for Kira. 'You'll have to make the rest on foot.'

'I can do that.' He nodded, if Kira could drag him for five days across the peaks and valleys of these mountains then he could bloody well pull himself up one small hill for her. He smiled, and the thing about that, was once he was there, she would have no choice but to listen. She would not leave him out in the cold, that much he knew, and unless she physically dragged him back down the valley, she could not get rid of him, sooner or later she would be forced to listen.

'I would wait until you have news of young Raven,' Harvey offered. 'My only piece of advice.' Adam nodded, a few days waiting with the knowledge that he would be going back up the valley and sleeping on the steep slopes of the mountains was doable. He would use the time to come up with a counter argument, he still thought having a team would be a good idea, he just had to come up with a more diplomatic way of selling it to her. He had made a mistake in blurting it out like that, taking her by surprise, but he wasn't going to make that mistake again. He would find a way to convince her that this was the best idea, just like he convinced her to go on the journey in the first place.

Chapter Four

Adam gritted his teeth as he bumped along the back of the snowmobile. He was once again on a sled, only this time he was moving much faster and the sled was purpose made for carrying casualties. Uncle George had been part of the rescue team in his day and although he still worked at base, he no longer went on searches. Adam had found the rescue sled in the garage, and was now, unbeknownst to Uncle George, bumping along on it. He had no doubt that his uncle would have thrown some form of hissy fit if he knew what Adam was up to. He held on the sled a bag of things he might be able to win Kira over with. She was a woman of the mountains, the earth and the stars, but she had a weakness for sticky buns, books and hot chocolate.

'Are you all right?' Harvey shouted from the front of the machine. It had been a long time since he came up this way.

'Fine!' Adam shouted. Despite the young man's words, Harvey could hear the strain in the man's voice. Shaking his head at this ill-conceived plot, Harvey continued on, bumping along the uneven track beneath several feet of snow. He really should make an effort to come up here more often, Harvey thought as he neared the point of divergence. He could make the few hundred metres of climb up the steep slope to the house, if he took his time. He had only been to the house on a hand full of occasions and only ever on John or Ava's request. They treasured their privacy and isolation, they wanted their daughter to grow up at one with nature, and she was not going to have that when there was a constant stream of people coming and going from the house. As it was, Kira had played naked in the streams and bare chested in the woods deep into her childhood. She knew how to hide, how to conceal herself and her parents had encouraged, not begrudged, this freedom of hers. They had both grown up in cities, which had only increased their hunger for the wilderness.

'Here we are!' Harvey pulled the machine to a stop, lifting his head in the direction of the house. He would have liked to go up there today, to see her, but today there was going to be fireworks and he wanted no part of it. Best for Kira to believe that Adam had made it up here on his own accord. Helping the young man to his feet, Harvey adjusted the bag on his back for comfort. 'How's that?'

'That's great. Thanks Harvey.' He turned to shake the man's hand and Harvey could see the earnestness in his face.

'You can thank me by keeping my name out of the conversation of how you got up here to begin with.' Harvey smiled as he turned away. 'Keep your phone handy for when she chucks you out. I'll come and pick you up.'

Laughing at the wink Harvey gave him Adam looked up at the steep slope. 'Here goes.' Taking a deep breath, he started his ascent, slow, cumbersome and very tiring.

Kira was coming around the corner of the house, her arms laden with firewood when she saw movement in the trees.

Freezing she focused her eyes, thinking, hoping that she might have an easy kill tonight. She loved hunting, but she certainly did not mind when something strayed into her back garden, providing her with meat for a few days or weeks. Tonight however, was apparently not a night for an easy meal, her eyes widened at the sight, her heart jumping into her mouth in surprise.

'Adam?'

He looked up from his laborious climb, his face red with exertion, his lungs panting for air as he exhaled plumes of steam.

'What the hell? Are you crazy?' Dumping the logs on the porch she approached him with careful confident strides. Part of her wanted to stand back and watch him struggle up this hill but the other part, the stronger part had her throwing her arm around his waist in support.

'Erm...' He panted, pleasantly surprised by the power in her embrace. Her body felt stronger and fuller than the last time he had seen her properly.

'Possibly.' He collapsed on the steps of the porch as she stood back shaking her head in awe. 'Thanks,' he gasped.

'You're crazier than I thought you were. What were you thinking?'

'I wanted to see you.' His breathing was still dominating his words but the truth in his eyes were unmistakable. 'We need to talk, and you weren't going to come down to town so...'

'You brought the mountain.'

'What?' He pulled a confused face.

'If Mohammed won't go to the mountain, we'll...'

'... bring the mountain to Mohammed,' they finished in

unison. 'Right.'

'Come inside,' she said brushing past him to collect the logs, if he made it all the way up here on his crutches, he could certainly make it into the house without her.

'You've been out?' His eyes fell on the smouldering coals before registering the nod of her head. Running, he presumed.

'You look good.'

'Thank you.' She certainly felt a lot better. 'I've been training.'

'I thought as much. Wish I could.'

'Why can't you?' She tilted her head, wondering why it was that people allowed their injuries and illnesses to stop them from doing what they wanted. He looked at her, confused, wondering which one of them it was that was going crazy here. He was in a cast nearly up to his groin, all he could do was sit around or hop around on his crutches.

'Erm…' His eyes went to his leg before a frown creased his brow.

'You made it up here didn't you?' she challenged. 'There is nothing wrong with the rest of your body is there?'

'I guess not, but…'

'There's no better time than to build up the strength in your upper body. You can't run or walk or cycle, true, but there are other things you can do. Training is not just the physical either, you could train your mind.'

He shook his head. 'You're right. You are absolutely right.' That is why she was who she was. She didn't accept failure and she used setbacks as learning points, training opportunities.

'Raven is doing well.' He blinked at the rate with which

her head shot up.

'Is she home?' The eagerness in her voice surprised him, she had hardly blinked when he came up with news about the car crash victim last year.

'Erm, no, not yet.' Her shoulders dropped slightly, and he got the impression that she would have dumped everything in an instant to run down the valley if she thought the girl was back.

'What exactly happened?' Adam was curious, apparently the girl had been talking about wolves and faces in the fire. Kira was busying herself with hot drinks, her head low as she thought about his question. She was still trying to figure it out for herself, she was unsure about the wolves, but she felt a connection with this child and so had they.

'I don't know if you'll believe me if I tell you.' She sighed, clearly overwhelmed by the event, whatever it was.

'Try me.'

She lifted her eyes to his, the green pulling her along into a deep green forest, lush with moss and grasses, overrun by springs. Birds were singing a melodic tune, leading her deeper and deeper into the forest. Suddenly he appeared in front of her, the wolf, the creature with its green eyes. Kira blinked on a sharp intake of breath, leaving Adam wondering about what she had seen in his eyes. 'I'm not entirely sure myself,' she started, handing him a mug before folding herself into her own comfortable chair. Her eyes were focused somewhere beyond the glass of the window as she relayed the tale to him. He saw the colour of her eyes change along with the emotion as the words spilled over her lips. He was enchanted by her tale, it was the kind of stuff legends were made of and he had never known Kira to lie. She was as connected to the earth as the roots of the trees outside, it only made sense for the creatures of the forest to see her as one of their own.

'Wow.' He breathed a quiet exclamation of astonishment as she moved her eyes to his, wondering if he believed her. She didn't care what the rest of the world thought about her, she was unperturbed by their whispering and pointing, let them think what they want, she knew the truth. She found though, as she sat there, that she very much cared whether or not Adam believed her.

'Have they been back?' He has never had any close contact with wolves and like most people feared them. Kira shook her head in answer. 'Not that I know of.' Her eyes moved to the window again. 'Their songs had grown quiet. I think they must have found another member to fill the space.'

He wanted to ask her what she meant but her face changed, and she fixed her eyes on him.

'So, why did you come up here?'

It took him a moment to still his head from the reeling change of topic and find his words before obliging to her penetrating gaze. 'I came to apologise,' he said, 'for my rash, and callous, decisions about returning to the glacier.'

He felt his stomach contract into a tight knot at the darkening of her eyes. 'I'm sorry,' he said, pleading for forgiveness with his eyes. 'I didn't mean to wipe away the importance of it to you, and me,' he added at the slight light of confusion. 'I understand what it means to you and I understand why you want to do it right.'

Kira stared at him unblinkingly, unaware that he could read her every emotion in the flashes of her eyes, the twitch of her muscle and the changes in her breathing. She was both relieved and cautious, excited and yet unnerved.

There was a very slight inclination of her head before she turned to tend to the fire. He felt the muscles in his body relax as he sat back in the sofa and watched her as she worked on the fire, hunched on the hearth, her bare toes clinging to the stone for balance.

'How old were you when you made your first fire?'

He saw her head tilt to the side with thought, she liked this question. Closing her eyes for a moment she thought about it, trying to remember.

'I think,' she started and moved away slightly from the roaring fire, 'I think I must have been about five.' She glanced up at him. 'The first time I did it properly, on my own. I used to help my dad with setting it, but it was a while before I was patient enough to do it properly.'

'Do you have any pictures?' he wondered out loud, trying to imagine what she looked like as a child.

'No.' Linking her arms around her drawn knees she leaned back against her chair and, tilting her head back, closed her eyes in memory. Adam's eyes followed the strands of pure white silk as they slid over her shoulders and tumbled to the ground. His eyes tracing the lines of her face as he committed them to memory. She must have been drinking those meal supplements the hospital had given her, he thought, because the stark, sharp angles of her hips and face were filling in, smoothing the curves and brining her back to the healthy Kira he knew so well. 'We never owned a camera and I suppose we spent so much time together that photographs were irrelevant. We never thought a time would come where we would need pieces of paper to remind us of each other.'

'Would you have liked to have a photograph of your parents?'

'I don't know.' She sat forward and crossing her legs leaned closer to the fire, staring into the flames. 'I don't need one, I can see their faces all around me.' Her voice was just a whisper. 'They are in the stars and in the wind, in the snow and in the fire.' Adam wished that he could move forward and put his arms around her, draw her closer, but yet again his injury prevented him from doing this without breaking the moment. 'They are in my heart, and I guess that is enough.'

'Do you think...' He paused, unsure of how to pose his question. Her eyes moved to his and she detected the doubt in his eyes. 'Do you think you see them because they have not yet moved on?' The frown came slowly over her face, she had been wondering about this herself. 'I mean, do you think that you will be less aware of them, of their spirits once you have found their...' He stopped short, suddenly aware of what he was going to say.

'Bodies?' Kira finished for him before turning her eyes back to the fire. 'I don't know. I would like to think that they will still talk to me, but maybe you are right. Maybe they are still here because I have not yet laid them to rest.'

'That's not what I meant.' He rushed into the sentence, scared that she might be thinking that he was blaming her for something.

'It's all right Adam.' The warmth in her eyes stilled his hammering heart. 'I saw them on that glacier,' she admitted. 'I saw their faces right in front of me, as if they were there.' Her eyes were glued to his, sending shivers down his spine. 'It was them that kept me going. It was my parents that told me to stay strong, to keep moving, to remain focused. They physically held me up when all I wanted to do was collapse, curl into a little ball and give up.'

'I have never known you to give up.'

'No,' she agreed. 'They are the reason for that, it is because of them. They taught me to keep going, to keep moving no matter what. They told me to stay strong and believe in myself even when all the odds were stacked against me, there was no such word as failure in their vocabulary. I learned it at school and it astounded me. Why would you choose to fail at anything?' She smiled. 'I didn't understand. There is no such thing as failure, it is all in the head. You learn from your mistakes, that is why mistakes are made, for you to gain knowledge and become stronger. We would be nothing, nowhere if we never made mistakes, how would we learn?'

'That is a great outlook on life.'

'There is no other.' She looked at him with seriousness. 'What other way is there to live? To learn? To grow?'

Adam shook his head. 'I don't know. I guess people just have the wrong end of the stick in their hands. They don't see the world the way you do.'

'No, I guess they don't.' She turned away and looked at the fire again. 'That is the problem with the world; people don't see its beauty, they aren't connected to her anymore. They are ignorant or they fear her or exploit her, but they do not understand her. They have lost their connection and they don't feel her aches and pains, they don't hear her cries or her shouts of anger. They ignore her, they try to control her. They do not understand that she is uncontrollable, that we are under her wing, her guidance and protection and if we don't respect that, respect her, we will fall into decline. They choose not to learn from their mistakes and eventually that will lead to failure, because there will come a point where she will give out no more chances. She is patient and kind, but she carries a wrath unlike any known.'

Adam understood what she meant, and although it made sense to him, he did not quite live in the world that she lived in. He respected nature and the mountains, he listened to her groans and her rumbles of warning, but he didn't ask her permission like Kira did. He didn't lift his eyes and thank her for letting them tread upon her, maybe that is where he was going wrong. The Sherpas, make offerings and prayers to the mountains and who knows better than those who live at altitude on the slopes of the highest mountain range on earth?

Why did the western world think they were any better, knew any more than those who live so close to mother nature, cradled in her bosom? Why was it that experienced mountaineers would make an offering at the foot of the highest mountain on earth but would not think to stop and do the same in their own countries or even those frequented by mountaineers?

Kira could see the cogs turning in his head and wondered why he had never thought of it before, why he had never seen it or realised it? Sitting quietly, she allowed him to mull these thoughts over in his head and hoped that it would bring him to the same conclusion as hers; that they had to go back to the glacier alone.

'Perhaps we've got it all wrong,' Adam whispered, determined to try and get it right. He wished he could be more like Kira, more connected to the earth. He wished that he could feel what she felt, see what she saw. His eyes drifted over her body once more, she was gaining her strength back, she would be ready to go back up soon, if she chose. A terrible thought suddenly occurred to him, the violence of the fear it caused him, enough to make her head turn back to his.

'You won't go up there by yourself, will you?' She could hear the panic in the tremble of his voice, his face a mix of anguished emotion. 'I mean, you will wait, won't you?' he questioned with a slight pause in his words but no waver in his voice. 'Until I'm ready to go back up there with you?'

Adam's words over a week ago, down in the town had forced her to contemplate this thing that evidently scared him so much. She would go up alone if she had to. She did not particularly want to, but she would, if she had to. She knew the route, the pitfalls, the dangers, and she knew she could make it in half the time it took them the first time. She was not scared to move in the dark, despite the cold it brought.

'Kira?' There was genuine fear and anxiety in his eyes, as his heart hammered against his chest in response to this unknown. He suddenly felt as if she might pack her bags right now and head off without him.

The careful blue of her eyes was studying him, reading the apprehension and surprise in his face and body. She didn't want to lie to him and she would much rather complete this journey with him alongside her, but she would if she had to.

'I won't be ready to go back this winter.' She finally spoke, her words drifting clearly on top of the gentle stream of her voice. 'You should be ready by next winter.'

Adam nodded, determined to be so, despite any concerns from the doctors. He was not going to let her go up there alone, he could not even fathom the idea, it was, in his opinion, preposterous.

'What will you do until then?' There was still a slight edge to his voice, the concern not completely gone as she looked back at him.

'Live, learn, grow.' She smiled. 'Like I've done all my life.'

His eyes grew quiet as he saw the contentment in hers. He envied her that, the freedom and contentment she found in her life. Suddenly he longed for it, to be part of it, part of her.

'Will you teach me?'

'Teach you what?' She forced her eyes to remain on his, to read his features, and found her heartbeat increasing.

'Everything.' There was a sudden spark in his eyes as the word breathed into the space between them. 'Everything you know.'

Kira's eyes narrowed as her head tilted to the side, white hair spilling over her shoulder, and caressing the hearth. The blood was still there he noticed, at the ends of her hair.

'I don't know everything I know,' she said slowly, trying to make her thoughts understood. 'I simply live the way I was raised. The way I have lived for twenty-four years.' She took a breath, her eyes flickering to the fire. 'I do not know how to teach you how to live.'

'I guess it's hard to teach an old dog new tricks.' Her eyes narrowed momentarily at the resignation in his voice, making Adam mistake it for confusion. 'It's hard to change a lifetime of habits or perhaps someone's perception of the world if that is all they know.'

'Hard,' she agreed, 'but not impossible.'

There was a glimmer of hope in his eyes as he looked at

her, the corners of his mouth starting to turn up. 'So you'll teach me?'

'Your perception of the world is not so different from mine.'

'No, but I want to be able to feel what you feel and see what you see.' The passion and emotion on his face spilled over into his voice, filling the room with enthusiasm, and touching something deep down inside of her. It was good to have him back, up here, where he belonged. As if agreeing the fire suddenly roared up beside her, making her turn her head and bask in its heat.

'All you have to do is take off your shoes and allow yourself to be connected to the earth,' she said. 'There is no magic potion, no mystery. You simply have to be able to allow yourself to be connected to her in the most primal manner, by being one with her.'

Adam raised an eyebrow at this. 'You mean like, running naked through the woods?' he teased, seeing the spark in her eye and the colour on her cheeks, filling him with laughter. Kira threw a cushion at him as he let out a roar of laughter, batting it away.

'I don't think you are quite up to that level, just yet,' she smiled placing her feet on the ground and stretching herself to her full length. 'Perhaps you should start with sitting in the snow for several hours, without moaning.'

He let out another roar of laughter as she walked past him, inherently pleased with the teasing quality of her voice. Perhaps she had forgiven him, for now at least, and they were back on equal ground.

'How are you getting back to town?'

Her words shattered his illusion like a rock being thrown

at a stained-glass window. 'Erm… the same way I came up I suppose.' His eyes moved to the window, judging the light outside.

'… and how was that?'

Adam could tell that she was starting to prepare for her evening meal, but he could not see beyond the counter as to what she was preparing. 'Well, you saw me.' He pushed himself to his feet and adjusted the crutches beneath his arms.

'I saw you coming out of the trees,' she admitted, a small smile trying to break through her carefully arranged features. 'I can't pretend to know what happened before then.'

'What do you mean?' he exclaimed with mock shock. 'I came all the way up here to see you, climbing that hill on my crutches…'

Her eyes fixed on his, she could read the truths in his eyes, on his face, as he tried to hide it.

'Uh huh.' She turned back to the food. 'I presume he didn't come with you because he didn't want to be associated with this insane notion of yours.'

Adam smiled and hopped over to his bag. 'I'm not at liberty to discuss that, but I do bring a peace offering.' He grinned.

Her eyes lifted to his once again, before lowering them to the bag on the counter. He could now see that she was preparing enough food for both of them and felt a deep sense of relief and satisfaction.

'Ta-da!' He pulled the brown paper bag of sticky buns out of the rucksack and watched the twitch of her mouth as she tried not to smile.

'Very well.' She moved her eyes back to the food, still

trying not to smile. 'You can stay.'

She could only guess that the smile on his face was a reflection of her own and the rest of the bag's contents did nothing to diminish that.

The physicality of their bodies warmed by the heat of the fire, they sat in their respective seats, content, with their hunger satisfied. Adam was surprised at how well they had both eaten. Kira had obviously been working hard at getting her appetite back to normal, he however, had been struggling. The power of comfort and familiarity enlightened the sense of joy and contentment within them, breeding a great reluctance to move from the fire and indeed each other's company, despite the depth of darkness outside. Adam's eyes travelled over Kira's body, curled up on her chair, her hands cradling a mug of peppermint tea. She had tossed some herbs onto the fire, the scent of which was creating a very pleasant atmosphere in the room. The strong lines of her body were still the same, it still ignited a spark of desire within him as it had the first time, but there was a familiarity in them that allowed him to appreciate it fully. She had not come by her body by spending hours in a man-made gym but simply by living. He would be a fool if he did not appreciate this as much as he did her. Her lifestyle had awed and fascinated him when he first met her but now, that awe, had grown into an understanding and a great desire to be the same. He noted a slight twitch in her muscles, a tensing, moments before the voice of a wolf filled the night air outside. His heart jumped at the sound, fear his immediate reaction, but Kira's body remained motionless, but for the slight inclination of her head and the closing of her eyes as the wolf howled again. She was listening to the tone of the song, the accents and inclinations, trying to determine its meaning. She had moved herself, from simply being used to their voices, into a separate realm of appreciating it, with a desire to understand. Wolves were thought to be dark and dangerous by many nationalities, but Kira knew that there were also those who believed that they were descendants of wolves. She knew that it was rare for wolves to attack people, in fact they have been known to save those found injured.

She smiled as the next howl echoed down the valley, it seemed that they were content that everything was in hand down here, and had retreated higher up to their lair.

'What is it?'

Her head slowly turned to his as she listened to the melodic tone of the howl. 'Nothing really,' she smiled, pushing herself up and making her way outside, knowing that he would follow, slower and more cumbersome. 'They are just howling for the sake of it,' she said when she felt his presence behind her. 'They are a bit like humans, in the sense that sometimes our words carry meaning and other times we just talk for the sake of it, with nothing really being said.' She paused allowing them to enjoy the chorus of wolf voices filling the night air. 'Did you know that their saliva carries healing properties?' She turned her eyes to his raised eyebrows. 'It's the same with many animals, when they are wounded, they lick their wounds because of the properties in their saliva.'

It made sense, now that he thought about it. 'Hence the saying, licking your wounds?'

'Perhaps,' she smiled, her mind was still on the mythical creatures high up on the mountainside. 'Many people believe them to be symbols of power and violence, they use their totems to represent warriors believing that it would make them better fighters.'

'Totems?'

Kira tilted her head trying to think of a way to explain it to him. 'Totems are like symbols of people,' she started. 'Historically people believed that at some point in their lives an animal spirit would make itself known to them and become part of them, connecting them to the great mother. This spirit was a symbol of their personality, their power or perhaps their destiny. Wolf totems were given to warriors providing them with cunning, speed and strength.'

Adam leaned back against the railing around her porch, enjoying the vision of her changing features as she retold the stories her mother had told her. 'Some people believe wolves were once men and see them as brothers, others believe that they are descendants of wolves and yet more have attributed their native land to the guidance of wolves.'

'Wow.'

'There are many believes and legends.' Kira half smiled up at him, aware of his eyes on her. 'All you really need to know is that they are part of the land, the earth, and so part of us. They need to be respected and listened to just like every other link in the chain of mother nature. They need not be feared but a healthy respect is recommended.' Adam smiled ruefully at the glint in her eye.

A shiver ran down her spine, both from the cold, seeping through the raw wood beneath her bare feet and the intense way at which he was looking at her. Adam noticed that his own feet were still covered by socks and suddenly felt the barrier it created between him and the land. Kira wrapped her arms around herself, running her hands up and down as she stared into the night for a moment longer. Was he faster, less hampered Adam would have stepped forward and wrapped his arms around her, but before he could move she was turning away and returning to the warmth of the fire.

***

Crossing the natural threshold of the line of trees surrounding her home it was Kira who was brought to a stop at the sight in front of her. She had been out since before dawn and the sun was now reaching, with outstretched fingers, to that much desired midday position. Adam was leaning heavily on his crutches, his face dancing through a repertoire of masks she did not realise he held, as his one bare foot melted into the ice beneath him.

She could not help but laugh, the sound lifting his head to her windblown hair, red cheeks and sparkling clear blue eyes.

'How long have you been out here?' she twinkled, moving towards him.

'About thirty seconds.' He puffed out a few desperate breaths as he plunged his foot back into the cold. Kira laughed again, watching the skin turn bright red on his feet.

As a child she used to run out of the door without shoes on her feet no matter the time of day or year. She had learned quickly that foot coverings were much preferred for long days out, playing in the woods, especially in winter.

'If this goes well, you can always go and stand in the stream as the next step up.' Adam's head shot up in surprise, shock painting his features until he saw the pull of her mouth and the spark in her eye.

'Cheeky mare.' He grinned. 'If I had the use of both my legs you'd be in the snow by now.' Kira laughed heartily, they both knew the alternate truth of that statement.

'Well, you stay out here and...' She looked down at his feet. 'Do whatever it is that you are doing,' she grinned turning away. '... and I'll go inside and do something altogether more appropriate, like attempt to broaden my knowledge on medicine by a roaring fire.'

He didn't need telling twice, spinning round he quickly followed her into the house where he collapsed on the sofa, pulling his freezing foot into his hands and making her grin. She had always been full of the joys of life, filled with curiosity for the world when she ran out of the house, white hair flying, blue eyes shining. She never noticed the cold until her feet were like blocks of ice, refusing to respond to her commands.

'That might be better to attempt in summer, or spring.' Kira smiled offering him a mug of warm liquid.

'I just wanted to feel what you feel.' His face was flushed with colour, the experience having been invigorating.

Enthralled by his interest in her life she felt a warmth seep through her body, lighting up her insides as she pulled some books off the shelf and brought them over to the fire. It was her turn to teach him, like he had taught her so many months ago.

Chapter Five

Time passed, like a river running its course, sometimes slow and gentle meandering around long bends and sometimes fast and furious over rapids of activity. Adam and Kira's bond had been re-established and grown with mutual respect, admiration and interest in each other's views and thoughts. Two weeks had passed by, beneath them, as they floated on this gentle stream of understanding, before reluctantly they were forced to admit that they needed the outside world for something. Adam had a hospital appointment in a few days, and he needed to return to town in order to prepare himself for the two-hour journey south, in a car.

'What were your thoughts on tomorrow?' They were wrapped in an invisible cloak of comfort and Adam resented being pulled out from beneath it as Kira's words reached his ears. He had avoided the thought of leaving, as he knew he would soon have to, having enjoyed the gentle rhythm of their days up here. This home was special, not just because of the care that was taken in the building process or because of its inhabitants, but in its ability to ground you, to slow you and make you appreciate the smaller, simpler things in life. Food tasted better sourced from the ground and the trees, cooked on the wood-fired stove. The cold was more intense and the heat altogether more pleasing and comforting. The house carried the scent of the earth through its wood, its history and the herbs Kira liked to throw onto the fire. He was never tense or anxious when in this fortress of solitude, and he enjoyed being up here, alone with Kira. He had been training, like she suggested, whilst she was out on her daily runs or activities which he knew nothing about. She could disappear into the woods at dawn and he would not see her again until dusk when she appeared with a couple of birds or a hare or some other form of nutrition. She always looked calm and fulfilled, her face filled with colour fighting for dominance over her vivid blue eyes. He longed for the days when he could go out with her, see what she did all day in the valleys or up on the summits. She always left him something to keep himself occupied with and when he was not doing pull ups on the eaves or awkward one-legged press-ups amongst other things, he would lose himself in the books she left behind. There was a wide range of literature to keep his mind occupied, from legends to medicine, hunting or technical survival skills. There were books about plants, trees, animals, birds, bugs, mushrooms and most anything you could think off. He was trying to learn what Kira had lived all her life, in a short period of time. He was never going to be able to learn it all, he knew that, but he would learn and retain as much of it as he could. Kira knew that when spring came and was quickly followed by summer, they would be spending the great majority of their time outside, as she had as a child. He might feel confined now, with the cast, but once that was removed and he was allowed to move around again, the knowledge he retained from the books would become invaluable. He was already cleaning his own wound and redressing it the way she had shown him, using only natural herbs.

'I think, I would like to walk down.' He said slowly, his words even and calculated. 'Or hop.' He smiled, his eyes sparking as he searched hers for signs of disagreement.

'How long do you think you'll need?' There was no surprise in her tone, she knew better than anyone that you could do anything you put your mind to. There was no doubt in her mind that Adam would make it to town on his crutches, they just needed to be sensible and give it the time it needed.

'I don't know,' he looked at her thoughtfully, 'four hours?'

It was at the very least an hour's walk at a steady pace and the conditions underfoot would slow them. Kira nodded along with his estimation, it seemed reasonable. 'We'll prepare to be out all morning,' she decided out loud. 'I can always run into town should we run into difficulty.'

'I'm sure we won't,' he voiced, nodding to her retreating back. The sky was dark outside as she started pulling items from the cupboards, laying them out in preparation for transformation. She would make two different types of travel cakes and some broth to take down with them. Adam had not yet changed his dressing, having been pulled from sleep by Kira's gentle hands as she begged him outside to partake in the particularly beautiful sunrise that morning. His mind and body had been busy all day, periodically filling with the vision of her bathed in the colours of the sunrise, and preventing him from even contemplating the basic need of changing his dressing. Now, as he pushed himself out of the seat and went to join her in the kitchen, he turned his attention to creating the mixtures he needed to do just that. He smiled at the gentle tone escaping from between her lips, as it often did and she was unaware of, and engrossed himself in the preparation of his own medicines. Kira looked up and smiled at him, pleased with how well he had taken to her healing herbs, and at just that moment Adam thought he wanted to freeze time. He never wanted anything to change. This simple domesticity filled his heart with love and joy and he knew he could ask for nothing more. He longed for her with every fibre of his being, every muscle in his body screamed out for her touch, his lips itched with the need to kiss hers but she had kept herself at a distance. He had read the uncertainty in her eyes every time the electricity sparked between them. His willpower had increased to an unprecedented amount, he was sure, as he held back every day, every night from touching her, for fear of scaring her away, again. He needed to be with her, she was as part of him as his own limbs and to be apart from her felt like a stab in the gut. The thought filled him with dread and so he relented, he did not push her for fear of pushing her away completely. Her life was so different from his, she had no experience in these things and he understood that, but he didn't know how to make his feelings known without scaring her. There were times, like now, when they were working closely together, the warmth of their bodies mixing and blending until it sparked every time their skin touched or their limbs brushed against each other, that he believed she felt the same. His heart was hammering in his chest with the closeness of her and, if he listened carefully, he could hear the drum of hers as it tried to contain the rush of emotions. He sensed the twitch in her muscles, the sideways glance and the parting of her lips as she required more oxygen to satisfy the rapid beating of her heart. Her body was covered in goosepimples and for the first time since knowing him she wished he would just grab her and kiss her. The tension was almost unbearable as it built until finally, he stepped away. There was, an almost visible sigh in the air, as the vacancy of his heat was quickly filled by the surrounding air. Her heart dropped and just for a moment her lids closed. She would not have stopped him, had he touched her then. She would not have pulled away. The tension grew with every passing hour of every day, the only respite from it their time apart. Kira used the power of the elements to distract herself from these feelings, the intense cold of the snow in her hands, the force of the wind against her face and the flow of it through her hair. She focussed on this, on the feel of the ground beneath her feet and not on the warmth of his body next to hers by the fire.

Tomorrow their spell would be broken, their fantasy interrupted by reality as they descended into town, a stark reminder of what they have been through and the separation of their worlds.

'Do you want to come with me?'

His words were like a spear to glass, shattering the silence around them and drawing an end to the barrier of tension.

'To the hospital?'

Adam nodded. 'Raven might still be there, you could go and see her.'

He did not miss the flash over her features. 'Maybe.'

Her heart and her head had been with the girl, when it was not dominated by the presence of her emotions towards

Adam. She had thought about her often, about her strength and connection to the land. She wanted Raven to understand that she was stronger than she thought, that the weakness of her heart also made it stronger, made her stronger. She would go with Adam, she decided, if Raven was still there.

***

The journey to hospital was dominated by the soothing tones of the radio, filling the quiet space not occupied by warm blood and twitching muscles. The seat beside the driver was occupied by Kira's quiet presence, she was by no means primitive, or ignorant to the ways of the world but her experience in vehicles was limited. She measured the speed by which they were travelling in terms of how fast objects passed her by when she ran. The slow crawl out of town on thick snow and slippery roads was no more than walking pace. They had gradually built-up speed as the roads became better to a speed at which she might run, until they found themselves on the open roads of the motorways. Here the snow had been ploughed away from the surface of the road and salt carefully and evenly spread to allow the tyres of the car to stick to the road, and they were flying. They were moving faster than the flight of an eagle, and saw less than the majestic bird might be able to observe from its great vantage point in the sky. She did not understand the need for this speed, why would anyone like to move at such speed that they were unable to focus their eyes on any one thing for more than a couple of seconds? Her body struggled to comprehend the fact that she was stationary and yet in motion, and she felt her stomach take violent turns of unease as the world sped by. Her knowledge probably far surpassed that of those in the vehicle with her, yet she was unable to force her mind into understanding of her current circumstances. She wished she had some ginger to calm the nauseating effect the journey was having on her stomach. Struggling against the growing nausea she closed her eyes and focused her breathing, but it was not until George lowered the passenger side window, with the press of a button, and the cold fresh air washed over her that she started to feel better.

'Thank you.' George was unsure whether the words were meant for him, as her head was turned away into the breeze, but he accepted them nonetheless. The natural line of sight connected Adam's eyes with Kira's body, with her head turned he could see the curve of her neck where the wind lifted the hair from her shoulders, manipulating it into fluid patterns in the air. He wanted to run his fingers across the smoothness of her skin and press his lips against the curve of her neck. Shaking his head, he diverted his mind away from these thoughts and focused instead on the impending visit. It has been six weeks since they left the hospital, which meant that only a couple of months ago they were at the starting blocks of their journey. The journey that would shape their lives, and decide their future, at least for the next year. He could be sure that Kira would be part of his life for at least another year, one more year to understand her and find a way to make his feelings known to her.

Kira and George had found a space of mutual understanding, where they could accept the presence of the other without intrusion. George had not mentioned her parents again since that night in her home, though he had thanked her several times for saving Adam's life. He had managed to keep the building questions and curiosity to himself, finding the answers by watching and understanding her through both his own and his nephew's eyes. It was clear that there was not only a connection between the two but that Adam was very much in love with the woman. He could not pretend to imagine what lay within Kira's heart, and could only hope that his nephew's feelings were not misplaced.

'Here we are.'

Kira's eyes opened as the vehicle slowed and turned off the large, fast road onto a smaller one. Overwhelming noises and smells had her searching for the button to make the window slide back up as a barrier between her and this world. An ambulance had driven them back to town and she had been comforted by the gentle rocking of the vehicle, whilst cocooned in its dark sides. She had not seen this side of the world on that occasion or indeed any other and she found that she did not like it. The car park was filled with vehicles of all shapes, sizes and colours with people of the same description moving around everywhere. The black surface of the road seemed menacing against the dirty grey snow, heaped on the sides of the road as people stepped over these, or ploughed straight through them without any indication that they even knew it was there.

'I'll drop you at the door.' George's voice broke through her confusion, violently jerking her back into the present. Suddenly she really did not want to get out. 'It's too busy, I'll have to go find a parking space further down.'

'No worries, thanks Uncle George.' Adam was unbuckling his seat belt and starting the struggle of getting himself out of the car when Kira's attentions snapped back into focus. Moving with speed and agility she managed to get herself out of the car, and moving around to Adam's side, slipped her arms beneath his shoulders, pulling him backwards out of the vehicle. It was only this focus that allowed her to temporarily ignore the melee around them. She tried to keep her attention focused on him, holding onto him more for her own support than the support she offered him.

'You can let go now.' Her arm was still around his waist and he could not move the crutches into place to allow him to walk. 'Ki,' he said gently, forcing her eyes to focus on his. 'You can let go now.'

'Oh, sorry.' Moving her arm away she suddenly felt very exposed.

'Come on,' he said and led her in through the big doors into the hospital. Inside it was cool and calm, the only drawback being the unnatural smell of antiseptic that filled her senses. She remembered it from when she woke up after their journey.

'We'll go and find out where Raven is.'

Kira used the sound of his voice and the edges of his words to keep herself grounded, as long as he was here, she would be okay. 'We're early so we can go and see her before I have to go for my appointment.' He looked to her for confirmation and smiled slightly at the unease on her face. She wasn't so much scared as uncertain, and he could understand why. He would probably feel the same if he came across a pack of wolves in his back garden, no, in fact that would scare the shit out of him.

He enjoyed the warmth of her close presence as she stayed near him, seeking reassurance from his confidence in this world that was so unfamiliar to her. She nodded her acceptance of his words and followed his progress as he guided them to the children's ward, it was not until they were within the guarded boundaries of this ward that she felt herself relax. The sound of children filled the space as some played quietly in the corner whilst others made loud sound effects and laughed giddily at their playmates. They smiled at Kira and Adam as they passed, some waved and much to her astonishment one girl ran forward and threw her arms around Kira's leg. She looked up at her with adoring eyes as Kira's hand came across the child's brow, smoothing the hair back. Children sensed the purity and power within her the same way that the animals did, and she found herself smiling, as much at ease with them as she was in her own home.

Adam would have taken her hand to pull her along, if he didn't need both of his on the crutches, as it were his voice was enough and she once again fell into step, following him down the corridor. Kira was not prepared for the rush of emotion that ran across the child's face, or that which leapt into her own heart before coursing through her veins.

'Kira!' The joy on her face was sheer and unadulterated as she pushed herself up onto her knees, throwing her arms around the woman once she was close enough to do so. The fragile spindly arms were warm around her neck and Kira felt herself responding with a gentle touch she reserved for small animals. 'I'm so glad you're here!'

Peeling her arms from around Kira's neck the girl sat back down in bed. Her colour was high and her body felt warm, yet she was smiling with uninhibited joy. 'I'm going home today!'

'That's great.' Kira smiled, tucking the apprehension

about the child's mild fever behind her words. She was intensely aware of the other two pairs of eyes staring at her.

'Kira, this is my mum and dad,' Raven said, suddenly looking every bit, the child she was.

Kira moved her eyes in the direction of the others and found a hand outstretched over the bed. Lifting her hand, she placed it in the woman's, finding pain in her eyes. 'Thank you,' she said looking straight into the deep blue of Kira's eyes. 'You saved Raven's life.'

There was a moment of silence as their gaze reflected mutual respect and understanding before it was shattered by a harsh tone. 'She would not have needed saving if she hadn't gone up there in the first place!'

The venom penetrated her skin like a knife through butter as Raven's head dropped, her shoulders slumping. Adam must have been aware of the malice in the voice as he had instinctively moved forward, closer to Kira. An awkward silence filled the room, lying just above the heavy weight of accusation as Kira felt no need to offer an explanation. Her eyes returned to Raven's who glanced shyly up at her from beneath heavy lids. Her father was obviously angry with her, or perhaps with Kira.

'Erm…' The need for convention overwhelmed Adam as he struggled for words to fill the heavy silence. 'I've got an appointment in an hour,' he said loudly, 'for my leg, so I twisted Kira's arm to come with me. We wanted to see how you were doing.'

Raven smiled. 'I'm good.' There was a slight pause. 'I'm going home today.'

'So you said,' Adam smiled, '… and I might get this cast off today.'

'Really?' She was excited for him, though she didn't know why. 'That's cool. Will you keep it?'

'I don't think so,' Adam laughed. 'I'd be glad to be rid of it.'

Raven nodded. 'You'll be quite slow when that comes off won't you?'

'I'm slow now!'

Raven grinned, her fingers had found Kira's and she was holding on to her as if her life depended on it. 'I'll be slow too,' she smiled. 'We could go for walks together.'

'We could,' Adam nodded. 'We can watch the snails pass us by.'

'…and the turtles!' Raven grinned unaware of the simmering anger and resentment of her father. Kira on the other hand was very much aware of it, she could feel it like a physical presence in the room and shifted uncomfortably beneath its weight.

'Would you mind staying with Raven for a while?' Kira's eyes lifted to the other woman's eyes as she slipped her arm through her husband's. 'We haven't had a chance to have lunch yet.'

'Of course,' Kira nodded. 'I'll stay until you get back.'

'Thank you.'

They watched as Raven's dad was nearly dragged out of the room, before a sigh escaped the young girl's lips. 'Sorry,' she said. 'My dad is a bit overprotective.'

Kira smiled back putting the child at ease. 'I think all dads are.'

'Is yours?'

Kira felt Adam's body stiffen beside hers, but she felt no tension at the child's question. 'He was,' she said. 'In his own way.'

'Was?'

'Both my parents have been gone for ten years.'

The larger number caught Adam's attention, and he suddenly realised the truth of her statement.

'Oh, I'm sorry.'

'Don't be.' Kira smiled brushing the hair away from the child's face. 'They are always with me.' She touched her heart. 'In here.'

Raven looked from Kira's hand to her own chest. 'Maybe you could lend them to me. I'm sure they will make my heart stronger.'

'You can borrow them any time you like.' Kira smiled. 'They will give you the strength they gave me.' She pressed her hand against Raven's small chest, allowing the heat to filter through her pyjamas and penetrate her skin.

'I can feel it already,' the girl whispered putting her own small hand over Kira's.

'Erm…'

Kira lifted her eyes to Adam's. 'I've got to go,' he said. 'Shall I come back here for you?'

Kira nodded and with another smile to the child he turned and hopped away on his crutches. 'I think you gave me some of your strength anyway.' Raven whispered, looking deep into Kira's eyes. 'Up on the mountain. The doctors said I shouldn't have survived for so long without my medicine, and out there.' She looked to the window but finding the view unsatisfying returned her eyes to Kira. 'I miss the mountains.'

'So do I.'

'Kira?' There was a flash of embarrassment through the

girl's eyes. 'I thought I saw something.' Her words were hesitant, encouraged only by the woman's gentle steady gaze. 'When I was out there by myself.' She paused and looked away, sighing quietly as if maybe she was wrong. Maybe her parents and the doctors were right, maybe she had just imagined it.

'The wolves?'

Raven's head shot up at the words, her eyes filling with wonder. 'They were real?'

Kira nodded. 'As real as you and me,' she smiled. 'They came to find me and led me to you.'

The girl was astounded. 'You know them?'

'As much as I know any other creature in the forests.' She pondered. 'As do you.'

'What do you mean?'

'They were protecting you,' Kira said. 'Guarding your body while you were unconscious, keeping you warm until they could find me.' She wondered for a moment if this was too much information to be giving a child. Would she understand or would she think that all wolves were her friends from now on?

'How old are you?'

Raven blinked, pulled further away from this magical world Kira seemed to live in. 'Eleven,' she whispered.

'When I was eleven, I was hunting in the forest, and running up the mountainsides, by myself.'

'All I'm allowed to do is watch TV, or read. I'm not allowed to run.'

Kira smiled sadly. 'I was born in those mountains, I am part of them.' She looked into the young eyes for understanding. 'We all have different parts to play in life, we are provided with challenges that will make us stronger, if we allow it to. This,' she said gently tapping the girl's heart. 'This, is not a weakness, it is a challenge, and challenges are symbols of strength. They were designed to test us and allow us to learn from them.'

'What can I possibly learn from a sickly heart?' Raven was despondent. 'Why can't my challenge be to run up a mountainside, or to kill a deer?'

'You have a special challenge.' Kira leaned forward, allowing her hair to spill over onto the bed, floating between the fingers of the girl. 'You have something that I will never have. You have a different kind of strength than I do, than Adam does and even that your mum and dad have. Your challenge was designed for you, because you are unique and only you can overcome it. I can't, your mum can't, your dad can't and not even the doctors can, only you can.'

'How?'

Kira smiled at the slight tug on her scalp as the child played with her hair. 'By believing in yourself. By being strong and being the best that you can be. You cannot compare yourself to others, because they do not have your challenge or your strength. Only you do.'

Raven's eyes darted to the door as her parents reappeared, making Kira's head drop slightly as she moved away from the bed.

'I should go.' She smiled at the girl. 'Stay strong.'

'Will you come and visit me?' It was a plea of desperation tugging at her heart as she looked into the sad blue eyes.

'Of course,' Kira smiled, 'and maybe when you are stronger you can come and visit me.'

She detected the light of hope in both Raven and her mother's eyes which were quickly overshadowed by the harsh dark words of her father. Kira allowed her eyes to remain on the girl until she looked back up, extending her meaning and information once again before quietly moving away.

Her thoughts were occupied by the events that had brought Raven so close to her heart, she felt connected to the child. She wanted Raven to recognise the power Kira saw in her eyes, the inner strength which would carry her through difficult times. Kira was no stranger to difficulty. Her life was by no means easy, but it was the resilience she had been taught that provided her with the ability to recognise the inner strength she possessed. It did not appear by magic and through the years she had to learn how to use that strength and resilience to accomplish anything she put her mind to. Kira had never doubted that she could do anything she wanted, as long as she put the work in. That is what she had been taught and in honour of her parents she kept living these values, despite their disappearance. She could have given up. She could have fallen apart, gone to live with Harvey in town. She could have gone to school, university and got a job, but she didn't. She was raised with the earth, the moon and the wind. The mountains were in her blood, there was no getting away from that. She found herself ripped out of thought as she reached the fracture clinic without thinking, her eyes immediately finding Adam's.

His cast was gone, the relief on his face, as his eyes met her eyes, was as complete as it was in her heart. His smile carried a hint of promise now that his leg was free of its constraint and Kira felt a sense of complete relief wash over her. She had to press a hand against the wall to ground herself. Her knees growing weak as the weight was lifted off her shoulders, she had not realised how much anxiety she had been carrying about his leg. He was still leaning on the crutches, but his leg moved freely and seemingly without pain, only the raw new skin over his wound remaining as evidence of injury.

Kira had done what she had to on the mountain, to keep them both alive. She knew that not setting his leg would have caused infinite more pain and discomfort, and they would not have made the distances they did. She knew she had no other choice than to attempt to set his leg, but the decision had weighed heavily on her shoulders. To this day she had carried the fear that she had done something wrong, had caused damage to nerves or vessels that could prevent him from regaining the full use of his leg, but as he approached, she could tell by the smile in his eyes that everything was going to be okay. His words of confidence and elation washed over her like a warm summer breeze as he told her about the doctor's complete satisfaction. He had never doubted Kira's abilities, her decisions or the power of her healing herbs. He had felt the healing of muscle and tendon, the mending of bones and the knitting together of skin as day after day, first she and then he, cleaned and redressed his wound with nature's own medicine. He had no doubt that the fresh air, positive energy and exercise had done him good, aiding in the healing of his physical injury, as much as the mental scars he carried. He was convinced of nature's healing powers as Kira had been all her life and was starting to slot neatly into her life, accepting her beliefs as his own.

The journey home was filled with quiet hope and great

expectation of the year ahead as they mentally prepared themselves for their second journey, back to the river of ice. Adam was eager to return to the mountains, her home in the woods which was starting to feel like his own.

Their days fell into a comfortable routine of no routine as Adam determinedly did his rehabilitation exercises, carefully and thoroughly every day, combining them with the training he had been doing before the cast was removed. Kira had grown accustomed and reliant on his consistent presence, providing aid, assistance or advice where he asked for it. She became used to just having another breath in the house, she was no longer alone, and the contentment with which it filled her took her by surprise. As the hours of daylight grew and the power of the sun increased day by day, melting the snow beneath their feet, another visitor made its way up the track to her house. It was with the first green leaves poking from beneath the snow, that her home welcomed the fragile young girl who had pushed herself to the very limit of existence to see Kira. Raven's presence became as normal and expected as Adam's and as the days grew longer and the temperature increased her home was filled with voices. Footsteps echoed off the walls and bounced into the warm dry air, shouts of glee mingled with splashing water at the streams as laughter and joy filled her house. Raven's health was improving with exercise, fresh air and positive stimuli. Her fragile frame was filling out with good food and a healthy appetite, and not even her father could deny the good her trips into the mountains did her. Her face was filled with colour, her eyes sparkled with joy and her hair shone a blue black with health. Gone was the pale complexion, dull eyes and lacklustre hair. She had enthusiasm for life and a hunger for the knowledge of anything natural. Adam listened as Kira answered the girl's many questions and revelled in the deep curiosity of her nature. He was learning, not just about plants and rocks and the natural world but about legends and gods and mythical creatures. Raven showed a particular interest in wolves, and sometimes when the girl was rapt in the sound of Kira's voice as she relayed information or told of legends, he found himself watching the two. Kira had easily fallen into the role of teacher and mentor. The girl looked up to her with a kind of hero worship and when she sat with the girl in her arms in front of the fire, he wished that it was his hair she was stroking and his cheeks over which her breath whispered. He had taken on the responsibility of ensuring Raven's safe journeying to and from the mountain home, and often found himself carrying the sleeping figure down the mountain after an exhausting day of living and learning. He missed his nights alone with Kira, wrapped in the comfort of her company and calming presence just as much as she did. Adam's presence at her home had been constant and complete, satisfying, and she missed him. She struggled to fill the empty space his absent form left behind, when he escorted Raven back to town. She enjoyed the child's company and was glad to see her growing fit and healthy despite the weakness of her heart, but she found herself longing for those quiet winter nights alone with the man that had followed her so foolishly when they were just kids. She smiled when she remembered their first meeting, the excitement, confusion and adrenaline that had dominated the day, and then looking around her empty home after they left, felt herself deflating ever so slightly. Although the nights were short in summer, they stretched out like long empty vessels of questionable cargo as she wondered each day when they left, how she would fill the evening. She felt a guilty sense of relief as her heart jumped every time he appeared from beneath the thick cover of trees, alone. Raven could not come every day and she treasured these days alone with him. She could no longer hide the fact from herself, she was in love with Adam in a way she had not known possible. She struggled with the unfamiliar feelings and emotions, knowing that he was so much more experienced in these matters than her. Her skin burned with excitement every time she found his eyes on her, her heart leaping with exhilaration and anticipation as it slammed against her chest, sometimes throwing her off guard. She knew when he was looking at her, she could feel his gaze linger on her shape whether she was hunched over a plant with Raven, or when they were quietly sipping at soup in front of the fire on a rainy day. Their bond grew, their connection being reinforced every day with more and more strings of mutual respect and admiration that bound them together. Every brush of his skin against hers was agonisingly electrifying, every meeting between their eyes growing with passion as increasingly Raven caught onto the atmosphere and distanced herself from them. She watched them from the side of the stream as they splashed and laughed like children, or from her perch at the counter as they sat close together in front of the fire. No word of affection had been spoken between them, though their love was as obvious to her as the sun in the sky.

'He likes you.'

Kira and Raven were sitting in front of the fire, their heads hunched close over a book as Kira taught her the medicinal values of plants. Her voice was a confident whisper, her eyes on the profile of Kira's face.

'What?' Kira tore herself out of the world of herbs, focussing her eyes on the child.

'Adam,' she said, her voice still low but no longer a whisper. 'You do know he likes you, don't you?'

Kira's eyes remained on the girl's for a very long time as she tried to read the meaning behind the colour. 'Of course he does,' she smiled. 'He's my friend.'

Raven's eyes rolled in their sockets as she shook her head. 'That is not what I meant.' She looked closely at the emotion on Kira's face, as her eyes found his form beyond the window. 'I like him,' Raven said following her eyes. 'You like him too, don't you?' The child's eyes were on her face again, but she did not turn to meet them.

'Of course I do,' she whispered, aware of the hammering of her heart. 'He's my friend.'

'That is not what I meant.'

It was this whisper of the child's words that was echoing through her mind as she watched him approach through the cover of trees. He was alone and sensing a change in the air she shivered slightly despite the warmth of the sun.

'Morning.' Her eyes were lifted to the mountains, their peaks ever covered in snow, when he spoke. She had trouble tearing her eyes away from them as he came to a halt next to her, following her gaze.

'Snow?'

Kira's eyes darted to his, reading the mischief in them and smiled. 'No, not down here.' It was only August.

'Just change.' She looked curiously into his eyes, unaware of what she was searching for.

'What kind of change?' His eyes were moving between the pull of hers and the curiosity of what she read in the peaks.

'I don't know,' she said quietly before pulling her eyes away. 'Where's Raven?'

'She's gone to the city for a check-up.' He saw the flash through her eyes and rushed to reassure her. 'It's just a routine check apparently. She said she has them every three to six months.'

Another shiver ran through her body as she looked into his eyes, unsure of what it represented.

'Are you all right?' His eyes changed as he recognised the fear and doubt in hers. 'What's wrong?'

Kira tore her eyes away, unsure of what it was in his aura, that had filled her with a sense of pain and sadness. 'I'm fine,' she smiled, shaking her head. Maybe she was just worried about Raven. 'I just need to get out.' Her eyes darted to the summits again before glancing over him as she turned away with a frown on her face. Something didn't feel right. A light breeze toyed with the hair around her shoulders as she turned away, drawing Adam's eyes to their length. He looked at it, always awed by the length and colour, and found himself wondering when the blood of the ptarmigan had disappeared from the ends of her white mane.

Kira's mind was struggling to deal with the conflicting thoughts and emotions as they walked deep into the forest, away from the house and the mountains. The feelings between her and Adam had grown into huge spirals of colour that tangled in the air between them every time they were together. The tension was undeniable, but the small dark twist in the space around him alerted her of pain. He might not know it himself yet, but she could see that he was going to hurt her, and for that reason she wanted to remain at a distance. She didn't invite him along on this walk, yet she did not ask him to leave when he followed. She was intensely aware of his presence, as he was of hers, allowing his fingers to brush against hers as they walked. He walked with ease, the strength in his leg growing every day, and he relished the freedom and ability to keep up with her. He had hated the times when he had to watch her turn around and walk away from him in a rush of emotion. Her breath caught in her throat as his hand brushed against hers again, finding cohesion. His fingers lacing through hers sent shivers up her arms and electric currents down his spine. The sun was warm through the trees and though he felt the tension in her limbs she did not pull away. He had seen her eyes close momentarily as she relented to the feel of his strong fingers between hers. An image flashed through her mind, the first time he had done that, up at the pool, before their journey. Suddenly, without warning, her hand slipped from his as she ducked down, disappearing beneath the undergrowth. Adam stood for a minute, confused, before copying her movements and pushing through the thick vegetation. To his surprise the land beyond dropped away steeply and he could see her moving down the slope with purpose and into the water at the bottom. This was a stream Kira had come to as a child, it was her hiding place where she came to dream. Her feet and legs were bare as they had been all summer and she walked straight into the water, without stopping, without thinking. The water rushed to enfold her in its cool embrace, eager as Adam's arms were to wrap around her. The cold reached the level of her chest before she stopped and quietly slipped beneath the surface. Adam was left staring at the surface of the pool, still and devoid of life. Had he simply stumbled upon the stream he would not have known that she had just slipped beneath the surface. It was a long time before the dark of the water was once again broken by the white of her hair, the blue of her eyes fixing on his as he watched from the bank. There was no place for words between them, every available iota of space was filled with emotion, and need, as she pulled herself from the stream. The sun was breaking through the trees, casting its long rays of heat on the rocky outcrop at the head of the stream. Kira's body knew the space well, moulding to the contours in the rock as she closed her eyes against the bright light. The cold water of the pool had been a pleasant escape from reality as it calmed the torrent of thoughts, like a healing poultice does a fever. Her mind was clear, still and she wanted to keep it that way. She needed to remain focused and so, fixed her attention on the way the sun dried the cold drops of moisture on her skin, warming her body. She was aware of his eyes on her as she had been over the last few months, but his words were still as his eyes feasted on her beauty and strength. He could see himself wiping the strands of hair from her wet cheek, and as she opened her eyes, filling his vision with the intensity of their colour, he would bring his lips down onto the moist red of hers. He had to cough and look away to stop himself from going too far. Kira's eyes opened and when he turned his gaze back, he found her eyes on him. She said nothing as they stared at each other and she wondered if she could allow herself just one small slip in concentration. Just one kink in her focus as she so desperately wanted to know what it would feel like to be held and kissed by someone who truly loved you. She had dreamed of being in his arms, though she had dismissed these dreams as a combination of friendship and a desire to know more about the realms of love and passion.

'Have you ever been to the sea?'

His voice was almost unrecognisable as his words struggled to make sense in her head. Sitting up she wrapped her arms around her legs, shaking her head, even as a far-off memory played through the shadows of her mind.

'I think you'll like it,' Adam said still looking at her intently. 'It's full of power and emotion.' Thoughts of the tempestuous sea reminded him of her and he was unable to take his eyes of her, much as he always had trouble tearing his eyes from the violent thrust of waves.

'We should go. I'll take you.'

There was a brief inclination of her head, had he been closer to her he would not have been able to stop himself from touching her. Across the stream he saw her rise, the muscles in her lean legs beautifully defined as she came down from her outcrop of rocks and came to sit next to him. She wanted to feel the weight of his presence, she knew things were going to change and she wanted just one chance of knowing what it felt like. The heat was almost unbearable where their skin touched, and she was very aware of the steadily increasing thumping of her heart against her chest. Her eyes were on the ground between her feet as her lips parted after swallowing past the excited apprehension. Adam's fingers were running through her hair, she could feel its tug on her scalp and was sure she could feel the hammering of his heart in the muscles pressed up against hers. Her eyes moved slowly to his feet before drifting up his legs and coming eventually to a rest on his face. Their faces were turned to each other the need clearly visible in each other's eyes, Adam's fingers were trembling when they came up to her face. Never before had he dared to make such a move, he stopped when his hand was wrapped around the side of her face, his thumb stroking her cheek as he looked into her eyes. He saw in them, what he had wanted to from the moment he met her, his own desire reflected in her eyes. He saw the faint flash of embarrassment and for a moment thought she was going to pull away, but he held her gaze, held her face in his hand and started to move his lips closer to hers. He could already taste her, he knew what she would taste like, he knew her better than he had ever known another person. He knew her scent and her warmth, he could read the emotion in her eyes and across her face. He could cause tension in her muscles and he knew how to release it. She tried to keep her eyes open, keep them focused on his but the power of emotion pulled her lids down and when she was sure his lips were going to touch hers, he was suddenly violently, unnecessarily ripped away from her. The foreign sound rang through the forest surprising them both and making them jump. Kira's eyes shot open, her heart hammering in her chest with shock, she had never heard his phone ring before.

'Dammit!' His eyes found hers. 'Sorry.' He was sorrier than she would ever know because the name flashing on the screen was what was bringing change. Kira could see the twist in the space surrounding him grow as his eyes went back up to hers guiltily.

'What the?' He stared at the screen in confusion, he had never answered Sally's questioning email on why he had dismissed the idea of this glacial exploration almost as quickly as he had come up with it.

Kira did not need to see the name on the phone to know that things had changed, she could see it in the tension of his muscles, the guilty confusion on his face and the dark twist. Pushing to her feet she felt deprived, wronged in a way that she could not explain. She didn't know what was happening, but she could almost feel the betrayal in her bones.

'Ki, wait!'

He didn't know himself yet what was happening, but he did not want her to run away like this, from this. He rushed to chase after her, but she had gone into stealth mode and she was gone. Try as he might he could not hear a sound giving away her heading and he knew from experience that she could be gone for hours. Running a hand through his hair, he sighed heavily falling back down to the ground as he pulled his phone out, listening to the voice mail.

Chapter Six

Kira had become accustomed to Adam's arrival without Raven, but not of the child's arrival without him.

'Raven?' The exclamation from Kira ended in a question mark as the girl appeared from behind the trees. She waited a few moments, expecting another body to emerge from the woods but when it remained motionless, but for the work of the wind, she moved towards the girl. Her face was flushed, her hair wild as her eyes sparkled.

'How did you get up here?'

'I walked!' she said triumphantly. 'All the way!'

Kira's eyes widened at the revelation, concern about her parents' reaction in the forefront of her mind. 'By yourself?' She asked cautiously, unwilling to dampen the wide grin on the girl's face.

'Yes, no, I mean; yes, I walked all the way by myself, but my dad walked me up until I told him to turn around.'

Kira raised an eyebrow. 'Your dad?'

Raven nodded eagerly. 'I didn't want him to know where you lived, I know you don't want people to know.' She paused briefly catching her breath. 'So, I told him it wasn't far and made him turn around before I went off the track.'

Kira was frowning as Raven stared at her with big eyes, willing the woman to believe her. 'The doctors were really surprised at my tests,' she explained. 'They can't figure out why I'm so strong.' She giggled. 'They asked me what I've been doing, and they say it's impossible for my heart to be getting stronger, and yet it is! I know what it is even if they don't.'

Kira smiled, the girl's enthusiasm contagious. 'What's that?'

'Magic,' Raven said, grinning. 'You are magic, you made my heart stronger.'

Raven threw her arms around Kira's waist, hugging her tightly. 'I'm not magic Raven,' Kira said gently, 'but the earth does have powers we cannot begin to pretend to understand. I have no qualms believing in miracles.'

'Oh, I brought you something.' She pulled away quickly leaving Kira reeling from the loss of comfort. 'It's from Adam.'

She didn't see the flash across Kira's face as she wondered about the change she had seen in his aura. The feel of him still almost tangible, despite the couple of days of absence since he had left her a hastily scribbled note that he needed to take care of something in town. He had rushed down the valley after finding out that Sally had decided to come and see him in person, tired of being ignored. He didn't want somebody to send her up the valley in the direction of where he might be, and risk Kira running into her unexpectedly. He needed to sort this before she got the wrong end of the stick.

'Here!' Raven pulled a small rectangular object from her bag, shoving it in Kira's hands.

'He said sorry that he couldn't come.' Raven saw Kira looking at the worn object with confusion. 'It's a tape recorder,' Raven explained. 'Here,' she reached out pressing the play button as they both leaned forward against the rush of wind to listen.

'What is it?' Raven looked up, confused at the sound.

'I don't know.' Kira frowned. 'Let's go inside.'

She didn't ask the question that was itching in the forefront of her mind. There was nothing that tied them together, no promises had been made and he was free to do as he pleased, yet she was very much aware of the absence of his presence. The last time she had seen him was on a height of emotion unlike anything she had ever experienced, and his absence caused apprehension to grow in her stomach. Inside, away from the rush of the elements Kira deciphered the buttons on the tape recorder, and rewinding it, played it again. The sound was much clearer, and she could feel herself being rocked to a gentle rhythm of roll and crash, time after time. 'It sounds like the wind.' Kira said thoughtfully. 'Only it's controlled, timed, rhythmic. It's always the same.'

She glanced at Raven, and suddenly the light sparked in the girl's eyes. 'It's the sea!' Raven exclaimed, turning her eyes to the tape recorder for confirmation. Her shiny black hair bobbed up and down with her head as she agreed with herself. 'Listen,' she paused. 'There's the roll of the wave, then the crash on shore and the swish as it pulls back again.'

Pleased with herself she smiled at Kira, looking for understanding but finding only a faraway look in her eyes. 'Haven't you ever been to the sea?'

Kira was unsure whether the memory was real or

conjured but the smell of salt overcame her senses as she played the sound again. A sticky layer over her skin and the itch of sand became almost tangible. She must have been. Adam was right, the mere sound of it spoke of carefully controlled power and grace. She could fall asleep to the sound of this rhythm. She already loved it as much as she did the aching howl of the wind. Pulling herself out of thought she resolved to listen to the tape again tonight and turning to Raven smiled at the child. 'So, what would you like to do today?'

Raven was in her element, never before did she have the opportunity to be completely alone with this woman she idolized and she didn't even know where to begin. There were many times that she had wished to be alone with Kira, to ask her the questions that burned in her heart and mind, but suddenly all of these eluded her. It was not until they were lying on the hot rocks of the outcrop at the top of the pool she had visited with Adam, that Raven started to remember her questions.

'Kira?' There was a slight pause as she stared up at the rays of sun filtering through the canopy above. 'How do you know so much about... everything?'

There was a long pause as Kira contemplated the answer, the silence forcing the girl to tilt her head to the woman beside her. 'Are you magic?' Her words were barely a whisper over her young lips, as if she was afraid to ask it out loud, in case she scared it away.

Kira pushed herself up onto an elbow and looked at the girl. 'I'm not magic,' she said gently. 'I was born in these mountains. If I shut my eyes, I can find my way home, just like you can find the way from your room to the bathroom in the dark, because it is what I know.'

The girl looked at her in awe. 'You know so much, though.'

'I grew up with the whispers of the hills in my ear, the brush of the wind on my skin and the earth beneath my toes. I have watched wolves pup and young deer take their first steps, I have learned to watch, to listen and to learn.' Raven's eyes were large with awe. 'My mother taught me everything she knew, as did my father. They were two very different people, and I was taught to be both gentle and strong, compliant and independent.'

There was a frown on the girl's face, alerting Kira that she did not understand everything that was being said. 'I was taught to listen,' Kira said simply. 'Listen to the mountains, the streams, the earth and the animals, they tell you all you need to know. Watch them, learn their behaviour and you will never be caught out.'

'Can you talk to animals?'

'No more than you can,' Kira smiled. 'I can, however, listen better than others.'

'Can you teach me?' Raven whispered. 'To listen?' There was only a slight pause before she spoke again. '... and do everything else that you can do?'

It had taken Kira all her life to know what she knew and there was a lot more to learn. 'I can show you how to teach yourself everything that you are capable of doing.'

'Can I learn how to listen to the mountains and the animals?'

'You can do anything you put your mind to.'

'... and you'll show me how?' she asked eagerly.

'I'll show you how.'

Her voice was soft and gentle as she smiled encouragingly down at the girl, watching her as she lay back down, closing her eyes against the sun. Her fingers were brushing across to rough texture of the rock as she learned how to stay grounded.

'Kira?' Her eyes remained closed as she asked her next question.

'Do you love Adam?'

The answer jumped, with her heart, into her mouth as she felt her stomach to a backflip, moments before her head was able to take over and analyse the question. What is love, what does loving somebody mean? Kira concentrated on the heat on her closed lids as the butterflies in her stomach tried to make sense of this all-consuming, confusing emotion. Was loving somebody the notion of wanting to share everything with them? Was it that the thought of them could creep up on you at any moment, and take you by surprise? Did you long for the company of their presence when they were not there, or for the warmth of their embrace? Was their face the first one you saw when you opened your eyes in the morning and the last one before you closed them again at night? Was it them that you wanted to rush to and share the facts of your life with, share memorable moments with? Did they carry the ability to hurt you more than anything else ever could? Was that love? Opening her eyes, she fixed it for a moment on the filtering sunlight before moving it onto Raven.

'How do you know?' she whispered to the girl whose eyes were already on her. Raven pushed herself up, crossing her legs in front of her as she studied Kira. 'I don't know. I guess you think about them all the time,' she paused. 'They make you laugh, they can take away your pain or hug away your sadness. You know you love somebody when you want them with you whether you are happy or sad, even though they sometimes make you angry. Kira smiled at the girl. 'Do you love somebody Raven?'

The girl blushed, pulling her eyes away. 'No, not love,' she said eventually. 'Just like, but it doesn't matter anyway, he'll never like me.'

'Why do you say that?'

She shrugged. 'I just know.' There was no self-pity or remorse in her tone as she pushed herself to her feet. 'I'm only eleven anyway,' she grinned. 'It's not like I'm about to get married or anything.'

Kira laughed, pushing herself up beside the girl. 'Let's go back.' She lifted her head to the sky, noting the sun's westerly travels. 'I'll walk you home.'

'You don't have to,' the girl said suddenly. 'I asked my parents if I could stay over, Adam said he would walk me home tomorrow.'

'Oh.' Kira was just able to suppress the rush of emotion welling up inside of her. 'Great.'

Raven smiled as her small hand slipped into Kira's, drawing the intense blue eyes downward. The girl's narrow bare feet were sinking into the soft ground of the forest as she walked with her shoes, forgotten, in her hand. Hearing the cry of a bird Kira tilted her head up, causing her hair to sink even closer to the ground, and from the sky the eagle could see the two figures. They were bound by nature, exactly the same and yet their appearances were in stark contrast to one another.

***

Kira and Raven were in a quiet introspective mood as they had been for most of the previous evening. They had sat by the warmth of the fire as Kira relayed legend upon legend to this girl who was so hungry for knowledge. Eventually the talking had stopped, and Kira had found her arms wrapped around the warm body of the sleeping child, her cheek resting on the soft black hair. She had felt complete and somehow empty. Her life had changed since she met Adam as she first became accustomed to having company, and later welcomed it. Now she longed for it. She no longer wanted to be alone and though she still treasured her independence, she wanted to return from a long day out, alone with her thoughts and be able to share her discoveries with someone. She had become dependent on Adam's friendship, and now with Raven in her life she had found a new role. She was teaching, mentoring and nurturing the young person. These new roles were fulfilling her in a way she had not thought possible, blossoming in the unconditional love and trust of the girl. Kira had never known any other kind of love. Her parents had loved her unconditionally and without reproach. They had nurtured and supported her, but they were not afraid to set her straight if she was wandering off the path. This parental love was all she knew, it was what she felt towards Raven, and what the girl felt towards her, but the love she felt for Adam was different. It excited and frightened her. The unpredictability and doubt confused her, though the power of it excited her.

'Good Morning.'

Kira jumped guiltily as her eyes shot open, the

movement bringing a twinkle of amusement to Adam's eyes as he smiled down at them. They were lying with their backs on the ground, the early morning sun on their faces.

'Morning.' Kira blushed slightly feeling the butterflies in her stomach as he stared down at her, amused by the colour on her cheeks.

'What are you doing?'

'Reading the clouds,' Raven said seriously, oblivious to Kira's state of mind as her eyes flickered to Adam's before fixing on the sky again. Tilting his head Adam looked up to the sky for a moment before turning his gaze back on the women. Kira's eyes were dark with emotion as he found them on him.

'Can I join you?'

Raven automatically shifted up, this small action bringing a smile to Kira's face. The girl had so much room in her life for others, it was an automatic reaction for her to create room for him, despite the wide-open space around them. Kira did not move, the lie of the land provided more than enough room for him to join them. Her heart quickened at the feel of his presence as the air changed beside her where he lay down between them. There were shivers running up and down her arms as her lips parted, to allow more oxygen to enter her lungs.

'What are we looking for?'

His arm was so close to hers she could feel the hair on his skin standing on end, brushing against hers. Raven was speaking but her words eluded Kira as the tension between them grew. She had wanted to see him since the day at the stream when he nearly kissed her, but now that he was here, she didn't know what to do with herself. She wanted to know what that phone call was about, why he had rushed off into town and had not returned for days. She had questions to ask, but she could not ask them with Raven there. Adam's arm had rolled closer, the warmth of his skin pressing against hers. Her eyes were closed when he turned his gaze on her, the rapid movement behind her lids visible as she swallowed past a knot of emotion. His heart was hammering in his chest as he filled his eyes with the beauty of her. He had to tear his eyes away as guilt washed over him, he didn't know how to tell her what he needed to. She didn't like the idea of having other people on the glacier, he understood that, but he did not want her to go through what they had already gone through. He could not bear to see her so beaten and broken again, and there was safety in numbers. He had a hard time convincing Sally that they didn't need a helicopter, but Sally was not a mountaineer, she was a glaciologist. She had no interest in walking for four days to reach a destination when it could be made in one, by helicopter. Perhaps if she met Kira, she would see what he saw and understand, but he wasn't holding his breath.

'Can I go to the stream?' Raven wiggled with unease at the growing tension between Adam and Kira. Jumping to her feet she posed the question as Kira pushed herself up into a sitting position. 'Of course.' She tilted her head at the anxious movements of the child. 'Just be careful and come back at midday to let us know you're okay.' Raven nodded and ran off without a second glance.

'She seemed anxious.' Adam was sitting up beside her. 'Do you think she's okay?'

Kira nodded, Raven was very intuitive and she knew it was the currents of emotion between her and Adam that had sparked her actions.

'She's testing the boundaries of her independence.' The words sounded realistic enough to her. Adam followed the shape of Kira's limbs as she pushed herself up and strode away. 'Are you?'

His voice was loud enough, and quick enough, to stop her before she could turn the corner.

'I'm fine. Why?'

Pushing himself to his feet he quickly closed the distance between them. 'I'm sorry for rushing off the other day.' Sorrier than she could possibly imagine. He would have sorely liked to finish what they had started. 'I wouldn't have left if it wasn't urgent.'

Kira nearly shrugged, and catching herself she turned her eyes away before he could read the emotion in them. 'No problem.' Striding around to the lines of vegetables growing behind the house she kneeled down to start tending to them.

Adam frowned, he thought she might at least have been a little upset about it. 'Don't you want to know what it was about?'

'Your business is your business.' She was fighting to keep her tone even, trying to ignore his looming presence behind her.

'It involves you.' Neither of them was prepared for, or indeed expected, the frustration in his voice. Her fingers ceased their work in the ground as she paused for a moment, controlling her breathing before standing up and facing him.

'What do you mean it involves me?' Her tone was calculated, her eyes clear and cold as they fixed on his.

Running a hand through his mop of hair he looked about him for inspiration. 'Can we go inside?'

'Why?'

'... because I don't want to you give the opportunity to run away.' The brutal honesty in his words alerted her that this was serious. He was done tiptoeing around the issue, skirting around the edges of the tension.

'Why would I feel the need to do that?' There was an undertone of steel in her voice as she stepped forward facing him like an opponent.

'I don't think you are going to like what I have to tell you.'

Folding her arms across her chest, her bare feet planted in the ground she fixed the cold steel of her glacial eyes on him. 'Go on.'

He took a deep breath, trying to assess the likelihood of her running and prepared himself to chase after her if he had to. 'That call the other day,' he paused seeing the flash of emotion, as she remembered what he did, the thought settling him. 'It was from a friend of mine, who had just arrived in town. Unexpectedly,' he added, eager to plant the seed that he had not invited her. 'She is a glaciologist.' He saw the quick flash of surprise as Kira struggled to control the reeling emotion in her head. Her body twitched and she had to move to keep her balance. His words were like a physical blow to the chest, as she grasped at the trailing ends of information scattered about her. It was all starting to make sense and as she stood with a handful of information, she looked at him with shock, the force of which taking her breath away, never mind her words.

'I did not invite her Ki,' he said quickly. 'She showed up because I had retracted my words about the glacier. I had rung her back the same day, telling her to forget about it, it was a stupid idea and that I did not want her to entertain it. I had asked her not to pursue it, but she is a scientist and she is hungry for adventure and power. She wants to establish herself in the field, make her name known and this glacier is her opportunity.'

He paused when her eye contact finally failed, her head lowering to the ground. She was shaking it to try and organise the overload of emotion. Her body was no longer controlled as she stumbled slightly, reeling from the information. Waves of betrayal washed over her as that dark twist jumped out from his silhouette, knotting her in hurt.

'Ki.'

She couldn't take anymore, she couldn't believe that he would do this, that he could tell her one thing but do the complete opposite. She had trusted him. She had believed him when he said that he understood, she thought that they felt the same about this. She thought that come winter they would be going back up there, together, just the two of them, but he had lied. He stood here in front of her, on her land, in front of her house, surrounded by her mountains and lied to her. There was fire in her eyes when she looked back up, barely masking the pain.

'How could you?' Her voice did not mirror the strength in her eyes, as it too chose to betray her. 'I trusted you.' Her voice wavered as she quickly turned her eyes away, blinking away the tears. She had never felt pain like this before, it was like somebody had pressed their fingers through the flesh on her chest, penetrating the protective barrier of bones and was clenching their fist around her heart.

Adam felt his life implode as she stumbled backwards, the hurt in her eyes like a knife in his heart. He had done exactly what he was had been trying to avoid. He was hurting her, again.

'Ki, just wait,' he pleaded. 'Just let me explain.'

'I don't need an explanation on betrayal.' She couldn't look at him, there were tears in her eyes as she gasped for breath. 'The feeling speaks for itself.'

'No.' He stepped forward, adamant to stop her from running as she stumbled backwards, disorientated by the spinning of emotion in her head. She was reaching for the wrong end of the baton and he could not let her run with it, it would be the end of them.

'Kira, stop! Just listen to me.' The desperation in his voice echoed through the trees, making Raven's head lift to the rustling of leaves. She sat quietly in her hunched position in the water watching the light dance through the trees and listening to the wind. Rising to her feet she looked about her, it was as if the wind was sending her a message.

'I...' Kira was shaking her head. Never before had she experienced betrayal like this and it hurt more than she could ever imagine. There were no words as her stomach knotted into an agonising cramp, her arm flying across it in protection. She had to get away, the world was spinning, she no longer felt safe in her own world. She closed her eyes for a moment to gather her bearings, but when she turned to leave, she found her progress stunted by a sharp tug. Her eyes flew open, focusing on Adam's fingers around her wrist.

'Don't run away from this,' he pleaded. 'I know it's a shock, but it doesn't need to mean anything. Just because she is here doesn't mean that she will be going up to the glacier.' Kira could see the doubt in his eyes, there was no way he could stop Sally and her team from reaching the glacier. He did not own the mountain, he had made a great mistake and he didn't know how he was going to fix it. Wrenching her wrist free she looked at him for another moment before her muscles sprang into action. He was not quick enough and all he could do was follow as she disappeared into the trees. He was not going to let this go, he was not going to give her a way out. She was going to have to face this, he had to make her understand. He was not yet as fit or strong as he had been before the journey and he could not even keep up with her then, so he found himself in a familiar position as he had to concede defeat on the chase, coming to a stop. His heart was hammering in his chest as he looked around for signs of her. It had been easier in winter, over seven years ago when he could just follow her tracks. Taking the time to catch his breath and gather his bearings he focused his attention on his surroundings, there had to be a way of tracking her.

Kira was flying. The freedom she felt from the utilisation of her muscles as she swiftly covered the ground beneath her feet, barely touching the surface, would not come. Today she did not feel freedom and peace, she felt like she was being chased. She was running away from the dark pain that had settled in her gut behind the house. She was running from the feel of his fingers laced through hers, the electricity of the nearness of his skin, the warmth of his presence, the longing of his embrace and the hurt in his words. She could not run from the hurt inside of her. She tried but the further away from him she moved the more acute the pain became in her heart. Her mind was not where it was supposed to be, she could not focus, and the forest took advantage of her distraction as a tree put out its foot, tripping her up. She was flying through the air, and moments later crashed into the ground, skidding for a few metres before coming to a halt against a tree. Gasping and moaning she curled into a little ball, trying to protect the pain in her body.

The tears came then as she lay unmoving on the ground, teeth gritted against the pain as all she could see was the dirt beneath her face. She could not roll over to watch the clouds rush past in the sky, or to feel the sun on her skin; the pain was too much, devouring her from the inside as her body shook from the force of the tears. She was not raised to mistrust people, she had no reason to believe that people might say one thing to appease you whilst they actually did another. Her naivety, her trust in the human spirit, had been her downfall as she took this perceived betrayal, much harder than anybody else might have. She had never been lied to or hurt by the darkness that can be carried within the spirit of a person. She did not know what it felt like to be hurt like this. She had not built up a resistance to it like so many others do from childhood. She was open, raw, exposed, and it hurt more than the disappearance of her parents had. Tears had pooled beneath her face, turning the ground into a small muddy puddle as her eyes opened to a sound. There was no attempt to disguise the sound, as the thrashing of a human body through the trees broke through her senses. She barely had time to think before she was on her feet, and running at a tree, swung herself into it. A shock of pain rushed through her and swallowing a groan she gritted her teeth against the pain, closing her eyes until she could force it into submission. She was not ready for the memory to come rushing through her when Adam stepped into the clearing. It was obvious from the marks on the ground what had happened, and he stopped to look around for signs of her.

Suddenly she was seventeen again, sitting in a tree and looking down at a boy, the one that had been tracking her. Why was he following her? The world was white around her, the cold wind had stilled for this moment as he looked around him in amusement.

Adam looked at the skid marks on the ground and followed them to the tree against which she had finally come to a stop. The ground was still warm from her body and the moisture on the ground fresh, he did not allow himself to think where it had come from. In his surveillance of the scene, he had walked straight past her and though she was in no condition to fight him, something inside of her took over. Instinctively she was behind him and moments later he was on the ground gasping for breath.

'Bloody hell,' he choked out as she straddled him, her hand holding his shoulder to the ground. 'It's been a bloody long time since you've done that.' He was caught by surprise, no doubt, but the words died in his mouth as he saw the look in her eyes. They were haunted with pain, the pain that he had caused her. Her face was streaked with dirt, tell-tale tracks running down her cheeks where the tears had scoured them clean. Her eyes were red rimmed. She remained quiet, motionless as he stared up at her, not knowing what to do next. She should not have done this, she should not have confronted him. She should just have stayed in her tree until he left, but now she had to do something. Her thighs tightened around his body for just a moment before a flash of pain controlled her features and she loosened them again. She was about to get up, he could tell, and he did not want her to leave.

He had no time to consider what he was doing, but

taking advantage of her momentary distraction he rolled her over, pinning her to the ground. The surprise was clear on her face, as she found herself in the unfamiliar position of staring up at him.

'Get off me,' she growled with fire in her eyes, the hurt was still there but with it a fire of defiance. She did not like not being in control, but despite her strength he had the physical advantage. She tried to kick and roll him over, her hips thrusting up and to the side, but he forced her back to the ground.

'No, not until you hear me out.'

'I have heard everything I need to hear,' she breathed before suddenly gasping for pain as his knee dug into her ribs. He saw the flash and the change of her eyes as her mouth opened wide in shock.

He felt his heart rate spike but he had to remain in control, if he let her up she would be gone, and he could not let her walk out of his life. 'Ki? Are you hurt?'

Her eyes fixed on his again. 'Let me go.'

'No.' His voice was softer, gentler as he looked into her eyes. 'I can't Ki. I can never let you go.' She struggled to read the emotions in his eyes, confused by the contrast between his body and his words. Her own body was reacting in a way over which she had no control, as she felt the tension seep out at the warmth of his eyes. Her skin started to tingle as he sat staring down at her. His fingers were still around her wrists pinning them to the ground, but the weight of them no longer felt threatening, in fact she welcomed the sensation it ignited within her skin. Her heart was hammering against her chest the way it had been that day by the stream. His eyes were roaming her face, unable to settle on any one place, until it fell on her lips. They were red from emotion, a small drop of blood in the corner from where she had hit her face against the ground. Her smooth cheeks were covered in dirt and one was scratched with pinpricks of blood. Her eyes and her hair were wild, but the colour changed once more as he looked into them and he thought them the same colour as a few days ago, by the stream. This time no phone was going to interrupt him and with both their bodies heightened to the full, hearts hammering, adrenaline pumping, breath catching and longing desires filling them, he brought his lips down on hers. It was like a shock of electricity through her system, jolting her hips and forcing them into his groin. Shocked, she tried to move away but he held her still as he looked deeply into her eyes. 'I love you Kira,' he whispered. 'More than I've ever loved anything in my life, and I cannot bear it if you walked away from me.'

Her entire body was tingling with the sensation and despite her shock she found her body longing for more. She said nothing as he read the emotion in her eyes and lowered his lips to hers again, this time there was no shock or hasty retreat. Her eyes closed as she welcomed the taste of his lips, her body shivering with pleasure at the touch of his warm skin. His fingers released her wrists as they found the curve of her waist, her arms immediately wrapping around his body. She had never experienced need like this, the feel of him beneath her hands had her searching for more, her hips flexed and with the assistance of his hand on her ribs she felt a sharp gasp of pain exploding from her mouth.

His hands froze, his eyes opened as he looked at the flush on her face. 'Are you okay?'

Another pain shot through her ribs as she tried to take a

172

breath to answer him.

'Where are you hurt?' He rolled off her and gently moved her hand away from its protective barrier over her ribs. 'Let me have a look.' His fingers were gentle as he peeled the layers of clothing away from her skin, a grimace jumping to his face. There was a graze on her side, but it was the bruising around the ribs that had him looking up in concern. 'What happened?'

'I fell,' she gasped, pushing herself up into a sitting position. 'I think I hit a rock or something.'

'I think it's broken Ki.' He pulled a face. 'We should get you to a hospital.'

'No.' She stood up, gasping at the pain as she doubled over. 'It's okay.' She forced herself up. 'I can make a poultice.'

'It doesn't look good Ki.' Adam frowned. 'I'm pretty sure you've broken at least one rib.'

'Let's just get home,' she gasped. 'I can examine it when we get back.'

Adam shook his head, he wasn't going to win this one and he didn't particularly want to start another argument. 'All right,' he sighed. 'Come on.'

She was realistic and sensible, if she thought it too severe to treat herself, she would go to hospital, but she knew that depending on how bad it was, there was not much more the doctors can do, than what she could do at home.

'What happened?' Raven came bursting through the door running at them, her eyes wild as she looked at the pain on Kira's face, never mind the dishevelled state she was in.

'I fell,' she explained. 'Could you please get me a bowl

of warm water Raven?' The girl nodded and ran back inside as Adam settled her on the porch. 'Is there anything I can do?'

She peered down at the wound wondering about the cuts and bruising. 'Erm… you can get some calendula if you like.' She didn't think it would make a massive difference, but it could promote healing and it would make him feel useful. Nodding he disappeared into the house leaving her alone on the porch. Inside she could hear voices as Adam and Raven helped each other with their tasks. She smiled upon hearing the soothing tone of Adam's voice as he reassured the child. She tilted her head back, closing her eyes against the burning left behind after the tears. She felt exhausted, completely drained, and wished that she could just slip off into a slumber.

'Do you want me to do it?' Raven was already kneeling beside Kira as she opened her eyes. Her top was pulled up above the wound and she nodded to the girl as she gently dipped the cloth in the water and started to wash the dirt away. Raven's fingers were sure and gentle as they cleaned Kira's wound, her eyes flitting up every so often in search of Kira's for reassurance. Finishing her job, she rose to her feet, the cloth still in her hands. 'Can I do your face?' Nodding Kira closed her eyes, enjoying the sensation of being cared for as Raven gently cleaned the dirt off her face and from her wounds.

'Thank you,' she said, smiling at the girl when she had finished. 'You did a fantastic job.' Letting out a sigh of relief she smiled. 'Can I do anything else?'

'Not just at the minute, thanks Raven.'

Raven nodded and picking up the bowl emptied it over

the side of the porch before going inside. Feeling confident and proud of herself, she slid the kettle onto the warm part of the stove before standing up on a chair to look inside the medicine cabinet for some herbs.

Straightening her back Kira pushed herself forward and perching on the end of the chair lifted her clothing to examine the injury. Her fingers gently prodded around the area, finding the most sensitive spot before tracing the rib. Although painful, she did not think that it was actually broken, maybe just cracked. The pain was at its worst only when she took very deep breaths, or pressed on the tender area as Adam's knee had done. An image flashed through her mind suddenly making her blush, she could hardly believe that less than an hour ago he was on top of her, kissing her. The natural response of her body astounded her.

'What do you think?'

Her eyes shot up to the concern in his voice, his brow furrowing into a frown as he looked at the wounds, and bruising.

'It's all right,' she whispered lowering her top. 'I don't think it's broken. I'll treat it with a pain poultice tonight.'

Adam half sighed but he knew the doctors wouldn't, couldn't really do much more. 'Will you come into town with me?'

'Why?' She closed her eyes, tired of trying to analyse the colour in his eyes or the emotions on his face. She didn't want to read into his words or try and guess ulterior motives. She was exhausted and all she wanted to do tonight was sit in front of the fire with a good book.

'Because I don't want to leave you up here alone, and I have to walk Raven home tonight.' He didn't want to leave her at all, and he wanted to continue their conversation, he wanted to make sure that she knew the truth. He didn't want to leave it until even tomorrow because it only gave Kira a chance to rationalise away her actions and feelings. He had waited long enough to take her in his arms, and he was not going to give her an opportunity to talk herself out of something.

'I've been alone up here for years, I think I'll be okay.' He smiled at the hint of sarcasm in her tone, something she had only recently started to develop, something she had learned from him.

'I've made you some tea.'

Kira opened her eyes to the sight of Raven with two mugs in her hand. 'This one is yours.' She handed it to Kira.

'Thank you Raven.' She smiled and instead of asking the child what she had put in the tea she brought her face close to the mug and inhaled the aroma. Closing her eyes again she continued her breathing trying to decipher the contents.

'Willowbark.' She opened her eyes for confirmation and saw the girl smile.

'For the pain,' Raven explained doing a little hop of excitement. 'What else?'

Kira closed her eyes again. 'Camomile, lemon and lavender.'

'Yes!' Raven smiled. 'Is it okay?'

'It's perfect.' Kira smiled. 'Thank you.'

She looked at Adam who was sipping at his tea as he watched them. 'What's in Adam's?' Kira grinned making him stop and look at them with concern. 'Camomile and mint.' Raven said looking at him. 'He needs to stop stressing.'

Kira laughed at the look on his face, the action jolting a

176

quick sharp pain in her ribs. 'Ow,' she whispered placing a protective hand over the injury.

'So, you'll come into town?' He frowned, making Raven look from one to the other.

'No thanks,' she gasped. 'I think I'll just stay in tonight.'

Adam sighed looking to the sky for the time of day. 'We should get going Raven, I think your parents are eager to have you back before dark.'

'Okay,' The girl said dejectedly. 'I'll come back tomorrow Kira, to make sure you're okay.'

'Thanks Raven.' She touched the child's arm. 'You did really well today, thank you.'

She nodded before retreating inside to gather her things.

'Hey Ki?' She turned her eyes to him, the look in his eyes sending shivers of anticipation all over her body. 'This is not over, just so you know,' and without warning he leaned down and kissed her full of the lips, the force of it pressing her into the chair, leaving her breathless when he finally pulled away.

'I guess the answer is yes then.' Raven's eyes were on Kira's, reminding her of the question she had been asked the day before, the smile on her face filled with amusement. 'Come on Romeo.' Raven grinned at Adam as he pulled himself away from Kira, her newfound confidence making all of them smile.

'She won't like her, you know.' Adam looked into the eyes of the girl walking by his side, their cool blue carrying a wisdom far beyond her years.

'Who's that?'

'Your friend, in town. Kira won't like her.'

Raven looked up at Adam as their feet carried them down the familiar path through the trees. The blue of her eyes now carried a permanent spark, her black hair was thick and shiny, and her face constantly carried a healthy glow. Nobody could understand why this child who had been so ill for so many years suddenly appeared so healthy. The heart condition she was born with and which had been so carefully managed would surely have been her undoing one day, and yet here she was; she looked healthier than she had ever been, and she was getting stronger every day.

'What makes you think that?'

Her head tilted to the side as she studied him, wondering how he did not see it, did not hear it. 'It's in the wind,' she said pulling him to a stop. 'Listen.'

Tilting her head up, her eyes closed as she listened to the rush of the wind through the trees, the tone and accents as it brushed and bend around the steady trunks. 'It feels like change.'

'You're starting to sound like Ki.' Adam smiled, he was fond of the child as Kira was.

'Is that a bad thing?'

'No, no it's not kiddo. Come on, let's get back.'

'Don't you feel it?' She still wasn't moving, and he was forced to stop and look back. He noticed for the first time that she was barefoot. 'I heard it today, felt it when I was by the stream. I thought the wind was trying to tell me something,' she frowned slightly, '... and then the two of you came back...' Her voice trailed off as she shook her head slowly and blinked.

'I don't know.'

'Come on.' He smiled putting a hand on her shoulder.

'It's been a long day, you must be tired.'

She was, her mind was whirling with the experiences of the day. How did Kira do it? How did she cope with the constant changes brought on the wind, the overload of sensory information, the way the mountains seemed to look down on you in judgement? She glanced at Adam once more with a slight frown on her brow, she didn't want him to hurt Kira.

He didn't want to, she could see it in his face. The confusion and the elements of his life was tearing him in two, but she feared he might.

'Adam!'

The voice pulled them both out of the silence of their thoughts, Adam had resolved to be going back up to Kira after he'd seen Raven home. This was the last thing he needed.

'Adam! Where have you been all day? I've been looking everywhere for you.' Raven felt her eyebrows knit together as the woman navigated the townsfolk to get to them.

'I've got some great news! I couldn't get hold of you…' Her eyes darted down to Raven, seeing her for the first time. 'Oh, hello. Who's this?' She glanced up at Adam before smiling back down at the child. Her feet were bare, the dirt reached up her calves with long fingers and even managed to have found its way to her face. 'It looks like you've been having fun.'

Her eyes twinkled with amusement as she looked back up at Adam.

'Sally, this is Raven.' Adam frowned slightly at the childish manner in which she was addressing Raven. They sometimes forgot that she was only eleven, she was smart and quick, her knowledge of Kira's world eking out ahead of his. She had a natural affinity with the world that lit up her soul, and made her seem much older in her wisdom.

'Have you two been up in the hills today then?' Raven's head simply tilted to the side as the woman continued her monologue. 'I guess I should get myself up there one of these days,' she sighed good humouredly. 'See what it's all about.'

She was pleasant enough, young and pretty but the space around her was a different colour to the townsfolk. It was predominantly red and gold with only a slight line of black and very different to Kira or Adam's. Glancing at Adam she saw a flash of brown, confusion, that had only in recent days started to develop. The glow that surrounded Kira always made her feel warm and loved as it radiated around them, like the colours of the sun on its arrival or departure. Her space was filled with purple, pink, orange and yellow, different days were dominated by different colours, but these are the colours she had come to associate with her friend and mentor.

'The mountains won't welcome you if you do not welcome them.' The voice was strong and melodic, speaking with a wisdom she had not expected from such a young child.

'Pardon?' Sally glanced down at the girl with half a smile.

'These mountains are special,' Raven said, not sure where the words or the knowledge was coming from. 'They are sacred, they protect the souls of our ancestors and they do not allow anybody into their hearts if they are not worthy.'

Adam looked almost as shocked as Sally, but where the woman laughed and dismissed Raven's words, he filed it in his mind to consider later. Raven was growing strong in both

180

body and mind.

'Is that what they teach you at school?' Sally laughed.

'No, it's what the earth and the skies told me.'

'Right.' Sally looked sceptical. 'So I guess Adam is worthy then? Seeing as he climbed the mountain.'

Adam sighed. 'Sally I told you, we only made it as far as the glacier...'

'Well,' she cut him off with a winning smile. 'We only need to get as far as that. Come on Adam, I've got something to show you.'

'Sally, can this wait? I have to walk Raven home.'

'She can find her way home from here, can't she?' Sally looked about her, her brown curls bobbing over her shoulders. 'You can pretty much see all the houses from here!' she laughed as Adam glanced back up the mountain; of course Raven could make it home by herself, but he didn't want to deal with Sally tonight. He wanted to go back up to Kira.

'You weren't planning on going back up there tonight, were you?' Sally pulled a face. 'What would you do up there in the dark?' Her face changed as she put her hand on his arm and smiled. 'Come on,' she implored. 'Have dinner with me and I'll tell you my exciting news.'

Raven's eyebrows disappeared into her hairline as she read the women's actions. The spark in her eye, the softening of her tone. Her hand was moving up and down Adam's arm in a way that neither he nor Raven liked.

'I'll be fine Adam,' she said loudly, making her presence known and looking intently into the woman's eyes. 'I'll tell my dad you walked me into town. Are you going back up tomorrow?'

Adam nodded. 'I'll come round for you in the morning.'

'Okay.'

Raven stood and watched as Adam got dragged away, his gaze flickering up to the mountains once more before they disappeared around the corner. She had a bad feeling about this. She did not know about Kira and Adam's plan to return to the glacier, nor of their arguments surrounding the matter but something about this just did not feel right to her.

Chapter Seven

'Jones is on his way.' Sally lifted the wine glass to her lips, watching him over the rim.

'What? Why?' Adam did not like the course this was taking.

'He is the best partner you ever climbed with,' she said simply. 'We need him.'

Adam frowned, she had seen the flash of hesitation in his eyes. 'You don't think we need him?' She lowered her glass, tilting her head as she observed him. '… or you don't think he's the best?' She felt a need to fill the empty space left by his silence. He had been the best, Adam agreed, until Kira.

'I thought the two of you parted on less than professional terms?' he finally spoke, ignoring the curious eyes of the people in the bar.

'We did,' she relented, sighing heavily. 'He is however the best and he agreed to come, because it's you.'

'What exactly do you want him to be doing up here Sally?'

She let out a little laugh, pushing herself up in her seat. 'You're kidding right?' She frowned at the silence of his non-response. 'Get us down the glacier Adam, what else?'

'I thought I told you I made a mistake.' He could feel the anger starting to boil in his chest. 'I don't want a massive-scaled operation.'

'I know.' She faced him over the table, eyes filled with determination. 'I'm keeping it small, but you need a partner, don't you? To go down the glacier with you?'

'I have a partner!' he growled. 'I don't want any part of this.' His eyes were throwing daggers over the table. 'I told you, I don't want anybody else up there.'

Sally was shocked into silence for just a moment. 'So why did you call me?'

'I told you, it was a mistake.' He didn't know how he was going to get through to her, she didn't seem to understand.

'You should not have come here.'

'I had no choice.' Her words were clear as ice. 'You would not respond to any of my messages.'

'That is because I don't want this matter pursued. You need to leave this be, Sally. You need to go home.'

She laughed again, amused at the passion in him. 'What has gotten into you? Do you not want to conquer this mountain? Do you not want to descend into the very core of her, and see what she is made up off?'

He hated that word 'conquer'. He never wanted to be the kind of mountaineer that went out to bag peaks, ticking the names of big mountains off his list and declare to the world that he had conquered them. That was not what it was about. He wanted to understand them, be part of them as Kira was. Respect them.

Sally was hungry for power, eager to establish herself at the forefront of this world. She was not happy fighting on the flanks, she wanted to be on the front lines, fighting with the big boys.

'You don't understand,' he said shaking his head. 'I have seen what that mountain is capable of. You may not understand it, or believe it, but what Raven said was true. She would not allow you on her if you are there for the wrong reasons.'

'This is ridiculous.' She almost laughed in frustration. 'Do you hear yourself? Mountains do not have feelings or personalities, Adam, they are mounds of rock and dirt. Big mounds, true, but they are just rock in some shape or form. They do not fight back.' She looked at him, oddly.

'I know it's been a while since we worked together Adam, but I am still the same person and yet you look at me with mistrust. I don't understand it. What's changed?'

He shook his head. 'I trust you Sally, I just don't like where this is going.'

'Why? I don't understand, it's a mountain. You like mountains. You climb mountains for a living. What makes this one so different, so special?'

It's her mountain.

The words were unspoken yet it occupied the space between them like a big white elephant.

'Is this because of that girl?' she said at last when the strain of their eye contact became too much.

'What girl? Raven?'

'No,' she said patiently, he knew what she was talking about, she could see it in his eyes.

'Everybody talks about her,' she said looking around the room. 'The woman in the mountains.' She paused to study the expression on his face. He could feel his heart hammering against his chest. He did not like the way she was talking about Kira. The dismissive tone in her voice. 'They talk about her as if she is some kind of hero, this mountain women. Is she?'

He didn't trust himself to speak. 'Is this it then?' Sally sat up, leaning forward across the table. 'Do you feel like you owe her something? Is that what this is about?'

Adam shook his head. 'You have no idea,' he said evenly, almost sadly. 'If you go up that mountain, you'd better be prepared to die, because if she decides she doesn't like you or like what you are doing to her she will make sure that you never do it again.'

'Is this the mountain we are talking about now Adam? The one with so much power?'

He pushed his chair out to leave. 'You are making a mistake.'

'Am I now? Or is it you that is making the mistake?'

He didn't bother to reply, he was fired up and despite the late hour and dark skies, he knew there was only one place he wanted to be tonight.

He pushed a note beneath Raven's front door before setting off towards the bridge, allowing the light of the full moon to guide him.

The familiar scuff of the door was not enough to pull Kira from the world beyond her dreams, and for a moment Adam stood in the seemingly empty room looking around in confusion. There was no sign of life, the fire was low but not banked, making him walk over to the pile of logs to add more fuel to the fire. This was more a home to him than any other place had ever been. He hadn't expected to find her on the sofa, ruled by sleep. Her breathing was calm and rhythmic but not very deep, her eyes were still behind her lids. Leaning down he put a hand to her brow but found no fever, she was not ill, and her deep sleep confused him. Putting his nose to the mug by her side he smelled the herbs but were unable to distinguish which ones she had used. Raven would know, he sighed quietly and lowered himself to the ground beside her. He really wanted to talk to her, needed to talk to her. He was frustrated and confused, and he needed her to help him make sense of everything. She had a way of seeing things clearly, of pulling apart a messy knot and laying out the strands in a neat logical order. His mind felt like a small child's finger paint palette; everything had made sense on its own, it had looked right, but somewhere he got carried away and now all the colours were mixed together, and he didn't know how he was ever going to get it clean again. A quiet moan escaped her lips, demanding his attention. There was pain on her face as his eyes drifted across her features. Her hair looked damp, smoothed back from her face, except for the lengths that had been pushed up against the cushions. The dirt had been washed from her face, the scrape where she had ploughed into the ground red and slightly raised on her cheek. Her lips were parted in sleep until another soft moan, followed by a whimper escaped them before she moved and licked her lips. Gently lifting the blanket away, his eyes fell on the familiar looking poultice on her exposed ribs. Her top was pulled up and the poultice had not been strapped, but merely left to dry as it worked its magic on her injured ribs. It felt cold to the touch. His eyes went back up to her face. He was very familiar with this poultice and if memory served him right it was truly effective for about four hours. It has been a lot more than that since they left her this afternoon and she was obviously in pain, it must be time for a new poultice. He hesitated only for a moment, wishing that Raven was there to guide him through the process, but he could probably do it himself. He had seen her prepare one, many times. Pulling himself to his feet he retreated to the kitchen, she would probably be awake by the time the poultice was ready. Checking the water level in the kettle he moved it onto the warm part of the stove before turning to the cabinet where she stored her extensive range of herbs and medicinal plants. His eyes moved over the bags and jars, reading the labels and pulling out the appropriate ones. He surprised himself with the amount of information he had retained as to the values and uses of the plants. He had been eager to learn, as Raven, but the girl managed to grasp things far quicker than him and seemed to retain a lot more information. She was turning into a regular little mountain girl, versed in the ways of the old world. Smiling to himself he pondered the way his life and values have changed since meeting Kira. He saw the world in a different way, it was like he'd been walking around with his eyes half closed for most of his life. Watching her, getting to know her, and learning the ways in which she had been taught had slowly opened his eyes to the real world. It was as if he now saw the world in colour where before it had been a dull, grey scale.

His hands stilled as he looked at the concoction he had created, it looked similar to the one on her ribs. Shrugging he turned his attention to the boiling kettle and poured the water over the herbs in the mug. He had added white willow bark as he knew it to be a pain relief, the rest was just for taste and he hoped he got it right. Carrying the two items he crossed the room to the fire and kneeling down beside her, lowered them to the floor next to him.

'Ki?' he whispered, watching her eyes moving behind her lids as a soft sound puffed over her parted lips.

Gently touching her face, he whispered her name again and waited for her eyes to flutter open. He smiled into the blue as her eyes tried to focus, a confused haze slowly disappearing.

'Hi.'

'Hi,' she whispered winching at the pain as she pushed herself up. 'What are you doing here?'

'I've made a poultice.' He held it up for inspection, a sheepish look on his face.

Kira grinned. 'Looks great. Thanks, it's about time I changed it.'

'I figured.' He sat back allowing her fingers to complete the familiar work, not trusting himself to touch her, now that she was awake and could respond to his touch.

'Here.' He handed her the tea when she finished, dumping the used poultice in the fire before whisking the bowl away to the kitchen where he rinsed it.

'Are you all right?' Kira pulled her knees up, making space for him on the sofa.

'I'm not sure,' he admitted, sinking down with a heavy sigh. 'I'm confused.'

She sipped at her tea, watching as he stared into the fire, thoughtfully. She had felt the same after they left, the confusion ruling her mind until she had stepped into the shower and allowed the water to pound the mess into logic. She had separated her thoughts and feelings, scrutinising them individually until she could find a box for them to fit in.

She was not used to being so emotional, or indeed so emotionally ruled and confused. The limitation of her knowledge and experience regarding this subject was what had allowed emotion to rule over sense. She still could not explain the tingle in her spine when he touched her, or find a reason for the acrobatics in her stomach at the sound of his voice but she accepted that. She accepted that some things could not be explained away by logic and just had to be felt, like the mood of the mountain, the breeze through your hair or the water on your skin. The feeling could not be explained, only experienced, and the way she felt when he was around was safe and complete.

'I don't understand,' he said running a hand through his hair. 'How do you do it?'

He turned his confusion on her, emphasising the fact that this was not a rhetorical question.

'How do I do what?'

'How do you make people understand?'

She frowned. 'I don't know what you mean Adam.'

He took a breath. 'How do you make people understand the power of this mountain or the need for respect?'

'I don't.' Her head was tilted towards his. 'You cannot make somebody believe in something that they do not feel, or do not understand. You will never get through to them if it is outside of their realm of understanding, so far removed from their reality. It is not my job to make people understand the mountain, nor would I want to.'

'You made me understand, believe.'

Kira smiled. 'No, I didn't.'

The sound of the fire filled the room as he stared at her incomprehensibly.

'You did,' he insisted. 'Didn't you?'

'Did I teach you how to feel the wind on your skin? Did I teach you how to appreciate the sound of the night or the sight of the stars?' She shook her head. 'No, appreciation cannot be taught nor can understanding.'

'You opened my eyes though Kira, you made me see the world in a different way.'

'Yes, but I did not teach you how to see the world.'

'Huh?' He was even more confused now, the look on his face making her laugh.

'It's really simple,' she said. 'We are all earth's children, we all have the ability to listen and learn from her, but we don't all have the opportunity or inclination to do so. I did not make you understand or believe.' Her head moved to the rhythm of her words. 'Perhaps you were more inclined to listen, more open to believe because of your history with this area...'

'... Or my history with you.'

There was a short silence as Kira processed the words, admitting to the connection that had been established when they were both young and filled with curiosity and emotion.

There was a slight inclination of her head as she accepted his words. '... But I did not make you believe. It was a choice and one only you could make. It is not something you can be forced into.'

'So, you don't believe that people's minds can be changed, to make them understand?'

'They can, but only by themselves.'

Sighing he fell back into the sofa, there was nothing he could do that would make Sally understand or stop her from proceeding with her plan. Kira saw the twist in his energy and felt a pang of regret, he was her friend. No, he was more than that, yet there was something that he wasn't telling her. They had not talked about this, aside from their argument earlier today, since the thought had initially occurred to him. He hadn't wanted to bring it up, aware of the torrent of emotion it released inside of her. He didn't want her to think that he had gone against her wishes, that he was betraying her, but he did not know how to broach the subject. He needed to tell her what was going on, for both their sakes, but he didn't know how to.

'You know that friend I was telling you about?' He glanced at her. 'The glaciologist?'

There was a brief inclination of her head, showing acknowledgement. Kira was tired, she did not want to talk about this right now. She allowed him to lift her feet over his lap and pull the blanket over them as he spoke. 'She's in town.' She already knew this, that is what their argument was about earlier today. Kira's eyes were being drawn shut by the warmth of the fire and the comfort of his presence. Despite the spike of ill ease at the mention of the glaciologist she found herself melting into the warmth and comfort. 'She wants to go up to the glacier Ki, and I don't think we can stop her.'

She was aware of the hint of anxiety in his voice, and even as her eyes closed, she felt the need to reassure him.

'We don't have to stop her,' she whispered. There was no point in fighting this she thought as her eyes closed. 'We just have to get up there before her.'

The heat behind her back was both novel and familiar. The sensation of his chest pressed against her back reminded her of their time in the tent last winter, all of that now seemed so long ago. Perhaps he had been right, perhaps they should have turned around after she fell through the ice, but then they never would have discovered those screws in the glacier wall. Kira was raised to heed the warnings, and despite that she insisted that they carry on with their journey. She hadn't known at the time what it was that had been pushing her, but she was starting to understand. Everything happens for a reason. Had she heeded those warnings, stuck to her teachings, and not rebelled against them in some small way, she might never have found any sign of her parents. Adam's broken leg and the journey back had been a dear price to pay, one that nearly claimed their souls, but something or someone had been looking over them. They had made it, and now they were planning on a second journey, this time only to the river of ice. The orange glow from the coals drew Kira's attention as she lay quietly, unwilling to move. She felt torn between doing what she wanted to and doing what she knew she needed to. During their journey they had often lain in the tent with their backs pressed up against each other. The feeling had been one of security and warmth, knowing that they were not alone. This feeling was different; his embrace still offered comfort and warmth, but his arm draped protectively around her, securing her to his chest and preventing her from rolling off the sofa, felt different. Smiling to herself she did not want to get up, she wanted to revel in this newfound emotion. This experience that was so new to her. She wished that the outside world could disappear and that the two of them could be left alone, here in her home, in the mountains. Her eyes fixed on the coals, her mind wandering to the information Adam had provided her with yesterday. They were in the last stretch of summer, it would not be long before the warmth would give way to snow, blown in on the wind. She needed to separate herself from the emotion that clouded her judgement, she needed to clear her head and make an appropriate decision about what to do next. The goal that had been driving her since their return, this year and for the nine years preceding that, was to find her parents. The time has now come for that goal to be realised, and she could not bear the thought of an army of people discovering her parents' bodies.

No, it had to be her.

Quietly as was her style and practice, Kira slid unnoticed from Adam's arms. She stoked the fire and peeling the used poultice from her ribs made her way outside. The sun was announcing its arrival in a wash of red and orange as her bare feet sank into the rich moist soil, sticking to her skin and creeping up her calves. She had been unaware of the rain that had fallen last night, washing the earth and cleansing the air. Her lungs filled with the familiar scent, the damp earth and leaves infiltrating her senses as her body led on, familiar with the course. She did not slow upon reaching the steep embankment and only came to a stop at the edge of the swollen stream. The rushing of water filled her ears, the sound washing over her like a powerful thundering waterfall, pounding out thought, emotion and memory until all that was left was water. Stepping out of her clothes she walked into the water, allowing its cold fingers to slide up, over and around her form, covering every centimetre of her skin in shivers, until finally her head too disappeared beneath the water, a flash of white the last visual evidence floating on the surface for a moment longer. She needed this, she needed to fill herself with the earth once more. She had allowed parts of herself to become consumed by human needs and desire. She did not long for material things but for the companionship of others, for voices and laughter in her home. She had revelled in her newfound roles of teacher, instructor and mentor. She had never entertained the idea that she had something to offer another person, and the process of sharing her world with others filled her with joy and contentment. This has however taken her away from her normal routine. The passing of time since their return from the journey had increasingly been filled with human contact rather than contact with mother earth, and she could not trust herself to make the right decisions if she was not one with nature as she had been before. She had been attuned to every sigh and whisper of the land when her entire life was ruled by it. She could not help but feel that the new distractions in her life had somehow detracted from her connection. She wasn't used to dividing her mind in this way, which was something she was going to have to learn if she wanted her life to continue in the direction it was moving. She needed to make time to be alone with the creatures of the earth, to listen to their voices and pay attention to their words. It was an astonishingly long time before Kira's head reappeared above the water, by which time the sun had shed its skirt of the horizon, and started to climb into the sky, baring all to the world. Adam had given her a lot to think about.

She had been overwhelmed by the powerful emotions which had taken her completely by surprise. The shock of what she could feel, based simply on his words and their perceived meaning, had sent her into a complete spin of confusion and irrationality. She did not want other people to discover her parents' bodies, but it was not the thought of this that had her running blindly into the trees. It had been the meaning behind his words, the perceived fact that this news meant that he must have betrayed her, gone against her wishes, and the power of this emotion was unlike any she had ever experienced. Total disbelief at the powerful blow to her gut had painted her in shame, anger, embarrassment and total confusion. She realised that she had to come to grips with these feelings, she could not allow them to cloud her judgement on this next journey. She needed to be able to act appropriately. The revelation of his kiss had wiped out the question mark that had been hanging over her head, but with this answer came other questions and challenges.

How was she going to remain objective about the journey? She could not allow him to sway her into including others in their journey, despite his argument of safety in numbers or speed in ascend. She needed to do this in a way that would please them, and satisfy the mountain gods. The mountains were holding onto her parents, she knew that their bodies were somewhere in that crevasse. The mountains had allowed Kira and Adam to be the holders of knowledge as to where her parents were. She could not help but think that they were finally ready to give them up, but they would not be happy if an army of non-believers descended upon them. She would be happy if she could just see them one more time, say her goodbyes and lay them to rest. The mountain could close her jaws around them and keep them close to her heart, as long as she had a chance to say goodbye. Kira knew that there was no way that she or Adam or anybody else could stop his friend from what she wanted to do. People were, at best, unpredictable as far as she could tell, and experience taught her that some would do anything in their power to get their own way. Adam's identification of his friend's hunger for power sends shivers down Kira's spine. She could not see this ending well, for anyone. She was concerned that despite what he says Adam might be persuaded to take part in Sally's expedition, as it was more familiar to him than what he had recently done with her. His experience was as a technical leader, assisting scientists in their studies by ensuring their safety. He was used to bigger parties of people, helicopters and equipment, and might just find it a little bit easier than her, to accept the premise and get pulled along. She could not, and had no interest in attempting to stop others from doing what they wanted, despite it happening in her back garden, on the mountains she knew so well. She could only hope that her skills and experience could get her up there before them and allow her to do what she needed to do before the mountain roared in anger, as she knew it would. She was going to have to be strong, she was going to have to distance herself from Adam, just a little bit. She was going to need to keep herself in check and not allow another outbreak like before. She had to expect the unexpected and accept that they were all just human and very capable of mistakes. Once she has laid her parents to rest, she could look to the future, find a new goal and work towards that, but for now this was her focus. Her goal was to close this chapter of her life, come winter, and she was going to have to draw on all her training and reserves of self-control to accomplish it. She did not want to do it alone, but she still stood by the fact that she would if she needed to, and if it was to be her last journey, then so be it. A shiver ran down her spine, making the hair at the back of her neck stand to attention as she moved out of the water. There was a change in the wind, and lifting her eyes to the sky she could see the clouds rushing past in a hurry. The snapping of branches and shuffle of feet reached her ears, snapping her head back into position. Neither Adam nor Raven was so careless in their footing, nor would they swear or pant like the sound reaching her ears. She stepped into her clothes and within seconds found herself high up in a tree, her form hidden by the leafy arms of branches.

Huffing and puffing the form stepped through the undergrowth muttering under her breath as she came to a still in front of the stream.

'Oh.' She wiped her brow, trying to smooth down the wild brown curls that were standing on end in the humidity. Kira sat motionless on her branch, blue eyes clear and focussed as she took in the actions of the woman. Her words were mumbled and spoken with an accent that Kira did not recognise, making it difficult for her to make any sense of the words. Falling to her knees the woman cupped her hands and brought the water over her face a few times before falling back and lifting her eyes to the sky. Her chest was rising and falling as she tried to catch her breath.

'Well,' she said out loud as if speaking to a companion. 'You can't say I haven't tried.' Sally was not unfit, her occupation demanded a certain level of fitness, but she did not particularly like climbing up mountains. She loved her job, glaciers fascinated her. She has done many seasons in Antarctica, spent many weeks on research ships and has seen some fascinating things without ever having to climb mountains like these.

'What is so special about it?' she whispered, just loud

enough for Kira to hear. 'Why this mountain, this glacier?' Pushing herself up she dropped her head, staring at the space between her legs and shook her head. There must be something about it if it caught Adam's attention. Pushing herself to her feet she looked about her. 'There must be a path around here somewhere.' Sally had simply walked out of the place she was staying and into the woods behind it. Her progress had been hampered by the thick undergrowth and uneven ground, yet she has made it a long way up the valley. She had briefly considered pulling the plug on the whole thing, on packing her bags and going home; but Adam's desperate attempts to stop her had caught her attention. His initial phone call had just queried whether she would be interested in exploring some glaciers, in an unknown mountain range. She had looked up the range and found out some fascinating things relating to legend and myth. The range itself had not seen much footfall at all, by what she could tell, and it was very likely that most of its peaks had never been summited. Now, she had no interest in being the first in summiting peaks, but the mystery around the whole range fascinated her. She could find only one reference to an attempt on it, which sadly had ended in tragedy. No one else has ever attempted it, apart from Adam that was. Sighing she pushed up the steep embankment hoping for a path. 'We'll soon see.'

Kira watched from her perch, the woman's words fitting into organised slots in her mind. This must be Adam's friend. She had realised as much whilst listening to the woman's monologue and had to push aside the unfamiliar feelings of jealousy knocking about in her stomach. She was young, and pretty. She was accomplished and she fitted perfectly into

Adam's world, unlike her. Her world was so far removed from his that she could never pretend that it would ever be any different. The noise stayed with her long after the person disappeared, and Kira followed cautiously, making her way home. Eventually it seemed that the path was found and with a sigh of relief Sally had set off downhill. The next time she was going up the mountain, it would be by helicopter.

Raven had not expected the woman to be walking down the path any more than Sally had expected to be encountering the child. Raven was deep within herself, focusing on her surroundings and yet unable to do as Kira did and be attuned to everything around her. She was relishing the damp beneath her feet, the way the ground rose up beneath her toes and tried to creep up her ankles as she walked. The smell of the rain was everywhere around her and everything looked clean, fresh, new.

'Oh! Hello.'

Pulled out of thought Raven jumped at the sudden voice, her hand automatically flying up to her heart. She was waiting for the change, waiting for something to happen with the pump in her chest and was surprised to feel nothing. No change.

'It's Raven, right?'

Raven lifted her eyes to the woman and felt another pang as confusion set in. What was she doing walking down the path, especially at this time of morning? It wasn't ridiculously early, but just too early for anybody to be coming down, except maybe Kira or Adam.

'Are you all right?'

Raven gathered her thoughts and focused on the woman

before nodding. Her eyes were pulled to the space surrounding her and Sally felt herself shiver, turning to see what the child was looking at.

'What are you looking at?'

'Your colours.' Raven focused her eyes on the woman's and tilted her head. Sally noticed that she was once again barefoot and on her way up the valley.

'You have great eyes.' She smiled, attempting to shake her feelings of unease. Raven smiled slightly, her eyes were nothing compared to Kira's, but Sally took it as a sign of gratitude and smiled with relief.

'Where are you going?' Sally asked looking around for a parent. 'Are you on your own?'

'Not far.' Raven was still staring intently at her. 'This is my home,' she said when the woman looked at her with confused concern.

Sally frowned at the slight enigmatic figure with her hypnotic eyes. 'I thought Adam said he would go with you.'

'His plans changed,' Raven said moving her eyes away and stepping to a side. She wanted to keep moving but she did not want Sally to follow her.

'Right, okay.' Sally smiled. 'I guess I'll catch up with him in town then.' She glanced at the girl and wondered about the strange half smile on her face. 'Are you sure you're okay?'

Raven's smile pulled up at both sides of her mouth. 'Are you?'

Sally realised she must look as if she'd been in the wars. 'Fair point.' She grinned. 'I guess I'll see you later.' Raven's eyes remained on the woman's back until she could no longer see her, only then did she turn around and continue her journey to Kira's. Smiling to herself, she though the woman was going to have a difficult time finding Adam in town. Her mind no longer on the environment surrounding her but on the strange sensation she's been experiencing around these three adults over the last few days she continued, unthinking, unseeing to her destination.

'Good morning.'

Raven jumped once more at the voice, she had not yet broken beyond the trees into the small clearing that held Kira's home, and had not expected to run into yet another person.

Her surprise disappeared when she registered the flash of white and then those deep blue eyes. Kira was smiling and Raven could not stop herself from putting her arms around the woman.

'Morning,' she mumbled into the folds of material as gentle hands ran down her smooth black hair. 'You surprised me.'

Kira smiled. 'Training. Next time you won't be taken by surprise.'

'What are you doing?' Her eyes darted from Kira to the tree and then quickly back at the woman. Frowning slightly, she refocused her attention on the person rather than the space around her.

'Collecting sap.' Kira held out the two devices in her hand. 'You hammer this spout into the maple and the sugary sap runs out.'

'Can I have a go?'

'Sure.' Kira emptied her hands into the girl's. 'Here.'

Her earlier encounter temporarily forgotten, Raven got engrossed in this small pleasure that many children her age have already done several times in their life. It was just one more thing she had been protected from, as the trees grew further away from town. Kira smiled at the joy on Raven's face and soon found herself engrossed in the child's joy as they lapped at the drops seeping from the spout, their faces and fingers growing sticky with the lifeblood of the tree. The sap would be useful in the making of travel cakes, it gave a different flavour to honey, more sugary-sweet. The sound of their laughter echoed off the valley walls as they approached the clearing, drawing Adam from behind the house. He had been trying to think of a way for Kira's garden to continue its growth even through the harsh winter months when everything was blanketed with snow. This would allow better supplies of fresh vegetables and she would not have to rely on the preserved, dried or pickled vegetables she usually did in winter. They were still laughing, their hands sticking to the buckets they carried as he came around the corner and watched them approach. Kira had not said much to him this morning and he was struggling to draw any information from her. Nothing more had been said about the journey, Sally or anything else that had happened. She smiled when he looked at her, folded her fingers around his when he touched her hand, she had not pulled away when he'd pulled her into his arms or kissed her lips, but she also did not make any approaches. When he let go, she let go. When he smiled, she smiled, but she did not talk about any of it. She had been gone when he woke up this morning and had returned hours later with the damp of the stream still clinging to her hair. Raven greeted him with smiles and excited chatter, allowing him to peel the steel of the silver bucket from her sticky hands. Kira just smiled at him, enjoying the scene of domesticity and hoping that one day it could be real, but for now it was going to have to wait. Instead of washing their hands Kira and Raven placed their hands in the dirt and pulled them out to see what had stuck to their skin. Raven enjoyed this unconventional method of learning as she did with everything else that Kira did. It was rare that they made use of books, so when they did, in front of the fire, after darkness had fallen or the weather had chased them inside, it was special.

They had gone for a walk, following the trail of berries and other edible plants and now found themselves at the side of yet another stream. All of these would be frozen in a couple of months Kira thought, staring into the water. Raven's eyes were on her, the event of the morning finally having found an opening to present itself.

Feeling the searching eyes Kira turned her own on the child, the look on her face telling her that she too had run into Sally. Kira looked away, momentarily overwhelmed by emotion once again before fixing her eyes back on Raven, determined to stay in control. There was a frown on the child's face. 'What is it Raven?'

'There is brown,' she said quietly. 'In your space, it was not there before.' Her eyes moved from the space surrounding Kira to the face of the woman that had become her friend. She saw understanding and resignation in her face.

'It's confusion,' Kira stated but offered no other explanation.

'It's in Adam's space as well,' she said pushing herself up. 'What's going on?'

Kira did not know how to explain something like this to

the girl, she did not know if she would understand. She did not even know if she understood.

'Is it to do with that woman? Sally?' There was a hint of distaste in her voice that pulled Kira out of her reluctance.

Kira could see the negative emotion swirling around behind the girl, she did not want her to get drawn in. Despite what the woman represented, or what Raven might think she represented, she did not deserve the scorn that was growing inside the young girl.

'Do you know her, Raven?' Kira thought carefully to find a way to bring her point across to the girl.

'No.' She shook her head. 'I met her last night, when Adam walked me home.'

There was fire in her eyes. 'So you do not know her?'

'No.'

'Then why do you dislike her so much?'

Surprised, Raven looked up at the woman. 'Because,' she said defiantly unable to find an explanation. 'I just don't,' she said. 'It's because of her that you are confused.'

'Do you know Adam?'

Raven frowned. 'Of course I do.'

'Do you dislike him?'

'No.' Raven's voice was rising with temper. 'I don't understand. What are you trying to say?'

'If I told you that my confusion was because of Adam would you dislike him?'

'No,' she said adamant. 'He is my friend. I know him and I know he won't hurt you.'

Kira nodded. 'If you had not known him? If you had met him on the path on your way up to the house and you found me confused, would you have disliked him?'

Raven thought about this. 'Maybe,' she said slowly starting to see where Kira was going with it. 'I guess, but then I would have gotten to know him and I would not...'

She stopped and looked at the smile on Kira's face. 'It is not for us to judge people Raven. Just like you would not judge the birds in the trees for making fruit fall on your head or for wolves who follow you up a path.' She stopped at the sign of memories flashing through Raven's mind. 'You do not know this woman, so you cannot dislike her for what you think she may or may not do. You were scared of the wolves, would probably have killed them if you had the chance, but they protected you. Without them you would not be here today,' she said bluntly watching the colour first drain then rise in the girl's face. 'Making rash decisions based on presumptions could cost you dearly.' She knew she was talking to herself as much as Raven. She too needed this reminder to stop herself from disliking someone she had not yet even met. It was not for them to judge and pronounce punishments, those privileges were reserved for the law and the gods.

Raven moved her gaze to the water, allowing the stream to carry her thoughts into a natural order as she tried to come to terms with these teachings.

'I don't know how you do it,' she said finally, her voice little more than a whisper. 'I cannot help but feel angry or upset. I resented other children for being able to do what I could not, I envied them, but you are always so calm, so level headed. You never get angry or blame others.'

Kira smiled. 'I do get angry Raven, and I do get upset. I would not be human if I didn't, but it's what you do with those emotions that matter. How you choose to react to them

206

is what defines who you are. I know that nobody is to blame for my parents' disappearance.' A cloud rushed past Raven's eyes, she didn't know much about this. Kira never spoke about it. 'I also know that nobody is to blame for what happened to me and Adam on our Journey.' She looked closely at the child, 'I was upset at the time, confused and for a long time afterwards I blamed myself for what happened.' Raven was looking at her with wide eyes, her small hand had automatically found its way onto Kira's. 'But,' she smiled, 'I figured it out, eventually. I came home and I tried to sort it all out in my head, and eventually it became clear. It was nobody's fault. It just happened and there is nothing you can do about it, you just have to push on, keep moving forward. Learn from you mistakes and your experiences so that you do not make the same mistake again.'

Raven sighed. 'I've got a long way to go before I can be like that.'

'You're a long way ahead of the rest of the world kiddo.' Kira pulled the girl closer to her, running a hand over her head. 'You're much further ahead than you think.'

'Do you think so?' There was a hopeful tone in her voice.

'Definitely. You just have to keep working and never give up. The stars will tell you the truth, the wind will warn you of change, and if you just listen to what these mountains, this land have got to tell you, you will go a long way.'

There was a long silence as they did just that. The voice of the land growing louder in their ears, the rush of water, the thunderous voice of the mountains, the rustle of the leaves as they whispered secrets to the wind. The damp earth rose up to meet them, enveloping them in its warm embrace, as the clouds rushed about in the sky, eager to go somewhere new. They could both feel the change in the air as the wind suddenly picked up. Raven sat up first, the feeling in her stomach making her look at Kira with concern. The wind whipped her dark hair across her face as dark clouds came rolling in over the mountains.

Kira's eyes were fixed on the rolling blackness approaching with speed. She felt Raven's hand slip into hers as the child moved behind her for protection, glancing up at the darkening of her eyes. 'A storm is coming.' The eerie nature of her whisper sent shivers up Raven's spine. Kira was speaking of the internal storm she could feel approaching.

'Kira! Raven!' Adam crashed through the trees, breathless, his eyes darting to the sky.

'Come on!' He held out his hand and Raven rushed to his side, feeling the secure lock of his strong fingers around hers. 'Kira!'

Tearing her eyes from the flashing light in the clouds she grabbed Raven's other hand as they turned to the sound of echoing thunder overwhelming the valley. The three of them flew down through the trees, their feet familiar with the terrain as the wind yanked at the women's hair, trying to stunt their sight. Crashing through the door Kira ran for Adam's phone on the kitchen counter.

'What are you doing?' Adam stepped in front of her. Thunder and lightning were dominating the mountains, the sound forcing them to shout. 'I have to call Harvey! Let Raven's parents know that she is okay!' Pushing past him Kira flew out the door and up the path to find some signal.

'No!' Raven yelled watching her through the window. 'Adam! Stop her!'

'I can't.' He had to hold the girl back as she too tried to run through the door. 'She'll be all right Raven.' He pulled her towards the fire. 'You know what she's like. She'll be all right.' The words echoed like wishes in his head as he sat with his arms around the child, trying to calm her as he prayed for Kira's safe return.

Kira was moving faster than she had done in a long time. Her eyes were on the dark clouds as they aimed their anger in vicious bolts to the ground. Somebody had made them very angry, she thought, veering off the path to a place where she knew she would find a signal. The wind was wild, playing havoc with the lengths of her hair, whipping them into knots as the first drops of rain reached her. It would not be long before the lighting also reached her. She felt alive, exhilarated for the first time in months, the wild weather, the anger of the gods both frightened and excited her. Her call was frantic, loud, and in the end she could only hope that two words made it through to Harvey. 'Raven! Safe!'

Her sprint home was even faster with the wind behind her and the lighting at her heels, adrenaline pumping, disguising the pain in her ribs. She crashed through the door, the excitement colouring her face as lighting struck the ground behind her leaving a wisp of smoke, the acrid smell quickly eliminated with the increasing strength of rain. She was soaked through, her hair plastered to her face as both man and girl ran to her side and threw their arms around her.

'Thank God,' Adam whispered his words, heard only by the ear against which his mouth was pressed and the gods of the world outside. His arms were so tight around her she could hardly breathe and it was not until Raven pulled away that she pressed her hand against his chest, gently applying pressure until his grip released.

The relief in his eyes was quickly replaced by anger as he grabbed her wrist and pulled her towards the bathroom. Raven could feel the tension in the room and moved back to the fire where she pressed herself into the corner of Kira's chair, pulling the blanket close around her. Her heart was hammering in her chest as the loud storm drowned out Adam's anger. 'Don't you ever do that again!' he shouted tossing a towel at her. 'What the hell were you thinking? Running into a fucking thunderstorm! You could have been hit!'

'I had no choice!' she shouted back, the towel forgotten in her hand. Who did he think he was shouting at her in her own home, questioning her judgement?

'Don't be stupid!' He stepped forward, starting to peel the wet clothes off her. Kira slapped his hands away, taking a step back. 'I had to let them know that she was okay.' There was fire in her eyes as a shiver ran down her spine. 'They would have been worried sick!'

'You could have died!'

'Don't be stupid!' She threw his words back at him. 'I know these mountains and these storms, I knew how much time I had.'

He was fuming, his body shaking with anger as hers did with the cold. 'That was stupid,' he said, stepping forward again. 'Anything could have happened. You know that as well as I do Kira. You cannot predict these storms and you took a big risk in doing that. Too big.' His hands were tugging at the wet layers sticking to her skin.

'Don't ever do that again.' The anger had been replaced by desperation as he looked in her eyes, her clothes in a heap on the floor. He knew exactly what he would have done had they not the child to consider next door. Tearing himself away he turned and moved quickly out of the room. Raven was huddled on Kira's chair, her arms around herself in protection. Adam lifted her off the chair, and feeling the fear shake her body, held her close against his own as they sat in front of the fire listening to the storm and waiting for Kira to join them.

The anger had gone by the time Kira came to join them and all that was left was quiet relief, and gratitude that she was still there. Adam had only experienced that terror once before in his life. Watching her run into the storm had been like watching her fall through the ice all over again. It was gut-wrenching. His arm opened to allow her in beside Raven and as the girl changed position to cling to Kira instead of Adam, his other arm came around them and found her hand. His fingers laced through hers, the physical presence of them settling the terror in his heart and the strength in them making him sigh with relief.

The heavens unleashed their fury on the land as lighting cracked on the ground around them. The roar of thunder filled the valley as torrential rain was delivered in sheets by the ferocious wind. Raven was hunkered down between the adults whimpering at the close crack of lighting. Kira had of course seen many storms out in the house, but none as bad as this. The ferocity of the storm surprised her, the wind was just right to funnel it down the valley and slam it against the house as storm-force winds threatened to lift the roof off her house. Adam's eyes lifted to the roof more than once as the wind howled and ripped and tried its level best to leave them exposed to the elements.

Kira's hand was absentmindedly stroking Raven's head as she tried to soothe the girl, unaware of the hum that had started within her throat. Closing her eyes, she was transported back, to a time when she had sat on the sofa clinging to her mother, terrified of the storm that raged outside. Her mother's voice had been pure and true, the words of the song had not mattered, it was the tone that had settled her as it was now settling Raven. The words came from somewhere deep inside of her; it was more than a memory, it was like a knowing filled with emotion as she sang the words to be true. The song spoke of mother nature and how she raised her children. She taught them with infinite patience and showered them with gifts, but when they disobeyed her, her wrath sent them cowering, huddled together in shelters. Her anger would eventually pass, and she would smile on them again, they would be washed clean of their sins and allowed to start over, to try again. The verses kept flowing out of her like a tap being left to run and her voice filled the room long after the lighting had moved on. The last notes of the song hung in the air and when Raven realised it was over, she lifted her eyes to Kira. Kira's eyes opened and found the orange flames licking at the walls of the fireplace. Smiling she said goodbye to her mother as she left the room and returned to her husband's side in the glacier.

'It's moving on,' Kira whispered listening to the thunder in the distance. The day had grown dark with clouds though it should still be light out.

'Do you know another one?' Raven's mother used to sing to her when she was a baby, she remembered that, but she hasn't done so in a long time. She was always so tired and Raven was left to tuck herself into bed. She enjoyed the sound of Kira's voice and her songs were like none that she has ever heard.

'I'll make some hot chocolate.' Adam pushed himself away from the warm bodies relieved that the storm had moved further down the valley. He had been really worried for a while, watching the roof in anticipation, wondering what they would do, where they could go if it had been ripped off. He had no idea that Kira could sing like that, her voice was beautiful and pure. It carried the same tone as the wind and the streams, somehow making them appreciate the storm despite the fear it was evoking in them. He carried the drinks over enjoying the sound of her voice as the words wormed its way through his senses and lodged in his mind. The singing eventually gave way to storytelling, the kind that Raven loved. Legend and folklore about man and beast living, fighting and surviving together. Some legends spoke of man and wolf being born from the same mother, others pitched wolves as dangerous and conniving — the enemy. In the end they all carried the same theme of the earth mother, and how she can both provide and take away as she pleases. Kira's mouth was dry, her throat sore from all the talking by the time Raven had fallen asleep. It was still early evening, the storm had moved on, but the rain and wind was still persistent. There was no question that they would stay the night. Kira could only hope that her message had gotten through to Raven's parents.

'Shall I put her in the spare bedroom?'

Kira nodded and allowed Adam to pick the girl up from her lap. His arms brushed against her flesh, leaving warm patches as he pulled away to move the girl. Putting a hand to her hair Kira pushed her fingers into the tangled mess which was now starting to dry.

'I've seen that before somewhere.' Adam smiled at the look on her face.

'Can you cut it off?' She smiled back at the memory and fell into the sofa. She had a comb somewhere that could deal with this but she didn't feel like getting up. Adam sat down next to her, pulling her into his arms and slipping his fingers into her hair.

'I'll do you one better.'

They sat for hours staring into the fire as Adam gently worked the knots from her hair, the tug of his fingers sending electric jolts down her spine. Adam couldn't figure out what it was within her that had made her run out into the storm like that. He had seen the storm clouds roll over the mountains in approach but he was not prepared for the speed with which it was travelling. His heart had jumped into his throat, he didn't know where Kira and Raven were, only that they had gone for a walk, identifying plants and food. It was instinct that had driven him to the stream and it was clear then that the storm had caught them as unaware as it had him. His only thought was to get them to safety, nothing else mattered, but for Kira, once again she thought not just of herself, she jeopardised her own safety to reassure others. Yes, Raven's mother and father would have been worried, but they would have just had to deal with it. He doubted that the call had made a massive difference to their state of mind and he couldn't justify the risk at which she had put herself.

'You really scared me today,' he whispered, the anger long forgotten. There was no blame in his voice, it was just an admission and maybe a question if she chose to answer.

'I'm sorry.' Her eyes opened and found the fire. 'It was instinctive.'

'You could have been hurt. Ki, you could have been killed.' There was mild frustration in his voice as if he did not understand. 'I know, I didn't think about that. I'm sorry.' She didn't regret what she did. She was good at reading the situation and she was a pretty good judge of herself. She knew she could make it if the storm stayed steady, never the less she did understand Adam's point. It was new to her, this compromise and justification of her actions. She never had to consider how others perceived her actions and never had anybody question them. He was not wrong, but neither was she.

'The worst of the storm has passed.' Kira noted. 'It's just rain and wind now. I would like to try and call Harvey again, make sure that they are okay and let them know that we are.'

There was a long pause before his fingers stilled in her hair. 'I'll go,' he said eventually. 'Raven might wake up and need you.'

'All right.' Kira didn't argue. It didn't matter how the message got to them, just as long as it got to them.

The familiar aroma of Kira's cooking had filled the house by the time Adam returned. Wet and windblown he stepped through the door, leaving a trail of water as he closed the door behind him and stepped out of his shoes. 'They're fine.' She could see the concern on his face. 'The town had taken a hit though. Harvey said the damage was significant but as of yet the severity is undetermined.'

'Is anybody hurt?'

He shook his head. 'They don't think so, though there

are some unaccounted for.'

He saw a flash through her eyes. 'Your friend?'

'They're fine.'

'They?'

Adam sighed. 'Yeah, an old climbing partner of mine have arrived in town today. Jones. They were having dinner when the storm hit, most people made it into shelters.'

The question in her eyes jumped out at him from across the room. 'Let's just deal with it tomorrow,' he said in answer to her unasked questions. 'Everybody is going to be focused on sorting the town out tomorrow, and finding those who are missing. They think some young men might have been somewhere up here.'

Kira frowned. 'I've not heard or seen anyone.'

'No, neither have I, but you never know.' He looked about him for a moment. 'I'll just get changed.'

Kira cast her mind back, trying to remember if she had seen any signs, if there had been any indication of people. She could come up with nothing. If there was anybody in the mountains, they were a lot further up than her home.

'I'll head back in the morning,' Adam said re-entering the room. 'Help sort the town out. Raven's parents are anxious to see her.'

'I'll go up.' Kira handed him a bowl and he smiled his gratitude. 'At first light.'

'Maybe you should just leave it to mountain rescue,' he said into his bowl, he wasn't really thinking who he was talking to. 'Those guys could be anywhere.'

'I can move faster than mountain rescue,' she countered. 'I know these mountains better.'

'True, but what will you do when you find them?'

216

'Oh, I don't know Adam.' She smiled. 'I'm sure I can think of something.' He was tired, she could see it in the slump of his shoulder and the look in his eye as he looked up at her in surprise.

'I'm sorry Ki.' He grimaced hearing his own words. If anybody could rescue those guys, she could.

'It's all right.' She grinned. 'They can't have gone further than the pool surely.' She looked at him as he shrugged. 'The second ridge?'

'I don't know Ki.'

'Hmm…' She turned her gaze to the fire. 'They would have stuck to the path, wouldn't they? They would have looked for a clearing in the storm, away from cliff walls and trees.' Her voice was quiet, contemplative as she wondered where they would have, could have headed. 'Got it!' she looked up suddenly. 'There is only one significant clearing they could have utilised, if they were in the area. It's only an hour or so away.'

Adam nodded. 'Can you show me on a map? I'll take it down in the morning to show the rescue team, that way I can send them in your direction.'

Kira nodded. 'Good idea.'

Chapter Eight

Adam and Raven were not prepared for the sight in front of them. Despite Harvey's words of warning, despite Adam's attempts to prepare the girl for what they might find, and despite the wreckage they had encountered on their way down, neither of them had expected the scene of devastation in front of them. The track had been littered with debris; they had to step over, under and even walk around fallen trees that blocked the path. Blackened trees smouldered deeper into the woods, the acrid smell of burning filling their nostrils. This scene was so different from the one Raven had walked through the previous morning. She wanted to close her eyes and remember the smell of the clean air, the fresh feel of dirt between her toes but all she could do was stare. Stare at the havoc that mother nature had wreaked upon herself. Kira had already left the house when Adam had drawn her out of her sleep that morning. She had wanted to talk to her, she wanted to ask her why? She wanted to know why she felt like this was a warning.

Even from the bridge they could make out the sorry state of the town. Partially torn-off roofs, trees down, electric cables damaged. Raven's hand tightened around Adam's as their eyes roamed the area.

'Come on,' Adam whispered squeezing her hand. 'Remember nobody was hurt.' That is what Harvey had told him, he hoped the news still stood. 'Let's go find your parents.'

The task was not difficult, her parents were milling about on the edge of town, trying to help, with one eye on the bridge in the distance. They had breathed a sigh of relief as they spotted the two figures, but did not allow themselves to relax completely until their daughter was in their arms and they could check her over for injury.

'I'll see you later Raven.' Adam ran a hand over the child's head. 'I'll go see where they need my help.'

'We're just clearing up at the moment,' the man spoke, taking Adam by surprise. Raven's dad was not a fan of them and had hardly ever spoken to him or Kira. 'Your uncle is over at Harvey's, helping with the clear-up. We have a town meeting at lunchtime when we will discuss what is to be done next.'

'Thank you.' Adam nodded. 'How is your house?'

'Still standing.'

'Just.'

Adam's eyes went to the woman by his side, reading the truth in her eyes. He noticed for the first time that the man's arm was in a sling and that there were grazes on both their bodies.

'I'll come and help as soon as I can.'

There was a brief nod of acknowledgement and acceptance. It appeared to all of them that Raven had actually been in the safest place she could have been last night.

'Hey! You! You ugly waste of space!' The powerful

voice reached Adam's ears and he could do nothing to stop the retort as he turned to face the owner.

'That's rich coming from the saddest excuse of a mountaineer I have ever met.'

The smile on his face was mirrored by the man who strode up to him with confidence. Their hands met in greeting before it was sandwiched between their bodies as they slapped each other on the back with enthusiasm.

'I dare say you could have at least cleaned up before I arrived.' Jones gave him another hearty slap on the back. 'Or was the storm my welcoming party?'

Adam shook his head. 'In all my life the town has never been hit this hard, to my knowledge.'

Jones's head bobbed up and down on his shoulders. 'She came in with a bit of force. Sal nearly perforated my ear drums with her screams.'

Adam grinned. 'Have you two kissed and made up then?'

They were walking in the direction of the bakery, his friend's explanation of the night before filled with humour and innuendo making him laugh. It was fair to say that their laughter was the only sound of joy in the town as people went about gathering the wreckage of their lives. Uncle George's house was apparently mostly all right, but Harvey's had lost most of its roof. Inside food debris littered the floor, colourful icing was smeared on the walls and they kept finding pastries and buns in the damaged machinery. Harvey could not help but grin at the splashes of colour on every imaginable surface. 'Found another one!' he laughed, pulling a sticky bun out from the gap between two cupboards. He held it up triumphantly before tossing it towards the dog that was sniffing through the debris.

'So aside from the storm,' Adam paused lifting his eyes to his friend, 'what are you hoping to find out here?'

Jones straightened his body, placing his hands in the small of his back as he bent backwards to stretch it out. They'd been sorting through the debris in front of the bakery, making piles of what was usable and what needed to be tossed. Jones was an attractive man, tall, strong, lean. His dark blond hair was just short enough that he did not have to worry about combing it, but not long enough to bother him. There were lines of experience around his gunmetal-grey eyes, which lifted to the mountains. 'Something amazing, according to Sal.' His tone was amused, and Adam found himself following his friend for a clearer view of the mountains. 'Apparently, up there,' his eyes were fixed on the summits, 'is something never before touched by human hand.'

He looked to Adam for confirmation. 'I guess it depends on where she is wanting to take you.' Jones was amused at the flash of anger in Adam's eyes.

'I thought you were taking us.'

A blow of derision escaped from his nostrils as he shook his head. 'I don't know what she told you mate, but I think it would be a bad idea for teams of people to go up there.'

'Why's that?' His feet had started moving him down the street, to where he could get a better view of the mountain. He was only half aware of Adam's presence beside him as he shook his head. He could not take his eyes off the mountain, it was like the summits were calling him, pulling him in.

'Have you been up there?' He had forgotten his initial

question. 'Sal says you've been up.'

'I've been as far as four days in,' he admitted. 'Got into some trouble on a glacier.'

Jones pulled his eyes from the mountain and fixed it on the emotion in his friend's eyes. 'What happened?'

Adam shook his head, he did not want to talk about it right now. 'Snow bridge collapsed,' he stated matter of factly. 'I broke my leg.'

A long low whistle emanated from the man's mouth. 'Bad times. Did you get evacuated?'

'No, we lost the phone down the crevasse.'

Jones's head tilted to the side as he analysed the words. 'Was this with the mountain girl Sal keeps going on about?'

Adam's head swung round for Jones to see the warning flash through his green eyes. 'I wouldn't put too much value on what Sally's been saying mate.' His voice was calm and calculated. 'She showed up unannounced, without invitation and despite my decision not to continue with this experiment. She's not pleased about my decision and won't heed any of my warnings. I would think twice about going up there if I was you.'

'So that is a yes then?' Jones grinned. 'She must be some kind of woman, this mountain girl of yours, to get you so fired up.'

Adam's brow knitted in anger. 'Seriously Jones, I wouldn't listen to Sal. You know what she is like, she'll do anything to get her name up there, but I'm telling you this is not the mountain to do it on.'

Jones took a breath as his eyes moved back to the mountain. 'Why? What makes her so special, so different?'

'I don't know,' Adam admitted, 'but I don't think she

wants us on her.'

Jones's eyes flitted to the frown on Adam's face, a feeling of excited apprehension tying his stomach in a knot.

'So, when do I get to meet this mountain girl of yours then?' He grinned changing the subject; the mountaineer in him already eager to see what secrets lay beyond those snowy peaks. Despite the humour in his voice Adam's remained calm as his eyes drifted towards the bridge where three figures were appearing.

'Soon.' His eyes reached across the stretch of land pulling Kira's up from the ground as she paused to let the two men cross before her. She had found them, wet, scared and tired but unhurt. They were exactly where she had thought them to be, and despite their ordeal or maybe because of it they had not stopped talking, all the way down the valley. She had allowed them to continue down the path whilst she ran home to get changed and caught up with them again on the way down. They were full of tails of bravado, the position of lightning strikes growing ever closer to their bodies the further down the track they walked. She had to smile to herself, she would not be telling anyone how petrified she had found them, huddled together against the chill of the wind on their wet clothing, except perhaps Adam. It was his eyes that drew her into town, the sight of devastation being observed out of her peripheral vision. She had no idea it was this bad. She stopped at the edge of town, allowing the men to continue on their own as she changed direction. Adam knew exactly what she was doing and set his feet into motion. He joined her on the perimeter of the town as she skirted around the outside on her way to Harvey's.

'You found them.'

Kira nodded, aware of the blond man heading in their direction. 'They were petrified.' She grinned her eyes twinkling, making Adam smile.

'Not that they would admit to that to their mates.' Adam mirrored her thoughts noticing the hand held protectively around her body.

'How's your ribs?'

Her hand dropped instinctively as she flashed him a guilty look. 'Okay.' She had pushed a bit too hard last night and this morning. The muscles around the injury ached as he pulled her to a stop. 'Let me see.'

She didn't stop his hands from lifting the T-shirt she had hastily pulled on, but it was not his voice that broke the silence.

'Wow! That's an impressive bruise.' Kira's head shot up to meet the man's eyes, momentarily drawn in by the warmth in its grey colour as Adam pulled the material back down, covering the injury. Jones himself was taken aback by the startling blue of the woman's eyes, standing in stark contrast to the white of her hair. He struggled to pull his eyes away, feeling drawn in by her beauty, as if it held some unexplainable power. Adam's voice finally cut through the strain of eye contact as he introduced the two to each other. She didn't speak nor accept his hand in greeting as her blue eyes darkened, staring unflinching into his. Jones lifted an eyebrow when she finally turned away and saw the amusement in Adam's as he shrugged. Kira had summed him up, in those few brief moments she could read his energy and form an understanding of what kind of person he was. She did not dislike him, he seemed nice enough, kind, the red colouring around him speaking of adventure and excitement.

She had been drawn by the grey of his eyes, a memory flashing through her mind, it was the same grey as one of the wolves which had led her to Raven. Slightly thrown by this connection she had turned away, Harvey's looked to be in a sorry state.

'I can see why you like her.' Jones's words were a loud whisper as they hurried after the woman. He had been stunned by her beauty and felt drawn to her, much as he expected Adam did. The warning flash in Adam's eyes made him smile as he wondered what was going on between the two, if anything.

Her legs looked strong beneath the shorts, despite their slimness as she walked with long confident strides, her white hair in a thick braid down her back. There was only the slightest hint of discomfort as she lifted her booted foot over the threshold of the bakery door and stepped inside.

***

'So let me get this straight.' Jones sat back in his chair. The three of them were having dinner, Kira had declined the offer as Adam knew she would, and retreated up the mountain. She would be back the next morning as people were only just finding the courage to creep from the comfort of their beds, and he would be there to meet her. He wished he too could forego this dinner and just go straight to bed. There was a lot to do; Uncle George's house only needed a few wayward planks replacing and a few tiles hammered back onto the roof, but was structurally sound. It would not take him long, but Harvey's needed a lot more work and then there was Raven's home. The place was barely standing, they would probably do better by just flattening the whole thing and starting from scratch.

'You decided that you wanted to traverse these mountains.' He paused. 'Thanks for the invite.'

'I did invite you,' Adam interrupted the sarcasm of his tone. 'You said no thank you. Remember?'

'Oh, was this about the time you said no thank you to Everest?' The men stared at each other. Jones had backed him on the decision to turn around on his previous Everest expedition; a few hundred metres from the summit the window had closed, and Adam had stuck to his guns, they needed to turn around. A heated argument at altitude had left them breathless but in the end the party had separated. Adam and Jones had returned to camp and those that returned with them were the only survivors of the expedition. Adam had decided to remove himself from that scene for a while. He needed to get back to basics, do what he loved doing for the right reasons. It was hard to remember who you were and why you were when you were surrounded by power-hungry, adventure-seeking big names who dragged you along in their wake of adrenaline. He had declined Jones's request to join him as leader on another Everest expedition, and instead returned to where it all started. To where he first fell in love with the mountains, and the art of exploration.

'Anyway...' Jones continued. 'So you come all the way out here, plan to do this major traverse, that has never been done.' His eyes found Adam's and saw the flash of hesitation. 'Find this woman, the myth, the legend.' He grinned, unaware of Sally's quiet snort into her wine glass. 'Convince her to go with you.' He paused taking a drink from the water glass beside him. 'So, off you go, into the mystical unknown, you fall down a crevasse.' He paused. 'Stupid. She saves you, hauls your ass out, sets your broken bone and drags you all the way back on an improvised sled?'

Adam nodded. 'Pretty much.'

'How far?' Jones leaned forward, astonished at the tale.

'Four days in... about fifty kilometres.'

'Well blow me Tuesday.' He sat back in awe. 'That is some kind of woman.'

This time Sally's snort did not go unnoticed and the men looked at her fleetingly.

'Oh, come on!' She sat up. 'Really?' Sally liked to have the attention on her, she did not like the way Adam's face softened as he spoke of this woman. She had always liked him but he had never so much as given her a second look, it was Jones who had paid her the attention she craved from Adam, until he too had found greener pastures.

'So you want to go back to this glacier?' Jones decided to ignore Sally's petulant jealousy and fixed his attention on Adam.

'Wanted,' Adam corrected.

'Why?'

'Why what?' Adam frowned confused by Jones's question and the looks Sally was throwing him.

'Why did you want to go back to the glacier?'

Sally sat up, paying attention. He had not actually ever given her a reason for this either. She had jumped at the opportunity to work with him again, and had asked no questions, but now as he sat in front of them, searching for words she too had to question his reasons.

'No one has ever been up there before.' The confidence in his voice did not match the flash of hesitation in his eyes.

227

'I thought it would be a good opportunity for us, all of us, to work on something new together.'

'So why change your mind?' Jones was not going to let this go. He could see the rationale behind Adam's words, but it felt as if there was more to it. It would be a nice project for them all to work on together, but this was exactly what Adam had walked away from a few years ago.

'I don't know.' Adam shrugged. 'I made a mistake. I wasn't thinking clearly when I called you.' His eyes shifted from Sally to Jones and back. 'I was frustrated with my injury, eager to get back out in any way I can, and I thought this would get me out quicker,' he paused. 'I soon realised I was wrong.'

'Why? Why do you think you were wrong?'

'I know I was wrong, because she does not want us on her.' He was leaning forward now, his elbows on the table. 'She's angry; that storm last night, it was a warning.'

Jones could see the fire in his eyes as he spoke each word with conviction. 'I don't know why she tolerated us for as long as she had. All the signs were there, we should not have gone up, we should never have gotten as far as we did. She is angry now, she won't allow anybody else on her.'

Sally laughed bitterly at his words which sounded convincing to his own ears. 'Come on Adam! Listen to yourself. It's a mountain!'

Jones was watching him with interest, he was obviously trying very hard to convince them not to continue entertaining this idea, and though he did not disagree with Adam's words or emotions he sensed something more.

'It's because of her, isn't it?' The vitriolic tone in her voice caught them both off guard as they turned their eyes on the woman. 'Don't look at me like that.' She sat up straight again. 'You're in love.' She turned to Jones. 'He's in love.' Her eyes drifted between the men. 'You would do anything she asked you. How do you know your judgements are sound?'

'Does that go both ways then Sally?' His eyes were hard. 'Can we assume your judgements can not be trusted either if you are in love?'

The tension grew around the table as her eyes glanced towards Jones making him shift uncomfortably in his seat. The three of them were all being reminded of Sally's questionable decisions underpinned by similar emotion. None of them had ever came as close as Adam just did to speaking it out loud.

'All right.' Jones sat forward. 'We are not here to tear each other apart or to question professional judgement. I think we are all tired and perhaps a bit stressed after the storm, so let's just take a step back.' Adam did not take his eyes off Sally, he did not like the tone with which she had spoken of Kira.

'I think we should call it a night,' Jones continued, aware of Sally squirming under Adam's stare. It dawned on him, as it did Sally, that Adam had not denied the accusation and though he did not think to question Adam's judgement, he did agree that he was very much in love with this woman.

'I've got to get up early.' Adam stood pushing his chair out. 'There's a lot of work to do around town, I'll see you tomorrow.' He was biting his tongue, angry at himself for ever calling them. This was exactly what he had walked away from and now he had invited it back, not just into his life but into the townsfolk's, into Kira's. Outside the air was already thick with humidity again, he could practically feel the heavy particles rubbing against each other, gearing up for another storm. Some part of him wished for another storm in the hope that it would scare Sally and Jones away. He regretted his rash actions, his thoughtless dialling of their numbers. He didn't want that part of his life to mix with this. He didn't even know if he ever wanted to go back to it. He was content here, with Kira. He could easily spend the rest of his life like this; living off the land, living with her. They didn't need anything else.

Jones had just waited long enough to look at Sally with heavy confusion before she had shot off a sarcastic remark. He had stood slowly, shaking his head sadly as he pushed his chair in. 'Night Sal.'

He did not see her deflate into the chair or drop her head in her hands.

***

There was a whirlwind of emotions circling around and through the foursome. Sally was distraught at the inability to curb her feelings and in doing so unfairly lashed out against somebody she hardly knew. Kira seemed like a lovely person, kind, strong and obviously always put somebody else's life, safety and happiness before her own. She seemed like the kind of person that could and would do anything, she would give you the shirt off her back or the shoes off her feet without thinking twice, and all Sally could do was stare at her with animosity and jealousy. Sighing heavily, she pulled her gaze away from the striking woman and once again reprimanded herself for her nasty thoughts. Kira had done nothing to receive her scorn and yet that was all she got. She found herself trying to belittle the woman at every opportunity, only to see the frowns of confusion on her friend's faces or the disappointing shake of their heads. Kira herself never rose to the bait that Sally dangled in front of her all too often. The townsfolk had been working hard over the past couple of weeks, clearing up the debris of the storm and putting homes and businesses back together. There had been another storm, less violent and shorter in duration, but enough to make people run for cover and children to cower at the sound of thunder. The air was now clear though the same could not be said for Jones's head. He found the whole situation massively intriguing. The mystery of these mountains drew him. Why had they never been climbed? Why have they not been explored? What was it that made people take a step back and shake their heads when he asked them about it? Why did they glance to the mountain with fear and admiration? Who was this woman, Kira? Why did people look at her in the same way they did the mountains and why was Adam so adamant that they should not return to this glacier? He had asked Adam time and time again, as they sorted through rubbish, built timber frames for houses and hammered slate onto roofs to tell him about Kira. He was fascinated by her. She disappeared at night only to reappear in the morning, nobody saw her leave, and nobody saw her arrive. Well, at least he never managed to. She was like a creature of the forest herself, and there was something about her that caused him great difficulty to keep his eyes off her. He had received a few warning glares from Adam, though his friend never said a word in the line that the two of them were together. Kira's eyes drifted to Jones's almost as often they did Adam's. She saw in him something different than she did the townsfolk, Raven or Adam. His eyes captivated her, haunted her in her dreams when they appeared in the face of a wolf. Who was he? He was not like Adam, nor was he like their other friend, Sally. The woman who seemed to despise her with every fibre of her being. She had seen the way she looked at Adam and could guess at the reasons for her scorn, though she would never react to it. She had never done harm to anyone, not by hand nor word and she would not start now. She had no reason to dislike the woman, but she did not have to be her friend. It was Raven that picked up on the swirl and drift of emotion that flowed between the four individuals like a river around obstacles. She frowned at the change of colours and shivered at the look in their eyes. Their minds were not focused, they were not listening, and the earth was trying to talk to them. Kira's colours remained mostly stable, but for a short burst of energy every now and them. Raven would feel it before she saw it. The change in her eye, the colours and then the fight as she tried to bring her emotions under control. She was much better at focusing her mind, she was listening, but not as good as she usually did. Her mind was covered in a thin film of fog that distracted her, that disrupted her connection. Kira herself struggled with this and removed herself from the tangible mix of emotions as soon as she could. Disappearing into the woods, she would take off her shoes, reconnect with the earth and force herself to listen. Her route home now included the stream with its deep pool every day. She felt the need to immerse herself fully in nature and wash away the dirty human emotions of the day. She was not used to so many murky layers in the hours of every day. Her home embraced her and for now she was content with the silence again. She was surrounded by noise and turmoil every day in town and relished the quiet of her home. On the odd occasion that Adam accompanied her home, they would both spend the dark hours in quiet reflection of the day. She did not stop him from lacing his fingers through hers or folding his arms around her. She enjoyed the warmth of his embrace and closed her eyes to memorise the feeling for when he was not there. Soon she would be walking away from him. She would be going up to the glacier and she didn't know if she would be coming back. Circumstances were changing, she could see it in the way Jones and Adam related to each other and it would not be long before she would have to make her move. She could not afford to wait until winter. She could only hope that the weaker snow would make the crevasses more evident, or better yet, with any luck the glaciers would be clear of snow.

Raven's hands stilled in their action, her head tilting slightly to the sky as her eyes closed. There was no breeze to play with her hair and strands of it stuck to her face with the adhesive of perspiration. The dirt was slowly rising, circling her wrists and rising up her forearms. Her feet were bare in the earth, a smaller replica of the woman's beside her. Kira stopped her work in the new garden they were creating in Raven's backyard. Her hand still full of seeds as she too lifted her eyes to the sky. The slight wind did not reach their skin but it whispered words in the branches of the trees, sending a secret through the leaves as they chattered excitedly. The girl's eyes opened and settled on the profile of Kira's upturned face.

'Did you hear it?' she whispered and watched Kira nod, there was misgiving in the girl's voice.

'What does it mean?'

'Change.' Her eyes descended to the concerned blue crystals of her young friend's. Raven shivered involuntarily. This was not like the change she had experienced before. She could feel the ache in her heart, read the warning in the skies. Kira could read the message in the perception of the wind, the movement of air was more a memory than a physical presence and, as the workers around them wiped at their sweaty brows, she knew it was only her and Raven that had felt it. Her eyes involuntarily found Adam's and moments later was pulled away to the grey of his friend's. They were talking about her, that much was obvious in the tilt of their shoulders and the tension in their backs. Adam frowned, he had not heard the message like the woman had, but he saw it in his friend's eyes. He too could feel that things were changing, and his frustration was fuelled by the confusion of not knowing what was going on.

'I don't like it,' Raven whispered, her eyes moving between Kira and the men.

'We don't have to like everything that is put in our path Raven, we just have to learn from it.'

Raven stood suddenly, throwing the dirt to the ground in agitation. 'I hate it when you're like this!' she said angrily, her eyes blazing. 'I don't like what is going on, and I don't understand why you are accepting it.'

'I have no choice,' Kira said quietly. 'I cannot stop their minds from thinking what they are thinking, nor can I stop them from doing it.'

'Why not?' The girl was standing now, her feet shoulder width apart, arms folded across her chest and defiance in her eyes. 'You can make them listen, you can make them understand, but you are not even trying.'

'Raven.' Kira sat forward on her knees. 'It doesn't matter what I say or do, they will do what they want to. I have no power over their decision.'

Raven turned her eyes to the men. Jones's gaze was still drifting in their direction, finding Kira's form every so often.

'Who is he?'

She didn't look at Kira as she asked the question. 'Why does he keep staring at you?'

Kira felt her heart skip a beat as her eyes once again found Jones's. 'I don't know Raven.'

That was the truth, she really didn't know what it was that pulled them together.

'Well, I don't like it. He and that woman are going to go up the mountain and I know what you are planning on doing.' Her eyes were back on Kira's now. 'I know that you are planning on going up there by yourself.' Her voice softened as she dropped to her knees in front of Kira. 'Please don't. Please don't do it.'

Kira's hand slid slowly over Raven's smooth hair, stopping at her cheek as she looked into the girl's eyes. 'This is something I need to do Raven.' She has never lied to the child before and she was not going to start now. 'I need to lay my parents to rest before anybody else finds them, and if that means I have to go up alone then that is what I will do.'

'No!' Her cry echoed down the street allowing the men to look up just in time for her to shake Kira's hand off and step away.

'You will die,' she whispered urgently, her blue eyes sparking with emotion. 'If you go up there by yourself you will die! I have seen it in the clouds.' Raven couldn't stand it.

She couldn't deal with it the way Kira was.

'What's going on?' Jones's words were still hanging in the air between them when Adam started to make his way down from the roof. Raven had turned and ran away into the woods causing alarm to rise in Adam. Kira had become more and more distant as the weeks of reparation to the town dragged on. Sally was doing nothing to help the situation, she did nothing but taunt and antagonise Kira, whether that be in front of her face or behind her back. Then at night, when Kira went home, she did nothing but apologise for her behaviour. She seemed distraught at the way she was acting, confused as to why and was blaming it on the urge to visit this magnificent glacier, as she put it. Everybody was confused by Sally's behaviour and Jones was doing his best to keep the peace between everybody. Sally was steadily busy convincing them that they needed to go up this glacier. Jones was listening, he had no reason not to, but Adam was doing his best to stop them, despite the urges to join them. He didn't like not knowing what was going on, and apparently Raven did. If anybody knew what was going on with Kira it would be her young apprentice, the girl who idolised her, who could read the signs like only Kira ever could.

'What's going on?' Adam brought himself to a stop in front of Kira, who had returned to her work in the garden.

'Raven is upset, she needs some time by herself.' She did not look up to meet his eye, she daren't, in case he could read the truth in them.

'What is she upset about?' His tone was not quite accusing, but as close to it as she had ever heard. She did not stop herself from finding his eyes this time. The darkness of the blue in her eyes startled him and he found himself taking

236

a step back.

'She is struggling to accept what will come to pass.'

Adam felt the fire building in his own eyes. 'And what exactly is that?'

'That is not for me to share,' Kira said calmly, barely able to keep the emotion out of her voice. She did not want to do this alone. She did not want the distance between her and Adam to grow any more than he did, but she had no choice. The mountain was calling, this was her last chance, and as if confirming her thought the mountain gave a loud rumble of acceptance, drawing her eyes.

Adam's eyes narrowed at the way she was looking at the steep slopes and snow-covered peaks. He could not bring himself to think about what she might be considering.

'I'm going to look for Raven.'

'She'll be at the stream.' Kira's eyes returned to the garden, she could leave at least this to the girl. Most of the work had been done in town, the debris was cleared away, businesses repaired, and re-opened, and now Raven's house too was nearly done. It would not be long before she set off on her next journey. She did not like to think about it, she did not want to go alone, but she had no choice. She would probably be starting her journey before the end of the week.

'Hi.' Kira's eyes lifted to the man, standing awkwardly beside her. Her eyes noticed his sturdy boots before travelling up his strong legs, taking in the shorts, dirty shirt and short cropped hair. He was once again mesmerised by the colour of her eyes, they were much darker today, filled with contrasting thoughts and emotions. She did not speak and as he moved the sun shone in her eyes making her blink.

'Sorry.' He sank down to her level bringing her eyes

down and away from the sun. She was truly a striking woman, with strong features, smooth sun kissed skin and those incredible eyes. Her white hair was tied back in a thick braid as it always was when he saw her.

'Are you okay?'

'Why wouldn't I be?' Her voice startled him, almost as if he did not expect her to speak.

'Is the girl okay?' He chose not to answer her question.

'She will be.' Kira's eyes moved to the woods through which Raven had disappeared and he saw something flash through her eyes.

'I have to go.'

'Wait!' He grabbed her wrist to stop her and was rewarded with her quick reflexes; in a moment he was on the floor, gasping for breath as her muscles tensed around his body, blue eyes blazing. He was stunned, much as she was, or Adam had been the first time she did it to him. Their eyes locked as they remained motionless, staring at each other. Jones's breath was still coming in ragged gasps as the power in her muscles both stunned and aroused him. Time faded into oblivion as he tried to find his words and Kira tried to find a way of explaining herself.

'Ki!' The desperation in his voice finally broke the spell as Kira's eyes lifted to find Adam, running towards her with Raven in his arms. He had barely a moment to register her position over that of Jones's, just long enough for her to see the flash across his face. She was on her feet faster than Jones had hit the ground. Raven was ashen, sweat beating on her brow but she was still conscious.

'What happened?'

He had never seen panic in her face as he did for that one

brief moment and his heart ached at the pain in her eyes.

'I found her at the stream, like you said, she was angry and...'

'Lay her on the ground,' Kira interrupted him.

'Raven, have you still got some medicine?' Kira's hand was running over her skin, trying to wipe the clammy moisture from her face before smoothing down her hair.

The girl nodded and Kira was gone in a second, not stopping to answer the shouts of support or offers of help. She tore through the house searching for the medicine briefly able to be thankful for the fact that the girl's parents were not home. Her fingers closed around the bottle as relief flooded through her and she rushed back to the girl.

Raven was still conscious and coherent enough to take the medicine, grateful for the comfort she found in the warmth and strength of Kira's arms. Kira sat on the freshly dug soil of the garden, her arms, legs and clothing covered in the dirt as she held Raven in her arms. Her heart was beating twice as fast as it should be, she knew she was responsible for Raven's state.

'I'm sorry,' she whispered into the girl's hair, closing her eyes and allowing the lone tears to escape. Adam did not like this, he did not like the state either of the women were in and he hated it even more that he did not know what it was about.

'Please,' Raven whispered weakly after a long time. 'Please Kira, don't do it.'

Kira's arms tightened around the girl and as she squeezed her eyes shut even more tears found their way through the pressured bottleneck. She could not lie to Raven, as much as she wanted to tell her that everything was going to be okay, she could not lie to her.

'Do what?' Adam's voice was strong after the weak whisper of Raven's and the quiet of Kira's non reply. His eyes were on Kira as she refused to answer him, her cheek pressed against Raven's head.

'Kira!' he said loudly. 'Do what?' She could hear the angst in his voice, the frustrated anger that has been building up inside of him.

'Kira!'

'Adam, come on mate.' It was Jones's arm that got swatted away as he tried to calm his friend down.

'Adam, you're making a scene mate. Just leave them be for now. Wait until you can talk in private.'

Adam stood for a moment watching Kira still refusing to look at him. He didn't like it, he did not like any of it, not the way Raven was pleading with Kira or the way Kira was avoiding his question, much less the way Jones was presenting himself as their protector.

'No, I'm not giving her a chance to run away. If you want to be a hero, watch the girl.' Adam stepped forward and took Kira's arm.

'Come on Ki, you need to tell me what is going on.'

'Not now.'

'Adam, you've got to stop her.' Raven pushed herself away from Kira and looked up at the man.

'Stop her from doing what?' He ran a hand through his hair. 'Ki, please you've got to tell me what is going on, come on.' He tugged at her arm and she threw him a look that reminded him of the way she threw knives at her wall.

'Kira please,' Raven begged. 'Just tell him. You can't...' There was a brief flash of amusement in Adam's eyes as the side of his mouth tried to curl up, at the look she had flashed him. Cutting Raven short Kira released the girl and stood up, wrenching her arm free from Adam's hold.

'Can you keep an eye on Raven please?' Her words and eyes were focused on Jones, much to Adam's annoyance as he grabbed her wrist to pull her away. He knew exactly what she would do next and released her, stepping out of the way moments before she could make contact.

Adam felt the tug of amusement once more as the annoyance jumped to Kira's face, he flashed Raven one last look before grabbing Kira's wrist once more, this time she did not protest. Jones looked on as they disappeared into the woods, his mind partially on the strength of the woman, alongside the thoughts of how well Adam knew her. He knew just how to act, what to say and when to push in order to get her to do what he wanted. They may not have known each other long, but they certainly knew each other a lot better than he ever knew anybody.

'Who are you?'

His grey eyes moved to the blue of the girl's as she stared intently at him, a frown on her face.

'I'm Jones,' he said calmly kneeling down beside her. 'Adam's friend.'

'I know that,' Raven said. 'I mean, who are you really?'

Jones frowned. 'I don't know what you mean.'

'Why do you keep staring at Kira?'

A red colour swept over the man's features as he glanced away, and in the direction the two had disappeared. Sinking down next to her he crossed his legs beneath him and stared at the ground for a long time before looking up at the girl. Her eyes were studying his form as if he was an alien creature to her. 'Are you one of them?' she whispered when his eyes finally met hers. 'Your eyes are the same colour.'

'One of who?'

Raven's head tilted to the side. 'The protectors.' She paused seeking recognition in his eyes. 'The ones that saved me. The ones that brought me to her.'

The lines on his face softened as pieces of the puzzle started to fall into place. Adam had told him how they had come to befriend this young girl, another story that had him staring at his friend in awe and disbelief.

'Why do you think I'm one of them?'

'Your eyes,' she whispered. 'You are always watching, because of the way you walk and the way you watch her. That is what the wolves do. They are always there, watching us, protecting us, even if we don't always see them. I can feel them.' She looked at him, willing him to admit that he was one of them, somebody that would protect and not hurt.

'I am not your enemy Raven,' he said finally. 'I watch Kira, and Adam and you because I think the three of you are incredible. I wish I had your belief, your way with nature, I wish I could still look like you do when you put your hands in the earth or when the wind brushes through your hair.

'I never used to be like this,' Raven said, she was sitting up now, facing him. 'Kira made me strong, she taught me, and she took away my weakness with her magic.' Her head dropped. 'Only, now it is coming back.' Her hand went to her heart. 'It's coming back because she is leaving.'

'What do you mean she is leaving?'

Raven's head lifted, her eyes roaming the space around him as his colours flashed and the wind whipped the hair in front of her face, making her gasp.

'Let go of me,' Kira said through gritted teeth, wrenching her hand out of his grip. He was the only person who could get her so riled up, make her so angry that it felt like the very blood in her veins were boiling. Adam grabbed her wrist again and as she turned to wrench it free, he grabbed the other one making her turn on him in anger. His face was calm, his eyes sparking with emotion. She could feel the pressure from his fingers lighting a fire inside of her that was unfamiliar. The heat of his body was close, she could see the pores on his face, practically feel the granules of dirt that was smeared across his skin.

'Not until you tell me what is going on.'

Her heart was beating so fast she thought it might jump out of her chest and run away; into the woods, up the mountain and dive into the glacier, where it belonged. She had never lied to him. She has never lied to anyone, she did not know how to, but she did not know how to tell him what she was planning. He would never let her go, he would do everything he could to stop her and she would be unsuccessful in her task. She would never be at rest, would never gain the closure she needed if she could not say goodbye to her parents. It tore at her heart to know that they were up there, waiting and she was taking her time going to them. She was fit and strong, the last injury aside, and she needed to go to them, now. She needed to put them to rest before Adam's friends descended on her mountains and either destroyed the sacred place or got swallowed by its huge jaws.

'Why don't you tell me what is going on?' Her voice was strong, calculated but the hurt in her eyes did not go unnoticed.

'What are you talking about?' Adam frowned. 'I'm not

the one that has been withdrawing myself, I wasn't running away and hiding.'

'I'm not running away.' She bit out the words, careful not to shout. 'I have never run from anything.'

'No,' he said looking at her. 'No, you haven't, so why are you not telling me what is going on?'

'What are your friends' plans?' Her head cocked in the direction of town, her tone as close to sarcastic as he had ever heard.

'By the looks of it Jones is more your friend than mine.'

Kira felt like punching him, like whipping his words out of the air and hitting him over the head with them. Her eyes were narrow in anger, her breathing loud and shallow as her face hardened.

'How dare you?' She tried to wrench her wrists free, but he only tightened his grip and for a moment there was panic in her eyes. He pushed her back against a tree and pinned her with his body, releasing some of the strain off her wrists.

'I am not letting you run away from this Kira,' he whispered loudly his eyes inches from hers.

'You may not have a choice.' Kira lifted her knee but he moved just in time for her to catch the side of his thigh. Her kneecap connected with his soft tissue sending a momentary shot of pain through his muscles, making him groan and loosen his grip on her. She tried to slip away, pushing him away from her, but he caught her arm again, yanking her back.

'What is going on?' he said angrily. 'What was Raven talking about?'

Kira was seething, his words had hurt, his strength was distracting and the feel of his body confusing. She did not know if she was coming or going and she hated it, she hated being so powerless.

'Tell me!' he shouted. 'What are you planning on doing?'

'What I've been planning all along,' she said finally, looking him in the eye. 'What we were planning,' she spat out the word as if it was poison in her mouth making his mind do a double take before it registered in his stomach.

'No way,' he said. 'No fucking way, am I letting you go up there by yourself.'

Kira blinked at the profanity escaping his lips as he half laughed, and half recoiled at the thought.

'Are you insane?' His face changed as he read the truth in her eyes. 'No way.' He shook his head, in a state of shock. 'Not a chance.'

'You cannot tell me what to do.' She wrenched her arm free and gave him a shove, sending him backwards in his unprepared state. His eyes widened at the defiance in her stance, she was actually serious about this.

'Over my dead body,' he growled lurching forward and wrestling her to the ground. 'There is no way on God's green earth that I am letting you go up there to drown in a fucking pool or fall to your death in a crevasse.' He shook his head. 'Not a chance.'

'Get off me!' Kira shouted, feeling the heat build up between their bodies. 'You have no right to talk to me like this, to tell me what I can and cannot do! I have lived here all my life! I have never needed anybody's permission to do anything and I am not starting with you!'

'Don't be stupid Kira.' He forced her arms to the ground to stop her from lashing out at him. 'It's not about permission, it's about safety. I can't in good conscience let you go up there by yourself, knowing full well the dangers that are up there.'

'I'm not the one who fell down a crevasse!'

Adam stopped, making sure she was looking in his eyes, paying attention to his words. 'No, but you did fall through the ice. Not even you are immune to the dangers of those mountains.'

Her body stilled beneath his as he stared at her, the fire in her eyes reaching fever pitch. Her body was no longer shaking with anger but with need. The tension that had been building was like a coiled spring ready to explode. She was unexpectedly reminded of the first time he had been on top of her like this. The feel of his lips against hers.

Her breath was coming in ragged gasps as her body cried out for him, her eyes refusing to leave his. He could see the need in her eyes, feel it in the tilt of her hips and the shivers on her skin.

'I cannot let you go up there Ki, because I cannot lose you.' His words were a whisper across her lips, so close she could feel the tingling of his lips as the words vibrated over them. The emotion in his eyes unlike any she had ever seen before.

'You have no idea how much I love you.'

There was no time for thought as his lips came down, pressing against hers. The warmth and strength in them conveying his urgency, the shift of her hips conveying hers. Kira felt her body, not melting but tense, lifting off the ground, pressing into the heat of his hardness. She wanted to feel every inch of his warm skin pressed up against hers, she had never felt need like this before, this urgency that sent agonising shots down her abdomen, confusing her insides and melting with the warmth between her legs. Adam pulled away, releasing a moan from her lips, sending electric currents through his body. Kira's released arms came up to his sides pulling him down, closer towards her, her hands slid beneath the material of his T-shirt grasping at the skin. She was desperate to feel his skin against hers. She didn't know what came over her but she knew that she could no longer fight it. His lips were moving down her neck, making her gasp at the surprising pleasure this small act evoked. His fingers were beneath her shirt, whispering over the bumps of her ribs and the neat blocks of toned muscle between them. It reached the point where hard muscle gave way to soft flesh and as his thumb slid below the tension of her bra, she gasped both at the sudden pleasure of his fingers on her breasts and the pain in her ribs as she pressed up against him. Adam shifted to relieve the pressure off her injured side and stopped the progress of his renegade thumb. Lifting her shirt, he brought his lips to the bruise sending another shiver up her spine, making her back arch in pleasure.

Lifting his head, he brought his lips down on hers. The kiss was long and deep filling her with all the pent-up emotion inside of him. When he pulled away her eyes were closed and he waited until they fluttered open and focused on his.

'Do you want to stop?' he whispered, aware that this would probably be her first time. Kira didn't need to think about it. They had made it far up the valley, they were not far from the stream with the deep pool and she could think of no other place she would want to do this.

'No,' she whispered, her hips moving in answer to his

question.

'Are you sure?'

Kira nodded and pulled him down towards her. She had never wanted anything more in her life.

The mixture of pain and pleasure took her mind to a different place, a place she has never been before. There was a mix of soft tender touches, hard muscle, exciting gasps of pleasure mixed in with short stabs of pain. Adam was gentle, patient allowing her the time to fully enjoy this experience. He loved the way her face changed as the feelings washed over her, the gleam on her skin excited him, the glazed look in her eyes sending him over the edge as her body moved beneath his. Her movements were powerful and graceful as with everything else about her. He never wanted to be anywhere else again, this was it for him. She was all he needed.

***

The gentle caress of cool water against her warm skin was calm and soothing after the exciting rough and tumble on the forest floor. Adam had joined her in the pool, a shiver running over his body, less adapted to the cold of the water. They were both spent, tired after the intensity of the emotion and as Kira closed her eyes and sank beneath the water, he kept his eyes on the spot where she had disappeared. The fear of losing her was in the forefront of his mind. They had taken this step, made this final connection and as far as he was concerned that was it. He was bound to her for the rest of his life, or hers, and the thought of the latter being much shorter than anticipated filled him with dread. Resurfacing, the water peeled away from her like a second skin, leaving a forest of droplets on the beautiful features of her face. The red glow of her cheeks stood out against her skin, matching the blue of her eyes and the red of her lips in intensity. Reaching out Adam pulled her towards him and wrapped his arms around her, kissing her.

She did not know what to say, so she said nothing, drowning in the warmth of his affections.

'I'll go with you,' he whispered. 'Name the time and we will go, just please don't go alone Ki.'

Holding her head in his hands, his thumb ran over the apple of her cheek, gently caressing the smoothness of it. 'Please, promise me you will not do this alone.'

She couldn't lie and despite the events that had passed and the intensity of emotion between them bringing them closer, she could not make that promise.

Leaning forward she pressed her lips against his, closing her eyes to hide the truth from him. She felt his arms around her back, his fingers moving up and down the length of her spine and, despite the tenderness, felt her body respond to his touch.

The second time was even better, though still sore the thought of what was coming excited her and allowed her body to be pulled closer to his. She could feel him beneath the water, the sensation new and alluring. Weightlessness aided their actions as her legs wrapped around his waist bringing them closer than she ever thought possible. His worries melted into the feel of her skin against his as all questions finally left his mind and he filled it with her, and nothing else.

The sun had sunk low in the sky by the time they were

able to peel their exhausted bodies off the heat of the rocks and set their feet in the direction of home. Raven's parents would be home by now, and there was no reason for either of them to head back into town tonight. They were closer to home than town anyway and the progression there was only natural. The evening slipped into darkness, which gave way to the quiet night as they found it difficult pulling themselves away from each other for even the smallest tasks. Kira knew that these could be their last close moments together and she wanted to savour them. She wanted to remember what it felt like to be loved and relish the experience of being loved in this way. Love that was not parental or friendship based, but loved in way that made her feel wanted, needed and cherished. She did not know if she would be coming back and wanted something to hold onto, in case she found herself alone, waiting for the inevitable. Adam was floating on the current of relief that was the knowing of her emotion. She was quiet and reflective by nature, her emotions only visible on the lines of her face, the flash in her eyes or the tension in her body. She didn't make her emotions known by the use of words and the uncertainty of it all had had his stomach tied in knots for weeks. Now those knots were untied, the tension had been broken. They were both calm and relaxed, their muscles earning a well-deserved break as they sat comforted by each other's presence. The glowing crackle of the fire was a perfect accompaniment to the wind that had picked up outside. Kira could hear the message as the wind slapped it against the house and closed her eyes against the truth. She did not want to do this alone. She did not want to leave him behind to venture back up the steep icy slopes. She would much rather stay here, wrapped in his strength, protected from the world, but the mountains had spoken. She could hear the beating of his heart, her ear pressed up against his chest as his fingers moved absent-mindedly through her hair. He was so alive, they both were.

A sliver of doubt crept into her mind, it barely had a chance to take root before a loud slap of wind pushed the door open, slamming it against the wall of the house and making it bounce back halfway.

'It must not have been closed properly,' Adam said standing up to close the door, but Kira dropped her head. She knew what it was.

The message was clear. Go alone or do not go at all.

Chapter Nine

Kira shifted uncomfortably in the chair, her hair catching and snagging on the smallest imperfections on the seat, adding to her discomfort. She had been coerced into this meeting, something she was not happy with at all, though she knew why he did it. Sally had asked them all to lunch and knowing Kira would not agree Adam had set it up to happen at Harvey's. It was the only place he could be certain of getting her to. She felt naked, exposed with her hair loose and her mind unguarded. She was not prepared for this, she had never been in a situation like this and her body itched to move, to run away. Her eyes drifted beyond the counter where Harvey gave her a thumbs up, she rolled her eyes and turned her attention back to the table. Sally was speaking, but her words made no sense to Kira.

She had already been to the second ridge and beyond today, assessing the snow condition and stashing food. She knew how to package it and hide it so that animals were not tempted by its scent. She wanted to move fast and light and dropping food in various places would allow her to move with a lighter bag. She had not yet decided about footwear. She might need the boots and crampons on the glacier, but she would move a lot faster without them.

'Ki?'

Adam's voice pulled her back from the edge of the ridge and focused the blue of her eyes on his. The skin on her bare legs tingled beneath his touch, it felt like warm silk where his hand enveloped her muscles. She did not miss Sally's eyes darting from Adam's hand to her face and back to the table, nor the flash of longing in them. Sally felt it like a stab through her gut. She knew that she had been acting like a hormone-fuelled teenager, throwing tantrums and laying blame where there was none to be laid. She was trying to apologise, but Kira was distracted. Her mind was on something else, somewhere else. Only Adam's touch, his words could bring her back.

She looked at him in confusion before her eyes floated over the faces of the people around the table. She had an enormous amount of trouble getting the words to move from her mind to her mouth.

'Sally was apologising for...' Adam's words slowed, trailing off as he tried to find the correct words.

'For being a bitch,' Sally said suddenly, 'essentially.' Her eyes locked on Kira and she noticed for the first time the way the woman's eyes changed colour. The widening of her lids was a signal of surprise and Sally found herself shrugging. 'Sorry. I was out of order, the way I acted and spoke.' Her words trailed off. 'I have no excuse.'

Kira's head tilted in recognition of understanding, but the words still did not roll off her tongue.

'It's all right Sal,' Adam finally spoke. Kira had never really given the woman too much thought, other than the brief moments of jealousy that had washed over her in the parts of her mind, not occupied by thoughts of the glacier. Jones's grey eyes did not leave Kira's face, he too could now see what Raven and Adam had seen. Kira didn't really care what was happening around the table. These formalities of modern civilisation did not appeal to her nor carried any weight in her world. Her mind was wholly occupied by something else entirely, something that had her glancing out of the windows.

'We understand.' He grinned. 'Kind of.'

Relief washed over Sally as she sat back in the chair, blowing out a breath and drawing Kira's attention.

'When are you going up?'

The voice startled Sally; she had not expected the melodic tone or the strength with which it reached her ears, and for a moment her words were lost. Kira's eyes were now focused solely on Sally's, and even as Adam and Jones spoke at once assuring her that Sally was not planning on going up, she could read the guilt in the woman's eyes. Sally found herself unable to lie or even slightly bend the truth, something she was so good at, as Kira's eyes bored into her. It felt as if she was touching her soul, reading the truth in her heart with those intense blue eyes and Sally shifted uncomfortably, averting her gaze.

'A friend of mine is flying up in a couple of weeks,' she admitted, barely able to hold eye contact with anyone for more than a few seconds.

'You're joking.' Jones looked at her in total disbelief. 'After everything we've just talked about, all your grovelling and apologies, you are still going ahead with it?' He shook his head as she protested his words.

'Don't tell me you do not want to go up there,' Sally said

catching his eye. There was no anger in her voice or face, just curiosity.

'I do,' Jones said, 'but not like this.' His eyes roamed the room, skimming over Adam's face and coming to rest on Kira's for a moment longer, before finding Sally's again.

'They are right you know,' he said calmly, smiling, almost sadly, at his friend. 'I don't think this mountain is happy about having us here. You are making a mistake by forcing this expedition. You should try and listen some time.'

Jones had had enough, shaking his head he stood, pushing his chair out. 'You are going to regret this decision.' He felt Kira's eyes on him, but did not meet them until he was halfway through the door. Adam had turned his attention to Sally, trying to understand why she was so desperate to do this. He was still trying to stop her as Jones held Kira's gaze for a moment longer. Adam did not realise that Sally's mind was made up, nothing he could say was going to change her mind, much as he expected was the case with Kira.

Adam's hand ran down Kira's arm and found her hand as she stood. Jones had disappeared through the door and she had no further interest in this conversation. She had no more than two weeks to get up there and put her parents to rest. She did not want them moved, no matter what, she would do everything she could to make sure they remained in the heart of the mountain.

'Where are you going?'

'Home,' Kira said. 'I have work to do.'

She was only partially aware of the nod of his head as his words entered her ears and circled through her mind. Harvey was at the counter, watching with interest and she could see the gap in the trees through which Jones had disappeared. She was going to have to leave very soon.

'Listen with your heart,' Kira said focusing her eyes on Sally. 'Make sure you hear her when she warns you.'

Her eyes remained on the woman for a moment longer before she gave a brief nod and, slipping her hand out of Adam's, left the bakery. She did not wait for the woman's response.

Kira did not think twice about Adam staying behind, he felt it his duty to try and convince Sally not to go through with her plan, for everybody's sake. He had thought she'd put the idea behind her, accepted the fact that it was not going to happen, but Kira had known. She had seen it in Sally's body language, in the colour of her eyes and the lines on her face. She had known all along that Sally was planning on going through with it, and had probably assumed that he and Jones were going to go with her. That was why she had been so wound up, so tense and withdrawn.

Kira needed to clear her head, prepare herself for the task ahead. She had been laying down the foundations, putting in the groundwork, but now she had to get her mind into the actual task. Somewhere in the back of her mind she had been hoping that it would not come to this. She had no hard feelings towards the woman, but she needed to get up there before them. She did not know what she might encounter or what she would do once she found her parents, so she had to make sure she allowed herself enough time. She didn't know whether Adam was going to come up tonight, she didn't have the presence of mind to listen to his words as the mountains called her name.

She had grown more used to the shoes and was able to

cover far more ground in them than she used to. She had spent more time in town over the past two years than she ever had in her entire life before that. The extra time had given her experience in the shoes and she was now flying through the trees like she did with her own moccasins. Her feet carried her to the familiar stream which now held so many memories, but still contained the capacity to clear her head and refocus her mind. She hoped that Adam would stay in town tonight. She had to distance herself from him, clear her mind and body of any trace of him, of anything that might hold her back. She had given herself to him, mind and body, but part of her soul was still reserved just for her parents. She needed to deal with this before she could allow herself to give over to him completely.

She became aware of the cool fingers of the water, embracing her feet and sliding smoothly up her legs, over her knees, across her thighs, enveloping the shorts, then her hips and then the T-shirt. Her hair was floating on the water like a ghostly lily-pad, for just a moment, before the water swallowed her completely, taking her away to another world.

Jones was astounded at the sight of her, the speed and fluidity with which she moved through the terrain. He had heard the stories, but none of them came close to doing justice to what he was experiencing. She was like a creature of the forest itself, blowing through it like a gust of wind, fast and smooth, floating over the ground which he seemed only to be able to crash through. He was barely able to recognise her for the speed at which she travelled through the trees. A keen runner himself he set off after her, astonished at her speed and power. The thick cover of trees made his task more difficult and the noiseless way with which she covered the ground made it near impossible to follow her. It took every ounce of strength and endurance to keep going at a rate to merely keep her in sight, until she finally disappeared through a thick hedge of vegetation. He stopped and watched, waiting for her to reappear and when she didn't, he followed cautiously. Pushing his way through the vegetation the branches scraped at his flesh, making him wince with the discomfort. He came through just in time to see the white circle of hair floating on the water only to disappear below the surface.

'What the…' His voice whispered into the air, the leaves picking up the words and tossing them about before releasing it up into the sky. His breath was coming in fast gasps, his muscles were burning. There was no sight of her for a long time and he was starting to think he had imagined it when the shadow of her figure appeared beneath the water. Backing away through some vegetation he crouched down, watching as she surfaced. Her eyes were closed, her hair slicked back from her face as she lifted her head to the breeze for a moment. She had to keep her mind clear, Kira thought, walking back out of the pool. Her clothing was clinging to her body, the material of her shirt exposing the flesh of her toned abdomen, drawing his eyes. He had caught a brief glimpse of her before, when Adam was looking at her bruise and just for a moment, he envied his friend. Shaking his head, to clear it of thoughts that could get him into trouble, he refocused his eyes on her. She was peeling the shoes from her feet, leaving them beside the stream before setting of on a run again.

'Fuck,' he whispered and jumping from the bushes slid across the uneven slope before finding his feet and racing after her. He didn't know what he was going to do when he found her, but he could not stop himself from running after her. It was like she was a magnet and he a mere scrap of metal, with no will of his own, being drawn along. She had a power, not just physical, a magic as Raven had described it.

Suddenly she was gone.

He raced along for a few more moments hoping that she would come back into sight but he was out of luck. His lungs were burning, his legs aching as they brought him to a reluctant halt. Staring into the distance he thought about the fruitless chase and threw his hands in the air, cursing himself for the impulsive chase. What exactly was he hoping to gain from this? Kira, for once was able to stop her natural instinct and instead of flooring him she swung down from the tree, landing quietly behind him so that when he turned, he was faced with her, a couple of metres away.

Jones jumped involuntarily.

'Where did you come from?' His hand flew to his chest trying to still the rapid beating of his heart. She did not answer, and he knew that he was the one that should be giving answers.

'Are you okay?'

'Why wouldn't I be?'

It was by no means difficult to keep his eyes on hers, for all her physical beauty it was the intensity of her eyes that drew him most. She hardly ever spoke to anyone aside from Adam, Raven or the guy at the bakery, and the clarity of her voice took him by surprise every time. He had no answer to her question and they stood staring at each other in silence. Kira's eyes left his briefly, to glance up to the summits, before returning to his. She was anxious to get away, to distance herself from everything and everyone.

'You're going up there.' It was more of a statement than a question, and she did not feel the need to answer him.

'I'll go with you.'

He thought he saw a flash of amusement in her eyes as she turned to walk away.

'Wait! Kira!' He rushed to her side, falling in step beside her as she turned to move down the valley. 'I didn't mean it like that. I really want to go up there.' He paused glancing sideways. 'You know this place better than anyone, so I'm told. Take me with you.'

Kira stopped and looked at him. 'What makes you think I'm going up there?'

'The look in your eye.' It was honest, straightforward, and she liked that. 'I assume that is what your argument with Adam was about?'

Kira's eyes had lifted to the skies, the wind was blowing through the trees, rustling the leaves.

'Why?' she asked when she had finished listening.

Jones frowned, confused for a moment before the words fell into place. 'I want to feel it.' His words were heavy with emotion making him blush slightly. He didn't know what it was about this woman that made him feel comfortable to share his inner most thoughts with her. 'I believe you and Raven. I can feel the power of the mountain. I want to know what it feels like to be surrounded by so much… magic.' He finished on a grimace. 'For lack of a better word.'

Kira smiled at his sincerity. 'You don't need me,' she said. 'Open your heart and listen, she will tell you when you are ready.'

The sun had started to duck beneath the horizon, the chill

of the wind on her damp skin and clothes making her shiver.

'I have to go.' Her eyes drifted to a point beyond him. There was movement in the trees and after a moment her eyes met his again. He could not read them, and after a minute she turned away.

'Take care on the way down.' Her eyes scanned the trees again before settling on his for a moment longer. Something was confusing her, he thought, as she frowned and turned away.

'Stick to the path, it's easy to get lost in the dark.'

Her words had hardly registered in his mind before she had disappeared. The strange light of dusk aiding her quick escape. The wolves would watch over him, she thought, leaving him staring after her in confusion.

Night fell quickly and with the darkness came the howl of the wolves. Kira's head lifted from her food preparations, her ears tuning in to the sound, her mind filing it in category. It was strange that they had so readily accepted Jones, like they had Raven. She could not make the connection, as she could with Raven. They had protected her because of the hidden abilities they had sensed in her. They had accepted her and brought Kira to her, but with Jones she didn't know. She couldn't see where the connection lay, but she knew better than to question it. Adam must have gotten waylaid. He was not coming up tonight. In a way she was glad because she could set off tomorrow. She was packed and ready to go, her mind was clear and if he had come home tonight, she might have had trouble leaving. On the other hand, she would have liked the feel of his reassuring arms, the comfort of his warmth and presence to see her through the next journey.

As it happened, in the end the earth and mountains knew best. Everything happened in the way it was supposed to, they, dwellers of the earth, did not need to know the reasons. It was enough that the mountains knew.

**

She could not allow herself the luxury of lengthy goodbyes. She allowed no emotion to break through her hard-won defences as she made her breakfast, cleaned the fireplace and re-laid the fire. She had checked and double checked her bag. She had mentally gone through what she had stashed and where. She had even written it down and stuffed it in the lid compartment of her bag; she could take no chances. She was going alone, that was risk enough and she was not completely stupid. She had written a note, leaving details of her route and expected day of return. She was being conservative with her timings, if she got into any trouble, she wanted to know that somebody would come and find her. She knew it would only be a day, or two at most, before Adam found her note. She also knew that there was a one hundred percent chance of him wanting to come after her and a ninety-eight percent chance of converting that want into action. The only thing that could possibly stop him would be the weather, or the sense his friends might talk into him, and she was not holding out for either of these. She did not look back into the house before pulling the door closed behind her — she knew everything was ready. The bag felt light on her shoulders, and she had to remind herself that it was because of the fact that it was summer, and not because she had forgotten something vital. She was not scared, she was not anxious, but her mind betrayed her as a memory dragged on her shoulders, like a physical weight, taking her back to the last time she had shouldered the bag. Shaking her head to clear the image Kira forced her feet into motion, descending the porch steps without a backwards glance. Her legs and arms were bare as the first part of her journey would not require any protection, and her feet were covered only in her own moccasins. Her heart was beating a reassuringly steady rhythm in her chest as she allowed muscle memory to take the lead. She did not have to think about her direction of travel, her body knew the way. She did not have to concentrate on the state of the path, and though the morning was dark and still around her she had no light. Her feet knew the track like she knew the way to her fireplace. Her thoughts had turned inwards, the time for complete focus would come, but for now she could still allow her mind to drift. The weather had been forefront in her mind, and after studying it for the last couple of weeks she had calculated that she had another weather window of approximately five to seven days. Kira thought about her journey, reminding herself of the pitfalls they had previously encountered, and bar any incidents there should be no reason why she would not be able to complete her journey in that time. She did in fact believe that it should be done in much less time than that; the weight of the bag was less on her shoulders, the ground much more accommodating without snow in the lower regions, and being alone she knew she would walk deep into the night. She could not stop thoughts of Adam from entering her mind if she tried; the void of human warmth accompanying her up the familiar path tugged at her heart. He had said that he would come with her, so had Jones, but — Kira shook her head, — by then she was convinced of the fact that she needed to do it alone. She did not know why. She would not have minded Adam's presence, she would have welcomed it, at one point she had thought there was no way she could do it without him, but now things were different. She did not know how or why, but the progression of events over the last month had led her to the belief that she had to do this alone. Raven knew it, it had upset her and for a moment Kira wished that she could have said goodbye to the girl. She knew that the girl's relapse was due to the stress caused by her own thoughts and actions. It was her fault that Raven was once more fighting with herself, but if she could only get this done... If she could just finish this chapter of her life, then she could move on, then they could move on.

Everything would fall into place, it always did.

Kira was both excited and nervous about the next chapter, the next step of her life. She knew her life would never be the same again, Adam had changed her in a way she had not thought possible. He had opened her eyes to a world of new adventures that was just waiting to happen. She could not imagine her life returning to the way it was before him. She could not imagine her home so quiet again; without the sound of footsteps and laughter. Raven and Adam had both brought light and life into her once empty home. She had not realised how empty it was, until they had filled it with their bountiful spirits. They were her best friends, and she did not know how she ever thought she could go through life without any. Nobody has ever thrived in solitude. Community dated back to the cave dwellings of the Stone Age, or round houses on hilltop forts during the Iron Age. She was naïve in thinking that she, woman alone, could live happily, thrive and become all she could be, alone. Had she never met Adam, she would not have learned the techniques needed for modern mountaineering. Had she not met Raven, she would never have found the passion of teaching within her, or the limitless love she had to pour into another's heart.

She would be lying to herself if she dismissed the aching in her heart.

She still cherished days of solitary exploration and connection with her environment, but she no longer wished for those times to stretch into weeks. Her face had become a familiar feature in town and though the townsfolk still held her in very high regard, they no longer stared at her in wide-eyed awe. They smiled and nodded their greetings, appreciating her for who she was, and the unique skill set she brought to town. They had at the very least four people's survival to thank her for. She no longer loathed the days she had to go into town, though she still preferred her own home and its surroundings.

The rising sun, casting long shadows of light through the trees, drew her out of thought stealing her attention to the beautiful display of nature. Sunrise in the woods gently coerced a world usually hidden by the earth's ability to reflect light, to the surface. Kira marvelled in the wonder of nature; its ability to create fanciful environments in which you could lose yourself had captivated her since childhood. As a young girl she had often sunk to her haunches near a stream as the light rose behind her, waiting for fairies to shake their wings and make the earth sing with their laughter. This world has not yet lost its wonder, and she had a long way to go before she would lose her imagination. Her feet had stilled along with her mind as she watched the light filter through the trees, knowing that it would not last long. She wondered briefly, how many people ever got the opportunity to see this. She would have to bring Raven up one morning, she thought. The girl would love this magical display of nature. The sun quickly ascended into the sky, and as the magic light disappeared Kira pushed on. She had taped extra padding to the waist belt of the bag, there was no better teacher than experience and reflection, making the bag fit much better. She did not feel the need to hook her thumbs beneath the shoulder straps in order to keep the weight more equally distributed. She felt strong and though the diminishing bruise on her ribs no longer carried much pain, she knew she needed to be mindful of it. She had come to the conclusion, through careful treatment and observation over the past three weeks, that the bone must just have been bruised or at the utmost — cracked. It could not have been broken or she would have suffered more pain for much longer.

The familiar view of the permanent snowline beyond the line of trees brought her mind back to the present. She had made good time, as she thought she would. She needed to push ahead while she could, because she was going to have to be extra careful on the glacier, she could not afford to take any chances. There was no partner to pull her out of a freezing pool, or to stop her from falling down a crevasse. No, she was not taking any chances; she was not walking over any snow bridges. If she had to walk a whole day to find the edge of a crevasse, then that is what she would do. Any snow still left around the lower regions would have been weakened by the heat of the sun's rays. If a snow bridge could collapse in winter, it was even more likely to do so in these late stages of summer.

Her mind automatically made comparisons to the last journey, and despite her best attempts to keep the memories at bay, she could not fight them off. The previous journey with all its adventures played a very significant part in who she now was. She didn't want to forget it, nor ignore it, but she didn't want to think about him right now. Thinking about the previous journey meant thinking about him, and at this stage it would only make her question her decision. The differences were stark; the air was different, warmer, thicker, and heavier to walk through. The cold tang of crisp ice crystals in the air, was replaced by the smell of warm earth. The scent of pine and maple drifted through the air, mingling with the earthy aroma and sticking to her skin like the tacky sap of the maple tree. She did not stop as the ground beneath her feet turned to ice, nor did she so much as pause at the pool where Adam had first touched her. The momentary section of thought, delivered in memory by her subconscious mind, was more than enough to throw her off track. Shaking her head, she pushed away the feel of his fingers lacing through hers and focused on the ridge. She had no partner, no backup if she was to come off, so she needed to be careful. The weight of the bag still altered her balance, and though she was more used to this now, she found that she still had to concentrate on it, perhaps more so than more experienced mountaineers. Pausing at the bottom, Kira allowed her eyes to drift the length of the now very familiar ridge, allowing herself the time to take stock whilst digging out some food and water. There were no cornices this time. The edge of the cliff was in clear sight and she would not have a misplacement of footing as she had before. The travel cake made up of summer fruits, picked by the hands holding them, and those of some very close friends, melted in her mouth. The sweet tang of maple juice reminding her of time spent with Raven. Her eyes closed momentarily as her thoughts drifted to her friends. 'No.' Her eyes shot open on the spoken word; she could not allow herself to think of them. The determination of her being seemed to seep out of her, filling the air around her, as she moved with purpose. The bag was back on her shoulders, the waist belt clicked into place and, as the sound echoed around the still cliffs, she lifted her eyes to the ridge. It was still early morning, she thought she could make it to the big pool at the foot of the slope of doom, at the very least. She had set off earlier than they had done previously, her bag was lighter, she knew the way and she had many more hours of light than they had had in winter.

There was a quiet determined calm surrounding her, as her body progressed without any need of encouragement, or conscious thought. The hard rock of the ridge felt familiar beneath her feet. The sharp edges were clearly visible and the last prints in the old snow, the only prints in the snow, was hers from the most recent training venture. She took some comfort in the fact that she had been up this ridge very many times and yet her prints were the only ones on it. Taking care she focused her mind on the task, ensuring that each foot placement was secure. She felt safe and confident but there was no room for complacency. Just because she had been up here tens of times did not mean that this could not possibly be her last. This was what made Kira special; her ability to remain humble, and to respect the dangers of the environment through which she travelled, whilst moving through it with confidence. Every journey carried risk, but most risks could be managed very effectively. Life would after all be very boring without any risk. Making use of both her hands and feet, Kira scrambled up the last steep section of the ridge, ascended the short vertical climb, and came to a stop at the top, as she allowed her eyes to gaze over her surroundings. She used to run every day. She used to find herself on some pinnacle or outcrop, high above the rest of the world, gazing down into the valleys, appreciating her environment. These days had been important to keep her connected to her heritage. It had filled her with a sense of achievement, and she fulfilled it with a sense of purpose. She was training. All her life she had been training, and now the adventures were beckoning. Adam had told her about many mountains, summits that her parents had told her about. The distance between her and some of the most iconic summits in the world was almost unperceivable. He had already asked her to go with him, to be his partner in all future expeditions. He wanted to take her to the Alps, the High Atlas and the Himalayas. It seemed as if a great part of their time together was spend pouring over maps. The excitement it brought to her heart staring at those maps, dreaming about adventures, was very different to the excitement she felt standing at the head of that second ridge, looking down into the valley. The routes and summits Adam had told her about had been done, they were tightly controlled, but this has not. These mountains were untamed, untouched and she wanted them to remain that way, the way her parents had left them. Her mind was filled with them, wondering if they too had ever found the contrast of snow beneath their feet, and the heat of the sun on their skin this intriguing. The altitude gained had brought a chill to the air, and though it was not quite cold, it was definitely not a summer heat. Pulling her eyes away from the view Kira set her feet back in motion, pushing on as the sun reflected off the white of her hair, bathing her in a golden light. She did not want to stop yet. She needed to cross the saddle and summit the next hill, which should bring her down to the foot of the slope of doom. The care she had taken on the long ridge had pushed the sun further up in the sky. She could make it across the slope and camp on the saddle at the other side, she decided. She was starting to believe she could make it to the glacier in two days. This would allow her enough time on the second day to possibly reach the crevasse. Kira was not irrational; her mind and thoughts were clear. She knew she needed to keep her energy up and, thankful for her forward planning, found the place where she had hidden some food. Smiling to herself she unwrapped the package as she set her eyes on the next summit. It contained some cold meat and travel cakes, all of which she continued to consume in her progress up the next hill. The climb was long and hard, it had been a while since she had expended so much effort with the bag on her back. Stopping for a moment, her eyes danced around the peaks in view as she took the time to have a break. She had fallen short on her consumption of water last time and tried to force herself to drink more. There was no timely voice reminding her to drink water, and so she found yet another part of her life where Adam had seemed to slot in so seamlessly. The climb had taken her longer than anticipated, she still had to descend to the big pool, refraining from falling in this time, cross the slope of doom and hopefully cross the lengthy distance to the foot of the next climb. It would be good if she could start the day with the technical climb, or move around it, before heading down the valley on the other side and across to the glacier. Pushing on, Kira set her sights on the next goal.

***

'Adam! Adam!' Raven still looked pale, the effort with which she walked concerning him as he quickly made his way to her side. Her breath was sticking in her throat, as she struggled to force it out. Her heart felt like it might jump out of her chest as her eyes darted about her, shooting up to the mountains and back to him.

'What's wrong?' Adam lowered himself to her height, pushing the black hair out of her face as the sun beat down on them from its high position in the sky. Raven had not slept well, her dreams had been haunted by nightmares; visions she didn't want to see. Her parents were concerned and did not want her to come out today, refusing to listen to her pleas and explanations. They did not understand; she was frantic with worry.

'It's Kira.' She finally pushed the words out finding his eyes. 'I saw it last night, in my dreams.' She stopped, gasping for breath. 'She's gone.'

Adam looked at the girl, first in confusion and then in horror. 'What do you mean she's gone?'

'I think she's gone up the mountain. That is what I was trying to tell you the other day, she was going to go up there by herself.' Raven's face was contorted in worry, her breath coming fast and shallow as her voice reached a pitch hard for him to understand.

'Hold on.' He looked around him before taking her hand.

271

'Come on,' he said, starting to guide her towards Harvey's and slipping in the back, apologised to the baker for their intrusion. 'Sit down Raven.' Adam pulled a seat closer before lowering himself down next to her. 'Take a breath and tell me again what you just said.'

Harvey handed the girl a glass of water, there were tears in her eyes as she tried to take a deep breath, quickly gulping at the cold liquid.

'I heard it in the wind,' she whispered. 'A while ago. There was danger in its message and then it was the clouds, it showed me what she planned on doing.'

'Going up to the glacier, alone?'

Raven nodded. 'Last night, I could not sleep. I could hear the wolves, even down here I could hear them.' Her eyes were glowing with concern and apprehension, looking enormous in her small face.

'They are protecting her,' she said, 'but something is going to happen.'

'What do you mean?'

Adam's blood had run cold in his veins. He knew she would do something like this, he should have stopped her. He should have gone home last night, but he got distracted by Sally's pleas and passionate explanations. He had felt the need to convince her not to fly up there, when he should have been with Kira. If he had been up there, she would never have been able to go up alone. He would not have let her, anything could happen.

'I don't know!' Her voice rose again in panic. 'I can't see it, all I can see is the black and red splashes of colour.'

'Okay,' he said placing his hands on her legs. 'Calm down. I'll find her.'

His voice was a lot calmer than his mind. His insides were churning, he felt sick to the stomach at the thought of her up there, alone. She would have left early and it was already past midday. She could already have fallen through that sodding pool. Harvey could see the turmoil in the man's eyes. He could hear the physical hammering of his heart against his chest. Adam had gone pale as Harvey dragged the apron over his head and ushered the girl outside. He needed to get her home, out of this stressful environment and then he could deal with Adam. Stumbling outside Adam felt as if his entire world was imploding, suddenly nothing else mattered. Nothing he did mattered, no achievement he had procured, or adventure he had pursued made any difference to this very moment. He would have given it all up if it just meant that things were different right now. The world inside his head was spinning, images blurring and, unable to still the moving print in his mind, he put his hand out against the wall of a building and felt the contents of his stomach retrace their path up his throat and empty onto the ground beneath him.

'Adam?' Jones rushed up to his friend putting a hand on his back. 'Are you all right mate?'

Another convulsion folded him in half as his body systematically emptied the contents of his stomach onto the ground, attempting to cleanse the darkness of his mind through the purging of his body.

'What the hell? What have you eaten mate?' Jones half laughed, until he saw the look on Adam's face as he lifted his eyes to meet his friend's.

'Shit,' Jones said, catching a glimpse of Harvey herding Raven away. The girl did not look in much better shape. 'What happened?' He knew it was Kira, it could not possibly be anything else. The three of them were connected and she was the only thing that could make both Adam and Raven look like this.

'She's gone,' Adam whispered wiping at his mouth, and just for a moment Jones thought she was dead. 'I have to go after her.'

Jones let out an audible sigh of relief. 'Fuck, mate, I thought you meant she was gone, gone.'

Adam did not look at him as he set off in the direction of his uncle's house. 'Raven says she's gone up the mountain. She has a head start, and she moves like the bloody wind.' Adam shook his head. 'I have to catch her up before something happens.'

'What makes you think something is going to happen?' Jones's eyes were pulled towards the snow-capped peaks, a vision of the woman, flying through the trees flashing through his mind. 'She's pretty sound in those mountains, isn't she?'

Adam nodded. 'The best I've ever seen, no offence mate.' He paused at the look on Jones's face '— but there is something about these mountains, I don't trust them and Raven saw something.'

'Saw something? Like what?'

'A vision, I guess.' Adam shrugged, he was hastily pulling gear out of the closet and off the shelves wondering how far he could get today.

'A vision?' The scepticism in Jones's voice did not slow the progress of Adam's hands. 'I can probably make it to the second ridge by dark,' he mumbled.

'What?' Jones's head snapped up at his friend's mumbling. 'You're going today?'

'I'm going now.' He pushed past Jones and through to the kitchen where he pulled a bag full of ration packs out of a cupboard.

'Fuck it!' Jones threw his arms in the air. 'Is there enough of those things for me?'

Adam stopped and looked at his friend. 'I can't ask you...'

'Shut up you bloody numpty,' Jones cut him off. 'Just give me some of this shit and I'll meet you in town in half an hour.'

Jones' hands dug into the bag pulling out packets. 'How many days of food will we need?'

'Five?' Adam shrugged. 'At a guess.'

'We can pick something up in town and eat on the way up, that is one less meal to carry. I'll bring a rope, you know what kit we need.'

Adam nodded. 'Thanks mate.'

'Don't thank me yet buddy, I've not even packed my bag yet.' Jones threw him a lopsided grin and rushed out of the house, his hands full of ration packs.

'What's going on?' Sally tried to stop him in town, but Jones just brushed past her. 'Sorry Sal, can't stop, on a mission.'

'Jones!' she shouted after him watching him jog to the Hotel. 'What the...'

Sally stood in the middle of town, looking around her in confusion. People were going about their business, buying food, walking dogs and eating ice cream, but something did not feel right. Where was Adam, and that little girl, and what was going on with Jones? They were up to something. Spinning on her heel she headed in the direction he had appeared from only to find Adam hastily packing up the tent in the front garden.

'What's going on?'

Adam looked up to the familiar face, the confusion in her eyes bringing back memories of when the three of them were much closer, working together.

'We are going up the mountain,' Adam said, returning to his packing. 'I think Kira might have headed up alone.'

Sally's eyes grew wide. 'What? Why?'

'To get to the glacier before you, I imagine.' He pushed the tent into the bag before strapping the rest of the kit to the outside.

'Why?' Sally was genuinely confused. 'It's not a race is it?'

Adam stopped with the bag at his feet, looking at her. 'She's gone to find her parents,' he said at long last. 'They disappeared eleven years ago. When we were up there last year, I saw something. I saw screws, in the crevasse and Kira is convinced that it was them. She has gone back to the glacier to look for them and lay them to rest before the place is overrun by the likes of...' He shrugged. 'Well, you I guess, and what I used to be.'

'Used to be?' Sally was more than a little stunned at the tale. Why had they not said anything before?

'I've changed,' Adam said shouldering his bag. 'I'm not going back to that world, my life is here now, with Kira.'

Sally was left staring after him as he pushed through the gate, making his way into town.

'So tell me something.' Jones was stomping up the valley behind Adam, moving at a blistering pace. 'All this time you have done nothing but tell us how dangerous these mountains are, how foolish it would be to go up there. You have done everything in your power to convince us not to go.'

Adam was silent in Jones's pause, pushing on, wanting to reach Kira's house and find her there. He would be furious, but relieved beyond comparison. 'So why are we stomping up the mountain?'

'To find Kira.'

'Right,' Jones nodded at his back, 'and why is that again? I mean, why is it that she has gone up there in the first place? What are you not telling me?'

'What do you mean?' Adam indicated to the right, stepping off the path into the trees.

Jones was momentarily thrown off track as he looked around him. 'Aren't we supposed to be going up there? Where are we going?'

'To Kira's,' Adam said. 'We don't actually know for sure that she has gone, we only have Raven's fears to go by.'

'Right,' Jones said again. 'I'd hate to stomp all the way up there just to find her lounging in front of the telly when we get back.'

Adam smiled at the image Jones's words created in his mind. 'Do you really think she is the type of person to own a telly, never mind lounge in front of one?'

Jones laughed. 'No, I guess not. She hardly ever stops moving that girl.'

Adam glanced over at the admiration in his friend's voice. 'She does,' Adam said evenly, keeping his eyes on his friend. 'She can sit still for hours; listening to the wind, watching the water tumble over rocks, or stand on the edge of a cliff looking into the distance.' He didn't know why, but he wanted Jones to have the correct picture of her. She was not just physically strong, fast and beautiful, there was a depth to her that he had never experienced before. A breadth of knowledge so wide he had never come across anything like it.

'Oh, right.' Jones half smiled, brushing off the intensity in Adam's eyes. 'I guess I don't know her as well as you do.'

Adam broke their eye contact and turned away. 'This way.' Breaking through the trees her home came into view and Adam moved ahead, oblivious to Jones.

'Ki!' he shouted pushing through the door. His heart sank as his eyes fell on the clean fireplace, subconsciously mumbling an expletive under his breath.

'What?'

'She's gone,' Adam said pointing to the fireplace. 'The only time I've ever seen that fire out was the day we left on our first journey.' Scanning the room his eyes fell on the note at the kitchen counter. Jones smiled, wondering at which point in the past three years since he had last seen Adam, he had started substituting the word expedition for journey.

'She left this morning.' He stuffed the note in his pocket, his eyes lifting to the kitchen cabinets. 'She's expecting to be back in five days, which means she is really pushing.' Adam pulled open the door to her medicines and rummaged through the herbs. He had completely forgotten to pack painkillers of any sort. His leg had healed well. The only time it caused him any trouble was after a long day of pushing it in the mountains, and he had not been out for more than a day and not with a heavy bag.

'What's that?'

'Willow bark, hemp, peppermint and ginger.' Adam put

the individual bags of herbs in a dry bag and stuffed it in his rucksack.

'Planning on some gourmet meals mate?' Jones followed him out of the house, waiting while he looked in once more before pulling the door closed. 'It's natural painkillers,' Adam explained descending the steps. 'I forgot to bring any pills and I don't know how well my leg will hold up.'

Jones nodded thoughtfully. 'How does it work? I mean, in case I need to jam it down your throat or something.'

They were moving up hill again, fast. 'Just steep it in some hot water, drink it as a tea, that is probably the easiest. You can chew the willow bark but it tastes like...'

'Bark?'

'Yeah.' Adam laughed. 'Pretty much.'

A long silence stretched between them allowing the forest to infiltrate their senses. The scent was intoxicating, the powerful aroma reminding Adam of the absolute nothingness of the smell of snow. He was not a big fan of snow at the moment, and he was certainly not looking forward to heading into the snowline. He knew he had to do it sometime, and the sooner the better, but he had hoped he could at least wait until winter. He wanted the snow to come to him, not the other way around, and yet here he was, pushing once more up the valley, into the heart of the mountains.

'So, do you want to tell me what is up there?' Jones broke the silence, his voice falling into step alongside the cracking of branches beneath their feet. 'Why is Kira so desperate to get up there? What is up there that is so important that she would risk her life for it?'

A huge audible sigh exploded into the trees around them.

'Her parents.'

Jones did a double take. 'I'm sorry, what?'

'Kira was born here, in that house, at the foot of these mountains.' Adam could see the snowline in the distance as the sun steadily worked its way to the western horizon; they were going to have to push to make it up the second ridge. He did not want to stop before they reached the first campsite he and Kira had used. 'She was raised on the mountain air with the dirt beneath her feet. She learned how to hunt when most of us were having play dates and sleepovers arranged by our mothers. She learned about the birth of the earth through legends and folklore, her mother was a healer and taught her everything she knew about the medicinal values of plants and herbs. Her parents were both mountaineers, her father trained her since she was old enough to walk.'

'Were?' Jones interrupted Adam's monologue making him look back over his shoulder.

'Yeah.' They broke through the trees and Adam headed straight over to the pool, the snow below his feet not going unnoticed. 'All her life, they were training, preparing themselves for this traverse that has never been done. One day, eleven years ago, they set off on the start of this epic adventure.' Adam paused, stopping at the edge of the pool, his mind running away with the memory of her.

'You're not thinking about jumping in are you?'

Adam grinned. 'No.'

His eyes lifted to the ridge, illuminated in the lowering of the sun.

'They never returned.'

Jones was stunned into silence as he followed Adam's gaze.

'We should keep going,' Adam said. 'I'd like to get to the top of this before setting up camp. Kira is probably past the slope of doom.'

'The what?' Jones asked shaking his head. 'Mate you have been holding out on me. I feel like there is much more of a story here than just the fact that she saved your sorry arse.'

'There is.' Adam half smiled. 'I'll tell you about it some time.'

Adam was digging in his bag and Jones, realising what he was doing, pulled out his own harness. 'How difficult is that ridge?' he asked, stepping into his harness and quickly doing up the buckles.

'It's not too bad.' Adam's eyes lifted to the ridge. 'Narrow and icy but steady going. There is a short climb over by that pinnacle of rock.' Jones followed the pointed hand and nodded. 'After that it eases off and opens up to the west, we'll head north to the summit and then bear west. We can camp up there tonight. We should be able to reach the glacier by tomorrow, bar any unexpected events.' Adam tossed the end of the rope to Jones as he had done with Kira all those months ago and tied into his end coiling the rope across his chest.

'So what happened?' Jones enquired once they had established a rhythm on the ascend of the ridge.

The rest of their journey to the top of the ridge was dominated by the sound of Adam's voice, repeating Kira's story. Jones listened avidly, as Adam took him on a journey through the young girl's life; the years as Kira had retold them, the emotions, the long empty hours of quiet guilt, anger and longing. Jones had to laugh at the picture created in his head, when told about Adam and Kira's first meeting. He had experienced something much the same as that. He loved the fact that Kira continued to take Adam by surprise, flooring him several times over, as even Adam laughed at the memory. 'The last time was down there,' Adam said pointing to the pool before losing himself in the story once more, forgetting about the incident by the stream.

'This was the first warning,' Adam said upon reaching the top of the ridge. His tale had been woven to the point of their first journey. 'We reached this point, there was a cornice of about a metre. We knew it and took measures to avoid it, but Kira must have misjudged the distance; she stepped over the boundary and we heard the loud crack. I don't remember ever moving so fast,' Adam said shaking his head. 'We chalked it down to nerves, but really we should have listened.'

'Why, what happened?'

The sun had disappeared below the horizon, the light of dusk the only thing accompanying them on route to their first camp. 'We camped over there.' He pointed Jones in the direction and they set their course to the campsite.

'The next day we went over this summit.' He looked up to the towering peak. 'Her parents' map showed a different route to the one we wanted to take, and we couldn't figure out why. So, upon reaching the point of diversion we stopped and looked around, trying to come to some conclusion as to why they would have gone the longer way around. I was looking the other way when she walked out into the opening and the next thing we know, there is a loud crack.'

'No.' Jones was gripped. 'Ice?'

Adam nodded. 'There is a large frozen pool, covered in

snow, not shown on the map. We had no way of knowing. That was our second mistake.'

'What happened?'

Adam blew a breath out of his puffed cheeks as his head half dropped. 'She went through.'

'Fuck.'

'Yeah. That moment, watching her disappear beneath the ice was quite possibly the worst moment of my life.'

'You got her out, obviously, because she is still here.'

'Right.' Adam nodded. 'We should have turned back. She was in a bad way. It took two days to fully rewarm her.'

'How long was she in the water?'

'Too long. I don't know how she did it, she didn't even drop her bag. She was just there, holding onto the edge, kicking whilst I sorted a rig out.'

'That's insane!' Jones could think of nothing other than to laugh.

'That was our second mistake,' Adam said. 'She convinced me to keep going. We should have turned back. If we had turned back at that point, we would have been fine.'

'Sounds like she was pretty determined to get up there.'

'She was. We can camp here.' He dropped his bag, immediately pulling out his head-torch and the tent.'

'So you kept going, and then what?'

Adam took a breath. 'Well, we had to get around the pool and our best option was traversing the slope to the north of the pool. It was tenuous, risky but our only option really. The slope was loaded, it was just waiting for an excuse to let go. It would have been fine if it was only Kira, she is light and fast, but I stepped on a bad pocket. We felt it go and ran like fuck to the other side. I only just made it out, she was ahead of me.'

Jones shook his head looking at Adam. 'This sounds like an absolute epic!' Adam nodded. 'Fuck mate, I have to take my hat off to you, I would not have kept going.'

'I guess we shouldn't have, but we were so far in by now that turning around was just not an option anymore. That was our third mistake.'

'Sounds like you must have gotten a foul ball in that inning.'

Adam nodded. 'She gave us one more chance and we ignored her, our next mistake would be our last.'

'The crevasse?'

Adam nodded as they continued to pitch the tent in silence, it was not until they were both settled inside that Adam spoke again. 'Perhaps we should never have been on it in the first place.'

'Perhaps not,' Jones agreed. 'So, is Kira essentially just looking for her parents' bodies?'

'In a manner of speaking.' Adam shuffled around so they could start the stove and cook some dinner. He wondered what Kira was having for her dinner. He wondered where she was and how she was feeling. He hoped she was eating enough, drinking enough and that she wasn't cold. She would be alone in the tent tonight, not something she was used to, and the cold would be more invading without the warmth of his body next to hers.

The tent felt so big around her, the empty space which used to be filled with Adam's form was now home only to her rucksack. At first, she had enjoyed the extra space in the tent, but now as she sat quietly, eating the food that reminded her of him, she felt empty. She was forcing herself to eat, she didn't like the food, but she knew she needed the calories. She had learned from their previous journey and she was not going to make the same mistakes again. She was already inside of her sleeping bag, her slight form silhouetted in the light of her head-torch. It was quiet, so quiet. She wondered if he had found her letter yet, if he was on the mountain. Perhaps he was just on the other side of the hill, maybe she should wait for him, they can go on together.

'No,' she said out loud, shaking her head. 'Don't be stupid Kira. He's not here. Now just shut up and eat your food. You have a big day tomorrow.'

She hoped Raven was okay.

'Stop it!' she reprimanded herself. 'Focus.'

She needed to get to the crevasse, she needed to end this chapter of her life. She really wanted to move on to the next one.

The night was cold and long, despite the summer hours and it felt much longer than it had on their previous journey. Sleep would not come as she lay shivering in her sleeping bag, curling up into a little ball in order to try and conserve some heat. She didn't remember being this cold last time. Her mind was running away with her again; what's the point? she thought, opening her eyes to the darkness of the tent. What's the point in lying awake, shivering? 'There's no point,' she whispered pushing herself up. She might as well get on with it; have some food and get going. She couldn't be sure what time it was, as she made sure she had a proper meal and a hot drink to refuel her, before she started packing up. She knew the route and it would probably be light in a couple of hours anyway. She calculated that by the time the sun rose she should have reached the hillocks on the other side of the climb. The glacier was not far from there and with any luck she would be with her parents before the end of the day.

The cold darkness had her dressing in winter gear before she pulled the technical boots, that Adam had bought for her, onto her feet. They were insulated, warm and dry, and she would probably need them soon anyway. The darkness folded around her the moment she stepped out of the tent, and she felt like she had been transported back in time. Everything around her was a sea of white, odd shapes illuminated against the blackness of the night sky. Her head tipped back, allowing sheets of her white hair to fall below the line of her bottom, as she looked up to the star-filled sky. The morning was clear, like the black waters of a deep spring, untarnished by dirt or human debris. The air was cold on her skin, the crystals stabbing at her lungs and reminding her of how much she used to love winter. She considered herself to have had a mild disagreement with winter and, at the moment, he was not her friend. He was more of an acquaintance that she tolerated but did not necessarily choose to be around. She was here because she had to be, because she had unfinished business. She would treat him with civil respect as was her duty, but she would not revel in his friendship, not at the moment. When this was over, she wanted to go away; she wanted to go to the sea that Adam kept telling her about and revisit some of those memories. She wanted to go and find some sunshine and forget about winter for a while. The crunch of the snow beneath her boots motivated her feet to move faster. She was passing through the valley on the north of the climb, the same one she had dragged Adam through on their return trip. The valley had seemed endless back then and she was preparing herself for a long haul as she kept her head down and got on with it. She could hear the sound of the waves, imagine the shape of them as they crashed against the shore. Adam had told her that there were places where you could climb on the cliffs above the crashing waves; she wanted to go there. She wanted to be suspended on the rock above the crashing of the waves and she wanted to go to other places. He had brought books up to her home, guidebooks, photo books, maps of the world. He had shown her all these wonderful places, and though she knew they existed she had never been tempted by them. She had never needed anything other than that house and these mountains, but now she did. She needed so much more. She needed him. She needed Adam and she needed to get away from here, just for a while, so that when she came back things would look new again. She could fall in love with it again, because at the moment she did not like these mountains. As much as she loved them, she loathed them. They were absolutely everything in her existence. They held her heart and ambition and had stopped her from being all she could be. She had allowed herself to be trapped by them. She had allowed them to hold her here, to retain her attention, to remain her focus for so many years. She was finally crawling from the bottom of the valley, reaching the exit point and she did not feel the need to turn back. In perfect symbolism of her thoughts Kira reached the end of the valley; the saddle opened up in front of her and she could see the hillocks, illuminated by first light, in the distance. She did not stop, she was doing well; she was fuelled by purpose and determination. She would stop just before the glacier and refocus her mind. Her stride was long and confident, her feet sinking through the snow. The hat on her head was pulled low over loose hair. There was no wind and so no need to tie it up. A small part of her wished that she could stand in front of her parents as the last time they had seen her; dressed in home-made leather leggings, soft down winter underlayers, peeled from the pelt of the beast whose meat they also ate, and a well worked, soft overlayer, like the one she wore in winter. She wanted them to be able to recognise her when she arrived, but somehow, she also felt like she needed to go as who she was today. She was no longer that fifteen-year-old girl. She had grown into a woman, she had changed, even before Adam's arrival she was a different person to the girl they had left behind. Now, she was even more different. Physically and emotionally, she was a woman, every tiny dreg of girlhood was gone, and she could only hope her parents would approve. Kira recognised the lateral moraine of the glacier, a feeling of cold fear running through her veins like liquid. She had disliked this river of ice right from the start.

Stopping at the edge of the moraine, she stared out over the vast frozen expanse as her mind remapped the route they had previously taken. She had an incredible visual memory which allowed her to pull pictures from her mind and place them into reality. She could practically see the two of them moving over the ice, retracting steps and changing direction. She was prepared for going slow, but she also knew that this ability of hers would help her move over the ice much faster than the first time. She could simply retrace their route, checking for crevasses with the snow probe as a backup. First though, she needed to refuel, refocus. Dropping her bag, she pulled out some food and despite the lack of an appetite pulled out more items than she would usually have done. She had a feeling that she was going to need it. She sat facing the glacier, going over the route in her mind until she had it memorised down to almost every step. She drank from her refilled water bottle, checking the measurements on the side to make sure that she was drinking enough, before she could put it off no longer. Pulling the draw cords tight on the bag she flipped the hood back over and clipped the buckles shut. She was not looking at the glacier as she swung the bag onto her back, the red standing out against the white of her hair.

'Okay,' she whispered, blowing out a quiet breath. 'Let's do this. You and I.' She stepped onto the ice and felt the cold power reach up through her boots, circle her ankles and shoot up her legs. 'This is the last time,' she said calmly. 'I promise. I just want to find them and then I will leave you alone. That is all I ever wanted, to find them. Please,' she pleaded. 'Please just allow me to find them and say my goodbyes. You can keep them, I won't move them, I just want to say goodbye.'

The monologue was allowing her to move over the glacier without fear. Her feet finding the familiar path as the probe slid easily through the snow, hitting the ice beneath. A song came into her head, a folksong her mother used to sing to her; the tune came first and then the words started to roll off her tongue like they belonged. It had been stored in the back of her mind, for this day. The slow rhythm of the song harmonised with the quiet of the air, the mournful tone slipping between the cracks in the ice, filling them and allowing her to walk over them unharmed. The song carried her along on a wave of distraction as the probe slid through the snow, sometimes hitting ice and sometimes slipping into air. She changed her course in accordance to its answer, each prod a question, a request of permission. The sun was climbing in the sky as she progressed onwards, slowly, glancing up every so often to map the route. She remembered the crevasse they had stepped over, now visible beneath the thin layer of snow. She did not even need to use the probe, she could see the other end and stepped over carefully. She was not far from the crevasse which she thought to be holding her parents' bodies. She would have to make sure her anchors were absolutely bombproof. They had to be one hundred percent secure because it would be her only way in and out. She did not know what lay beyond the lip of the crevasse. She did not know how deep it was, if she even had enough rope, but she had to try. Her mind ran out of lyrics as her feet came to a stop. No more than twenty metres away, she could see it; a large, long split in the ice. She recognised it immediately; she hadn't known if she would. The memory hit her in the pit of the stomach. She could see herself fighting with every fibre of her being to keep Adam from plummeting to the bottom of the crevasse, and dragging her along with him. She could feel the strain in her muscles as she gritted her teeth and fought against everything that was willing them to fail. That day, that moment, was the culmination of what she had been training for all her life, but now that was over, and she was back again. She had encountered no difficulty on this trip, no warning signs or cries of anguish from the mountain. Kira moved forward, still probing the ice despite the accurate memory of the crevasse free zone. She forced herself not to walk right up to the edge and peer into its dark depths like she wanted to. She moved to the side, a good distance away and shrugged the bag off her shoulders. She would stay calm, she would set up some anchors and she would check them several times over. Time was on her side, there was no rush this time. She purposely kept her back to the crevasse as she set up the anchors, praying for some sign from her parents. Last time their presence had been so strong, she could almost touch it, but today there was nothing. Nothing but quiet. Blue skies above, white ice below and blue glacial veins even further into the heart of the mountain. The scratch of her axe against the snow and ice was the only sound filling her ears, overwhelming her senses, keeping her focused. With two T-shaped slots dug she slid a sling around one of the axes before she dropped it into the slot, pushing it into the ice as far as it would go. She went through the motions of securing one end of the rope to the anchor before attaching a safety prussic to the rope and clipping it to her harness. She needed her other axe to cut a slot in the lip of the crevasse, for the rope to run in. She turned her attention to the crevasse before slowly starting to make her way to the edge. Taking a deep breath Kira lowered herself to the ice, and lying down on her stomach, peered over the edge. It took her mind a while to register the three-dimensional shapes of ice within the blue guts of the ice river. Her eyes scanned the walls, searching for the bottom and found a labyrinth of tunnels, shelves, platforms and deep, endless holes. She wished she had thought to bring another axe or some stakes to use as anchors. She would need her axes and crampons to move along the narrow walls. Her eyes scanned the walls again, and as the sun moved less than a degree in the sky, it caught the reflective surface of a shiny screw; blinking like fairy dust in the sky and causing Kira's heart to leap. She focused her attention on the object and soon found a line of screws leading around the corner and out of sight.

Frowning, Kira pushed away from the edge and moved further down the length of the crevasse to try and get a better view. She followed the line of screws, noticing where they disappeared beneath the ice.

'Must be an ice cave,' Kira mumbled to herself, deciding to move her anchors to allow her decent to bring her to the entrance of the cave. She could lower herself just enough to see into the cave, and then she could make a decision. She moved confidently; with accurate, measured steps and movements, digging slots, sliding slings over shafts and pushing axes into ice. She tied her knots and double checked them, she equalised the system and triple checked her knots. She checked her anchors again, checked the slings were sitting right and that gates were screwed shut on the karabiners. Then she checked her knots again. She sat back into the ice and looked at the system before pushing herself forward and checking everything again. She could find no fault, and she could no longer procrastinate; the time had come. She checked the equipment on her harness, made sure the ascenders were secure; they were her only way out. She had run out of things to do, things to check and so with one hand on the rope and the other on the descender she started walking backwards, loading the system, checking it, loading it, checking it.

She was on the edge.

Her body stilled, her eyes closed. A breeze picked at the ends of her hair and ran its cool fingers over her scalp. The earth stilled and spoke to her, the sun danced across her face. She looked like a photograph, trapped forever in this position, leaning back over the edge of the crevasse. Her eyes opened, slowly, the blue punched at the sky with an insult, making the lesser colour retreat in inferiority. She heard the whisper of her name and, with a deep breath, she started to descend into the jaws of this river of ice.

Chapter Ten

The coldness of the ice walls swallowed her whole, covering her entire body in a long shiver. She was only just over the edge and already the world above the surface had been forgotten. Every sense was overcome with this completely unique, new world. The flow of water down the mountain had frozen in its progress of least resistance.

It felt as if she had found a secret door to the innermost centre of the flow of water. The liquid having stilled for her, with the aid of freezing temperatures, creating a snapshot of the world inside a stream. She was surrounded by the most tangible world of three-dimensional shapes, and colours never before experienced by her optical nerves. The smooth flow of icy curves called out to be touched, forcing Kira's body into motionless suspension in an attempt to take it all in. She leaned forward and brushed her fingers across the wall. It felt coarse beneath her glove, unsatisfying. Pulling her hand away, she conjured a quick few loops into a simple knot, locking her descender in place, and preventing her from plummeting to the end of the rope, before pulling off her gloves. The exhalation of breath froze in the air in front of her, coating her face in tiny ice crystals. Tucking her gloves away to ensure they did not fall down the crevasse, she once again leaned forward and tried to run her fingers over the wall. It was rough, not smooth as anticipated and the dry coldness of the ice made her fingers stick to the wall. Pulling it off she winced slightly as the patch of skin, which was in contact with the ice remained to be so. A bright red drop of blood fell from her finger and carried on down the empty space beneath her. Kira wondered if the drop would be frozen by the time it reached the bottom of the crevasse. The injured finger had found its way to her mouth and as she lifted her eyes first up to the descender in front of her and then up to the blue sky far above, she pulled it from between her lips and shoved her gloves back on. A long deep breath blew through the crevasse like a breeze as she undid the knot and allowed herself to descend further down the gaping hole. Every metre of descent brought her closer to the heart of the mountain, the guts of the earth, but further away from the safety of the surface. She glanced up only to see the edge move further and further away as the sound of cracking, popping and squeaking surrounded her. Her eyes moved around this foreign world, taking in curves, lines, cracks, stalactites of ice, all the while trying to connect the sound to the movement. This glacier was by no means dormant and unmoving, she could hear the faint bubble of water on the far side of the thick ice walls, lubricating the heavy frozen river and allowing it to move down the mountain. The friction between rock and ice created heat which melted a layer of water which acted as lubricant. A loud crack, quickly followed by a pop had Kira's head turning just in time to see a huge chunk of ice fall from the roof of the crevasse and tumble through the air, bouncing off the walls until it could no longer be heard. She had no way of knowing how deep this crevasse was, she only knew that she did not want to test it. The air settled as the noise dissipated, along with the rapid beating of her heart. Kira tilted her head down and looked to the line of screws. The roof beneath which they disappeared was just that, a roof and not a very deep one. It was no more than a couple of metres, just enough to have been able to fool Kira. She realised that she was going to have to descend a lot deeper into the crevasse in order to find the starting point of the ice screws, and with it, hopefully her parents.

'Right,' she whispered to herself, glancing to the lip of the crevasse and wondering how far off Adam was.

'Come on Kira, move.'

Fixing her eyes on the descender, she once more allowed the rope to run through the device and slowly lower her deeper into the quiet cold. She hadn't allowed herself to think of what she would do once she found her parents. She knew she wouldn't be able to get them out and she didn't want to. What would she do with their bodies on the surface? They would want to remain here, as part of the mountain. The slant of the roof finally changed and, looking up, Kira reckoned she must be at least thirty metres from the top. Her eyes turned back to the roof as it deepened and slanted away from her at a sharp angle. A few metres lower she should be able to see into it, fingers crossed. Her heart rate increased with every moment's worth of thought of what she might find, until it was hammering loudly against her chest, filling her ears and drowning out the alarming cracking of ice. She couldn't bear to think of them in obvious pain, the anguish frozen on their faces or bodies for all eternity. Holding her breath, she lowered herself another few metres until, finally, the roof opened up into a deep corridor.

She stopped suddenly, frozen, her heart skipped a beat and for a moment it did not feel as if it would restart. Then her eyes found the screws, like a modern-day version of Hansel and Gretel's breadcrumbs, leading her to her parents. There was a shelf, about a metre away and two metres down from the roof, she could practically see her father looking out of the cave, trying to see a way out. She could feel him turning the screw in the ice, hear the sound of ice being carved away and see the gate click shut on the quickdraw. Shaking her head to clear it of the vision she looked back down at the shelf, wondering how she was going to get to it. She could take a swing, she might just make it, if her anchors held and her crampons got purchase. She frowned for a moment, remembering what Adam's crampons had so kindly done to his leg upon digging into ice. Kira looked around her again, looking for anything that could help her out, allow her to reach the shelf safely. The nearest screw was probably reachable if she leaned over as far as she could and push off the ice. Maybe, just maybe she could get a quickdraw in and guide her rope closer to the roof. Her fingers were already going over the kit clipped to the loops on her harness; she had a few quickdraws, some slings, screw gate karabiners and two prussics along with the ascenders.

'Okay,' she whispered to herself looking at the screw and then the quickdraw in her hand. The last thing she wanted was to be losing any kit to this monster, she could not afford to risk dropping the quickdraw or even leaving hold of it. She needed to remain attached to as many anchors as she could.

'Okay.' Her voice was quiet, calm. Her eyes bright, like the ice itself, and focussed as she unclipped a sling, unravelled it and clipped it to the belay loop on her harness, before clipping the quickdraw on the other end. She blew out a quiet breath, forcing herself to focus, her eyes drifting to the clear blue sky above, watering as she blinked against the bright light. The quickdraw was now secured to her harness, which would stop it from falling to the ground if she dropped it, but also immediately securing her to the screw if she got it clipped.

'Come on Kira.' She took a deep breath, focussing her cool blue eyes on the screw before starting to move. Slow and controlled she leaned over, tensing the muscles in her core and digging her crampons into the wall of ice, carefully finding her centre of gravity as she reached out towards the ice screw. 'Come on,' she whispered, her body at an exaggerated angle, a tense straight line, reaching out, inches away from the screw. She moved her fingers lower down, to the bottom of the karabiner as her body stretched out even further. Her muscles elongated, stretched to their limit, white hair tumbling down at a right angle with her body, reaching for the bottom of the crevasse. Her muscles were trembling with the effort as she tried to inch forward.

'Come on, come on,' she whispered, it was just out of reach. She froze in her position, looking at the screw. Focussing her mind on the attachment point, she was only about an inch off, she only needed a small push and a hundred percent focus. She could do it.

'Okay,' she breathed, looking at the ring, her eyes focussed, visualising the attachment point grow in front of her eyes.

Focus.

The world around her disappeared as every ounce of her

energy focussed on this one small ice screw and the karabiner in her hand. She did not want to clip it and then swing back, she wanted the load on her anchors to remain as static as possible. So not only did she have to clip the karabiner through the hole, but she also had to then grab the quickdraw to stop herself from swinging out, and risking her anchors moving.

Everything was quiet. The only sound was her own breath in her ears, it was like hunting; you had to be patient, wait for just the right moment, and then, when the time was right, and there was no way you could miss...

Move.

It was a short dynamic move, her muscles contracted and released sending her forward, her eyes remaining on the screw as she moved forward in slow motion. The karabiner slipped past the attachment point on the screw only to reach the point at which gravity took over and started to slip back to its point of origin. Kira remained focused and watched the sharp end of the open karabiner slip through the hole on the ice screw. The gate clipped shut and her fingers folded around the webbing of the quickdraw. There was a slight jerk as time snapped back into place, a breath of relief escaping her lips. She moved quickly, not wanting to tempt fate, and slipped the rope through the second karabiner on the other end of the quickdraw.

Good girl.

She looked up sharply as the sound reached her ears, trying to see where it had come from. The sky was still clear and blue, the edge of the crevasse devoid of human life. Lowering her eyes, she looked into the cave. She could not see the end of it despite the light bouncing off the light-coloured walls and illuminating the corridor. Her eyes found the second screw. If she could clip into that one, she would be able to descend safely to the shelf, without risking injury or death.

She lowered herself just beyond the next screw, allowing enough slack in the rope for the sideways travel before locking her descending device off again. She went through the process of finding another quickdraw, clipping it to the sling still attached to her harness and then focusing her eyes on the screw. It seemed closer than the previous one and with any luck she would reach it.

'Okay,' she breathed, digging the sharp teeth of her crampons into the wall of ice again before slowly starting to tilt her body. Her muscles contracted, released, stabilised as she found her point of balance. Her breathing was slow, calm and rhythmic as every fibre of her being focused on this process. Leaning over further, she could feel a slight scrape beneath her feet.

Shit.

She would have to be quick, she was slipping. 'Come on Ki.'

It was not until after the quickdraw was clipped, and the rope fed through it, that her own words reached her ears.

She half smiled to herself, leaning back the other way to look to the edge of the crevasse. Surely, he could not be far off? He must be close, she could feel him in her head, egging her on, telling her to stay strong to keep going, to never give up, just like her dad always had. He was the only person who had ever called her Ki, ever, and she liked it. The edge of the crevasse remained clear, empty of any sign of human presence and she had to force herself to look away. She had come here for a reason, and she was not going to stop until she had found them. Fixing her eyes on the shelf she carefully lowered herself down until she could reach over with one leg and pull herself onto the ice. She stepped onto it, carefully, testing its strength despite the metres of frozen water below it, she did not remove her rope. She had more than enough length to remain safe and attached. If anything happened, she wanted to know that she was still attached to the surface via this stretch of nylon and webbing. She had left her bag up top, having only stuffed a couple of snacks and a head-torch in her pockets. She didn't know how long she would be down here, but she didn't want to stay for too long. The crevasse had come to life once more as it moved around her, moaning as she glanced over her shoulder every couple of steps. She was fighting a nervous energy as she moved deeper down the corridor of the ice cave, feeding the rope out as she progressed, her eyes everywhere. Her heart was hammering in her chest, her breath was no longer calm, her muscles ached from the tension in them, her stomach complained violently of the stress she was heaping upon it. The tunnel grew narrow, the walls started to close in on her. She could feel the cold creeping closer, trying to touch the material of her clothing, trying to reach beneath and coat her skin with a thin layer of ice. Her head swung round, suddenly, quickly, as an overwhelming urge to run overcame her. Her hair was still moving at the motion it had carried through as her eyes widened in fear, her heart jumping into her chest.

Kira.

Her heart stopped. The panic left her eyes as she closed her eyes and listened.

Keep moving, you can do it child.

'Okay.' She took a breath, stilling her racing heart.

Focus. Move.

She moved forward and within two more steps she could see the end of the cave. The light had been swallowed by the ice and in the shadows, she could see the outline of one big lump. She had to lick her lips to stop her mouth from running dry and with her eyes on the lump she dug out her head-torch, securing it to her head before closing her eyes and flicking the switch on the light.

She stood with her eyes closed, knowing that when she opened them, she would have completed her task. She knew they were there. Slowly, with her heart hammering loudly in her ears, she allowed her eyes to open as the shape of their familiar forms came into view, inch by precious inch.

The emotion was instantaneous. Knocking her backwards and taking her feet from beneath her. Her hand flew up to her mouth as her knees gave way and she plummeted to the icy ground, tears pouring from her eyes.

There was nothing she could do to stop them.

After eleven years she had finally found her parents.

She could not find her feet, she could not move towards them. She was no more than two metres away from them, and yet they were so, so far away. The permanent sub-zero temperatures had infiltrated their flesh, freezing the molecules of flesh and blood and keeping them preserved. They looked exactly as they had eleven years ago, but for the lack of colour on their skin and the film of ice around their bodies. The glacier was keeping them to herself, that much she knew. Her tears ran silently from her eyes, like a leaking tap as she inched forward, the ache in her heart almost unbearable. Despite years of knowing that they were gone, it was hard to believe that they were actually dead. Nothing could have prepared her for this moment. Her father's arms were wrapped around the smaller body, her mother's head resting on his generous chest. Her eyes were closed and so were his. They looked at peace. She could see no signs of injury from this distance, but she knew for them to not have been able to make it out, there had to be. She was reluctant to investigate, unwilling to allow herself an opportunity to ponder their pain. They had not made it out and that was all that mattered in the end. The reasons behind it made no difference to the truth of the facts.

Inching forwards her arms stretched out towards them, she wanted to touch them but…

Tears filled her blue eyes as she looked at them, her hands stopping short from making contact. She did not want to cause any damage, she wanted them to remain like this, forever. The ice would preserve them for a long time to come. They looked, just as they always had, clothed in their own home-made garments, as she had been for most of her life. She felt different as she sat, kneeling in front of them in her modern clothing. She found that with the high wicking, light modern clothing Adam had introduced her to she could wear less of it and be just as warm as with her own clothing. It was less bulky and increased her agility and movement. She felt, just for a moment, like a fraud, like she had betrayed them. They were not talking to her, like they had before; it was ominously quiet in the cold cavern. The only sound was the popping and cracking of ice over the huff of her own breath.

'I'm sorry,' she whispered as tears spilled over her lids.

'I'm so sorry. I tried to find you…' Her head dropped as a sob caught in her throat and she shook her head, slowly.

'I miss you so much.'

She didn't know what to say or do, it was as if she was frozen in time with them. She could not move from her kneeling position in front of them. She was only mildly aware of the cold pressing through her knees, and all she could feel was the warmth of their presence surrounding her. Her heart was filled with a longing ache, unlike anything she had ever experienced, she was unaware of the ice cracking behind her, the noise rumbling down the corridor as blocks broke free from the roof of the cave and crashed onto the shelf. The world around her disappeared as she sat motionless, just as her father had taught her. The tears were turning to ice on her cheeks as they lessened, the blue of her eyes having taken on the colour of the crevasse walls. She sat staring at them, unable to move, unable to make herself leave. She was alone in this world.

Time was slipping away as the cold started to pull at her flesh, causing her muscles to shake in an attempt to warm her body. She was oblivious to the way her hair was turning into icy clumps against her back, looking more like the ice beneath her knees with every passing minute. The shivers turned into violent shaking and still she did not move, she couldn't. Her stomach churned with the thought of leaving them behind. Her inner strength, perseverance, tenacity, resilience and determination had a limit after all. She did not hear her father's whispers. She could not focus, she could not move.

***

Jones's eyes drifted over the tense form of Adam's body ahead. They had done this before, tens of times, they had walked at a distance, tied together checking for crevasses, yet he had never seen Adam so tense, so distracted. He was pushing the snow probe in one spot and then stepping on another, he knew Adam had been here before but that was no excuse for this lack of focus.

'Adam!' His voice carried easily across the distance between them, there was no way that the sound had not reached his ears, but still he pressed on. Probe one place, feet in another.

'Fuck's sake,' Jones mumbled under his breath. 'Adam!'

The man did not respond. Jones grabbed the rope with his gloved hand and yanked hard, watching Adam jerk backwards and quickly fall on his axe.

His head was down, he was waiting for the rest of his friend's weight on the rope and when it didn't come, he lifted his face out of the snow to see Jones a couple of metres away, closing the distance between them.

'What the...'

Adam pushed himself off the ground and faced the man's grey eyes.

'My turn.' Jones grabbed the probe out of his hands and took the lead.

'No, I know the way better, we'll get there faster,' Adam protested. His mind was so full of Kira. The vast expanse of ice stretched out in front of them, they were not far off, he should be able to see some sign of her.

'We'll end up at the bottom of a crevasse sooner all right.' Jones faced him. 'You are not concentrating. You have to remain focussed.'

Adam ran a hand through his hair. 'You're right, I'm sorry.'

Jones nodded. 'Come on.'

'Hold on.' Adam was staring in the direction of the crevasse, he was sure he could hear the low rumble of ice tumbling down steep slopes. His heart lurched, making him feel sick.

'Did you hear that?'

'Hear what?'

Adam was staring to where the sound had come from.

'Is it that way?'

Adam nodded. 'We should be able to see her, it's not far away.'

'Well, you did reckon she was at least half a day ahead of us, that might mean that she is already down the crevasse.'

Bile rose in his throat at the thought and he quickly swallowed past it and focused his eyes on the distance.

'I think it was crevasse free from here,' he said, 'but you go ahead, let's try and remain in control.'

Jones nodded, he did not like the way Adam had swayed unsteadily on his feet. 'How's your leg?' he asked starting to move on.

It was hurting, he was plagued by a constant dull ache which was doing its absolute best to drive him insane. 'It's all right.' He raised his voice so that Jones could hear his answer in the growing distance. He took some willow bark from one of his pockets and put it in his mouth. It would have to do for now. He didn't think he was going to stop for a brew for a while. Best case scenario, they found her at the top of the crevasse. Regardless of what had passed before that was by

306

far the best option for him. Worst case…

Well, he didn't really want to think about that. It seemed to take a very long time to cross the empty white space between them and the crevasse. Jones had stopped and was staring at something on the ground. His eyes were running from a point just above him all the way down to the edge of the crevasse.

Adam rushed up to his side in fast confident strides, feeling his stomach sink all the way into his shoes. 'Do you recognise the rope?' Jones' words filled the space between them.

Adam nodded, swallowing past the lump in his throat. 'It's mine. I left it at home.'

Jones looked up into Adam's eyes, reading the destination he described as home, not as his uncle's house.

'I'll set up another system, next to it.' Jones shrugged the bag off his shoulders. 'Why don't you use her line as a safety and move to the edge to see if you can spot her.'

Adam nodded, he was already unravelling a prussic and twisting it around the rope, it was not loaded and he had no idea how to feel about that. If it was loaded it would mean that she was definitely at the end of it, in what state he could not hazard a guess, but at least he knew she was there. The unloaded rope could mean that she had somehow come off it, the rope got cut or she abseiled off the end… but she was not that stupid. It probably meant that she got down to a place where she could safely move around without the assistance of the rope. He moved to the edge, visibly swallowing at the fear in his throat.

'Kira!' he shouted down the crevasse before he even reached the edge. No reply. Sinking to his knees, he lowered himself to his belly, and peered over the edge just as she had done. 'Kira!' Her rope went straight down and then disappeared below a sloping roof. He could not see her or hear her, but he could hear the cracking of the ice.

'Shit.'

He pushed himself up and quickly moved away. 'I can't see her.' All the colour had drained from his face, he felt dizzy and for a moment he had to sit down to remain in control of his legs. He felt sick, like he had when he found out that she had gone. He could not imagine his life without her. He didn't know what he would do if he lost her.

'I'll go down,' Jones said checking the knots in his system.

'No.' Adam's head shot up. 'I'll do it. I can hear the ice moving, it wasn't like that before.' His head moved to the gash in the vein of the mountain. 'I don't think it's stable.'

Jones's hands stilled in its preparation as his eyes found Adam's. 'Should we be going down there at all?'

'No,' Adam said without hesitation, 'but there is nothing you can do to stop me.' His eyes were fixed on the place where her rope disappeared over the edge. 'There is no way I am going home without her.'

'Fucking hell mate.' It wasn't a reprimand or an exclamation of insanity. It was a quiet awe at the power of this woman. Jones felt much the same, though he knew Adam loved her more than he could pretend he had ever loved anybody.

'All right.' He shook his head. 'You check this set up and I'll check it again when you are done. I'll remain up top and you can give me a shout if you need anything.'

Adam nodded and moved towards the rigging as Jones

moved over to Kira's. Kira's was a very good set-up. Solid, tidy. He could see every loop of every knot, it was done with care and precision. The Y-hang was perfectly equalised, spreading the load between the two anchors. Some movement had slipped her slings slightly out of place and he moved to push the axes back into the snow and re-align the slings. The rope was frozen beneath his fingers and he had to wonder how long she had been down there. He didn't like to think what he would do if Adam found her in a less than satisfactory state. His eyes lifted to find his friend's back, he was adjusting something on the rigging. Jones blew a breath out of his cheeks, he was just going to have to be prepared for anything.

'All right?'

Adam nodded. 'I just tidied the knots.' He turned his attention to his own harness, retrieving the kit he would need. 'You check it again.'

Jones smiled, his knots now resembled Kira's a lot more, and he wondered if it was Adam that had taught her or Kira that had taught Adam.

'It's sound.'

Adam nodded, as he attached his descender to the rope. 'I don't think it's a bad idea to get in touch with the town,' Adam said against his own will. There was a gnawing feeling in his gut, warning him that they were going to need support. Jones nodded as Adam walked backwards and, without a pause, leaned back descending into the very crevasse that Kira had hauled him out of all those months ago.

The sound of cracking ice overwhelmed him as it echoed off the walls of the crevasse making his stomach pull into a tight knot. 'Kira!'

He did not go slowly as she had, he did not have to look and search. He had no time to appreciate the colours, shapes and sounds. The ice was moving, it was cracking and popping. He was very aware that not only could big blocks of it fall off, but the entire crevasse could close down with them in it.

'Kira!' There was no answer, no sound other than the warning of the ice. 'Dammit,' he whispered angrily, feeling the emotion build up and threaten to spill over the edge. He tried to stay as close to her rope as he could, oblivious to the temperature drop or the eerie atmosphere inside the crevasse. He had only one thing on his mind and he had to get to it before it was too late.

'Fuck.' He stopped where her rope diverted beneath the roof of the cave.

'Clever girl.' He smiled at the way her rope was attached to the ice screws and wondered just for a moment how she had reached it, before realising he was going to have to do the same. He moved further down before locking his descender off in the same way that Kira had. He reached for the rope pulling on it to bring himself closer to the ice screw...

Kira felt herself being yanked backwards. At first it was a small tug as Adam tested the tension on the rope, and then a violent pull yanked her off her knees sending her flying backwards and slamming into a block of ice that had fallen from the roof. She sat still, her breath rasping out of her raggedly. She had no energy to move. The tension relented as he grabbed hold of the quickdraw and placed his own to hold his rope in the same position. She felt another sharp tug making her catch her breath and briefly pulling her out of her trance before that too relented. She had no idea what was going on. Her brain was not working the way it should, she didn't even know where she was or why she was there anymore. Her eyes found her parents' frozen forms and she wished she could find the energy to crawl over to them and fall asleep in their arms. Just one more time. She wanted to fall asleep in their arms one last time.

Pulling himself beneath the roof Adam felt a sudden punch in the gut as a big block of ice fell from the roof to join its predecessors already starting to block the passageway. Kira's rope was running through the blockage.

'Ki!' he shouted in frustration, fumbling with his kit. 'Shit, shit, shit.' He could feel the fear building up inside of him. 'Oh, please God, don't let her be beneath it.'

A moment of clarity had him moving to the edge of the shelf and tilting his head to the opening of the crevasse.

'JONES!' He summoned every ounce of strength to compose himself and waited for the answer of his friend's voice. 'GET A HELICOPTER UP HERE!' He didn't care how he was going to do it, but he just knew it needed to be done.

'Fuck.' Jones moved back from the edge and ran for the satellite phone. He had no idea what was going on, but the desperation in Adam's voice had cut through him like a samurai sword.

'Kira! Answer me dammit!' Adam was stumbling through the blockage hoping to find her rope on the other side. 'Please God, please,' he pleaded. The ice was so cold, his clothes were sticking to it as he scrambled over the broken pieces, the light was fading fast on the other side of the partial blockage and he stuck his hand in a pocket to find his head torch.

'Ki!' His voice echoed off the sides of the corridor, trembling with fear. He didn't know what he was going to do if he couldn't find her. 'Ki!' His light finally fixed on his head it flicked on, illuminating the corridor and her rope travelling down it.

'Thank fuck,' he whispered running down the corridor only to find more blocks of ice obstructing the path. He ran around them until his eyes fell on the two figures at the end of the corridor. His body took over before his mind could do a double take; his stomach convulsed as tears filled his eyes and everything still held within his stomach poured out in violent spasms. Kira was hardly aware of his presence. Her brain was all but switched off.

'Oh God, oh God.' Adam pushed himself away from the sick and stumbled closer to the bodies. It couldn't be her, but God it looked just like her. She was the absolute spitting image. It took him another moment before reason kicked in; this had to be her parents, there was no doubt in his mind. There was no way it could be Kira, despite the shocking resemblance, so where was she?

'Ki!' He spun round and found his vision punching him in the gut as his brain registered the body against the shard of ice.

'Ki.' He ran towards her falling to his knees and putting his hands immediately to her face. She was so cold, her skin was like ice, her lips were blue. 'Oh God, no. Kira!' He lifted her eyes to his, they were the same colour as the walls around them. 'Kira, can you hear me? Look at me.'

There was no response and his eyes travelled over her body for signs of injury. Shards of ice were stuck to her knees and looking back he saw the place where she had been pulled from.

'Oh God, sorry.' He leaned forward and pressed his lips to her head. 'I'm so sorry Ki,' he whispered realising that it was him who had pulled her from the spot, he had been using her as an anchor and the guilt overwhelmed him.

'Ki,' he said again urgently, she needed to respond, he could not lose her, his world was collapsing in front of his very eyes. 'Kira, you've got to fight this.' His whisper was urgent, his hands warm against her cold skin. 'Kira please you have to focus, you have to concentrate,' he urged her, he wasn't going to give up. He was not going to lose her to this mountain. She had gotten him out of here, so he had to do the same. 'We have to get you out of here.'

A word penetrated her senses as she lifted her eyes to his and he saw the flash of recognition through her eyes, a spark of life.

'Okay,' he whispered with relief, running his hands down the side of her face. 'Let's get you out of here.' He stood up and gently pulled her away from her icy seat, she offered no resistance as he slid his arms beneath her and lifted her from the ground. His heart was in his mouth with every step, but every step closer to the entrance was a step closer to getting her out and warmed up. He paid attention to where he was stepping, careful not to tread on their ropes with his crampons. He couldn't adjust the slack on either of their ropes with his hands occupied, but the shelf had felt pretty stable and he just had to hope for the best. If the worst came to the worst and the shelf collapsed, they were still attached. It would be an almighty drop and jerk, but they would not plummet to their deaths. He was going to have to stop to untangle her rope from the first blockage. His only options would be to untie the rope from Kira's harness and pull it through the blockage, hoping that it wouldn't put up too much of a fight, he could adjust the slack then.

Her hair was like shards of ice trapped between his arm and her body. He could feel the sharp edges dig through his clothing and had to stop himself from wondering how long she had been down here, alone.

Why hadn't she moved? His eyes glanced down to her colourless skin and blue lips, as her head rested against his chest, her eyes closed.

'Ki,' he whispered giving her a jiggle. 'Ki, you've got to try and stay awake,' he pleaded as her eyes opened. 'Keep your eyes open. Fight it, I know you can.'

She didn't appear to be injured, so why had she not walked out when the roof started collapsing. He heard another loud crack and increased his pace, reaching the blockage and carrying her through to the other side before lowering her to the ground. He felt sick, but at least she moved when he put her down. She was not like a brainless ragdoll. It didn't take him long to attach a sling between the two of them, securing her to him whilst he found himself having to cut the end of the rope to free it from her harness and pull the loose end through the obstacle. He was surprised at how easily it slipped through and hastily tied another knot back into her harness. The rope was stiff with the cold, making the tying of the knot very difficult. He made short work of the rest of the cave and finally stopped at the edge, putting her down on the ground before shouting up to Jones.

Kira had finally reached the limit of her reserves. All her life she had been training, pushing herself, stretching her abilities. All her life she was testing the boundaries, pushing for that point where she could no longer push. All her life, she had not reached that limit. She had come close on their first journey. It had taken everything she had to keep moving and get her and Adam out of there, but in the end, even as she gave up and collapsed into Harvey's arms, she still had something left in the tank. Today, now, here, she had reached her limit. She physically, and mentally, had nothing left to give, she was at the complete mercy of others. She had no strength to focus, to move. All she had was a cold empty loss. She felt her heart aching at the distance between her and her parents, aware of leaving them behind once more. Her mind was fighting hard against sleep, everything inside of her screamed for her to give up, to just close her eyes and go to sleep. She could do that, she could go to sleep and all the pain, all the heartache would disappear. She would be with them once more, but something was stopping her. She felt hands tug at her harness, she felt herself being lifted from the ground, she felt fingers brush away the tears on her cheeks and warm lips on her cold forehead. She was not aware of the ice cave collapsing behind them. She did not feel the rumble of the mountain as it swallowed her parents' bodies, hiding them from the world for as long as it pleased. She could just hear the whispers, but she could no longer tell if it was coming from inside of her or from out there, somewhere.

Keep fighting.

Stay strong.

'Come on Ki,' Adam pleaded as they travelled up the crevasse. 'Stay awake!' Her eyes shot open and after a moment found his. 'Fight it!' he shouted. 'You are better than this, you are stronger.'

She forced her eyes to stay open, tried to imagine the blood flowing through her body, warming her. She had never felt so indifferent, so numb. She was not cold, nor hot, but the look on Adam's face told her that something was wrong. She had been in that cave for a long time. She had been in there since the morning and moving up the crevasse the light outside barely registered on her optical nerves.

Adam and Jones were both working incredibly hard to haul the cold motionless body out of the crevasse. Jones's heart was beating fast from the exertion but by the look on Adam's face it was nothing compared to the painful racing of his friend's as he hauled the woman he loved over the edge of the crevasse. Jones rushed forward, feeling a stab of pain at the motionlessness of the woman. He grabbed her by the shoulders and pulled her clear of the edge. He had never seen her look like this. He never thought she could be anything less than strong and powerful. Her extraordinary beauty still stood out against the paleness of her skin and the blue of her lips, but there was a dull glaze over her eyes which seemed to pale with every passing second.

Adam's eyes lifted to the sky, the sun was slanting toward the west. 'Have you got a helicopter?' Adam was rushing towards them and the men both started pulling kit from their bags. They needed to get her warm and they needed to do it fast.

Jones nodded. 'It was scrambled but it will be a couple of hours at the very least.'

A powerful roar of frustration and anguish exploded from Adam's throat and echoed off the wall of the mountains around them. 'Fuck's sake!' His eyes went to the sky again as he breathed a quiet, pleading prayer.

He wiped angrily at the tears on his cheeks as he piled as much insulation on the ground as he could before starting to undo her harness. 'Get the stove going Jones.' Adam barked. 'Get some hot water on.'

'Kira,' he said loudly tugging at her harness. 'Kira, listen to me.' He leaned forward as he worked on the gear. 'You are not going to give up. You are going to fight. You are going to go to that place inside of you where I know you have more. You are more than this. You have more than this.' He paused, dropping his head onto her chest in a moment of despair; it would be dark by the time the helicopter got to them. Everything always felt worse in the dark.

'Please,' he whispered. 'Please Ki, you have to fight. You cannot give up.'

'We'll get a shelter around you guys,' Jones said calmly. 'Keep the heat in.'

Adam nodded as he removed his own gear before quickly pulling out her sleeping bag from her bag and zipping it to his, like he had done before. He pulled a foil blanket from his bag and opened it, lying it inside the sleeping bag before starting to peel her clothes off. The only chance she had was body heat. Nothing else was going to help right now. It wasn't long before they were inside the sleeping bags, the foil blanket covering her cold skin and his chest pressed up against her ice-cold back. His breath caught in his throat as his body jumped away from the cold. A quiet expletive escaped from his lips before he closed his eyes and pressed closer, folding his arms around her and pulling her into the fold of his body. The pose was familiar to him and feeling a slight flutter of her fingers he could do nothing but pray for the heat to seep out of him and into her.

There was nothing he needed more in this life than for her to live. They filled the sleeping bags with hot water bottles and after a while Jones crept into the shelter to add his heat to the cocoon. He sat quietly on the edge of the shelter as Adam held Kira in his arms, begging her to warm up. They did everything they could. They tried to get warm liquid inside of her and put energy gels into her mouth. It seemed like forever before the whooping sound of helicopter blades could be heard outside of the shelter. Jones's head shot up at the sound and moments later he was scrambling out of the shelter. He had cleared a perimeter of crevasses earlier and when it started to get dark had laid out lights ready to be activated. He rushed about getting the guiding lights on and wondered how long they had been waiting as he guided the helicopter to a safe landing. He had called in with a situation update and they were well prepped for Kira's transportation. The medics filed out of the helicopter as if they've been doing it all their lives. Jones filled them in on the situation and put himself at their disposal as they nodded acknowledgement and confirmed their plan. A blur of activity followed in the powerful draft of the helicopter which could not be switched off in case it did not start again. The pilot was none but the very best of high-altitude helicopter pilots and his face was set in concentration as he focused on keeping the craft hovering. He had taken off almost as soon as they had landed, fearing that the landing gear might get frozen to the glacier. Jones was finding it difficult to tell what was going on what with the noise and bustle of movement, but the helicopter crew seemed to have it well in hand. He was hustled into the helicopter after the stretcher and Adam, wrapped in a blanket. All their bags had been loaded and before he knew it, they were carefully retreating from the glacier.

The medics were working on Kira, getting warm liquid directly into her body via an IV, injecting her with he didn't even want to know what, and the other crew on board was coaxing Adam back into his clothes and the story from Jones.

Adam looked like he'd aged ten years in two hours. His face was pale and drawn, pain evident in the lines on his face. His head was in his hands for the best part of the journey as silent sobs tore through his body, he couldn't get near her as the medics worked, keeping careful track of her vitals. She was beyond hypothermic. He knew the stories of children making miraculous recoveries after falling into frozen lakes and could only hope that Kira would be the same. She was no child, she was the strongest person he knew and she would not give in to the fight. She would battle until the very last moment, until she physically could not anymore. Adam did not so much as look at anybody other than Kira as they finally reached the hospital and she was rushed through into an emergency room. Adam and Jones had done absolutely everything they could. Their experience in these kinds of situations, had aided in their quick judgement, and their fast acting had probably saved her life. She was not out of the woods yet, the doctors had said, not by any means, but they could satisfy themselves with the fact that they had done everything they possibly could have, to help her recovery. They had stopped the plummeting temperatures of her body and started the incremental increasing of it by their actions. Adam had refused to leave her side. He felt sick to the stomach at the thought of her not waking up, he didn't think he would ever see her in such a position. She was empty, completely and utterly drained. She had been exhausted after their first journey, but this was beyond even that. She had sat too still for too long and the cold had taken hold of her heart, dragging her into its claws of submission. She had been rushed away from him, leaving him standing alone in the corridor, feeling lost and empty. They hadn't even told him what they were going to do, and it was hours before he saw her again.

'Ki,' he whispered leaning close and stroking the hair away from her face. 'Ki, please don't leave me.' He pressed his lips against her forehead, pleased to feel a difference in temperature. 'Keep fighting Ki, please, keep fighting.'

***

'What is going on?' Raven was beside herself, her heart was racing with fear and anticipation. 'Please, Daddy, just tell me what is happening.'

'Raven, calm down.'

He could see the panic in her eyes, the veins stood out like blue snakes against her ever-paling skin. She had not been well, the past three days had felt like an eternity as the healthy glow of summer started to disappear, and the weak child of winter started to return. The burden of knowing what was going to happen had weighed heavily on her young shoulders, and the ignorance of specific details hammered against her heart doing its very best to weaken her.

'Sweetheart, please?' Her dad kneeled in front of her and rested his hands on her shoulders. 'You have to try and calm down.'

Raven shook him off, the wild panic returning to her eyes as her heart raced ever faster, the sweat was glistening on her brow and she swayed slightly, unsteady on her feet as the oxygen struggled to reach her brain. 'I'm trying,' she said, 'but I don't know what happened, I can't see what happened.'

Her panic had started as a seed of concern, days ago when she first felt like something was wrong. It had steadily grown into panic upon discovery of what Kira was actually planning on doing, and then the blind summit of panic was reached when she knew for certain that she was gone. She knew that Adam would find Kira, but she couldn't see the rest. She had heard the helicopter, she had seen the concern in her parents' eyes. She had rushed outside to hear the apprehension and worry in the townsfolks' words. She saw the pain in Harvey's eyes and the worry in the slope of his shoulders. Sally, that friend of Adam's, was walking around ordering people about. Raven had run out to ask her what was going on, but had been brushed aside and told to go home. Somebody had picked her up and carried her home, depositing her into her father's arms and she had been like this ever since. Raven suddenly stopped in the panic and tilted her ear to the window. He had seen her do this many times, she was listening, to the wind or the birds or something.

She was always listening. She turned her eyes on her dad and with a sudden calmness she opened her mouth.

'Is she dead?'

He felt his stomach drop at the words. He really had no idea, but Raven seemed to have a gift for knowing these things and the mere fact that she had spoken the words send a ripple of fear through him. Kira had done so much for her, for them, for the family and the town. Losing her would be a great loss to the town and he didn't even want to begin to think what it would mean for Raven.

'I don't know,' he said seriously pulling her closer again, seeing the pain in her eyes. 'We haven't heard anything, and as far as I'm concerned; no news is good news.'

He felt her sway and caught her as her knees gave way. Her eyes were rolling into the back of her head. 'Raven!' he said trying to stop her from disappearing into that world. 'Raven look at me.'

She fought hard.

She thought about Kira, about everything she had taught her. She thought about being strong, about never giving up and she fought against the powers that were trying to push her under.

'Raven you are stronger than this,' he said when her eyes met his. 'We were wrong, your mother and I. We thought you were weak, but you are not, you are strong. You have to fight this. Kira would want you to.'

'Daddy, I don't want to die.' Tears were pouring down her face. 'I don't know if I can live without her.' Raven still thought that her and Kira's lives were connected. That Kira was providing her with the magic that she needed to make her heart strong.

'You are not going to,' he said with tears in his own eyes. 'Neither of you. You know how strong she is, she will fight just as she would want you to. Now, you have to calm down. I will take you to see her tomorrow.'

Raven nodded and allowed her father to lead her to a chair where he wrapped her in a blanket before moving to make her a hot drink. She sat quietly, staring unseeingly into the distance. She could hear nothing, the wind was still, there was no clouds to read, no flames to dance a scene in front of her eyes, she was completely blind to Kira's state and she did not like it. She had nothing to go by but the feeling in her heart. It was still beating and that must mean that Kira's was as well.

'Daddy, I think she is okay.'

Her mind reached out, searching across the vast expanse of distance separating them. Her hands were folded around the warm mug, her nostrils filling with the scent of hot chocolate. Kira loved hot chocolate.

She said it was her weakness, that and sticky buns. Raven smiled, she thought Adam was Kira's weakness and her strength, and she was his. A shiver ran down her spine and was quickly followed by a sense of warm liquid. She could practically feel it washing through her in exactly the same way it was flowing through Kira's veins as she lay motionless in the hospital bed, her eyes closed. Her lids were hiding the blue emotion, depriving Adam of the opportunity to read her innermost thoughts and desires. He could tell by looking into her eyes what she was thinking and how she was feeling, sometimes even before she could. He wanted to peel her lids back and look for the strength he knew was hidden inside of her. The monitor above her bed was showing her vital signs and he could not stop his eyes from wandering up every few seconds to see if the temperature had increased. He felt sick every time he looked at the machine beside her bed. Her body was covered in heating pads that were individually controlled but it was the memory of what had passed before the pads that had his stomach churning. They had struggled to find a pulse on her in the helicopter, the medics were doing CPR as she was rushed into a special room. The doctors had already made a decision based on the information received from the helicopter that they were going to drain the blood from her body, heat it externally and then pump it back into her. The thought horrified him, but she was taken away without so much as a cursory glance in his direction and returned hours later in the state she was in now. The procedure had taken the edge off the cold but there was still work to be done. She was out of danger but the doctors reminded him that it had taken more than an hour for her temperature to plummet and would certainly take longer to climb back to normal. He had to be patient. He had to wait and allow her body to gradually re-heat. This was not like when they had jumped into the glacial pond and she could not stop shivering for hours, nor was it like when she had fallen through the ice and could not control the violent convulsions of her body for over twelve hours. It tore at his heart to realise that she had gone through all those stages, alone, sitting in that crevasse, watching the lifeless bodies of her mother and father. His eyes returned to the pale skin on her face, never before had he been able to see the oxygen-laden, life-carrying blood flow its course beneath her skin. Her hair melted away against the white sheets, like silk ribbons, disappearing beneath the covers of the hospital bed. Wiping away the moisture from his green eyes he rested his head in his arms, face down on the bed. His fingers were closed over hers, the coldness of her skin bringing more tears to his eyes. They could not tell him if she would be okay, if everything would be normal. They didn't know how long she had been so cold for, they couldn't possibly make a judgement. She was in the right place now. They had done the best they could, now they just had to wait, wait for her body temperature to slowly rise back to normal.

Wait for her body to deal with its injuries.

Wait for her to wake up by herself.

Wait.

Wait, and then they would know.

Adam lifted his head from the bed and raised his eyes to the monitor.

The temperature had gone up a fraction of a degree. Sighing he allowed his gaze to drift over her face again before dropping his head back to the bed. He was so tired.

Chapter Eleven

Contradictory emotions were washing through her like waves as she found herself trapped in a comforting darkness. She was standing alone, the blackness creeping closer as the walls around her grew ever higher. Kira lifted her head to the growing boundaries, her white hair standing out against the black of the night.

There was no temperature in this world. No heat or brush of cold. There was no wind, no light, no water. There was only pure, quiet darkness.

She felt comforted by the lack of life, the lack of any need to act, to fear or to fight. Frowning she shook her head as something scratched at the edge of her mind. The darkness suddenly seemed threatening, like it was isolating her from something better. Something was calling her back from the depths of the heightening boundaries. A longing was making her tilt her heat to the pinprick of light, far in the distance. It was a very odd sensation walking through this absolute darkness, a void, an empty cavity of space and time, feeling both at home and completely alone. Suddenly, without warning, a fear appeared out of nowhere and grabbed hold of her senses. The hair on the back of her neck stood on end as her head spun round to seek out the danger. She was focused, her eyes piercing through the black and scanning the surrounding darkness, but there was nothing. Nothing, other than the black void. Her heart increased its hammering against her chest, a lump forming in her throat making it difficult for her to swallow. She could feel the danger, propelling her forward, chasing her towards the light. Her feet started moving beneath her as instincts kicked in, sending her flying through the darkness.

Come on Ki.

The words reached her ears as she raced through the unmarked territory, making her look back over her shoulder in confusion. The black was overwhelming and the familiar sound alien in this dark space. Her feet kept pushing her forward as her heart raced to pump oxygen through her body to keep it moving. She could feel the danger, following at a distance. The light was growing, incrementally, in front of her eyes. The monsters were not nipping at her heels anymore, but they were not yet behind her either. They had not yet given up and she was fighting. She was fighting to keep pushing, to lose this unknown fear in the maze of walls behind her, and she was fighting against the fear in her heart, this fear of the unknown.

Don't stop. Keep fighting. Please Kira, don't give up.

Her legs were feeling heavy from exertion, the adrenaline wearing off as the danger seemed to leak away into the background. Kira felt dirty from running through the dark, her feet were slowing to a fast walk as she stumbled on. Tilting her head, she could see the light, it was still there, far away, but a symbol of hope none the less. Her breath was ragged in her chest, her lungs burning as her muscles ached.

She was fighting back tears, torn between giving in to the dark and fighting to reach the light. There was a gentle pressure on her hands as she dropped to her knees, her head bowing to the ground. She was so tired.

Confused, she struggled to find the strength to lift her head. She didn't know where she was or how she had ended up here. Everything just felt so hard in the darkness, her head felt too heavy for her neck, her shoulders slumping with the effort of supporting the weight. Her hand was burning from an unknown heat, the pressure increasing and jumping to her other hand.

What is going on?

She lifted her head as anger started to simmer below her skin. Tilting her head, she focussed her intense blue eyes on the pinprick of light in the distance, the voice was echoing through the tunnel of light. The smouldering coals of a forgotten fire was being sparked back into flame inside of her, a fight that felt so natural started to boil in her veins.

Move.

That was all she needed. A flame of hope and determination sparked into action as the word echoed off the dark walls around her. Her muscles tensed for a moment, eyes focused on the light, and then she leaped into action. She was being propelled forward by an inner need, a desire, a strength and instinct she could not question. The distance to the light was hard to judge, her mind felt foggy as she blinked and tried to clear it. The lack of light meant she had nothing other than the pinprick in the distance to focus on; she could not see the obstacles around her, she did not know this darkness as well as she did her forest, her mountains. She could feel the closeness of the empty void, but not the obstacles in the way and instead of flying over all the obstacles she found herself stumbling over at least half of them. Every time she crashed to the ground, she pushed herself back up and kept going, but she could feel the determination weakening. Her resolve was crumbling with every sharp blow of pain that bolted through her body as she ran into obstacle after obstacle. It was not long before she could hear her own laboured breathing in the blackness around her. She stumbled over an obstacle and fell to her knees. A sharp pain shooting up the joints making her gasp in pain. Tears were stinging behind the heavy lids of her eyes which she struggled to keep open. She could feel something warm and sticky on her skin but was unable to identify it. Her hair was sticking to her clammy skin in dirty clumps as she tried to fight through the thick forest of doubt and fear.

'Kira.'

Her head shot up at the gentle familiar tone. The voice was different, laced with concern and woven in hope. She felt a gentle pressure on her fingers and lifted her hand to try and see what it was. It was too dark, she could see nothing. The pressure increased as the small voice reached her ears again.

'She moved.'

There was surprise and excitement in the voice as Kira jumped to her feet. She was spinning around, looking for the origin of the voice.

'Ki? Can you hear me?' A different voice.

Her heart was hammering in her chest as she tried to find her voice, to shout out to them. *Yes, yes, I can hear you*, but there was nothing. She opened her mouth to scream but nothing came out. Frustration had the tears building in her eyes, a painful lump in her throat making her gasp for breath.

'Keep fighting Ki. You can do it. You can beat this. You are stronger than it, keep fighting.'

Kira stopped in her frantic search for the voice.

She closed her eyes and listened to the words. She had to focus. She could not fight if she did not know where the danger lay. Taking a deep breath, she opened her eyes again. She had to find a way out of this darkness.

'Okay.' She breathed, focusing her mind on the darkness around her. She stood perfectly still, listening, trying to feel any change in the air around her, trying to clear the murky water from her mind. She closed her eyes against the blackness, feeling her breathing settle into a slow rhythm as a picture slowly began to form in her mind.

Everything was white, the air was cold and still, but there was an urgency in her heart. The white started to dissolve into shades of blue until the crevasse had formed around her in perfect three dimensionality. Everything was exactly the same; the flow of the water frozen in time, the cold coarseness of the ice walls. The intense glacial blue colour of the guts of the crevasse, and the bright red drop of blood. Kira focused her attention on the drop of crimson in the icy world of white and blue. It stood out in her mind, creating a focal point for memories to rush to. She felt her heart rate increase, as the events of the past seventy-two hours slowly started creeping toward the circle of light she had created around herself. Visions of isolated incidents jumped out at her as she struggled to catch the tail end of each vision and file it in order in her mind. She had no idea how long she remained there, suspended between the dark and the light, watching a film of the past three days play out on the walls of the crevasse. She could see the fear in her own eyes, feel the pain and elation at the discovery of her parents at long last, and once again found herself fighting the battle between staying with them and returning to a world of light. There was a warm pressure on her hands, a longing in her heart as she felt the heat seeping through her cold skin and warming her flesh and blood below. She was not raised to give up. She had been taught to move, to run, to fight and to never give up. She had been taught to sit quietly and listen to the earth, to hear the wise words in a stream, the soft whispers on the wind and to heed the warning of the mountains. She had been taught to read the signs, to know when to move and when to remain motionless. She had been taught to wait patiently but never had she been taught to give up. She could feel the fight start to build inside of her. She was becoming more aware of the world beyond the dark walls. She could hear voices, feel the pressure of warm hands. She was aware of movement, of the intonation of words. She could isolate the voices and she knew she was not far off. Her mind felt like it was on fire, her eyes itching from exhaustion. She knew where she had to go now, she could hold on to that pinprick of light, growing in front of her eyes. She could find the fight inside of her and focus it in a single direction. The pressure on her left hand was from small fingers, colder, more anxious than from that on her right hand. Her right was folded into a comforting gentle warmth, she could feel the strong fingers laced through her own cool, motionless ones. They applied a constant gentle pressure, giving her something to focus on. She wanted to reciprocate the feeling of hope in the gentle pressure, but despite her best efforts it was merely a small flutter, barely a pressure, against Adam's warm skin. The whisper of movement was just enough to make his eyes flutter open from its exhausted sleep and focus on her fingers laced through his.

They had definitely moved.

A gnawing feeling of concern and utter helplessness was manifesting itself as frustration in Adam's actions.

She should have been awake by now.

A wave of frustration had him on his feet and pacing away from her, the tail end of his emotions reaching the child, still perched beside the bed. Raven looked up, feeling the emotion sweeping around the room as it exuded from Adam's tense body. Her arm slipped from where it had rested across Kira's waist as she lifted her head from the bed. She didn't like that Adam was so anxious. His eyes were darting between the monitors and Kira's still, motionless body. The heating pads had been removed.

'She should have been awake by now,' he mumbled running a hand over his hair, his words sending a ripple of fear through the girl. Her temperature had steadily climbed through the night and had reached its goal hours ago. He had thought that upon reaching that magic number she would simply open her eyes, and everything would be fine again. The doctors had looked at him in pity as he expressed his concern about her not being awake yet.

'It takes time,' was all they could say. Nobody could tell him when she would wake up, if she would. They could not predict if the extreme temperature drop of her body had caused any lasting damage, they simply had to wait until she woke up. Nobody knew for sure how long she had been hypothermic and so it was hard to make any guess, educated or not, about when she would wake up and what state she might be in.

He was adamant that she would be fine. She was a fighter. He was sure that any minute now she would open her eyes and smile at him. Those minutes had dragged into hours and now he was fighting with himself to keep the faith.

'Come on Ki.' He paced back towards her leaning over her as Raven moved out of the way.

'Come on Ki, wake up,' he urged her and waited, watching for any flutter of movement behind her lids.

'Wake up,' he said again, more urgently, his voice carrying more strength. 'You have to wake up. Come on Ki, fight it. Fight it!'

His face was inches from hers and somewhere behind him he could feel a gentle shake. His eyes travelled down her body, but it was not Kira that was moving. It was Raven, trying to bite back the sobs as she watched Adam fight against his own fears, fears which were now reaching out towards her and colouring her world with bleak shadows. He sighed as he saw the pale, tear-streaked face, aware that his action and anxieties were probably not helping the child's state.

He moved away from Kira and reached out to the girl. 'Come here.' He pulled her into his arms and she melted against his chest. 'I'm sorry,' he whispered as the small body shook in his arms and he was once more reminded of her connection to Kira. She had grown strong under Kira's gentle care and guidance. She had become as much a part of the world Kira lived in as he could only ever hope to be. Her connection to this fearless guardian of the earth was stronger than his, perhaps he should be listening to her rather than his own doubts.

'It's going to be all right,' Adam whispered as Raven cried into his chest. Her small hand seeking out the motionless one on the bed and folding her fingers around them.

She wanted to believe him, she wanted to trust in his words, but she could still not see or hear anything. The wind was not talking to her, the birds had abandoned their song and sat quietly on the windowsill watching, waiting. Nobody could reach Kira, not even the earth or the mountains themselves. She was completely alone in this and she was going to have to fight her way through, by herself.

'I can't feel her,' Raven whispered after a long time. 'I can't reach her.' Misinterpreting the words Adam moved away to allow Raven the space to get closer to the woman on the bed, frowning when he saw Kira's hand in the small one's.

'What do you mean?' he asked cautiously as his eyes found Raven's.

'She feels so far away,' Raven whispered. 'I can't reach her.'

A tear was running down her face as she tore her eyes away from Kira's face and focused them on Adam's. He felt a sudden jolt as her blue eyes fixed on his. He could see Kira in them. A thought suddenly rushed through his mind making him almost double over in pain. What if Raven was her replacement? What if Raven was sent to them because Kira was going to leave? He couldn't bear it, he couldn't entertain the thought for more than a moment. Raven saw the colour drain from his face before he spun around and headed toward the door. She couldn't read the expression on his face, but she could feel his pain, it stabbed into her gut like a sharp knife.

She couldn't see what he saw, she could not possibly know how much she resembled the life and strength of Kira just then. Adam had never felt pain like that, pure mind-numbing, life-changing, nothing-else-mattered kind of pain. He stumbled blindly through the door only mildly aware of a sharp pain as he crashed against a hard shoulder. Strong hands gripped his arms, trying to make him stop but the power was overwhelming. The fear and loss swirled through him like nausea. He pushed on, moving away from the pain and out through the hospital doors. The cold hit him like a sledgehammer, freezing in his lungs as he tried to take a breath. Frozen lumps of breath were blocking his airway making him gasp for breath as he stumbled down the steps, uncoordinated. Voices echoed around him, bodies blurred in front of him. His foot caught on something, he could not lift it. His world was spinning, darkness closing in on him. He could not force the oxygen into his lungs. He was lost, completely and utterly. He was no one without her, his life had no meaning if she was not in it. If she could not live then he did not want to, either. It all seemed so pointless. The pain was slowly taking over every cell of his body, pummelling it into submission, freezing the life in it and forcing it to a standstill. He could not bear it, he could not fight it. He was going down and he didn't even care. As darkness descended the rush of moving bodies blurred into one big blob before everything went black.

Raven felt him going down. She felt his fear and pain. His overwhelming rush of helplessness and hopelessness punching her in the gut. Jones looked into the room where Adam had rushed out of, Raven's face was paling in front of his eyes. He was torn between rushing after his friend who was in an obvious state of despair and wanting to comfort the child who was clinging to Kira's hand. He looked away to see Adam disappearing out of sight and by the time he looked back Raven's eyes were rolling into the back of her head.

'Shit.' He ran forward as her body wobbled on the edge of balance. Her brow was covered in a film of sweat and as her eyes rolled back and her body slumped, he pushed his arms beneath her, stopping her from tipping off the seat. He stood for a moment as the air settled around him. Everything was quiet for just a moment before a loud continuous beep exploded into the room. Jones had no idea what was going on, he was still coming to terms with Raven's sudden and dramatic collapse when a mob of staff rushed into the room, wide-eyed surprise and shock on their faces. The last thing they had expected was for Kira's heart monitor to shout at them in desperate warning. She was stable, she was showing signs of life, she was beginning to wake up. Jones was pushed out of the way, the child being mistaken for being asleep rather than having suffered a collapse. He was on the edge of the room, Raven grey and slack in his arms, Kira's pulse monitor on her finger. The medical staff was still rushing around trying to find the cause of alarm, confusion reigning until one nurse stepped out of the melee and looked calmly around her. Her eyes fell on the grey colour of Raven's skin, the sweat on her brown and the unconscious state. Alarm bells were ringing in her head; that child was not asleep. She started to move as her eyes travelled over the small body before coming to rest on the small fingers, the pulse monitor still clinging to it, barely.

'Oh my God.' The nurse paled as she ran towards Raven,

lifting her out of Jones's arms as she shouted orders into the room. Jones watched as Kira lay motionless, oblivious to the turmoil around her. Raven's clothes were being cut away, electric pads placed on her chest. A shock was sent through the pads as her small body arched off the ground. Jones felt as if he was standing in the eye of a storm watching havoc being wreaked around him. He had no idea that Adam was being wheeled into emergency, his collapse an unknown. He could not watch this child die in front of his eyes, and Kira did not look much better. It seemed that an intricately woven web was being torn to shreds as the strands that connected these three people got ripped apart, separating their lives.

The only thing that remained steady and unchanged in their immediate world was the unmoving state of the woman on the bed. He moved towards her, fixing his eyes on her face and closing his eyes as he slipped his hand beneath hers.

There was no thought process, he was acting on instinct, an instinct that he didn't even know he had.

The world stilled around him. A feeling of motion was pulling at his mind, dragging him beyond the boundaries of the conscious world. Suddenly he was moving, fast, the forest ground beneath his feet flying past at an alarming rate. The world around him blurring as he passed through trees and leapt over streams. His breath was loud in his ears, his heart hammering against his chest as his grey eyes focussed on a figure in the distance. His vision appeared to be a lot closer to the ground, the notion throwing him, but the movement did not stop. The ground turned to ice beneath his paws as he ate into the distance between him and the figure. It felt so right, so natural and yet so surreal. She was standing with her back to him, staring up to the mountains. Her white hair reaching desperately to the ground, trying to connect to it, as her bare feet turned red in the ice. He opened his mouth to shout her name, but a short sharp yelp escaped. Jones shook his head, confused, before trying again. The sound reached his ears as a bark, making him look down at his chest in shock. Where had that sound come from? A moment of utter disbelief followed, as he became aware of the new body he found himself in. The fur felt warm and comfortable, the instincts sharp, his eyes keen as he stared at the woman in front of him. He could feel her confusion and her fear. He had to stop her from moving further up the mountain, he had to bring her back down. Raven needed her. Adam needed her. Without her they would never be the same again. Accepting his new role, he found a howl deep within his chest and lifting his head to the sky belted it out, long, loud and clear. The sound reached Kira's ears, penetrating through the fog and tugging her head around. Her eyes focussed on the grey of the wolf's. She smiled as she recognised those eyes and moved toward him.

'I knew you were one of us.'

He yelped, trying to tell her to come back with him, that she needed to save Adam and Raven. Her eyes lifted to the sky in the direction from which he had come before turning back to the mountains.

'I have to leave you now,' she whispered up to the sky, and for a moment Jones felt his heart lurch. 'I'm sorry I cannot join you.' There were tears in her eyes, resembling the pain in her voice. 'I really want to be with you, but I am needed down here.' She looked towards Jones.

'That is why you are here, isn't it? To lead me back?' He yelped his reply and she nodded, the decision had been made for her.

'I love you,' she whispered to the mountains, tilting her head once more to the majestic peaks and listening for an answer. The breath of wind across her cheeks was enough, and tearing her eyes away she turned back, fixing her blue eyes on the wolf. There was a slight inclination of her head, not quite a nod, making him tilt his own head to the side as he watched her. The breeze had gone, the air was perfectly still as Kira stood motionless, watching him. He did not expect the sudden burst of motion as a moment later she was shooting past him, flying down the mountain side, gliding over the snow, guided by the connection she had with those in her life. Astounded he leapt into action, following her down the snow and into the treeline. He lost sight of her as she flew through the trees, finding her way back over the territory she knew too well. The wind blasted colour onto her face as she leapt over obstacles, her muscles devouring oxygen as she swerved around the trees, skimmed over puddles and drifted over the dry vegetation on the forest floor. In the distance she could see the end of the trees, she could smell the smoke from her fire. She was nearly home.

Jones jolted awake, his head flying up, his heart beating wildly in his chest. Kira's eyes were moving behind her lids. Raven and the staff were gone. They were alone.

'What the heck?' He looked around, confused. Had he been dreaming?

Jumping up he pushed out of the room, he had to find both Adam and Raven. They had to be there when she woke up. He didn't know where the urgency came from, nor how he knew, with absolute certainty, that she was about to wake. He didn't know why it was so important for Raven to be there when she woke but he just knew it was.

Finding them was easy, Adam, having regained consciousness in the emergency room had made his way to Raven's bedside. The difficult part was going to be getting Raven to Kira's room. The girl was in ICU. Her heart had failed, it had simply stopped in its action of fuelling her body with oxygen-rich blood. She was on machinery keeping her heart and lungs working, and there was no way she was going to be let out.

'We have to get her to Kira,' Jones said urgently looking at Adam. Adam's face was strained, he could feel the life draining out of him as he looked at the child. How could this happen? How could she have been so well a week ago, running, playing, laughing, learning like a normal healthy child, and now she was dying. Her heart had simply stopped.

'Adam, I know this sounds crazy but you have to believe me. Kira is going to wake up and Raven needs to be there. They are connected. I don't know how it works, I don't know how I know it, but I just do. She will be fine, they both will, but we have to get her to Kira.'

Adam looked at him in despair. 'There is no way they will let us move Raven,' he whispered as he filled with guilt. Somehow it had to be his fault, both of these women who had played such a massive part in his life lay unconscious, unresponsive.

'Then we'll move Kira,' Jones said suddenly. 'Come on.'

He grabbed Adam's arm and by the time they reached her room Adam had pulled himself out of his hole. He had to keep believing. He had to keep fighting and trust that everything was going to be okay. Kira was strong and Jones was right, she was connected to Raven. When she was doing well so was Raven, this turn for the worse in the child had to be connected to Kira's state. The men did not try to convince any of the staff to allow them to take Kira. Adam paused as they reached her bed. Her eyes were moving rapidly behind her lids, her fingers were twitching.

'Oh my…' He looked at Jones who was grinning.

'Told you,' he said before turning to the door. 'Now come on, let's get her upstairs before she wakes up.

They moved fast, with confident speed and precision, removing the tabs and wires from her body, ignoring the warning beeps. Adam's arms went around her like he had been doing it all his life, lifting her off the bed and striding out of the room. He had one focus in mind and nothing was going to stop him from getting to it. Raven and Kira were connected, and he could not imagine life without either of them. He would do whatever it took to bring both of them back into this world of life and consciousness. He ignored the words of warning, the voices of pleading, and the hands and bodies of several staff as he progressed toward the ICU. He was like a rugby player, in the championship game. He had the ball and he was reaching the goal for the game-winning try at any cost. It was mind over matter, he had learned that from Kira. Keep going, no matter what. He kept moving. He kept hold of her, nobody was going to pull her from his arms, nobody was going to stop them. His heart was hammering against his chest, the shockwaves pulsing through Kira's body. She was aware of movement again. Her feet were off the ground, but she was still moving. She could feel the comforting warmth and familiar hardness of Adam's chest. She smiled as a feeling of content happiness spread through her. There was a slight tug on her arm, a brush against her legs as she frowned and looked to the culprit. There was nothing, but even as she looked at her arms, she felt the tug again. She gasped at the shock, Adam's eyes immediately going down to her face.

'She's waking up,' he said evenly, struggling to hide the emotion coursing through him. He was aware of the burly men around him trying to stop him, but the purpose in his stride made them step out of the way. There was something about the way he was moving, something about the woman in his arms and the mission they were on that made the men look after them in awe. Jones was fighting off the hands grabbing at Kira's body, pushing a tunnel through the bodies for Adam to move through. The doors of the ICU were shut when they reached them but Adam simply turned his back to the doors and pushed through despite the calls of protest that followed him through. Staff in the ICU jumped to their feet, confused about what was going on. Adam pushed past them, into Raven's cubicle and waited for Jones to move the child before lying Kira down next to her. Everything stilled as the nurses looked on in silent amazement. Nobody knew what was going on, but the moment was so powerful that nobody could find the will to protest. Kira and Raven lay motionless beside each other. Kira was being pulled back down into the darkness, the warmth and comfort of Adam's arms had left her and she could feel fear and danger pulling at the edges of her cloak. Jones sat down on the opposite side, his hand closing over Raven's. This had to work. Adam's fingers were laced through Kira's and he applied gentle pressure trying to make her aware of his presence. Raven and Kira's bodies were pressed up against each other.

'Come on Ki,' he whispered. 'Fight it.'

She was back in the woods, everything was covered in a blanket of snow. The cold cut through her like a knife, making her shiver. Adam looked up at the goosepimples on Kira's arms. She felt lost. She didn't know why she was back here. Turning around, she allowed her eyes to travel over the view, taking in the woods in as much detail as she could. There was movement beyond the trees, eyes. Kira stopped and focused her eyes on the equally spaced glints of light in the dark. Suddenly eyes started appearing all around her and she felt her heart increase in its rhythm as she turned once more, taking in the view of eyes. Movement made her spin back around as she came to a sudden stop. One pair of eyes were growing as they neared her. A short yelp broke the silence. A breeze lifted the hair off her back and made it dance across her shoulders as she stood still, the blue of her eyes standing out against the white backdrop of snow. She felt calm and reassured, as if she was exactly where she was supposed to be. The wolf yelped again before turning away, and without hesitation she followed him. Her fingers curled around Raven's hand on the hospital bed as she followed the wolf in her dreams. She knew where she was going. She dropped to her knees in the snow, pulling the child up into a sitting position and waiting for her eyes to open.

'Raven,' she whispered. 'It is not your time to go yet child, you have to get up.' Raven's eyes opened and found the blue of Kira's. 'You have to fight Raven,' she whispered. 'You are the only one that can pull yourself through this. You have to fight.'

A look of relief washed over the girl's features. 'Are you okay?'

Kira nodded. 'Come on.' She stood, pulling the girl to her feet. Raven stumbled, making Kira stop. She could not pull them both through. She had just enough energy to push herself back up the slope and through the door of her home. She could not carry Raven.

'Come on Raven.' Kira forced the girl's head up. 'Fight it.'

Raven pulled herself back up, forcing her feet to start moving. The path was difficult to navigate in the dark, it was steep and tiresome. Raven had to stop every few steps to take a breath and search for the energy to keep moving.

'I don't think I can do it.' There were tears in her eyes as she looked up at Kira. 'I really want to, but...'

'Fight it,' Kira said. 'You are stronger than this Raven, fight it. You can do it. You have to keep telling yourself that you can do it.'

Raven's head dropped for a moment.

'Fight it!' Kira shouted so loudly in the dream that a sound escaped her mouth, shaking both their bodies. The crowd around the bed had grown, and a collective gasp ran through them as their bodies jerked to the movement in their dreams.

'Come on Ki, come on Raven,' Adam whispered, staring anxiously down at them, one hand on Kira's right hand and the other over Raven and Kira's clasped hands in the middle of the bed. 'Fight it.'

Jones's head was down, his eyes closed as if in prayer as he played his own part in this world, nipping at their heels and forcing them in the right direction.

Raven's feet were dragging, her head down as they trudged uphill. It took all of her strength to keep going. The pull on her arm was getting heavier with every step. Kira stopped and turned to the girl.

'Raven.' She dropped to her knees in front of the child. 'I cannot carry you through this.' Her heart ached at the sound of the words. 'I wish I could, I wish I could do this for you, but I can't. This is your battle to fight. This is your fight to win. You have to find that strength inside of you, the strength I know you have. You have to look deep down inside of you and find that well of reserves. You have to dig deep and push through. You can do this. You are strong, you have the mental strength to do this. You may have reached the limit of your physical strength, but your brain always keeps something in reserve. You have more. You have what it takes to get through this, through anything, but you have to choose to do it. You have to choose to fight, and you have to do it alone. Nobody can make this decision for you, nobody can fight this battle for you, only you can.'

Raven looked deep into Kira's endless blue pools, searching for the strength she would need to get herself through this.

'Are you leaving me?'

'I will never leave you,' she said. 'Even when you can't see me, I am there.' She looked to the light, it was only a few steps away. 'You have to do this last bit by yourself,' she said turning her eyes back to the girl. 'To prove to yourself that you can.'

Kira leaned forward and pressed her lips against the girl's clammy forehead. It tore at her heart leaving this young girl to fight this difficult battle by herself, but if she wanted to live she would. She got a small glimpse into what it might have felt like for her mother to leave her behind all those years ago.

'I'll see you on the other side.' She smiled and turned away, walking towards the light.

It took everything inside of her not to turn around and run back to the child. She wanted to pick her up and carry her over the final hurdle, but she knew that if she did Raven would take even longer to recover next time. She needed to believe in herself, she needed to know that she could do this by herself, that it was her strength that was carrying her through, not Kira's.

Kira stopped on the very edge of consciousness and closed her eyes. This was her last chance, once she was through there was no turning back. She felt Raven move behind her and with a smile stepped through. Raven was going to be fine.

Chapter Twelve

The silence in the room was palpable. The tension thick enough to be cut with a knife, like a snow shovel slicing through several layers of snow and hitting a rock beneath with a metallic clang. One moment everything was still, motionless except for the movement in both Kira and Raven's bodies. These were good signs, neither of them had done much of anything since being tucked up in their respective beds. Kira's hand was still covering Raven's and, in a moment, Adam saw the tension in them relax, a visible breath of relief left Kira's body, and as moments grew into seconds everybody's eyes had focused on Kira's face. She was close, Adam could tell she was on the verge of waking up. 'Come on,' he whispered leaning closer, urging her on, pulling her through the vast expanse of light. Seconds turned into minutes and, just when the staff were about to give up and return to their duty of settling patients and making sure that everybody was where they were supposed to be, Kira's eyes fluttered open. The intensity of the glacial blue colour stunned the medical staff into silence as Kira felt Adam's relief wash over her in a wave of emotion. He was laughing and crying as he reached forward towards her, his relief a physical presence in the room.

'Ki, thank God,' he choked out, unable to describe the emotion that was coursing through him, he could not put a limit on the relief he was feeling. He could not put into words the feeling of complete desolation and hopelessness at the thought that she might not wake up. She was in his arms, pressed against his chest as he swallowed back tears, trying to bite back the sobs that managed to escape through his carefully guarded gates. 'Thank God, thank God,' he whispered into her hair, tangling his fingers in the strands of white silk as he pressed her head against his shoulder. The staff had slipped away for a moment, giving them some privacy, but Jones had not looked up; he was still locked away in that world, watching over Raven as she struggled up the hill. The last few steps seemed to be the hardest, her body would not obey her commands, her legs refused to carry her weight and she sat helplessly, staring up at the light, doubtful if she could make it.

Kira couldn't find her words any more than Adam could. It felt like so much had happened over the past few hours, never mind the last days or weeks. She was exhausted with the effort of battling through those obstacles, of fighting with everything she had, just to push through the boundary. The stretch of light was longer than she had anticipated, testing her, making sure she was ready to come back. She could only hope that Raven could find the strength to push through, to keep going. Adam was laughing and crying at intervals, pressing his lips against her head, her cheeks her mouth and running his fingers over her skin. He could hardly believe she was awake, that she had pulled through. He pushed her away slightly in order to look into her eyes; struggling to believe that she had come back from the poor state that she was in. Her body felt heavy as she struggled to hold herself up, her lids fighting against gravity as she tried to keep them open. Her skin was still pale and dark shadows circled her eyes.

'Ki,' he whispered. 'You did it.' Her eyes fought against the pull of sleep, finding his eyes. 'You did it.' He was smiling, tears running down his face. 'Thank God.'

She had felt better in the dream, stronger. Here she just felt weak and tired. Adam allowed gravity to pull her back down as he laid her back next to Raven. Her head turned, finding the pale, dark-haired child next to her. Her hand immediately found Raven's folding around the small fingers.

'Raven...' Adam was going to explain what had happened, but Kira's mouth opened, making him stop.

'She's coming,' Kira whispered, her words barely audible. She had to keep believing that the child would pull through, would fight through. She knew that Raven had it in her to do it, she just didn't know if she was in a position to find that well of strength. Adam had never felt relief like the waves coursing through him. Every time he looked at her, he felt a new wave wash over him. It felt like a dream, it was so difficult to explain and with each new wave that reached him, his fingers increased their grip on her hand.

Kira tilted her head to face Raven, she wanted to be closer to the child.

'Come on Raven.' Her words were mumbled, but in her head they were clear, and she knew Raven could hear her.

She was shuffling, struggling to get her arms around the child, she wanted to pull her through, like Adam had pulled her through.

'She's going to be okay,' Adam whispered as he helped

Kira put her arm beneath the child and pull her closer. He leaned forward putting his arms around both of them, as he noticed that Jones too, was still holding the girl's hand.

Jones was still on the other side, urging her on. He was nipping at her heels, nudging her with his nose, trying to get her to stand up.

Come on Raven.

She lifted her head to the light, her dark hair slipping over the dirt of the earth, collecting strength from the source of all life.

Raven leaned forward, falling onto her hands and knees. She was so tired.

Stay strong. Keep fighting.

She felt something soft and warm slip beneath her arm and started for a moment, as the grey eyes appeared from between her chest and arms. She gasped as the colour registered and allowed him to support her as she pushed herself to her feet.

'Come on Raven,' she whispered to herself, lifting her foot; it fell forward, and her body followed, unbalanced. 'Keep moving.'

She could sense the warmth and support from the other side of the light. She knew Kira was there, waiting. She had to stay strong, she had to keep fighting. She could not give up, she had to prove to herself, to everybody, that she was strong. She wanted to make Kira proud. Kira had been through so much, had come so close to death and still managed to pull through, so she could do it as well. Kira had made her strong, had helped her heal and taught her how to live. Now was her chance to prove that she had learned something, that she could fight just as hard as Kira could.

She was not weak. She was strong.

She was strong and she could beat this.

Her knees gave way and she stumbled to the ground once more. Jones's body jerked beside the bed as he nudged the motionless child, keeping her awake. Raven looked up and lifted her arm over the wolf. She sat still, just for a moment, enjoying the warmth and comfort. He had saved her once and he would save her again. Jones nudged her again and she leaned forward, her hands pressing into the soft dirt, her knees scraping against the rocks as she started to crawl forward.

Kira pulled her even closer and whispered into her ear. 'Come on Raven, you are stronger than this. I know you can do it. Fight it. Fight it!'

Raven felt a surge of power as she pushed forward, her muscles tensing before releasing like a coiled spring, a short burst of energy had her diving forwards, through the light, crossing over the line between light and dark. Jones ran forward and leapt through the light, his body jerking awake as he gasped for breath. Adam's head shot up, confused at the look on his friend's face. He did not know what to think of Jones's reaction, he didn't know where he had been. All he knew was that in Kira's world anything was possible, and even the most mystical and fantastical sounding things carried truth. Jones pushed himself up, his breath still ragged as his eyes focused on the child's face. His eyes wandered briefly over Kira's features. He had known she was awake, but the confirmation sent a rush of relief through him nonetheless. Her eyes were closed but her grasp on the child was firm.

'Come on kid!' Jones barked, making Adam's head turn

in surprise. His voice was rough and unfamiliar, but Jones did not so much as blink.

Raven felt the tears running down her face, she was crawling through the light, it seemed endless and she didn't know if she could make it. She was alone now, completely alone. Kira was gone, the wolf had gone, now it was up to her.

The dirt was rich beneath her body, she could smell the nutrients as her face pressed against the ground. She took a deep breath, inhaling the familiar scent and ran her fingers over the soil. She loved the feel of dirt beneath her feet, squishing through the gaps between her toes. She could feel the wind on her skin, and see the leaves rustling, high up in the branches of the trees. If she gave up now, she would never again see this, feel this. She would never again feel the rush of the wind through her hair, she would never again hear its whispers in the leaves. Should she give up, she would never again feel the soil against her skin as the scent filled her senses, she would not again feel the warmth of the fire as she watched a scene being danced out in the flames. She would never again hear the howl of the wolves, feel their sensitivity and power, she would never again dig in the garden or pull out the vegetables she had planted. She wanted to pull through. She wanted to go home and learn about ancient medicines. She wanted to learn more about the mountains, the stars and the earth. She wanted to swim in the streams and grow healthy on the vegetables she planted and the meat she hunted. She wanted to be like Kira and the only way to do that was to be strong, to never give up, and to be herself.

Raven lifted her head once more from the ground and

pushed herself to her feet. It took every ounce of energy she had, every last reserve of mental strength but she pushed through, she kept her feet moving. Her eyes were fixed in the distance as she took one steady step after another. The tunnel narrowed, the distance shortened, until finally, with a smile on her face, exhausted from the effort she pushed through the barrier.

Kira felt the moment Raven pushed through. Her eyes opened at exactly the same time as the child's and their eyes locked. A spark lit the room as the woman and child looked at each other.

They had a connection, that could not be denied, but it was only the internal strength of each individual, that had managed to pull them through at the end.

'You did it.' Kira smiled as tears spilled over her lids, and splashing onto Raven's face, mixed with the girl's own tears.

There was a great sense of relief, a collective sigh as the room itself let go of the breath it had been holding.

No one could pretend to know what the future held. Nobody knew how long Raven's road to recovery would actually be, or what the path would hold, but they had hope. She had pulled through when nobody thought she would, she had fought hard and showed the tenacity and resilience in her spirit. This kid would not give up. She would fight for as long as she could which brought a smile to everyone's lips.

Relief washed over Kira as she felt Raven's heart give a confidence-boosting thud against her own chest. Nothing could have prepared her for that moment when she had to leave Raven behind, but she was glad that she had made the right decision. She closed her eyes against the exhaustion as tears still escaped her lids. The only thought that was running through her head was home.

She just wanted to go home.

***

The clinical white of the hospital walls was discomfiting, the mattress was hard beneath her exhausted body and the blankets scratched against her skin. Kira's head was tilted towards the window, her eyes fixed on the green life beyond. The windows were open, allowing a cool breeze to carry in the scent of the earth and changing seasons, caressing her skin with timeless gentleness and care. Individual leaves on some trees were eager in their rush to autumn, starting to change their colour much to the amusement of the other vegetation. The first signs of summer coming to an end were appearing, but it was still early, it would be weeks before the scorning leaves would follow in pursuit of their eager forerunners. She had done nothing but sleep for the past few days. Her body had been hammered into the ground, pummelled into submission as she had finally pushed it to its very limit. She had never come so close to stepping over the boundaries of her strength and capabilities as she had in the last few days, and she was paying a heavy price. Her organs were faster in accepting the healing properties of warm life-giving blood than her muscles were. She felt weak when trying to stand on her own two feet; this weakness was different to that which she had felt after their first journey. That was a physical exhaustion, one through which she could push herself, but this was different. It was not just her body that was tired but also her mind. She was not as quick and sharp in her thought process. Words did not come easily and quite often she would drift off to sleep on a train of thought. She didn't like this feeling of weakness, she wanted to go home and rebuild her strength. She wanted to sit in front of her fire. She wanted to tend to her vegetables and allow the earth to heal her. She was not going to recover in this place, not to the person she was before. Adam was outside, discussing terms of her release with the doctors. They didn't want to let her go yet, they were worried about her being able to take in and retain enough calories. She was struggling with the hospital food and her meals were being supplemented by high calorie shakes and purees. She didn't like them, just as she hadn't liked the stuff they gave her in the hospital last time, but she consumed them nonetheless. She needed to get out of here. They both knew that she would do, and feel, much better in her own home with her own food. Raven was still in hospital, her heart was weak, and she was being monitored carefully, but she was in high spirits. Her positivity was infectious and every time they went to visit her, Kira came back feeling stronger. The sun dipped away behind a cloud and Kira's eyes dropped away from the window with a small sigh. She so desperately wanted to be outside. She wanted to feel the earth beneath her feet, the tingle of the wind on her skin. She wanted to touch the bark of trees and inhale the earthy rich scent of nature. She felt incomplete without the sheer walls of the mountains towering above her, or the trees of the dense wood surrounding her. Her eyes travelled to the door as moments later Adam stepped through, quickly followed by the doctor. Her eyes found Adam's, searching for the answers beyond the green colour. The doctor's words drifted over her, buzzed around her like a lazy bee, struggling to find a place to land. She could tell by the look on his face, the spark in his eyes, and the way he held his body that they were going home. She knew the doctor's advice was important, but she had heard it several times already, it was ingrained in her memory. She knew what they thought she needed to recover, but she knew with absolute certainty, with every fibre of her being that all she needed was the strong healing powers of home and its surroundings. The hospital had done all it could to heal her physically, now she had to heal her mind in order to further heal her body.

A wave of relief washed over her as the doctor left the room, leaving them alone. Adam moved closer, the intensity of his emerald green eyes captivating her. How had it come to this? Her heart hammered against her chest at his nearness, her skin tingled in anticipation of his touch, as unexpectantly she was thrown back to their very first meeting.

She had been so young, in body and in mind. A part of her had feared people, feared the fact that they might take her away from her home. She was only fifteen when her parents had left her home alone as they set off on their journey, never to return. Kira had spent months jumping at the slightest sound, running for cover, thinking that somebody was going to come and take her away. She was not ready for the powerful reaction of her body, two years later when she met this boy. His green eyes were as wide as saucers, his cheeks red from the cold, his lips parted as his breath rushed out of him in fear. She was sitting on top of him, her knife to his throat. Her blue eyes piercing through the hard shell of his gemstone-coloured eyes, like a knife piercing a hole through leather. That was such a long time ago. Her mind and body had both reacted to the feel of him beneath her, the sense of his strength and open mind. Never in her wildest dreams had she thought that they would ever meet again, and here they were.

'What are you thinking?' Adam ran his fingers across her cheek brushing away imaginary strands of hair; he just wanted to touch her. She was real, she was still here.

'I'm just remembering.' She smiled, stilling his hand and gently applying some pressure, wondering if the memory would shoot into his mind as it had hers.

His face changed as a grin pulled at his features. 'Remembering how you floored me and pinned me to the icy ground?' There was a hint of amusement in his voice, his eyes sparking as she let out a laugh.

'Something like that.'

'I dare you to try it now.' The colour was dancing in his eyes, filling the room around them with colour and excitement.

Kira grinned and pushed herself up in bed before pushing the blankets away and swinging her legs over the side. 'Be careful what you wish for.' Her voice was full of laughter. 'I'm pretty sure I can still take you.'

Adam's laughter reached the corridor, tugging at a cord which released a bucket of relief and joy over Jones's head. He didn't know how it had happened, but he felt connected to these people and this place. His heart had jumped out of his chest the day he arrived in that small sleepy town, huddled at the foot of a magnificent mountain range, and ran off into the woods. It had felt like coming home. All his life he had been searching, for something, or somewhere. He could never settle, and now he knew why. He pushed through the door to find Adam packing Kira's stuff, still smiling to himself, oblivious to Jones's presence. Moments later the bathroom door opened, and Kira stepped through; she stood tall, the muscles in her arms and legs looked strong, determined to carry her home. There was a healthy colour on her skin, her white hair glinting with a healthy shine as her blue eyes twinkled at the prospect of going home.

They had one last thing to do before heading back to the mountains.

Kira didn't want to leave Raven behind. She wished the child was well enough to return with them, but she still had some recovering to do. Her room had been transformed, she was surrounded by her own colourful possessions and comfortable reminders of home. There was a smile on her face and colour to her cheeks when they had gone to say goodbye. Kira had promised that when Raven was well enough to come home, she would come to town to lead her into the woods. Raven yearned for the healing powers of nature just as much as Kira did, and she knew this. She wanted to leave Raven with a positive prospect, something to look forward to and to work towards.

Now, finally she was standing once more on the edge of two worlds. The point where her two worlds met and merged. The bridge no longer felt like a line, a separation point between these two very different parts of her life. The boundaries had merged. A seamless integration of two worlds had taken place. The sun was still warm on her exposed skin, but she could smell the change in the air. Kira closed her eyes, she could feel the warm coarseness of the wooden bridge beneath her bare feet, the brook was bubbling enthusiastically, flowing below the structure. She could smell the cool water, feel it rushing over her skin, bringing a smile to her face. Familiar sounds, smells and feelings crept forward out from the cover of trees, one by one making themselves known to her. Reintroducing themselves into her life. She felt as if she had been gone for years, instead of days. Her eyes still closed she moved forward, stepping off the bridge and tilting her face to the snow-capped peaks of the mountains, allowing the sun to warm her skin as the emotions warmed her from the inside. The light breeze was brushing over her body, lifting her pure white strands of silk, and tossing them about her back and shoulders. She felt first Adam, and then Jones, follow her over the bridge. The air changed around her as they came to a standstill on either side of her. They closed their eyes and lifted their faces to the mountains, offering their silent thanks, and unknowingly binding themselves to the peaks. Jones felt a stirring in his heart, a prickling on his skin and as he opened his eyes, he saw the other two had done the same. Kira was smiling, the blue of her eyes once more an offering to the mountain gods. They had come home.

Jones looked from the mountain to Kira and then Adam, a curious feeling of anticipation and excitement bubbling in his veins. Kira smiled as she caught his eye. She could see it as he felt it.

'Let's go home.' She fell into step, Adam and Jones momentarily startled at her sudden movement before quickly following her lead.

This was the start of a lifetime of adventure, they could feel it in their bones.